THE LAST CONFEDERATE

BOOKS BY GILBERT MORRIS

THE HOUSE OF WINSLOW SERIES

1. *The Honorable Imposter*
2. *The Captive Bride*
3. *The Indentured Heart*
4. *The Gentle Rebel*
5. *The Saintly Buccaneer*
6. *The Holy Warrior*
7. *The Reluctant Bridegroom*
8. *The Last Confederate*
9. *The Dixie Widow*
10. *The Wounded Yankee*
11. *The Union Belle*
12. *The Final Adversary*
13. *The Crossed Sabres*
14. *The Valiant Gunman*
15. *The Gallant Outlaw*
16. *The Jeweled Spur*
17. *The Yukon Queen*
18. *The Rough Rider*
19. *The Iron Lady*
20. *The Silver Star*
21. *The Shadow Portrait*
22. *The White Hunter*
23. *The Flying Cavalier*
24. *The Glorious Prodigal*
25. *The Amazon Quest*
26. *The Golden Angel*
27. *The Heavenly Fugitive*
28. *The Fiery Ring*
29. *The Pilgrim Song*
30. *The Beloved Enemy*
31. *The Shining Badge*
32. *The Royal Handmaid*
33. *The Silent Harp*
34. *The Virtuous Woman*

CHENEY DUVALL, M.D.[1]

1. *The Stars for a Light*
2. *Shadow of the Mountains*
3. *A City Not Forsaken*
4. *Toward the Sunrising*
5. *Secret Place of Thunder*
6. *In the Twilight, in the Evening*
7. *Island of the Innocent*
8. *Driven With the Wind*

CHENEY AND SHILOH: THE INHERITANCE[1]

1. *Where Two Seas Met*
2. *The Moon by Night*

THE SPIRIT OF APPALACHIA[2]

1. *Over the Misty Mountains*
2. *Beyond the Quiet Hills*
3. *Among the King's Soldiers*
4. *Beneath the Mockingbird's Wings*
5. *Around the River's Bend*

LIONS OF JUDAH

1. *Heart of a Lion*
2. *No Woman So Fair*
3. *The Gate of Heaven*
4. *Till Shiloh Comes*

[1]with Lynn Morris   [2]with Aaron McCarver

GILBERT MORRIS

the LAST CONFEDERATE

BETHANYHOUSE

Minneapolis, Minnesota

Published by Bethany House Publishers
11400 Hampshire Avenue South
Bloomington, Minnesota 55438

Bethany House Publishers is a division of
Baker Publishing Group, Grand Rapids, Michigan.

Printed in the United States of America

Library of Congress Cataloging-in-Publication Data

Morris, Gilbert.
   The last Confederate / by Gilbert Morris.
     p.   cm. — (The house of Winslow ; 1860)
   Summary: "Having returned from the West and settled in Virginia, the Winslow family is pitted against their Winslow relatives from the North as the nation totters on the brink of war"—Provided by publisher.
   ISBN 0-7642-2952-4 (pbk.)
   1. Winslow family (Fictitious characters)—Fiction. 2. Virginia—History—1775–1865—Fiction. I. Title. II. Series: Morris, Gilbert. House of Winslow ; 1860.
   PS3563.O8742L37   2005
   813'.54—dc22

                           2004026013

To Dixie Lynn Morris
and Andrea Necole Smith.
May you both grow up to be
handmaidens of the Lord.

GILBERT MORRIS spent ten years as a pastor before becoming Professor of English at Ouachita Baptist University in Arkansas and earning a Ph.D. at the University of Arkansas. A prolific writer, he has had over 25 scholarly articles and 200 poems published in various periodicals, and over the past years has had more than 180 novels published. His family includes three grown children. He and his wife live in Gulf Shores, Alabama.

CONTENTS

10

PART FOUR
THE PRISONER

THE HOUSE OF WINSLOW

★ ★ ★ ★

THE
HOUSE OF WINSLOW

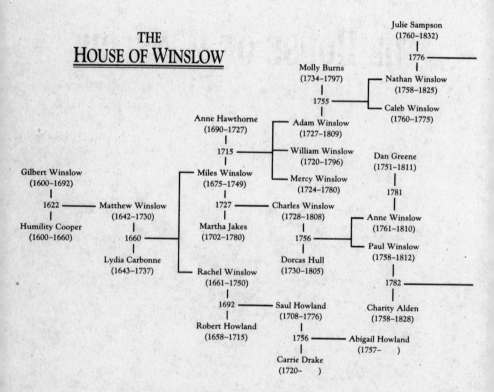

Gilbert Winslow
(1600–1692)

1622 —— Matthew Winslow
(1642–1730)

Humility Cooper
(1600–1660)

1660 ——

Lydia Carbonne
(1643–1737)

Miles Winslow
(1675–1749)

1727 ——

Martha Jakes
(1702–1780)

Rachel Winslow
(1661–1750)

1692 ——

Robert Howland
(1658–1715)

Anne Hawthorne
(1690–1727)

1715 ——

Adam Winslow
(1727–1809)

William Winslow
(1720–1796)

Mercy Winslow
(1724–1780)

Charles Winslow
(1728–1808)

1756 ——

Dorcas Hull
(1730–1805)

Saul Howland
(1708–1776)

1756 —— Abigail Howland
(1757–   )

Carrie Drake
(1720–   )

Molly Burns
(1734–1797)

1755 ——

Nathan Winslow
(1758–1825)

Caleb Winslow
(1760–1775)

Julie Sampson
(1760–1832)

1776 ——

Dan Greene
(1751–1811)

1781

Anne Winslow
(1761–1810)

Paul Winslow
(1758–1812)

1782 ——

Charity Alden
(1758–1828)

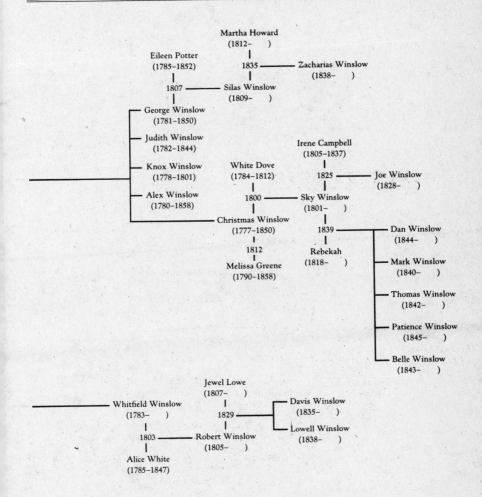

Martha Howard
(1812–   )

Eileen Potter
(1785–1852)

1835 ———— Zacharias Winslow
(1838–   )

1807 ———— Silas Winslow
(1809–   )

George Winslow
(1781–1850)

Judith Winslow
(1782–1844)

Irene Campbell
(1805–1837)

Knox Winslow
(1778–1801)

White Dove
(1784–1812)

1825 ———— Joe Winslow
(1828–   )

Alex Winslow
(1780–1858)

1800 ———— Sky Winslow
(1801–   )

Christmas Winslow
(1777–1850)

1839 ———— Dan Winslow
(1844–   )

1812

Rebekah
(1818–   )

Mark Winslow
(1840–   )

Melissa Greene
(1790–1858)

Thomas Winslow
(1842–   )

Patience Winslow
(1845–   )

Belle Winslow
(1843–   )

Jewel Lowe
(1807–   )

Whitfield Winslow
(1783–   )

1829 ———— Davis Winslow
(1835–   )

1803 ———— Robert Winslow
(1805–   )

Lowell Winslow
(1838–   )

Alice White
(1785–1847)

PART ONE

THE YANKEE

★ ★ ★

(November '60—April '61)

CHAPTER ONE

FUGITIVE

★ ★ ★ ★

Captain Hubbard nodded with satisfaction as the *Dixie Queen* nosed into Richmond just as darkness fell on the James River. The ship was seventy feet long and thirteen feet eight inches deep, which allowed it to navigate the narrow river with few problems. Over the top of the levee Hubbard saw the yellow glow of the lantern lights on Cherry Street, and even over the drum of his pounding engines he heard the sound of a band playing a tinny marching song. *Must be some kind of military shindig goin' on*, he mused. The war furor that had shaken the land all through the year of 1860 often resulted in such celebrations.

The captain's eyes lighted on the large white sign with the black 3 on it. "Mr. Tyler," he called out of the wheelhouse window, "there's our dock—get your lines out and make fast!"

The ship bounced off a piling with a heavy *thump*, and the deckhands scurried around, attaching the lines to the dock.

"Lower the plank—lively now!" Tyler, the first mate, shouted. He looked up at the wheelhouse and bellowed in a bullhorn voice, "Cap'n, you want to unload tonight?"

"Wait till morning, but take that stowaway to the jail as soon as we're anchored well."

"Aye, sir!"

Tyler turned. "You there, Mason," he called, "see that the

ship is secure, then give the boys leave to go into town."

After issuing the order the first mate walked along the deck until he came to a small iron-bound door near the port paddlewheel. Pulling a key from his pocket, he unlocked it. "All right—come out of there!"

No one answered. Tyler lit a lantern hanging on the outer wall, and entered the small, dark room. It was a storeroom packed with rope, cables, paint, and gear of all sorts. He swung the lantern around until the light fell on a figure asleep on a coil of rope. The sailor grabbed the arm of the sleeper with his meaty hand and pulled him roughly to his feet, snarling, "You can sleep in the jail, boy!"

He held the lantern high, his piercing gaze checking the stripling before him. The boy stared at him with eyes strangely bright. The red splotches on his cheekbones indicated high fever. He was perhaps two inches short of the mate's six feet, but so thin that his clothing hung like sacks. His jet-black hair was almost invisible against the shadows, and there was something foreign in the angular planes of his wedge-shaped face. When the vagabond had been discovered hiding in the small runabout the previous day, the captain said, "Looks too young to be much of a criminal," but the mate insisted that the boy be locked up and turned over to the sheriff at Richmond.

Now Tyler felt sure he had been right, for there was a wildness in the boy's face. The mate took a firmer grasp on the thin arm and jerked his prisoner out of the storeroom and down the deck, cursing him for dragging his feet. When he stepped off the gangplank onto the wharf, the sailor was pleased to see that the man sitting on a bale of cotton wore a star on his checked shirt and a gun in a worn holster.

"You the sheriff?"

Before the man with the star could answer, one of the young loafers leaning against the wall of a warehouse spoke up. He was a short man with an enormous walrus mustache that wiggled as he said, "Him? Not no way, sailor boy! This here's jest ol' Shippy Williams."

"You keep yore mouth shet, Dooley!" Williams glared at the other, then said loudly to Tyler, "I'm William Shippy, deputy around here. "Whatcha got here?"

"Fugitive, I reckon."

"Looks like a fugitive from the poorhouse to me," Dooley said. He moved closer to examine the prisoner. "Why—he ain't nothin' but a nubbin', sailor boy!"

"I tol' you to keep yore oar outta this, Dooley!" Shippy snapped. "It ain't none of yore business! Now, then, you want me to arrest this here feller?"

"I reckon," Tyler replied. "He stowed away on the *Queen*. He's probably running away from something—the law, most likely. Must be some kind of a wanted poster out on him." He stared at Shippy carefully. "You sure you got the authority to take him in?"

"Authority! See that badge? And you see this hogleg?" Shippy pulled the old cap-and-ball Colt from the holster and waved it under the mate's nose.

"Watch out with that thing!" Tyler snapped. He looked at the silent prisoner, then glanced over toward the lights of town; the music was getting louder and he wanted to get started on his own celebration. "Well, you got him, Deputy." He shoved the prisoner toward Shippy, who took a sudden step backward and put the huge bore of the pistol on the boy's chest.

"Watch yourself, Shipp!" Dooley hooted, following the pair down the wharf. "He's a dangerous character, ain't no doubt. Probably robbed a Sunday school picnic or some other such bad business."

"Git on there, you," Shippy said, poking the prisoner with the huge pistol. "An' I don't need none of yore help, Dooley Young. Best git on 'bout yore own business."

But Dooley was not to be denied. He followed the deputy closely, giving him a constant flow of advice as they passed through the gap in the levee and walked down the incline to the south end of town. The jail was at the north end of Cherry Street. They continued oh in the dark across the grassy field that led to the cobblestones forming the main street of Richmond, Virginia.

The prisoner stumbled and almost fell once, and it was evident that he could not go much farther. By the time they reached Cherry Street, the lights from shops and saloons cast their glow over broad avenues lined with buggies and filled with horsemen.

Ordinarily Richmond would have been relatively quiet at this time, but now crowds cheerfully jostled one another as they celebrated. A six-piece band was making its way up the street, playing "The Girl I Left Behind Me" with more volume than accuracy.

Several times the trio passed by saloons, from which wafted out to the street a wave of raucous noise and the odor of raw whiskey. The restaurants were doing a brisk business, and the smell of cooking pork mixed with the smell of whiskey.

Several times Shippy stopped friends to explain importantly that he had arrested a man, while Dooley pointed out the dangerous appearance of the prisoner. Finally they came to a squat red brick building with JAIL written over the door, and Shippy shoved the prisoner inside. He tried to slam the door to keep Dooley out, but the little man was too quick. He slipped inside and grinned at the large man behind the desk. "Hidee, Shurf Bailey. Your deputy's done made an important arrest."

"Will you shet up!" Shippy yelled. "*I'm* the deputy, and I'll do my own talking. Sheriff, I want to report—"

"You'd best put up that cannon before you do any reportin'," Sheriff Bailey suggested softly. He was such a huge mountain of a man, made even bigger by the heavy fur coat he wore, that the soft voice seemed to come from someone else. He carefully watched as Shippy put the pistol away; then he continued peeling the large apple almost hidden in his big hands. He listened as Shippy rambled on for five minutes, carefully closed the gold-handled knife, slipped it into his vest pocket, and leaned forward in the cane chair.

"What's your name, son?" he asked, taking in the pale face, the red spots on the cheeks, and the trembling hands.

"My name is Novak—Thaddeus Novak." The boy looked up at the sheriff defiantly.

"How old are you, Thad?"

"I . . . eighteen."

"No you ain't," the sheriff said, noting the slight hesitation. "Maybe you will be in a couple of years." Then he asked abruptly, "You wanted for something where you come from, Thad, or are you a runaway?"

"Well, shoot!" Shippy broke in. "You don't speck he's gonna come out and admit it, do you, Sheriff?" He pulled at the handle of the pistol with irritation. "You want me to lock him up till we find out what he's did?"

"I ain't done nothin'," Novak protested. "Nothin' but steal a ride on that boat." His eyes were black as night, but dull with fatigue as he stared at the sheriff.

Bailey carefully picked a choice spot on the apple and bit off a small piece. He chewed it slowly, tasting the flavor. The long silence that followed was interrupted only by the man's soft munching. It seemed as if he had forgotten the youth before him. Then he looked at Novak and said mildly, "You know, I think that's right."

"What!" Shippy yelled. "You mean to tell me yo're gonna turn him loose?" His face flushed with anger and his beady eyes almost popped out of his head.

"Ain't no paper out on him that I remember, Deputy," Bailey answered. "If we undertake to lock up every kid that stows away on a riverboat, we'll need a sight bigger jail than this one. You just go on and do some more patrolin'."

"What about him?" Shippy protested, as he edged toward the door.

Bailey took another bite of his apple. "Dunno," he said, then smiled as Shippy slammed the door with a loud crack.

"What you want, Dooley?"

"Ah nothin', Shurf," Dooley replied, grinning. "Jest thought I'd see what this here dang'rous criminal might do."

"Looks to me like he might keel over." Bailey nodded toward the boy. "You sick, Thad?"

"I'm all right," he said stubbornly, staring at the sheriff with distrust. Then he shrugged and added, "Guess I've felt better a time or two."

"Got any money?"

"If I had, I wouldn't have stowed away on that boat, would I? Can I go now?"

"I reckon so."

Bailey turned to Dooley. "I'd say the best thing for him to-night is the Mission."

"Ah, Shurf—not ol' Pitchfork!" Dooley groaned. "If this kid ain't sick now, he *will* be after a dose of that preachin'!"

"Won't hurt him none," Bailey shrugged.

"You go with Dooley, Thad," the sheriff told the boy. "Looks to me like you need to get around some food and then into a warm bed." He examined the thin face, wondering at his slightly foreign look. "Come see me tomorrow; maybe we can make some medicine."

Dooley steered the boy out the door. "He's a good shurf, Thad. Lots of that breed would of chucked you into the pokey on general principles."

"What's this mission thing?"

Dooley had to lean forward to catch the words, and he saw that the boy was almost out on his feet. Grabbing Thad's arm, he said, "Aw, it's jest a place where the Methodists git the drunks together and preach at 'em. But the good thing is that after you get preached at you get some real good grub. Ol' Miz Hollis, she does the cookin'. And they's some cots to stay the night on."

"I don't want—!"

"Oh, it ain't all that terrible, Thad."

Dooley guided the boy through the milling crowd to a side street. He noted that the stowaway wore only a thin coat and was shivering from the bite of the frosty wind that whipped around the corners. The young man made a mental note to bring one of his own worn but serviceable coats to him.

After they had walked a short distance, Dooley pointed at a frame building where the lamplight spilled through two windows. "That's it," he told Thad. "I reckon they put it this close to the saloons so's they wouldn't have to carry the drunks too far."

The two approached the building and stood under the hand-lettered sign over the door: RESCUE THE PERISHING. "Good thing you ain't got to stay out tonight," Dooley remarked. "It's startin' to snow."

He lifted the latch and pushed the door open, shoving Thad ahead of him into a room no more than twenty feet square. In one corner a large potbellied stove glowed like a huge ruby, around which six tattered men—all the worse for drink—huddled. A kerosene lantern hung high on each side of the room, casting a pale gleam on an assortment of battered chairs and a table with a Bible on it. Behind the table was a door, and Dooley nudged Thad. "That's where you get the stew and the bunks—

but you gotta put up with ol' Pitchfork first."

"Who's that?" Thad murmured weakly. He was feeling very faint and lightheaded now, and Dooley's voice seemed to come from a long way off, muffled and thin.

"Oh, he's the local sky pilot—preacher, don't you see? Now set down here, Thad. I gotta run and take care of some stuff. Jest set here and when ol' Pitchfork starts in on you, think of that good stew and warm bunk! I'll be back and check on you after a while."

Recovering some of his strength, Thad asked, "You know anybody named Winslow living around here?"

Dooley's eyes widened, and his mustache shifted as he grinned. "Boy, you better believe I do! Ain't nobody in these parts who don't know the Winslows. Why you askin'?"

"I . . . used to know somebody by that name. Worked in a mill with me. He said he came from around here. I thought I'd see if he'd come back here to his folks."

"Well, if he worked in a mill, he wasn't no kin to *these* Winslows, Thad. Mr. Sky Winslow is jest about the richest man around. 'Course, it might have been a poor Yankee relation."

"I guess." The boy stared into space for a moment, and finally asked, "Where'd you say these Winslows lived?"

"I didn't say, Thad—but they live south on the River Road— that's the one that runs alongside the levee." He studied Novak's face, then shook his head. "But they live twelve miles from Richmond, and with it beginnin' to snow, you ain't in no shape to make it." He slapped the thin shoulder and added, "I live down that there road myself, Thad. Tell you what—I'm headed home tomorrow. You can ride behind me. I gotta go right by Belle Maison—that's what the Winslows call their place."

Thad stared at the banty-legged young man. "Why you helpin' me? We ain't friends."

Dooley laughed and his bright blue eyes sparkled beneath his bushy brows. "Why, shoot, Thad! Mebby we might git to be. Anyways, I been down on my luck a time or three." He got up and walked toward the door. "Jest ride it out for tonight—and tomorrow we'll see." Then he was gone.

Thad felt more alone than ever before, even more than in the storeroom on the *Dixie Queen*. He slumped into a chair and watched the men around the stove.

The room was warm after the walk through the cold night, and Thad's head soon dropped forward and he dozed off. He thought once, *I ought to get away from here.* But the rich aroma of stew from behind the door held him and he decided, *I can stand it, I reckon.*

He awoke with a start, confused and in a panic. A large hand was shaking him, and he opened his eyes to see that the chairs were all full.

"Wake up, boy!" A red-faced man, heavily larded, was pulling at his arm.

"All right—I'm awake!" Thad growled, pulling away from the man's grip.

"Very well. See that you remain so!"

The fat man, obviously the preacher, straightened up and walked to the table at the front of the room. He picked up the thick Bible, surveyed the assortment of drunks before him, and drew his thick lips into a hard line. Shaking his head slowly, he began to moan in a blubbery whine: "Oh, *Gawd!* You see these miserable sinners!" He glanced upward, as if seeking for the Lord in the dusky ceiling, then continued his prayer in much the same manner, except that the longer it went, the shriller he became. By the time the man was finished, Thad's head ached with the sheer volume of it all. *Don't see how I can stand much more of this—even for grub!* he thought.

The Reverend Josiah Tate plunged into a sermon that was, if possible, even on a higher pitch than the invocation. He informed the wretches trapped in the cane-bottomed chairs that there was a hell, and that they were prime candidates for permanent residency. He reminded them that they had been *elected* for this fate (by some sort of divine process Thad didn't understand) and that they were undeserving of anything else.

Strangely enough, the piercing voice of the preacher did not keep Thad awake. Instead, he became accustomed to it and sat with his eyes half open, fighting to stay alert. The room grew hotter and he felt very sleepy, but knew he must hold his head up. Suddenly he was aware that something was wrong. He forced himself to focus on the preacher and was startled to find the man's fat forefinger pointed directly at him! The voice was screaming, "And *you*, no doubt, are the worst! All these men are from our town—poor unfortunate wretches that they are. Yet they are *true* men, good southern men! But you. . . !" He walked over to Thad and stabbed his thick forefinger at the boy's chest as if he wished to penetrate that region clean to the heart. "You," he shouted, "would ruin our southland! You are a benighted *Yankee* —and that is the worst of all sinners!"

Thad leaped to his feet, his head swimming with the effort, and cried, "I don't know what you're talking about!"

An oily smile spread across the round face of Rev. Tate, and he sneered, "You don't know *anything* about the North, do you? Oh, no. You're not from *there*, are you, boy?" He jabbed Thad's chest again and again as he continued to shout his questions, until the boy trembled beneath the heavy hand. "*You* aren't from that nest of vipers, are you? *You* have no knowledge of that godless place, which is reserved for the pit, have you?"

He would have continued his tirade until his victim lay prostrate at his feet if Thad hadn't jerked away and lurched toward the door. There he turned and consigned Rev. Josiah Tate to the lowest section of that region the minister had spoken of so harshly. He also told Mr. Tate *exactly* what he could do with the food and the cot for the night. Then as the man's pursed fat lips made a shocked round *O*, Thad laughed, threw open the door, and plunged out into the freezing air, slamming the door with such force that the lantern rattled against the wall.

Thousands of tiny flakes glittered in the light of the lantern. Thad's face ached with fever and from the heat of the room, and the falling flakes seemed to soothe his burning cheeks. Pulling the thin coat closer around his skinny frame, he walked unsteadily toward Cherry Street. At this hour most of the crowd had gone indoors or returned home, and Thad avoided the few left by crossing the street. He halted uncertainly, peering into the darkness where he thought the river lay, then made his way down a side street until he came to a break in the buildings. The snow had papered the ground with a thin layer, making the surface slippery underfoot. But Thad did not stop until he came to a broad road over which the dark form of the levee loomed. *Must be the River Road*, he thought, and turned to follow it southward.

There was just enough light from the crescent-shaped moon to reveal the ground if he bent forward, and he saw in the distance the light of a house beside the road. When he approached it, he almost stepped up on the porch to ask for shelter, but then he wavered and plunged on toward the next house. This, too, he passed, saying out loud, "Reckon I can walk twelve miles any day."

He began to call out the name of the place Dooley had mentioned, repeating it by syllables in cadence with each step:

"Belle—May—zon. Belle—May—zon."

The words had no meaning for him, but they kept his mind off the razor-sharp wind that whipped across the road, stiffening his face and numbing his feet. He passed a few more houses, but did not stop; instead, he plunged on, calling out "Belle—May—zon!" over and over again until he reached the end of town toward the open fields of the delta. The road wound with the meanders of the river, so he concentrated on keeping inside the perimeters of the white strip.

Time soon ceased to have meaning, and distance became the space between one step and another as he walked doggedly through the snow, now falling heavily.

After a while he could not feel his face; even his eyelashes were stuck together with snow crystals. From time to time he had to brush them off with his hands, which seemed to belong to someone else.

Finally he slipped, falling full length into the snow. He lay there, thinking very slowly and with great effort: *Gotta get up. Can't stay here.* He realized he might freeze to death, but his mind was so dulled he could not remember which way led back to town.

He tried to get up, but it took three attempts, and then he began to run, clumsily with flailing arms, but plunged into a shallow ditch beside the road. He couldn't stand up, so he pulled himself out by grabbing the thick weeds beside the road. Again he tried to get to his feet. *I can't do it,* he thought.

A strange sense of warmth began to flow through him as he lay there holding on to the weeds like a drowning man to a life preserver. He tried to rouse himself, but the warmth crept up his body and into his brain. He mumbled, "Just—a few—minutes—just—"

He drifted off and seemed to be resting in a warm feather bed. But someone was trying to get him to leave it! Someone was pulling at him, and he resisted, hating to leave the warmth that had surrounded him. He began to fight, crying out, "Leave me alone!"

Though he struggled, a strong hand grabbed him, forcing him out of the feather bed. Then he came out of his dream to see a black face not two inches from his own, the thick lips forming the words: "You cain't stay heah, white boy! You freeze to death!"

The man pulled Thad to his feet, and he felt himself being pushed against something hard. "I boost you inter da wagon—watch yo'self!" Suddenly Thad was hoisted high and fell onto a hard floor, striking his head. Sparks seemed to fly in front of his eyes, and warm blood trickled down his cheek.

"You wrap up in dis heah blanket," the man ordered, pushing the rough covering around Thad. He began drifting off to sleep at once, but a voice said sharply, "Wake up! You go to sleep now, you ain't nevah gonna wake up!" Then he called to the horses, "Git up!" The wagon lurched down the rutted road, throwing Thad from one side to the other with such force, he lost all thought of sleep!

Finally the rocking motion stopped, and he fell back, totally exhausted. He felt strong arms lifting him, and said, "I won't go to sleep!"

A deep bass laugh shook the heavy chest Thad lay against. "Dat's all right, white boy. Now, heah we goes!"

Thad drifted off, but knew that the black man had carried him out of the cold into a small room not much bigger than a closet. A cheery fire burned at one side. He managed to open his eyes, and his gaze fell on faces staring at him by the light of the tiny fire—they were all black! He smelled greens cooking, and someone made him swallow the stuff. Then he lay back and was plunged into the warmth of a smooth black darkness—safe from the icy storm raging outside.

CHAPTER TWO

BELLE MAISON

★　★　★　★

As always, the first thing Pet Winslow did when she awakened in the morning was to look out the window. She waited until the maid finished building up the fire, driving out the chill; then she threw back the covers and ran to the mullioned window. "Lucy—look!" she cried with delight. "It's like a fairyland!" As far as she could see, the earth glittered as the bright sun struck the unbroken snow. Dressing quickly in the clothing Lucy had laid out for her, she said, "Maybe we can build a snowman. And we can have snow cream!"

"Humph! It's jes' a big *mess*—thas all it be!" Lucy snapped. She was sixteen—one year older than Pet, and the rich food that the house servants ate had plumped her out until she was bursting out of her blue gingham dress. Her speech was slurred and lazy, but much clearer than that of the field hands. She had grown up as a maid to Pet and her sister Belle, and her ear was quick enough to pick up the diction of the white folks in the big house. "You wait right where you is!" she ordered as Pet made a dash for the door. "Whar you goin' widout no coat on?"

Pet snatched at the garment, drew it over her shoulders, then skipped down the winding staircase, passing through the large foyer into the smaller of the two dining rooms.

"Good morning, Papa—Mama," she called out cheerfully,

running around the large oak table to kiss both parents. Then she sat down and spoke to her brothers in a general greeting. "Hello—pass me the biscuits, Mark."

As she speared two of them, Mark Winslow, her oldest brother at the age of twenty, grinned and winked at his other two brothers sitting across from him, saying, "Pet's going to be late for the resurrection." He was the darkest of the brothers, and his high cheekbones revealed more of his Indian ancestry than was visible in Dan and Thomas. In fact, he looked much like a younger edition of his father, whose mother was a half-blooded Sioux. His hair was black as a crow's wing, and he was the largest of the three boys.

Tom Winslow at eighteen was more like his mother, having her clear hazel eyes and fair skin. Dan, at sixteen and the youngest of the boys, was fair as well. He alone of all the boys had the bright blue eyes that Sky had said most characterized the Winslow men. All three of them were outdoorsmen, expert riders and all good shots.

"Papa, can we go out for a sleigh ride today?" Pet asked, speaking around a mouthful of sorghum-soaked biscuit she had crammed into her mouth.

"Don't talk with your mouth full," her mother chided instantly. "You're going to strangle yourself one of these days, Pet." Rebekah Winslow didn't look her age. At forty-two, she seemed little different than when Sky had married her—and he often said so. Her figure was still slender, despite the six children she had borne, and her hair was the same bright auburn it had been when she had crossed the plains on a wagon train in 1839. All the children had heard the story—how she'd been deceived by a man, so their half sister, Mary, had been born out of wedlock. Sky had adopted her after he married Rebekah. Mary had married a businessman six months earlier, and they now lived in St. Louis. Joe, Sky's son by his first wife, was a successful lawyer in Richmond, Virginia. Every year he brought his wife Louise and their two boys to Belle Maison for a two-week visit. There had been a foster son, Tim Sullivan, but he had died of cholera at the age of sixteen.

Rebekah gave a half-whimsical look at Mark, saying, "You can't use the sleigh, Pet. Mark's going to take Belle over to the Bartons."

Sky Winslow caught the glance Rebekah gave Mark, and smiled at his oldest son. "Are you taking Belle or yourself over there?"

Mark flushed slightly under his coppery tan, and affected indifference. "Oh, I suppose it would be nice to see Rowena again."

"Oh, Mark Winslow, you *are* a sly one!" Pet grinned. Her blue eyes sparkled as she loaded her plate with eggs, sugar-cured ham, fresh butter, sorghum, grits and a heap of steaming mush. "You'd get mad enough if Vance Wickham beat you over there!" She shoveled a big forkful of eggs into her mouth, giggling.

"You're going to choke if you don't take smaller bites," Mark snapped. He was very fond of Pet, but he hated to be teased about his stormy courtship of Rowena Barton. "Mother, can't you teach this child some proper manners? She eats like a hog!" He was frowning, and swallowed a cup of scalding coffee so quickly that he nearly gagged, his face turning crimson.

"The way I hear it," Sky Winslow said solemnly, "it's not the local competition you have to worry about, Mark. I understand Rowena got herself a prize young fellow while she was away at school in Boston. Rich as Croesus—at least his family is."

Rebekah winked across the table at Tom and Dan, saying innocently, "You'd better start giving your big brother an extra prayer or two. It's not going to be easy to take Rowena's mind off a rich Yankee."

"Who cares about him?" Mark countered. "If she's crazy enough to fall for a Yankee, I'm not interested in her."

"He's in the army, isn't he, Mark?" Sky asked.

"Yes. I got it from Beau—but I ask you, Father, what kind of southern girl would get mixed up with a Yankee soldier when a war's coming on?"

"I pray there won't be a war, Mark," his mother said firmly.

"Not be a war!" Dan sat back and stared at her in amazement. "Why, Mother, you can save *that* prayer!"

"Dan's right, Mother," Tom agreed with a knowing nod. "There has to be a war. No way out of it now."

Rebekah looked at her three sons, and her eyes clouded. She saw Sky's expression, and knew there was no way their three hot-blooded sons could escape the war fever that was sweeping the South like an epidemic.

Sky shook his head, put down his coffee cup, and spoke slowly, regret in his voice. "I guess they're right, Rebekah. Gone too far to settle this issue any other way."

"Is it over slavery, Papa?" Pet asked. Her quick eyes caught the distressed look in her mother's eyes. "Why can't we just let the slaves go? Then there wouldn't be any war."

"If it were that simple, Pet," he answered, "I'd free all our slaves in a second." He had left the West Coast with a large amount of money made in the fur business fifteen years earlier. Land had been cheap in Virginia, and he had put his money in land, buying large tracts here and there, until now Belle Maison was one of the largest plantations in Virginia. All his neighbors owned slaves, and a large number of them had come with the original purchase of the land close to Richmond—but he had never liked the idea. He had often said to his wife, "It's not right, Rebekah—one human being owning another. I'm going to get out of it some way or other."

Sky had tried, but cotton farming requires many workers, and there simply hadn't been enough help to keep the plantation going. Winslow took some comfort in the knowledge that his slaves were treated better than any he knew of—pampered, his overseer called it—but he still had a guilty feeling.

When he brought his attention back to the table, Sky heard Tom saying to Pet with a superior air, "Why, you little silly, who'd work the fields if all the slaves were free? You? You can't even get to breakfast on time! Anyway, the North doesn't have any right to tell us what we can do with our own property!"

"They're probably going to try," Sky said sadly. "Lincoln won't let the thing rest."

"Well, it won't last long, Father," Mark predicted. "Why, you can just imagine what would happen to a Yankee army of factory workers! Any good Southerner can whip three Yankees any time!" This was a current doctrine among the young men of his class, the number varying from three to ten, depending on the speaker.

The conversation continued in this vein, with the three young men lightly speaking of the approaching war as if it were a fox hunt. Rebekah was glad when Belle came through the door, saying, "Hello, Mama—Papa. Sorry I'm late."

Belle Winslow was thought of as the most beautiful girl in the county. She was taller than her mother, and her figure was perfect—slim, yet fully rounded. Her hair was glossy black and straight. Large dark blue eyes with lashes that curled impossibly, lips that were full and red with no help from cosmetics, and a flawless skin—all well shaped, tidy and perfectly done. She had been the belle of every ball in the county since she was fifteen; and her father had once said in despair, "I'm going to have to charge room and board to Belle's beaus if they keep cluttering up the house!"

Pet glanced at her sister and smiled. That she was not in the least jealous of Belle was a minor miracle, but it was true. Her parents noticed that smile and looked at each other, thinking the same thought: *What a shame that Pet isn't as pretty as Belle, but isn't it wonderful that she has so many other fine qualities?* Not that Pet was plain, but next to her sister's delicate beauty, Pet's face seemed—well, strong. And as Sky watched her, he thought, *She's a strong child.* In fact, in some ways she was like another son to him. She loved every aspect of plantation life, and was as likely to be seen riding the fields with her father as helping her mother with the housekeeping.

Sophie, the oldest of the household slaves, came bustling in with an announcement. "That worthless Toby say he hafta see you, Massa Winslow." Sophie was nearly seventy, but she had been in charge of the children since they were babies. Now her little black eyes snapped with anger. "I tol' that worthless nigger to git—but he say you gotta speak to 'im."

Sky Winslow smiled. "I've not finished breakfast, Sophie. Let him come in here."

Sophie sniffed as she turned to leave the room. "I don't speck it mount to a hill of beans!" She stepped outside, and they heard her say shrilly, "All right, wipe yo' big feet now—and keep yo' hands offa things!"

The Negro that entered the door was very large and powerfully built. He moved carefully, as if he were afraid of breaking something. Snow glistened in his wooly hair, and he twisted a shapeless cap in his massive hands. Glancing balefully at Sophie, he said in a deep voice, "I's got a sick man in mah house, Miz Winslow."

"What's the matter with him, Toby?" Mr. Winslow asked. It was not uncommon for sickness to strike in the slave quarters, but it was rather strange for Toby to make such a direct report; usually one of the women would come to Rebekah, and she would see to the remedy.

Toby shifted nervously and his eyes rolled as he muttered, "Don' rightly know, Mistuh Winslow. He awful sick, though. Mebby die."

With slaves selling for a thousand dollars apiece, this was serious. "Who is it, Toby?"

The black man did not answer at first, which was strange. Finally he said, "I don' know who he is, suh."

"Don't know? Isn't he one of ours?" Mark demanded. "Is he from around here?"

"No, suh, he ain't from no place round heah," Toby replied emphatically. "I wuz drivin' back from town last night wif de new plow, an' I sees dis heah man. He wuz mos' buried wif snow, an' I almos' don' sees him. When I gets down, I sees he ain't dead—so I load him in de wagon and Jessie puts him in de bed at mah house."

"Well, he must belong to somebody," Mr. Winslow said. "All right, Toby. I'll come by and have a look at the fellow."

As Toby left, Tom frowned. "Well, that's strange. Toby knows everybody in these parts. Maybe he's a runaway."

"Wouldn't surprise me," Mark commented as he got up. "Not with all the abolitionists roaming the country. He may have decided to cut and run for the North. Well, Belle, are you going to the Bartons?"

"I'll be ready as soon as I finish my breakfast and pack a few things."

Mr. Winslow laughed. "Well, you can read a book until noon, Mark. You know her—she'll carry enough clothes to last through the Millennium!"

"I'm leaving in twenty minutes!" Mark announced firmly, and turned to leave the room.

"All right, Mark, take her over—and you might say hello to Rowena for the rest of us—if you can cut your way through her suitors." Then Sky turned to Belle. "You be back by Wednesday, you hear me?"

"Oh, I will, Papa." She smiled at his stern words, and rose to kiss him. "Pet, you'll help me pack, won't you? There's a dear!"

After the children were all gone, Sky went to stare out of the bay window. After a time, he turned and said, "You're worried, aren't you, Rebekah?"

"Yes. I'm afraid of this war talk. And I don't know about Mark. He's serious about Rowena."

"You don't think she'd be a good wife?"

"Who can tell, Sky?" Rebekah sipped at a cup of coffee. "She's never done anything but go to balls. After she gets married, she's got to do more than that."

Sky grinned, and came to put his hand fondly on her shoulder. "Well, that describes Belle pretty well, wouldn't you say? She'd starve to death in a pie factory! Doubt if she knows where an egg comes from."

"Oh, I know, dear." She raised his hand and kissed it, then got up, and he pulled her into his arms. She laughed. "Oh, Sky, I'm too old for that!"

"Like blazes you are!" He kissed her full on the lips. "You put all these young women to shame, Rebekah!" He held her close and said quietly, "Try not to worry. Let's pray that the North will show some judgment."

"Yes, because there's no hope that our folks will show any." Rebekah drew back, and her face was tight with apprehension. "Some of these hot-headed fools are acting like a war is some kind of Christmas picnic." She shook her head, adding, "Well, I suppose Rowena is no more empty-headed than the rest of them."

"Good thing we have Pet," Sky smiled. "She's got enough sense to make up for them all. If she can just decide to be a young lady and stop chasing around like an overseer." He sighed, then changed the subject. "Need anything from town?"

"I'll make a list for you, but first let's go see that sick man Toby picked up."

They followed the brick path around the house, walking past the smokehouse and several small out buildings. The slave quarters were almost a fourth of a mile from the Big House, but there was a beaten path in the snow leading to their lodgings. The quarters consisted of two rows of small cabins facing each other across a space of about fifty feet. Smoke spiraled upward from every cabin, mingling with the cold, crisp air. Most of the slaves were inside, for there was little work to be done during the winter.

I wonder how many factory workers have houses as warm as these? Sky wondered as they made their way to Toby's cabin. There were no finer quarters in the country, and Sky never looked at them without thinking how fortunate his slaves were. Most owners kept their slaves in leaky shacks, with gaps six inches wide that let in the wintry blasts.

All the cabins were the same: built of good pine lumber, with a brick floor and a small fireplace for heating and cooking. There were two small glass windows in each, and Winslow had heard that many of his fellow planters felt he had gone too far, providing such luxuries for slaves.

His thoughts were interrupted when a voice called from behind, and they turned to see Pet running lightly across the snow. "I'm going with you, Papa. Maybe I can help nurse him." She fancied herself a nurse, and Rebekah often said that Pet was good with sick people, so Winslow nodded, and she walked along with them.

"There's Toby," he murmured, and kept a tight grip on Rebekah's arm as they crossed the hard packed snow. Toby stepped back and let them in without a word, then followed and shut the door.

It was dark inside, but the tiny windows and the cheerful flickering light of the fire allowed them to take in the form of Jessie, Toby's wife, leaning over the single bed in the room. Their son Wash clung to her dress, hiding his head from the white people.

"Well, let's have a look at him," Winslow said, stepping forward to the bed. He gasped in surprise, "Why, this is no slave, Toby!"

"No, suh." Toby's face was impassive, and he added, "I nevah said he wuz, Mistuh Winslow."

Rebekah moved to stand beside Sky, and the two looked at the face of the sick man, for Jessie had wrapped him from head to foot in a ragged quilt. He appeared very young, and in spite of his covers, the outline of his body indicated an extremely slight frame. His cheeks were flaming red and his dark eyes were half open. They were large eyes, set in a wedge-shaped face that was planed down to a bone structure that had a foreign look. His hands were outside the cover, and though very large, they were thin and wasted. *His hands look like those of a worker,* Sky thought. The face itself, he noted, was hammered into a hardness only hardworking men have.

"Why, he's only a boy!" Mrs. Winslow cried. She put her hand on his forehead. "He's burning up with fever."

"Yassum, he is," Jessie nodded. "An' gittin' worse all de time!"

Pet crowded in beside them and stared down at the boy. "Is he going to die?"

No one answered, and then Winslow asked, "What do you think, Rebekah?"

"I think you'd better stop by Dr. Wright's on your way to town."

"Well, he may not be sober."

"Sober him up then! Now, take a wagon and have Toby bring him back, drunk or sober."

"All right. Toby, hitch up the light wagon." Then looking at the sick man, Sky asked, "Did he ever say who he was?"

"No, suh."

They moved away from the bed, Rebekah warning, "Jessie, better not give him anything more to eat before the doctor comes."

"He won't eat nothin', Miz Winslow."

It was nearly three in the afternoon before Toby pulled up in the circular driveway with the doctor drooped beside him on the seat. Rebekah and Pet went out and rode with them to the slave quarters.

Dr. W. G. Wright slumped in the seat, obviously in the last stages of a fierce hangover. He was seventy-one years old, and had been a large man in his youth. Now his bulbous nose was the fleshiest thing about him, for drink had burned the flesh off his body. He had gone through three wives and a sizable fortune, and now was the joke of the local medical profession. Rebekah

Winslow did not agree. She knew that despite the ruin of his life, there was more ability and shrewd knowledge in the aged drunk than in all the fine doctors in Richmond. It gave her some pleasure to let them know she thought so, too.

They stopped in front of the cabin, and Toby jumped out to help the women down. Then he took Dr. Wright by the arm, as the old man nearly slipped getting down.

"I'm all right—get your hand off me!" he snapped. "Let's get inside before I freeze! Go on in, Rebekah; you too, Pet. What in the name of common sense and the twelve apostles are you two planning to do here?"

He took over at once when they were inside, going immediately to the bed and yanking the cover down to get a good look at his patient. The young man was wearing an old shirt of Toby's, and it was soaked with perspiration.

"Looks like a plucked chicken," Wright muttered angrily, as if it were a personal affront. He began to poke at the boy's chest, then listened to the heart. Finally he threw the covers back over the boy, and said abruptly, "Well, Rebekah, what do you want me to do?"

"Why, treat the boy, of course!"

"Rebekah," he said in disgust, "you know as much as I do about fever. You can see he's got pneumonia—or almost, anyway. If you leave him here, you'll bury him inside two or three days."

"What about the hospital?"

The old doctor coughed and went to spit in the fireplace. Turning his watery eyes on her, he grunted, "You know my opinion of that butcher shop. He can die as well there as here, I suppose."

"Dr. Wright," Pet cried, "*you* must stay here and take care of him!"

"Got no proper place, Pet," he said. "Too crowded in here. Not enough air. What he needs is a quiet place with lots of air— and most of all, good care. Might make it with that."

"Mother, we can put him in the old storehouse next to the larder," Pet said eagerly.

"But—who'll take care of him?"

"*We* can! We have house servants all over the place gettin' in one another's way. And you'll stay and help, won't you, Dr. Wright?" She saw a refusal forming on his lips, and smiled sweetly, "I do believe I can find you some of that pecan pie you liked so much."

Dr. Wright stared at her for a long time, and finally a light of humor appeared in his red eyes. "Pet Winslow, you are *bad*! Bribing an old man with food is a sin, isn't it, Rebekah?"

Rebekah saw that he would stay, and asked, "Toby, do you need any help to take him to the house?"

"No, Miz Winslow. He don't weigh no more'n a bird!"

"All right, you give Pet and me about an hour to get the room ready; then you bring him up. You want to go with us, Doctor?"

"No, I'll stay with him. Pet, you find that pie while your mama's gettin' the bed ready." He looked down at the still figure and added sourly, "Better get a lot of it. Looks like this boy is going to be a real problem. Maybe he'll last out the week. If he does, he's got a chance."

It was late in the afternoon by the time Toby brought the unconscious boy into the room. The doctor looked with approval at the clean bed, the table beside it with the medicines he had ordered—and especially the generous slice of fresh pecan pie on an elegant luncheon plate.

Wright reached into his coat and brought out a small bottle of brandy. He uncorked it, lifted it to the light, licked his lips, then paused. With a gesture that was almost violent, he corked the bottle and banged it down on the table, addressing it in a hard voice: "Not one drop till this boy is either well or in his grave!"

CHAPTER THREE

NEW HAND

★ ★ ★ ★

Sometimes it was very dark and all he could see were the coals in the hearth, gleaming like red eyes at him. The light would flare so brightly that it made him shut his eyes and turn away. Faces would come and go, seeming to float so close he could see them clearly; then they would slowly dissolve as he drifted off again. Two faces he saw more than any others—one was old, with lines like a spider's web, and eyes dim and yellow in their deep sockets. The other was a young face, pale as ivory and framed by hair drawn up into a soft halo. He associated the old face with a rough touch and flinched when it appeared, but the young face always meant a soft voice urging him to drink, and a gentle hand holding his head up.

Other sounds would come to him as he tried to burrow out of the warm darkness that seemed to hold him like quicksand. Thick, dark voices spoke in a manner so odd he could not understand them. Then he would drop back into a heavy sleep, and all the noises would fade like the tide going out.

He finally rose out of the heavy sleep with an abruptness that confused him, like a swimmer who rises from the depths of dark waters, breaking through into a blinding sun in one instant. One moment he was groggy and confused; the next second his eyes opened and he saw the familiar old face not six inches away from his own.

"Well, it's about time you decided to wake up, young fellow!" the old man said. He shook his head in wonder, adding, "For a time there, I thought you were going to wake up with a set of wings—or maybe in a hotter climate!"

Thad opened his mouth to ask where he was, but his lips were so dry he could not speak.

"Here, boy, drink some of this." The old man placed a glass of cool water to Thad's lips, and he gulped greedily.

"Take it easy, boy, and drink slowly. I'm Dr. Wright, in case you're wondering." He sat back, observing Thad. "Now I don't want you to talk too much, but you should say a little, I guess."

"Where am I?"

"This is Belle Maison—Mr. Winslow's plantation. Do you remember how you got here?"

Thad thought about it, then answered weakly, "I was on a boat, and then I got off, and then—well, I remember being in some kind of a church. I remember walking in the snow—but that's all. Can I have another drink of water?"

Dr. Wright gave him another drink, then asked, "Are you hungry?" He smiled at the look on the boy's face. "I reckon you are. All you had for days is what little chicken soup we could ladle down your gullet. I'll go have some grub sent in—then maybe you can talk a little."

The doctor left the room stiffly, for he had spent long hours in the chair. He had remained at Belle Maison ever since Toby had brought him, and the effort had been draining. He walked outside, following the brick path toward the kitchen door. The snow was still on the ground, but it had been cleared from the walk, and the steps had been dusted with sand to give safe footing.

He climbed the steps, entered, and saw Pet and Sophie up to their arms in flour at a large table. Pet looked up and asked quickly, "Did he wake up?"

"Just now. Where's your mother?"

"She went over to the Taylors' early this morning. Mrs. Taylor's sick."

"She's always sick—or thinks she is," Wright responded

grumpily. "The boy needs something solid to eat. Battered eggs, maybe."

Pet went to the huge fireplace and dragged a massive black skillet away from the coals. Lifting the lid, she said, "There's lots of scrambled eggs here left over from breakfast."

"That'll do—and maybe a biscuit with butter."

She piled the food on a plate and covered it with a cloth. "I'll take it to him," she offered.

"All right," the doctor replied wearily. "I'm going to drink a gallon of coffee; then I'll be there. Let him have all he wants, I guess—just don't let him founder himself."

Pet left the kitchen, and when she got to the door of the small room she balanced the tray on one hand and entered. She walked over and looked down at the patient, who watched her steadily.

"Hello," she said cheerfully. "I'm Pet Winslow. Dr. Wright said you may eat as much as you wish." She didn't give him a chance to talk, but set the plate on his lap and pulled the cloth off. He began wolfing the food down so voraciously that she was afraid he might choke. She had never seen anyone attack food like this young man. Though weak, he brought the plate to his lips and raked the yellow eggs into his mouth, seeming to swallow without chewing! From time to time he picked up a biscuit with a trembling hand and stuffed the whole thing in his mouth, adding more eggs. Finally he washed everything down with a large glass of milk.

"Well, you *were* hungry, weren't you?"

Only then did Thad realize how crude his manners must have appeared as he wolfed down the food, and he flushed in embarrassment. He had never been in the presence of a young woman of this class. Her clothes were finely woven of delicately dyed material, not the cheap cotton the girls of his acquaintance wore. She was, he saw, not even as old as he. He noted the oval face surrounded by light brown hair that came down in an odd point right in the middle of her forehead. The dark blue eyes were large and well-set, and she seemed very much at ease.

He shifted nervously in the bed, trying to think of something to say. Her voice was not thick and mushy like those he'd been hearing in his sleep. Hers was softer and much slower than he was accustomed to. He sat up straighter and handed her the empty plate. "That was real good, miss." He looked at her more closely and asked cautiously, "I've seen you before, ain't I?"

"Oh yes. We've been taking turns nursing you."

"How long have I been here?"

"Nearly a week. Toby brought you in on the second—and this is the seventh." She looked at him curiously. "What's your name?"

Just at that moment, Dr. Wright came in, followed by her father. "Well, I see you got it all down," Wright said, then added, "This is Mr. Winslow."

"Glad to see you're feeling better," Winslow acknowledged. "Maybe you can tell us who you are."

"I'm Thaddeus Novak, Mr. Winslow. They call me Thad."

"Where are you from, Novak?"

"New York, sir."

"Bad time to be coming south, Thad," the doctor remarked. "Where are you headed?"

Thad hesitated. "Well, I was trying to get west—but I got sick."

Winslow asked, "Who are your people, Thad?"

"Ain't got no people."

"You must have someone," Pet said quickly.

"No, ma'am."

Winslow saw the stubborn line in the boy's jaw. "You know there's going to be a war, don't you, Thad?"

"Heard some talk. Don't know nothin' about it, though."

Winslow studied him for a minute. "Dooley Young said he met you in town. He told me you asked for the Winslow place."

A sudden flush touched Novak's cheeks, but he shook his head. "I was outta my head, I reckon. Don't remember nobody named Dooley."

It was obvious to Winslow and to the doctor that the boy was lying, but there was nothing to be gained by pressuring him.

"Guess if you'll give me my clothes, I'll be heading out," Thad said.

"You wouldn't go far, boy. You better stay here until Mr. Winslow gets some meat on your bones." He saw the boy frame a protest, so he added roughly, "Go to sleep, boy! I got too much invested in you to bury you *now!*"

They left the cabin and went back to the kitchen. Wright settled himself in a chair and said, "Pet, you wouldn't happen to have baked any more of that pie, would you?" He waited while she brought him a slice; then he lifted a huge forkfull to his lips. "Ahhhh! This is the best pie this side of Richmond, Sky!"

"I'm suspicious of that boy, Doc," Sky frowned. "He's not telling the truth."

"Well, who in blazes *is*, Winslow?" Wright demanded. "You've been caught up in this abolitionist scare. You reckon the boy is a Yankee spy?"

"Well, no—but who is he?"

"He's only a *boy*, Papa," Pet said.

"I don't think he's dangerous—but he's hiding something," Winslow insisted. "How long do you think we'll have to keep him—before he's well enough to make it on his own?"

"How should I know?" Wright asked sleepily. "Go ask them fancy doctors in Richmond. They claim to know everything."

"He'll be well pretty soon, Papa," Pet nodded. "He's just weak."

"You take care of him, Pet," Wright said, then turned to Sky. "Tell Toby to hitch up the wagon, will you? I'm going home to get drunk."

Sky shrugged. "I'll tell Toby."

Thad spent the next three days eating and sleeping, getting out of bed only for short periods as his strength returned. Much of this time he listened to Pet Winslow, for she had taken Dr. Wright's suggestion and had assumed the responsibility of preparing and bringing Thad his food. At first he was tense, but she never referred to his past or asked any questions about his personal life. From these conversations he learned a great deal about Belle Maison. Pet would sit nearby and tell him about the servants, the work, her family, the neighbors—all the things that made up her world. It was, however, a strange and foreign world to Thad! His life had been iron-hard, bone-deep in poverty, and a direct contrast to Belle Maison—the luxury of the food, the dress of the family, even of the house servants, was obvious.

Late one Thursday afternoon Mr. Winslow came to visit Thad

and found him sitting outside on a rock planter, enjoying the fresh air. Thad grew tense, but there was nothing threatening about the expression on Winslow's face. "Well, you're looking much better, Thad."

"Oh, I'm fine, Mr. Winslow—and I sure do thank you for helping me out."

"Well, I guess you'll have to give most of the credit to Toby. You'd have died in that snowstorm if he hadn't pulled you out." Winslow looked at Thad carefully, noting that the boy looked healthy. Thin, of course, but one day that frame would fill out. His hands were hard and calloused, and Winslow liked the boy's face. There was a stubbornness in the dark eyes, but that was fine with Sky Winslow, who himself was a stubborn man.

"Thad, I'd like to ask you a question, but don't answer if you don't want to. You're from the North—are you in any kind of service for the Union?"

"No, I ain't, Mr. Winslow."

The boy did not protest, and Winslow liked that. "I believe you, Thad. Now, I've got an offer for you. You can't go anywhere until this snow is gone, and you don't have any money, I take it."

"No, sir. I'm plumb busted."

"Well, I think we can keep you until you get your strength back—not here, of course, but in my overseer's cabin. He's got plenty of room and an extra bed. You can rest up and put some meat on that skinny frame—then we'll see."

The unexpected kindness was too much for Thad. He could only swallow and nod. Winslow saw this, and patted the boy's thin shoulder, "Well, you take it easy, Thad, and we'll be talking later."

Winslow went immediately to see Sut Franklin, his overseer. Franklin was a rough man who took little care of himself, a characteristic of most overseers. He was too hard on the slaves, and Winslow had to watch him carefully.

Franklin listened, then shrugged carelessly. "He'll have to take care of hisself, Mr. Winslow. I ain't no nursemaid."

"He won't require any care. See that he gets plenty to eat, Sut. Maybe we can use him around here."

"Not likely," Franklin returned quickly. "He's a Yankee, ain't he? We don't need his kind!"

Later that day Franklin came for Thad, taking him to the small house. "That's your bunk," he said roughly, then added, "I won't be here much for the next few days. Big poker game goin' on in town. You can get fed in the kitchen at the Big House." He was surly about it, and said nothing more to Thad until he left for Richmond that evening.

For two days Thad ate huge meals and walked around the property. His strength flowed back, and late on the second day, he went to the slave quarters and asked an old man with snowy white hair where Toby lived. The man said something, but Thad didn't understand a word. Thad could understand the house servants fairly well, but this old man sounded as if he had a mouth full of mush. Finally the man looked at him in disgust and pointed at a house right across from where they were. Thad went to the door and knocked. When it opened a large black man stood before him. "Well, look at you! Ain't you jes' all well, sho nuff!"

"I guess you must be Toby," Thad said, then hesitated, not knowing what to say next.

Toby turned quickly and called, "Jessie, look heah who's done come to see us." He opened the door wider. "Come on in, now."

Thad entered and took in the single bed stuffed with shucks, the stone fireplace with pothooks and black utensils—then glanced at the woman and the small boy. "I . . . sort of remember you . . . but not much," he apologized to Toby. "But I know you saved my life—so I came to thank you for it."

Toby nodded, grinning widely. "Why, you mighty welcome. I reckon you do da same fo' me."

"I sure hope so," Thad replied. "Well, I guess I better get."

"Wait a minute," Toby interrupted. "You et yet? No? You is a Yankee boy, ain't you?"

"Guess so, Toby."

"Well, you set right in dat cheer, and pitch inter some of dis catfish. You ain't nevah had no fish till you eats a mess of bull-head catfish!"

Thad sat down awkwardly, but soon the tension left him. He felt more at home in the small cabin with the slaves than he had in the Big House. Jessie was quiet at first and the boy, Wash, was bashful, but after a time, the woman began to smile and the boy came to stare up into Thad's face. The fresh catfish steaks had been fried in fat and were the most delicious Thad had ever put in his mouth. He allowed Jessie to fill his plate twice, then held up his hand, moaning, "No more! I'm plumb full!"

He stayed at the cabin until it was so dark he had trouble finding his way back to Franklin's. For a long time he lay awake thinking with a warm feeling of the friendliness of the black slaves, and wondering what it was like to be owned by someone. He thought of stories he'd heard in the North about slaves being beaten to death; then his thoughts drifted to Pet Winslow and how gentle she was. Finally he dozed off.

The Winslows had just sat down to breakfast the next morning when the sound of an axe on wood floated into the room. Sky got up, walked to the window and peered out. "Well, I'll be a—look at this, all of you!"

Pet ran to him, followed by her brothers and her mother. "What is it, Papa?"

"It's that young Novak fellow. He's cutting wood out there."

Rebekah watched the boy as he brought the axe down on a block of oak, cutting it cleanly in two. "He shouldn't be doing that, Sky!" she protested.

"I'll go tell him to stop." He hurried outside to the woodpile where Thad was lifting his axe. "Now, Thad, we can't have this!"

Thad dropped the axe, splitting the wood easily. "I've got to earn my keep."

"Plenty of time for that!"

Thad shook his head stubbornly. "No, sir. If you won't let me work, I'll have to move on."

Winslow stared at the intent face, thinking, *If all Yankees are as stubborn as this one, then heaven help the South!* He reached out and took the axe from Thad, saying, "All right, you can work, but not splitting wood. We have to cut a lot of ice this week. You can help with that."

"Cut ice? What for, Mr. Winslow?"

"Why, we cut it off the river and store it in our icehouse. Pack it with straw and it keeps through most of the summer. We sell it in Richmond, mostly. You go out with Toby tomorrow—but don't overdo it."

"I'll be careful, sir. I—I just can't sit around and do nothing!"

When Sky got back to the house, Tom asked, "What's he doing, Pa?"

"Says he has to earn his keep, Tom."

"He's still a Yankee, though," Dan insisted.

Sky Winslow stared toward the woodyard, then said quietly, as if to himself, "I don't think so, Dan. I don't reckon he's anything—not yet, anyway!"

CHAPTER FOUR

CHRISTMAS GIFT

★ ★ ★ ★

The day following his talk with Mr. Winslow, Thad had risen at dawn and gone to the lake to cut ice with Toby in a wagon fitted with sled runners. As they prepared to get into the vehicle, Toby cautioned, "Now you listen to ol' Toby. I didn' pull you outta de snow to hep you kill yo'self cuttin' ice. So you jes' kinda set back and take it easy till you gits plumb well." He grinned at Thad. "You know how to drive a team?"

"Me? No, Toby."

"Well, git in an' you can learn." The two climbed up on the seat, and Toby gave him the lines. "Hold dis line like dat—an' put dis 'un like dat. Now—jes' say 'Hup, Gyp!—Hup, Babe!'—an' you see how easy it is."

Thad called out to the mules, and was delighted with the ease of the ride. He had been in a horse-drawn streetcar in New York once, but it could not compare to the joy of sweeping along the icy road with the green pines whipping by so fast they blurred in his sight. He called out again, and was a little alarmed when the sleek mules broke out into a dead run. "What do I do now, Toby?" he cried.

"I guess you goes wif' 'em, Thad!" Toby laughed. "Let 'em go. Mebby dey run some of dat meanness outta dere system!"

Finally the mules slowed to a trot, and Thad began to look

around at the landscape. "This sure is flat country, Toby." As far as he could see there was no rise of ground higher than a five-foot knoll. The hardwoods that covered the horizon were bare, glistening with the casing of ice that loaded the smaller branches to the ground. The tall evergreens farther back from the river were topped with massive mounds of new snow. The fresh, clean air was like wine, bringing a crimson flush to Thad's cheeks. His eyes sparkled with new life. "Is it this flat everywhere around here?" he asked.

"Nooo, not ever' place. North of Richmond dey's some purty good hills—but dis is de Delta, Thad. Look, you sees dat little road up ahead? Turn da team dat way." He watched carefully as Thad guided the mules down a small side road, and nodded his head. "You gonna be a good driver, I allows."

Ten minutes later they arrived at a narrow lake, actually a small oxbow lake that was part of an old riverbed. Toby explained to Thad as they drove up the bank and descended, "Ain't much to it, cuttin' ice. We jes' take dis saw an' cut off some chunks. Den we take 'em to de icehouse an' cover 'em up wif straw. Next summertime we gets de ice and sells it in Richmond. Last July Mistuh Sky, he made nuff vaniller ice cream fo' ever' hand at Belle Maison!"

He led Thad out on the ice to a squared hole, saying, "See whar I been cuttin'? Now you jes' watch ol' Toby and see how to do it." He took the large bucksaw that had been shortened and fitted with a handle and put it in the gap. He drew it back and forth with his powerful hands until he had a straight cut, then picked up the hatchet he'd laid on the ice. "Ain't no need to cut but one way," he said, and gave the ice a hard blow. A rough square-shaped chunk of ice broke free. Toby reached down and flipped it to the ice, giving it a kick with his foot that sent the ice chunk skidding to the bank. "Dat's all dey is to it. A sight easier den cuttin' post oak wif a bucksaw."

"Let me try it." Thad took the saw and was amazed to discover how easily the ice parted. "Why—this is *easy!*" he cried.

"Humph! We'll see 'bout *dat* when it comes quittin' time," Toby sniffed. He let Thad work for a while, then made him rest. They took their time, but by noon a large supply of frozen slabs lined the bank and Toby called a halt.

They ate a lunch of cold chicken, thick slices of ham, biscuits with butter and peach preserves—all washed down with milk from a stone bottle.

After they finished, Thad looked at Toby and asked with some hesitation, "Toby . . . can I ask you something?"

"Reckon you can."

"Well, I ain't never been around—" He halted, not knowing how to phrase the question that had pushed at his mind for some time. "Well, I grew up in the North, and . . . ."

Toby gave him a quick glance, then chuckled softly. "What you means is you ain't nevah had nuffin' to do wif no black folks. Dat it?"

"Well—yes. All my life I've been hearing about how bad slaves get treated in the South. Lots of folks say some slave owners beat their slaves—and even worse."

Toby stopped smiling and gave Thad a sober look. "I tell you what I couldn't nevah tell no white man from round heah, Thad. You thinks we is treated purty good heah at Belle Maison, ain't dat so? And we is, fo' a fact! But most of de talk you hears up North is so on mos' plantations. I done seen some mighty *bad* things, Thad—an' ask yo'self what would happen if Toby gits sold to somebody who *ain't* so good to his hands like de Winslows. What if I gits sold to somebody like Solomon Spencer ovah in Louisiana? He done kill two of his slaves. Beat 'em to death wif his whip!"

Toby's voice got deeper, and a strange light fired his eyes as he whispered, "What you think happen to my Jessie an to Wash if I gits sold? I ain't nevah raised my hand to no white man, Thad, but if dey do dat to me—!" Toby broke off abruptly, and his face was rigid as he turned to look across the icy lake. His hands were trembling, Thad saw, and he could not say a word.

"Well, I reckon you want this war to come, then," Thad commented. "That's what they say will happen—all the slaves will go free. Lincoln says so."

"I don' know, Thad. I don' reckon dey's any easy way to fix up dis mess." Toby got up slowly and added, "I's gonna be a good hand fo' Mistuh Winslow 'long as I can. He's mighty good to me—but dey ain't all like him." He shook his wide shoulders and forced a grin. "Come on, now, let's git dis wagon loaded.

Mebby we git back late 'nough so's we don' hafta make 'nother trip till tomorrow."

They drove back slowly, the mules throwing their strength to pull the heavy load, and all along the way Toby was pointing out different kinds of trees, animal signs, and the best places to hunt coon and possum. He seemed to Thad so gentle for all his enormous strength, and yet the boy sensed the potential for explosive anger in the black man.

They unloaded the ice in a building such as Thad had never seen before. Only the roof was out of the ground, and a stone ramp led down to the chamber dug out of solid earth. Inside he saw rough-hewn chunks of ice stacked to the heavy rafters, and they guided their new store of ice into place, then covered it with straw. "Make good ice cream nex' summer, Thad!" Toby said as he closed the heavy door.

Every day they went early to the lake and cut ice, and by the end of the week Thad's strength seemed to have been restored by the fresh air, work, and good food. "I always was quick to get well," he said to Toby as they made their way back with a load. "Why, I bet I can work more now than before I got sick!"

Even as Thad spoke, a man on a bay horse caught up with the wagon, gave the two a cursory glance and rode on. Suddenly he pulled the horse up sharply, wheeled, and spurred the animal back to them.

"Well, I'll be dogged!" he said in amazement. Throwing his scarf to one side he exposed a massive mustache that covered the lower half of his face. "I been wonderin' what happened to you." He gave Thad a quick look. "Guess you don't remember me. I'm Dooley Young. Took you over to ol' Pitchfork at the Mission."

"Sure, I remember," Thad said. "Well, some of it, anyway. Never did get a chance to thank you, Dooley."

Dooley waved his thanks aside, and pulling at his mustache, said, "Well, I reckon ol' Pitchfork's preachin' was worse than I thought. When I went back to the Mission, you was gone, and all the preacher would say was that you wasn't no fit candidate for a Methodist! Guess you hurt his feelings, Thad!"

"I got sort of confused, I guess," Thad smiled. "Got out on the road and would have died if Toby here hadn't pulled me out of the snow."

"I remember you asked the where'bouts of the Winslow place," Dooley nodded. "But you shore was temptin' fate to start out walkin' to it in that storm and as sick as you was. You stayin' there now?"

Thad saw the intense curiosity in Dooley's sharp eyes, but said only, "I'm working for Mr. Winslow for a while. Long enough to get some traveling money."

Dooley knew better than to press the issue. "Well, that's real fine, Thad. Say, we're havin' a little Christmas party next week. Now, it'd pleasure me a heap if you'd come over and shove your feet under the table! All right?"

"Well, I'll try and come if I can. It depends on what Mr. Winslow has for me to do."

"Shore," Dooley nodded. He spurred his horse and wheeled her around with an expert hand. "We'll be lookin' for you, anyhow. You jest leave one little ol' red-haired gal named Julie May alone, you hear? I got that claim staked out!" He lifted the reins and left on a dead gallop.

"He sure can ride a horse," Thad said with admiration. "Is he friends with the Winslows, Toby?"

"Him? Not likely! Boy, you don't know much 'bout da South!" Toby shook his head. "Dooley Young an' his folks might git to set with the Winslows in heaven—but dey ain't nevah gonna git no invite to Belle Maison!"

Thad thought about that, then shrugged. "Guess it's the same here as in the North. Rich and poor just don't mix, do they, Toby?"

They cut ice every day except Sunday, and it soon seemed the natural thing for him to drop by Toby's house in the evening. Thad would play small games with Wash while Toby told tales of hunting and fishing.

On Tuesday Sut Franklin gave Thad a rude awakening when he said, "Novak, guess you ain't to blame for it, seein' as you ain't from around here—but you got to watch what you do on this plantation."

They were preparing to go to bed, and as usual, Franklin had been nipping at his bottle. His words were somewhat slurred, and there was uncertainty in his movements as he slumped to pull off his boots.

"What's wrong?" Thad asked in surprise. "Ain't I been doing my work right?"

"Guess that's all right—but you been hangin' around the niggers too much. You don't know no better, so I'm tellin' you; they ain't to be trusted! That's what I'm here for—to see they don't get uppity! Got to make 'em do what they're told." He stared at Thad and added in a hard tone, "And you ain't makin' it no easier the way you been cuddlin' up with 'em!"

Thad was silent. He had never considered it wrong to spend time with Toby and his family. He had little choice, for the only two classes of people on the plantation were the Winslows and the slaves. He wanted to ask, *You think I ought to go eat at the Big House?* but held his peace. He *liked* being with Toby and somehow could not feel guilty about it. "Did Mr. Winslow say that?" he asked.

Sut spat a stream of tobacco juice to the floor and cursed. "He ain't said nothin' because he's got more to do than watch a dumb Yankee makin' up to his niggers! *I'm* telling you, Novak— stay away from the niggers, or I'll run you off the place. Ain't you got no sense atall? Don't you know there's about to be a war over the slaves?" He spat again, then rolled into his bunk and mumbled, "You ought to be thankin' me—but I don't reckon you Yankees got enough manners for that!"

Thad was miserable, but no matter how hard he tried, he could not feel guilty. Who else was he supposed to talk with? He slept little that night, but finally said under his breath, "He's *wrong!* Even if he weren't, Toby saved my life and that settles it!"

The next day was Christmas, and the entire population of Belle Maison had a holiday. The smell of pies, cakes, baked meats, barbecue and other spicy aromas began to flow out of the Big House and from the slave quarters as well. Men and boys were run out of the kitchens with dire warnings, and they engaged in games and singing outside in the snow with a freedom Thad had not seen before.

It was nearly three in the afternoon when the slaves gathered in the barn where planks had been placed across sawhorses to make tables. Lanterns were hung across the ceiling to break the gloom, and the food was stacked high!

Hams, chickens, ducks, turkeys and wild game of every sort

covered one long table. A variety of steaming vegetables in huge pots filled a second long table, while another table bowed under the weight of potatoes with thick gravy, yams dripping in syrup, mountains of hot biscuits, corn bread, and rolls fresh from the oven. Farther down, a line of desserts was placed full length on yet another table: peach cobblers, apple pies, tarts, blackberry muffins, taffy, and candy.

Thad edged in close to Toby and Jessie for a time, then moved back into the shadows. Soon the master of Belle Maison entered with his family and the house servants. The slaves quieted down as Mr. Winslow raised his hand. "Let us thank God for the food." Thad expected a long prayer, but it wasn't. "Lord God, you are the source of all our blessings. We are unworthy servants. We know this good food comes from your hand, and we thank you for it—and for all the other good things that come to us. In the name of Jesus Christ, Amen!" He lifted his head, smiled and said, "All right, now, let's get at it!"

There was a scramble, and Thad stood back, watching with a smile as the slaves piled their plates high with food. As they retired to an open area to eat, continuing animated conversations, Thad discovered that their slurred speech was becoming clearer to his ears. At first all the slaves had looked alike, but now he found he knew a great many, having encountered them in Toby's company. Thad waited until the first rush was over before he went forward to get his plate. Some of the food looked strange to him, but having tasted Jessie's cooking, he knew it would be good. He sat by himself, noting the goodwill among the slaves as they laughed and slapped at each other playfully. *They sure don't seem to be as bad off as Lincoln says*, he thought. The whole matter of slavery had puzzled Thad ever since he had met Toby.

When the meal was almost over, the Winslows began to pass out presents. Thad had often thought of the younger member, Pet. Now she sought him out with her eyes and gave him a smile, which he was too bashful to return. He nodded and forced his gaze away to the other members of the family. He knew Mr. and Mrs. Winslow, and he had supposed that the three young men were sons. The one he couldn't stop watching was the beautiful girl with Pet. She was a Winslow, of course—the older daughter he had heard about. But he had not known that a woman could be so gorgeous! She was finely dressed and moved gracefully as she handed out gifts to the slaves.

Every time one of the slaves would take a gift, he would cry out "Chris'mas gift!" and there was a constant stream of giggles and shouts of pleasure as gifts were unwrapped. Most of the gifts were clothes, but there were candy and other small favors as well.

Thad was so engrossed that he was startled when a voice right beside him said, "Christmas gift, Thad!" He turned quickly to see Pet and the other girl standing there, each of them holding out a package. "This is my sister, Belle, Thad," Pet said.

"I've heard all about you," Belle smiled. "You've got a mole on your left shoulder, haven't you?" She laughed gaily at Thad's puzzled expression and explained, "Pet told me!"

"But, how—"

"Why, who do you think washed you off when you were unconscious?" Belle teased. "It was Pet!"

"Oh, Belle!" Pet's face turned a bright red. "You're awful!"

Thad was speechless. He stood there struck dumb by Belle Winslow's beauty.

Finally, Pet asked, "Well, are you going to open your presents—or just stand there staring?"

Glad for an interruption, Thad carefully removed the paper from Belle's large package and found a heavy wool coat and a red wool cap. He stared at them, then said "Thank you" in a breathless voice.

Pet thrust two small packages into his hands. "I made some cookies and knit some socks. I expect you won't be able to chew the cookies or tell one end of the socks from the other—but Christmas gift to you anyway, Thad!"

From across the room, Sky Winslow was watching the scene. He had just given Toby a pair of bright yellow suspenders that the black man had admired for some time. "Toby, what kind of young fellow do you make Novak out to be? Guess you've been around him more than anyone else."

Toby was donning the garish suspenders, but he paused to glance over to where Thad was standing in front of the two girls, looking very awkward. He snapped the suspenders into place, and said emphatically, "Well, I tell you one thing, Mistuh Winslow—dat Yankee boy is da mos' fo' work I ever seen!"

"That so?"

"Dat is de unvarnished truf!" Toby snapped the suspenders for emphasis. "He can almos' put a good mule outta work when he git goin'!"

Winslow nodded, as if it were something he expected to hear, then left Toby to drift over where Thad stood staring at the gifts in his hands. "Merry Christmas, Thad," he said.

The young man looked up and responded slowly, "Best Christmas presents I ever got." He stroked the coat softly and looked at the crudely made socks.

Winslow cleared his throat and studied the boy. "I've been talking to Toby. He says that if you could stay around and help, you two could fill the icehouse in a month or so. I'll pay two dollars a day if you want the job—and if that works out, maybe we can discuss a permanent job."

Thad stared at him in astonishment. "You mean, you'd hire a Yankee?"

Sky Winslow scowled. "Well, to tell the truth, Thad, being born in the South doesn't necessarily confer sainthood on a man!" Then he shrugged his shoulders. "Let's just say I'll take a Yankee who is ready to do a day's work over some of our southern 'gentlemen' who are too good to get their hands dirty. How about it? Do you want the job?"

Thad began to twist the button on his shirt. He seemed to have trouble speaking for a time. Finally raising his eyes, sparkling with new hope, he said softly, "I'll try to please you, Mr. Winslow."

CHAPTER FIVE

NEW YEAR'S BALL

★ ★ ★ ★

"Lucy—pull harder! I'll never get into my new gown if you don't hurry!"

Belle's maid heaved back on the strings of the corset, and Belle held tightly to the post of her canopy bed. She gave a gasp, crying, "That's it! Tie it quickly!"

Lucy finished lacing and tying the corset, grumbling all the time. "If you don't hold still, I ain't never gwine git you dressed! Now, hold up them hands and git this dress on." She took the bright red taffeta dress from the bed and Belle wiggled into it, then twisted impatiently, trying to see herself in the mirror as Lucy laced up the back.

Pet sat cross-legged on the bed, watching her sister curiously. She did not mind in the least that her parents felt Pet was too young to go to a ball—held this evening at Belle Maison. Next year when she was sixteen she could go—but watching Belle's excitement and frantic preparations for the New Year's Ball, Pet failed to understand what the excitement was all about.

"Pet, be a dear and hand me my locket," Belle purred. "Over there on the table—the gold one with the red stone." She took it from Pet, held it against her throat and sighed. "It's so *tacky*! I must have a new necklace before the ball at Deerfield next month. Papa will just have to understand that I can't go around looking like a scarecrow!"

"I think you look beautiful, Belle," Pet said. "Anyway, you're always the prettiest girl at the dances."

"Oh, I don't know about that, Pet," Belle replied with a trace of smugness.

Pet's eyes twinkled. "I'm sure you'll be the prettiest one there—unless Martha Sue Grimes comes." She was delighted to see Belle's head snap up, and added innocently, " 'Course, I think you're much prettier than she is, but you know what I heard—" She stopped. "Oh, my goodness, I didn't mean to tell you!" Pet clapped her hand over her mouth and pretended to be horrified.

"Didn't intend to tell me what?" Belle demanded. "Tell me!"

"Oh, it was just Beau Beauchamp, Belle. You know how he is!"

"What did he *say*?"

"Oh, I heard him tell Papa last week, 'I don't care if Martha Grimes *is* prettier than Belle, Mr. Winslow—her father doesn't have half as many acres of good cotton land as you do'!"

Belle's face was crimson with fury! Pet stared at her sister's expression, then fell into a fit of laughter. Belle ran to the bed and began beating Pet with both fists. "I'll kill you—you little beast!" she cried.

"Miss Belle, you gwine ruin dat dress! Now stop dat messin' round, you hear me?"

Belle straightened up and glared at Pet. "I'll get even with you for that! I'll tell Papa not to let you go to a ball until you're an old woman!"

Pet rolled over and smiled at Belle. "I don't care. Papa said I could go on the big coon hunt when the snow melts—and he said I could shoot one too. That'll be more fun than any old dance!" Then she jumped off the bed and ran to kiss Belle. "I was just funning you! You're always the prettiest girl at the ball. Beau said so, and so did Vance Wickham." She smiled at the sudden effect her words had on Belle, and whispered, "I'll bet they'll *fight* over you one of these days—maybe even a *duel!*"

Belle shivered with pleasure, but said, "Oh, that would be just dreadful, Pet! You mustn't even say such things!" She tried to look shocked, but her eyes gleamed. Assuming a prim frown, she picked up her evening bag, saying, "Well—I must go. I'll tell you all about it in the morning." She pecked Pet's cheek, then dashed out of the room. Pet heard her greet the other young women who had come for the ball. *They sound like a bunch of silly chickens!* she thought.

Downstairs the men were gathered around a large table set at one end of the ballroom in front of the huge bay window. It was a large room, thirty feet wide and nearly sixty feet long, composing half the first floor of Belle Maison. The other half of the house was across a wide hall—the kitchen, the small dining room, the library, and a parlor. The ballroom was kept closed most of the time, being used only for large groups or for dances such as this one.

As many as a hundred people had attended dances there, though that was too crowded for comfort. Only about half that number were gathered for this night's celebration—which was an informal New Year's Watch Party. It had been a tradition at Belle Maison for several years, and the cream of the aristocratic young people of the neighborhood maneuvered for invitations with cut-throat determination.

Around the table, lifting glasses in the first toast of the evening, were three older men—Sky Winslow, the host, and his guest, Seth Barton. Barton was the richest man in the county and looked the part. He was a tall man dressed in a fawn-colored frock coat and a snowy French dress shirt. The single diamond on his finger winked in the lights, and another shone in his dark blue cravat. He had the look of a man so assured of authority and power that it never occurred to him to accept anything less than the most prominent place. The other man was sixty years old, but looked older. He was Oscar Toombs, lieutenant governor of Virginia—a close friend of Barton's.

All the other men were very young, most of them twenty or less. Mark Winslow stood beside his best friend, Beau Beauchamp. Beauchamp was the largest of the younger set—six feet tall and bull-chested, but swift and fleet of foot, nonetheless. His eyes were light blue and glinted with quick emotion in the lamplight nearby. Vance Wickham stood across from Beauchamp and smiled at the larger man, his dark face in sharp contrast to Beauchamp's. He lived west of the James River, but was much involved in the affairs of the county. It was rumored that he intended to move to Richmond. Some had even guessed that his frequent visits to Belle Maison were part of a campaign to marry Belle.

The group also included Tom Winslow, Shelby Lee, a nephew of the famous general, and the Hardee twins, Gil and Robert, the best horsemen in the state. Next to the twins stood Will Henry, a pale young man, hopelessly in love with Belle, lost amid six or seven other young men who crowded close to the table.

The musicians had begun tuning their instruments, so as the men raised their glasses of sherry for the first toast, Sky Winslow raised his voice above the noise. "Gentlemen, I give you a toast—here's to the fine young men of our beloved South; there are no finer on the planet!"

Toombs and Barton added "Hear! Hear!" and they all drank.

"And to you, sir!"—Beau turned to Winslow as they refilled their glasses—"to you and your generation who have made our land an Eden! I give you the South, gentlemen!"

"And destruction to her enemies!" Gil Hardee cried out. After they had drained their glasses, Mark announced, "Here come the young ladies." He waved his hand languidly toward the broad double doors that seemed to erupt in a blaze of color as the brilliantly dressed young women entered. "I shouldn't be surprised if they didn't cause us as much trouble as the Yankees."

"Why, you're not courteous, Mark," Vance Wickham reproved sternly, but with a gleam of humor in his gray eyes. "I refuse to admit that any true southern woman could be anything but a joy." He looked directly at Beau with a mocking smile. "I'm sure Beau will say amen to that."

Beau swayed his heavy shoulders and bowed slightly. "I must concede to your superior knowledge of women, Vance." It was a dangerous speech, for Wickham's reputation as a womanizer was well known but never alluded to in his presence. It had been mentioned once, but in the duel that followed, the poor chap had taken a bullet in his chest, and no man since then had dared speak ill of Wickham. Beau, however, was a person who loved danger, and in his contest with Wickham for Belle's favor, he stared at the other man fearlessly.

Shelby Lee stepped forward, saying quickly, "Ladies, you are lovely," and the mood changed as Beau smiled and took Belle's hand, kissing it gallantly. "I believe the first dance is mine," he smiled. He was an intensely handsome man and confident in his own skills as he guided her out on the floor to the fast tune the musicians were playing.

"I declare, Beau," Belle said, "you're holding me too tight!"

He only grinned and held her closer. "You're beautiful tonight."

"Why, thank you, sir." She smiled up at him, pleased as always with a compliment. Then with a mischievous gleam in her eyes she asked, "What were you and Vance talking about when we came in? Was it about the war?"

"You'd hate to think so, wouldn't you?" Beau grinned. "No, Vance and I were about to go outside for a duel to see which one would get you." He knew she loved to be pursued, and his white teeth gleamed under his light mustache as he swung her around on the floor. "Tell me, sweet, which one of us would you rather have get the ball in the brain, me or old Vance?"

"Oh, don't be so *awful*, Beau!" she gasped, gripping his hand tightly. "You mustn't fight over me—it would be wicked!"

"But you'd forgive the winner, wouldn't you, love? I mean, you'd be honor bound to marry the survivor."

He laughed and they moved across the floor, conscious that they were the center of attention.

Mark glanced at them, and said to Rowena Barton, "I wouldn't be surprised if Beau asked Belle to marry him pretty soon. He'll have to hurry to get ahead of Vance, though."

"Which one do you think would make the best husband, Mark?" Rowena asked. She was a tall girl, like her father, and had his piercing eyes. Her mother had died at Rowena's birth, and she had practically ruled their home since her teens. She was nineteen now and could have her pick among the bachelors of the county, but apparently had set her sights higher than the locals.

"Neither of them," he said dryly. "Sooner or later they'll shoot somebody in a duel—or get wiped out in this war."

She frowned and shook her head. "I don't like to think of it, Mark." She hesitated, and there was an arch light in her eyes as she commented, "I met one of your kin when I was in Boston last month."

"My relation?" Mark asked in surprise, then smiled. "He's not the rich Yankee you fell in love with, is he?"

Rowena glanced at him quickly, noting that he was only half serious, and it displeased her. "No, that's another man," she replied. "I didn't know my affairs were talked about so much."

"Tell me about *your* young man."

"Oh, he's the son of one of Father's old friends. His name is Steven Williams. He's at West Point, and he came to a party with another soldier—Lowell Winslow."

"Never heard of him."

"He knew about *you,* though—at least he knew about your father. He comes from the Boston branch of the Winslows, he said." Rowena gave him a pointed look. "He's *much* better looking than you are, Mark—and he's quite a soldier, too."

"Guess I'll be taking a shot at him pretty soon, won't I?" Mark shook his head, depressed by the thought, then shrugged. "Well, if he's a Yankee, I guess he's no competition for me—for you, I mean?"

Rowena's eyes snapped with anger. "You're not in competition for me with anyone, Mark!"

He nodded. "That's right. Until the war is over, no man has a right to ask a woman to marry him."

"Oh, Mark, that's not so!" Rowena put her hand on his arm, her anger replaced by a soft light in her eyes. "We can't stop living because there may be a war, can we? There's always been danger in front of people. There always will be."

But he was sobered by the thought of a relative he'd never heard of who would be in the Union Army. "I wish the South had never gotten chained to this slavery business, Rowena. I hate it—but I'm tied to it. We all are. It's going to be a hard war."

She stared at him in surprise, for all the other men of the South were saying quite the opposite. She saw that the fatalism in him ran deep, and said quietly, "There's no rich Yankee I'm in love with, Mark. That's just gossip." Then she pulled him onto the dance floor and tried her utmost to drive away the gloom that creased his brow.

Three hours later there was a break in the festivities. The dancing stopped and the ladies retired. The men threw themselves into chairs pulled up before the fire, and talked while sipping their drinks. The huge fireplace that dominated the north wall had blazed all evening, but now the fire had dwindled down to a bed of glowing coals. "Lewis—have some logs brought in," Winslow said. "It'll get cold in here before midnight."

"What time is it?" Mr. Toombs asked.

Pulling a heavy gold watch from his pocket, Mr. Barton peered at it. "Going on eleven. I thought it was later."

"Shall we wait for the new year, Seth?" Sky Winslow asked. "Or are we getting past such things?"

"Certainly not!" Barton shot back. "Why, you and I are in the prime, Winslow! We'll have to show these young fellows what it's like when the company is formed."

"Are you really going to do it, Barton?" Toombs asked instantly. "I mean, have you actually decided?"

"Certainly! There's going to be a war. No man can doubt that, so we must move at once."

"Are you thinking of a command yourself, Mr. Barton?" Mark asked with a wink at his father. Every man in the room knew that the command of the company would settle firmly on Seth Barton.

"We'll have an election, of course," Barton informed him. "If I am elected, I will do my best to fill the post."

"Why, there's no doubt of *that*, sir!" Robert Hardee exclaimed. "With your military experience, who else *could* be chosen?" Barton had served briefly with the army in Mexico, a fact he managed to publish quite often.

The room began to buzz with talk about the political situation. Finally Mark remarked, "Well, Lincoln has already said he intends to free the slaves."

"He can try!" Beau retorted. His face was flushed with anger as he went to refill his glass. "I can't say that I'm of the opinion that the Yankees will fight at all."

Will Henry had remained quiet, but now he spoke up. "Maybe there'll be some way out of it—I mean, maybe we can work out a compromise of some sort."

"Compromise!" Beau snorted. "I'll give them this compromise: I'll promise not to shoot any Yankee that stays in his own land! But the ones who come here and try to tell us how to live—they'll get a bullet!"

"That's the way, Beau!" several of the young men shouted, and a hum of approval drowned out Will's protest.

The outer door opened, and Beau looked up to see someone come in carrying a huge red oak log for the fire. He supposed at first it was one of the slaves, but now he noticed it was the young man Mark had pointed out earlier. Beau's eyes narrowed as he watched the boy stagger to the fireplace and dump the log on the coals, sending the sparks flying wildly. Beau suddenly grinned and intercepted the boy as he started for the door.

"You the Yankee who came in on the *Dixie Queen*?" he asked, placing himself between the boy and the door. He glanced at his friends, winked broadly at Mark, then demanded, "Well, are you the Yankee or not?"

Thad stood there, confused and a little frightened. He had been asked by Mr. Winslow to keep close to the house during the party in case he was needed. He had listened to the music, and peered in through the windows for a time, then had settled down in the kitchen, talking to Lewis, the butler. He had eaten quite a bit of the rich food, and the warmth of the kitchen lulled him into a torpid sleep. He had been awakened when Lewis passed along Mr. Winslow's order for a log, and had brought it in. Now he looked around at the group of men who all seemed to be laughing at him.

Finally he saw Mr. Winslow nod, and he said, "Yes, sir. I came on the *Dixie Queen*."

"And are you a Yankee, boy?" Beau demanded.

"I don't know."

"Don't know! Well, where did you come from?"

"I came from New York." Thad tried to edge away, but the large man blocked his path.

"New York? Well, that's Yankee enough, wouldn't you say, fellows?" The group vocally gave assent, and Beau deliberately looked Thad up and down, then turned to face his friends. "Well, there he is, gentlemen—a real live Yankee! Anyone here afraid to face up to him in battle?"

They all stared at Thad as they would have stared at an unusual animal in a cage. He was not much to look at, Thad well knew. He had begun to pick up the weight he had lost during his sickness, but his clothes still hung on him loosely and his face was thin, making his eyes look too large.

He glanced at Mr. Winslow for help, and got a nod toward the door. He tried to walk around Beau, but just as he passed, the large man caught him by the arm and held him in a vise-like grip, saying, "Look at this fellow, Mark! Why, I'd be ashamed to fight against a bunch of men like this!" He gave Thad a shove, and caught off balance, Thad stumbled and almost fell.

"Now, Beau, that's no way to treat a servant." Sky Winslow moved quickly to stand in front of Beau. His voice was soft and he had to look up into the face of the younger man, but there was something in his eyes that made Beau freeze. He knew as well as any man in the room that Sky Winslow had been a mountain man in his youth, and in Oregon he had gone up against hardened gunmen—and lived to tell about it.

The crowd fell silent, caught up in the confrontation. Beau was a fiery-tempered man—but there was something deadly in the still figure of Winslow. Though he was almost sixty, there was such strength in his face and upright figure that no one thought of him as being old. He was a smiling man, known to be mild and easygoing—but there was something of a carnivore in him just now—and Beau quickly dropped his eyes.

"Sorry, Mr. Winslow. I was out of order." He reached into his pocket, and before Thad discovered what the man was doing, Beau put a coin in his hand, saying, "I apologize, young fellow. Take this and have yourself a good time. I see you're not a fighter, but that's not your fault."

"I'm afraid you're not quite correct, Beau," a voice said, and they all turned to look at Shelby Lee. He was the son of General Robert E. Lee's brother and a second-year lieutenant at West Point, first in his class. He looked a great deal like a younger edition of his famous uncle, and his fine eyes were gentle as they fixed on Thad.

"What do you mean, Shelby?" Beau asked in surprise.

Lee shrugged. "There are some pretty poor specimens from the North—just as there are in the South. But there are some pretty good young men as well. And they'll make good soldiers."

Beau did not dare contradict Shelby, but he would not back

down. "Do you mean a first-class fighting man could be made out of this boy?" he asked with a look of disbelief. He turned to Thad. "Are you a good shot, boy?"

"I ain't never shot no gun," Thad answered quietly.

"There it is, Shelby," Beau said with a broad smile. "Now you all just think—how many boys around here do you know who've never shot a gun?" They all recognized instantly that every boy, poor and rich, learned to shoot by the time he was able to hold a rifle.

Vance Wickham spoke up. "You can't be sure of what you say, Beau. Give this young fellow a gun and a little training and he might do pretty well." His eyes lit with an odd smile, "Remember that old king in the Bible who went out to war, and it says, 'A bowman drew a bow at a venture'—and it killed the king. Get enough fellows like this to throwing lead, and it could be pretty dangerous."

"Didn't look for you to start quoting scripture, Vance," Beau grinned slyly, then added with a frown, "But I don't think this fellow could hit anything by accident or any other way."

"Wouldn't put a little money on that, would you, Beau?"

Beau stared at Wickham in surprise. "Bet on what?"

"Well, you say this young Yankee could never be any kind of a soldier—that he could never learn to shoot. How much would you bet on yourself in a shootin' match against him?"

Beau threw his head back and laughed. He well understood that this was just a ploy of Wickham's to make him look bad, so he said, "How much do you have to lose, Vance?"

"How about two hundred dollars?" Vance returned quietly, and immediately the room grew still. They all had watched this pair come close to trouble several times—now it seemed imminent.

"At what odds?" Beau asked. "And how would it be handled?"

"I'd say let Shelby and Mr. Winslow arrange the match." Then Vance smiled sleepily and said the one thing that was calculated to goad his rival into action. "I'd like to take something away from you, Beau."

Every man there realized instantly that Wickham did not

mean cash, but Belle, and Beau's face flushed. "Done!" he said in a harsh voice.

The whole episode caught the fancy of the young fellows, and a yell went up. The older men tried to get the two to call off the bet, but the betting instinct was strong in the breed.

Vance said, "I'll have to have a little time to teach my man how to hold a piece."

"You've got until noon tomorrow, Vance," Beau replied. "I have too much to do to wait around for you to work a miracle."

Wickham put his hand on Thad's arm, saying, "Let's have a word outside, my boy." He led Thad into the foyer and turned to him. "Are your eyes good?"

"Oh yes, sir," Thad nodded. "I can see real fine."

"Good! Now hold your hand out." He took a gold knife from his pocket, opened it, and laid it across one of Thad's knuckles. "Now, hold that steady, Thad. See that line of light on the blade? Try to keep it steady."

Thad concentrated and his hands were almost rock-like. "Very good!" Wickham said in surprise. "You can see and you have steady hands. Now, you heard the bet I made with Mr. Beauchamp?"

"Yes, sir—but I can't beat him!"

"The odds are three to one, Thad. You'll get three shots to his one. In the morning, you meet me in front of the house. I'll teach you how to hit the target. Now don't get worried. If you can't do it, I'll understand."

"But, Mr. Wickham—!"

"Thad, those fellows laughed at you. I saw your face when they did that. Now, if you can do this thing, I'll give you the two hundred dollars—and more than that, you'll show those fellows you're a man!"

Thad looked at Wickham with glowing eyes. "Well, it's your money. I've always been able to hit anything with a rock—maybe I can do it."

Wickham was a little hopeful—for the first time, really. He had started it all to give Beau a bad time, but as he looked at Thad's face, he saw a look of such determination that he cocked his head and thought, *He's got spirit—maybe Beau will get a surprise in the morning!*

CHAPTER SIX

THE SHOOTING MATCH

★ ★ ★ ★

"Here're the rifles, Thad," Wickham said. "This is a Spring-field .58—a sweet-shooting gun."

Thad shivered in the cold and fervently wished that he'd never gotten into the affair. He had risen before dawn and come to the barn far away from the Big House to meet Wickham. Then they had walked about a mile through the snow, carrying the heavy rifles. Now the first light splintered the darkness and the brilliance of the snow hurt his eyes.

"To start with, I'll show you how to load," Wickham said. "Watch me carefully, because you're going to have to learn. First, you put the powder in." He pulled a paper cartridge from his side pocket and after biting it open, poured the fine powder into the rifle barrel. "Now put the bullet in." He pulled a conical slug from his other pocket, wrapped it quickly in a small piece of cloth, set it in the muzzle, then pushed it down firmly with a ramrod he'd removed from a mounting under the barrel. Next he pulled a small cap from his shirt pocket and put it on the tube leading into the base of the barrel. Finally, he pulled the hammer back with a click.

Carefully he handed the Springfield to Thad. "Ready to fire," he said. "I can load a rifle in twenty seconds, and some can do a lot better. Now, you just raise the rifle and look down the barrel. Put the bead at the end of the gun right on that target. Then—and this is the most important thing of all—you just squeeze that trigger. Hold your body as still as you can. Don't move a muscle except that trigger finger. All right—go ahead."

Thad looked down the long barrel of the rifle and put the tiny round bead on the piece of paper Wickham had put on a huge walnut tree fifty feet away. The bead wandered off, but he pulled it back and froze, holding the rifle steady for a moment— then carefully squeezed the trigger. There was a loud *crack*, a puff of smoke that got into his eyes and nose, and a kick of the Springfield to his shoulder.

"A hit!" Wickham cried in delight. He gave Thad a glowing smile. "Here, try it again." He passed him the other rifle.

Thad raised the weapon and with more assurance let the shot fly, and this time he saw the round dot on the paper not an inch from his first shot.

Wickham stared at the target, saying nothing. His face was a study, and he looked again at Thad with a strange expression in his eyes. Finally he said, "All right, let's move back." They retreated fifty yards. "That's a pretty good distance. Load the gun and take your shot, Thad."

Thad could not explain it, but somehow the rifle felt *natural* in his hands. It had been the same with the slingshot he'd picked up when he was ten years old. He never practiced, but it seemed as if he couldn't miss. In the gang fights that sometimes took place on the east side of New York, he had gained such a reputation that the older boys always took him along. After a time, just the sight of Thad Novak reaching for his slingshot was enough to cause the other gang to take to their heels. "How do you do it, Thad?" his friends would ask as he popped bottles and cans without taking aim. But he could never explain; it was just like pointing his finger.

Now that same feeling was in his hands. He simply swung the rifle up and pulled the trigger, almost in a single motion, and was not at all surprised when another hole joined the first two— this time touching the mark.

Wickham took the guns and loaded them this time, speaking with excitement. "You're a natural shot, Thad! I've seen it a few times. Why, you take the Hardee twins. Robert's been practicing all his life, but he still can't hit a mule from ten paces. But the first time Gil Hardee picked up a gun, he could hit dead center. We took him out squirrel hunting that day—and on his first time out, he shot seven times and brought home six gray squirrels! And that wasn't with a shotgun but an old Enfield rifle!" He finished loading the guns and said, "I think you can beat him, Thad—but in a real match, there's a lot of noise. Gil Hardee told me once that in a match he pretends he's in a big glass jar that shuts out all the noise. He just gets in, closes the lid, and all he can see is that bull's eye! Just try your best to ignore the crowd. I'll load the guns for the match. Well, let's get back."

Inside the Big House, the young people were finishing up a big breakfast of bacon and eggs and fluffy biscuits smeared with yellow butter and apple jelly. They had scarcely slept at all— the girls having stayed awake and talked; the men playing cards and talking about the war.

Mark said as he finished, "You ladies will have to excuse us for an hour or so. We have a little business outside."

"Oh, we know all about the shooting match, Mark," Rowena smiled. "You needn't think you're going to leave us out! Come on, girls, let's get our boots!"

"It's too cold outside!" Dan protested. "And besides, it won't be any fun for you."

"Why, I hear Beau is going to defeat the Yankee," Belle laughed. "I wouldn't miss it for the world!"

They quickly bundled up in warm coats and boots, and Sky said with a frown on his face, "Mark, I think this is a mistake."

"So do I, sir, but Beau and Wickham have gone too far to back down."

Beau came in at that moment with a rifle in his hands. He held it up, saying with pride, "Take a look at this, all of you—a new Whitworth!"

They had heard about the English-made Whitworths, the finest long-range guns in the world, and rushed over to admire the weapon. Beau finally retrieved it, then said, "Let's go whip this Yankee, boys!" And they rushed outside with a great deal of pushing and yelling.

Pet Winslow ran to catch up to her father as he followed the rowdy crowd down the road to an old log cabin a half mile away.

Noticing the frown on her face, Sky asked, "What's wrong, Pet?"

"It's not fair, Papa!" she said, biting her lip. She looked up at him with anger in her eyes. "They're making a fool out of Thad! Beau's been shooting all his life—and poor Thad's never even shot a gun. I think it's mean!"

Sky put his arm around her and gave her a quick hug. "Men do foolish things sometimes, Pet—and this is one of them." He looked at her with affection. "You're just the same as when you were a little girl—always taking care of every stray kitten or worn-out hound that showed up at the house—just like your mama, I reckon."

"Thad's not a dog or a cat! I don't want him to get hurt."

Sky said nothing, for he could not stop the match, but he resolved to make it up to the boy later. When they arrived at the old cabin, he saw seven or eight young fellows standing off to one side. "Why, that's Dooley Young!" he exclaimed. "Wonder what that bunch is doing here?"

They soon discovered that Dooley and his friends had finished a wild night of celebration in Richmond and had somehow heard of the shooting match. "They're all drunk," Beau said with disgust. He had no use for Dooley or for the small farmers that lived close to the river.

"Well, I guess we've had a drop or two ourselves, Beau!" Gil Hardee laughed. "You been puttin' away too much whiskey for a man who's goin' to shoot. I told you that last night."

"This isn't a real match!" Beau snapped.

"They think it is," Gil replied soberly, waving toward the line of slaves that had come to lean on the fence close to Dooley's crowd.

Dooley was anticipating this match, and moved forward, his eyes bright above his swooping mustache. "Hidee, Mr. Winslow. We heard about this here match and sort of figgered we'd like to watch—if you don't mind."

It was obvious that neither Dooley nor his friends cared a pin about whether they were welcome, but they appeared peaceful enough. "That'll be all right, Dooley, but you'll have to behave yourself."

"Me?" Dooley asked in obvious astonishment. "Why, Mr. Winslow, I am shocked! When did you *ever* hear of me doin' anything else?"

Winslow laughed, for he liked the feisty little man, and replied with a broad smile, "I do think I can recall a *few* times when you had to explain yourself to Judge Williams."

Sky turned from Dooley and walked over to where Beau was standing, and said, "They'll be all right, Beau."

"You ought to run that trash off, Mr. Winslow!"

Sky stared at him. "Beau, it won't be long before you'll be leading men into battle. Dooley is the kind of man that'll save the South—if it can be saved. You'd better be willing to learn something about him."

Beau's lips tightened and he shook his head. "We don't need that kind in our army! Give me men like *these*"—he waved his hand proudly toward his friends—"and we'll whip the Yankees!"

Winslow considered him soberly before he spoke. "You'll soon learn better, I hope."

Sky went back to stand beside Pet and Rebekah, calling out, "Shelby, state the rules and begin this thing."

Shelby Lee nodded and said, "I'll ask all of you to stand on this line out of the line of fire. There's been at least a little alcohol consumed lately, and I wouldn't like a bullet in anything but the target!" He waited until the spectators moved back, then continued. "The rules are as follows: Seven volleys will be fired—the first from 40 yards, then at distances increasing at 20 yards until the final shots are fired from 160 yards.

"The target will be these sheets of paper, six inches square with a cross to mark dead center. According to the bet, Mr. Beauchamp will get one shot; then his opponent will have three shots in which to do better. The first man to win four out of seven will be declared the winner." Shelby paused, then added evenly, "In case of hits that are very close, I will ask Mr. Toombs, Mr. Barton, and Mr. Winslow to select the winner. Understood?"

"Let's get on with it," Beau growled impatiently. He felt like a fool for getting himself in a match with a ragged boy, and wanted to settle the business. The only advantage he saw was an opportunity to get the best of Vance Wickham. He took his stance and looked at the white square fastened to the log house forty feet away.

Shelby called, "Fire when ready," and Beau fired instantly.

"Dead center!" came the cry from several of his friends.

Thad felt Wickham press him gently, and he came to the line and lifted his rifle, trying to remember all he'd been told. He was nervous, however, and sent his shot far to the right. He heard the jeer go up, but Wickham encouraged him quietly. "That's not bad, Thad. Just a little case of buck fever. Slow and easy this time."

Thad took the rifle and this time did better. The slug hit the square, but high and to the right. There was a murmur of laughter from Beau's supporters, but Thad caught a glimpse of Dooley and saw the little man wave encouragement. The third slug was again high and to the right.

"First score to Mr. Beauchamp," Shelby announced. "Move back to the next mark—sixty yards."

The second round was almost the same. Beau hit the mark dead center, and Thad sent three shots high and to the right. Wickham whispered to him, "The gun isn't true. Next time aim lower and to the left of the cross."

Beau hurried his next shot, hitting the square, but three inches off the cross, and a groan went up from his friends. "Now you git yore licks in, Thad!" Dooley cried out, and his companions cheered loudly. The aristocrats gave them a shocked look, realizing that Dooley and his friends had chosen, for some reason, to champion the boy from the North. Dooley caught that look, and his mustache twitched as he shrugged. "Well, I got an interest in this boy, seein' as how I sent him to ol' Pitchfork and nigh got him froze to death. Anyways, I don't figure he's a real Yankee!"

Beau ignored him, but Thad grinned for the first time. He stepped forward and fired—and a dot appeared exactly in the center of the cross. "Dead center!" the man who checked the target announced.

"Beau, you better stop foolin' around," Robert Hardee frowned. "It won't look good if you get whipped by that kid!"

"The score is now 2 to 1, favor of Mr. Beauchamp," Shelby announced, and the competitors moved back.

As Beauchamp went to the line for the fourth shot, Belle cried out, "Beat him, Beau!" and all the young ladies echoed her cheer. Beau took careful aim and put his bullet in dead center, and a cheer went up.

Thad stepped forward, and someone called, "You can do it, Thad." He glanced toward where Pet stood with her head lifted high, ignoring the displeased look she got from the others. He saw as well that Mr. and Mrs. Winslow were smiling at him.

The match had become more than a contest of skill. Beau Beauchamp, tall, powerful, and dressed in fine clothes, stood for one thing, and Thad stood for something else, he realized. Though he was not from the South, he was much closer to Dooley and his friends than Beauchamp was—and he was a million miles closer to the slaves! He saw Toby give him a huge smile and an encouraging nod, and knew that Beauchamp would never be able to make the slave do that!

Toombs exclaimed in alarm, "We ought to stop this, Barton!"

"Too late," Winslow said grimly. "We never should have let it start."

Thad put all three of his slugs close, but again Beauchamp was dead center. "Score is 3 to 1—Mr. Beauchamp!"

Beau grinned, and Gil Hardee told him, "Just one more like that, Beau, and we can go to the house!"

Beauchamp took careful aim, but just as he pulled the trigger, one of Dooley's crowd—or Dooley himself, Thad thought—let loose an unnerving scream and Beau flinched, sending his shot to the left of the paper. "Clean miss" was the call.

Beau's face was crimson. "I'll take that shot again, Shelby."

Vance Wickham remarked with a grin, "Think the Yankees will give you a second chance, Beau?" and a laugh went up from Dooley's crowd. At a nod from Shelby Lee, Thad fired, and missed by two inches, but still beat Beauchamp's clean miss.

"Move back for the sixth shot," Lee announced. "Score is 3 to 2—Mr. Beauchamp's favor."

The factions grew much noisier now, and when Beau put his sixth shot only one inch from center, Thad's supporters rent the air with their cheers. He could hear Pet above all of them, but did not look at her. He was feeling the pressure now, and did poorly with his first two shots. As he stepped forward for his next shot, he glanced at the crowd. Winslow's sons looked worried, but not angry—though others did. Then he saw Pet, standing beside her parents. Suddenly she smiled brightly and raised her hands in a token of victory. He turned and lifted the rifle, sending the slug dead center.

"The Yankee wins that round," Robert Hardee said in disgust.

"Score is tied at 3 to 3," Shelby announced. "Move back to the last line; the winner of this volley will be the winner of the match."

The partisans of the two men were louder than ever, and Beau took his time, holding his breath and placing his shot. "*Almost dead center!*" was the verdict.

"That's all right, Thad," Wickham murmured with a smile. "Get in that bottle now, and cork yourself in."

Thad heard the shrill shouts of the people. Then he deliberately tried to shut out everything except the white target—which now appeared very small. All at once it seemed as if the noise of the crowd was swallowed up in silence; he could hear only the heavy beating of his own heart. The target seemed to swell until he could see nothing else. He never remembered pulling the trigger, but he heard Shelby cry, "Almost dead center!" as the lookout pulled the sheets down and brought them at a dead run.

Barton took them. "Gentlemen, we'll adjourn to that grove to consider this matter." Winslow and Toombs followed him a short distance to a stand of oak, and there they examined the target sheets. "They're pretty close," Winslow said. The others agreed, and finally Barton said, "Well, this one looks a hair closer—but I can't be sure."

Barton was silent, then spoke soberly. "There's more at stake here than two hundred dollars. Beau will be one of my officers. If he loses this match . . ." He did not continue, but the other two knew his fears.

Toombs said quickly, "I think Beau has the best of it—slightly. What do you say, Winslow?"

Sky stood there, still thinking that the boy had won—but he knew that Barton and Toombs were thinking of the problem of morale. He sighed heavily, handed the sheets back with a nod. "All right. Let's get this mess over with."

They walked back, and Barton handed Shelby the target. "This is the winner."

Shelby raised his eyebrows, but said only, "Mr. Beauchamp is the winner."

Loud groans went up from Thad's supporters, but Beau's

friends drowned them out. Belle threw her arms about Beau, and the young men joined in, beating him on the back and yelling his name.

Perplexed by the outcome, Thad turned away. As he walked by Shelby, the man stepped in front of him, his hand extended. "Congratulations, young man," he said warmly. "You did *very* well!"

"Thank you, sir," Thad replied, glancing in Beau's direction. By the glare on his opponent's face as he looked at Thad, the boy knew he had made a bitter enemy.

Dooley and his friends were waiting to grab Thad. They pounded on his shoulders, and Dooley cried, "Boy, it's *our* turn now! You got to come and help us celebrate—we ain't even started good yet!" Thad was glad to get away, and looked back to see Pet give him a wave, then he left with the rowdy crowd, riding behind Dooley.

Vance wasted no time walking up to Beau. "Congratulations, Beau. Here's the two hundred."

Beau looked at the cash, then shook his head. "I hope you didn't think I was serious about that bet, Vance." He gave a hard look at the bunch of farmers riding out, saying, "That Yankee lied to us. He's shot before!"

Wickham was about to speak, but Shelby Lee joined them, saying quietly, "If all Yankees shoot like that one, it's going to be a long, long war!"

CHAPTER SEVEN

POSSUM UP AN OAK TREE!

★ ★ ★ ★

April of 1861 was ushered in by a hot breath, melting the dagger-like icicles hanging from the eaves and dissolving the old snow. Frozen roads turned to a rich brown soup, and the wagons mired to the hubs.

For Thad it was like the world coming to life. He had felt the pulse of Belle Maison the many long months he had cut ice with Toby, coming slowly to understand that the plantation was a little kingdom. The Big House was the palace, and Mr. Winslow, the king. Inside, the family ruled and the house servants scurried to meet the Winslow needs. Outside, a small group of slaves kept the grounds in order. The large open fields were ruled by Sut Franklin. He was responsible for the equipment, clearing the ditches, building fences, deciding when and where to plant, and giving the orders for the thousand and one details of getting the seed in the ground and the crops harvested. If Mr. Winslow was the king, Thad saw quickly, then Sut Franklin was the baron who carried out the king's orders. Once Thad talked with Mr. Winslow about it. It was the first day of spring plowing, and the master had come to watch as the mules pulled the plowshares through the earth, turning up neat slabs of rich, black bottomland.

"Well, Thad, you've been at Belle Maison for four months. How do you like it?"

"Oh, real good, Mr. Winslow!" he answered quickly. "Toby's going to teach me how to plow."

"I hear good things about you. Hope you decide to stay on."

"I'd like it fine, sir." He shook his head and added, "Sure beats working in a factory! But this is a busy place—something going on all the time. I don't see how Sut gets it all done!"

"He's a good overseer."

"Yes, sir, he is, but . . ." Thad hesitated and finally blurted out, "But he is hard on the slaves."

Winslow shot a quick glance at the boy. "I know he is," he said, regret in his voice. "I try to make sure he stays within bounds. What would happen to this place if the slaves weren't kept in order?"

"But—your slaves aren't mean."

Mr. Winslow bit his lip, and when he spoke it was as if he were trying to convince himself more than the boy. "No—but they're *slaves*, Thad. I guess you can't blame anyone for being unhappy with being a slave." He paused and looked thoughtfully at the plowmen following the teams across the fields. After a few minutes he turned and faced Thad. "One of these days, my boy, you yourself may be an overseer. And if you ever have the responsibility for a place like this—why, you, too, will become pretty hard."

Thad considered his words, then offered his thought. "I think they would do *better* if they were treated kinder, Mr. Winslow— not worse. That's the way I am—and I figure the slaves are no different."

Sky Winslow said evenly as he turned to go, "Perhaps you don't realize we're about to fight a war to prove that they *aren't* like us. If they *are*—God help us all!"

An hour later when Thad had a chance to speak with Toby he asked, "Do you think Mr. Winslow is a bad man, Toby?"

"He's a mighty *good* man, Thad—but I reckon he'd like to be a *better* one." Toby took a drink of spring water from the bucket that Thad had brought, and gave the boy a careful look. He knew Thad was having a hard struggle with the problem of slavery. "He jes' kinda caught in slavery—like *we* is. Slaves ain't got no say in what dey is—but de man dat owns a slave, why he's in a mess!"

"How's that?"

"Why, don'cha see, boy—if a man can be bought and sold like a gun or a hoss, den a man ain't no more dan a piece of property. Now, Mr. Winslow, he be a Christian man, and he don' want to think dat—'cause it would mean dat no man was more dan a hoss—and he knows de Bible say different."

"Guess you're right," Thad nodded. The thought had never come to him like that, and he considered buying and selling *people* with a new distaste. "Would you like to be free, Toby?"

Toby put his massive black hand on top of Thad's. "Feel dat hand, boy? It's warm—jes' like yo' hand. No different. I guess we all wants to be free, Thad." He added with a sober look on his face, "I see a darksome time comin'." Then he slapped his leg and started back for the plow. "Tonight is de night when we goes on dat possum hunt, Thad. Gets to stay fo' two days and two nights! Whooeee! We gonna have us a time!"

The subject of the possum hunt came up at supper in the Big House that night. Mark had followed Rowena to Richmond, and Dan, burning to learn more about the war, had gone along. Belle had joined them; leaving only Tom and Pet there with their parents. Sky said as he bit into his steak, "Rebekah, did you read that letter from New York?"

"Yes, I did." Rebekah sipped her tea, then asked, "Who is Whitfield Winslow, Sky?"

"Oh, he's one of the New England branch. I never met him—but I remember hearing about his father, Paul Winslow."

"Why, he's the war hero, isn't he, Father?" Tom asked. "The one who died in the War of 1812?"

"That's the one." Sky paused, his brow furrowing. "Pa told me one time that if Paul Winslow hadn't come and gotten him out of prison, I wouldn't have been born." They all knew the story of how Christmas Winslow, Sky's father, had gone to prison over a shooting affair; it had been Paul Winslow and his father Charles who had gotten him a pardon.

"And Whitfield is Paul's son?" Rebekah asked. "He seems to know a lot about the Winslow family."

"Oh, it's his hobby," Sky shrugged. "Goes around digging up

all the Winslows he can find. He's found a few he'd just as soon stayed lost," he grinned. "He writes once in a while to pry some more information out of me, but I don't know too much about our family."

"From his handwriting, I'd say he's getting on in years."

"You're right. He's got to be in his seventies. I haven't heard from him in the last few years, so I thought he'd died. His son is named Robert, I think. Like the letter says, Whitfield's writing a book about the Winslow family."

"You're going to be in a book, Papa?" Pet asked.

"Not too important—just a minor character, Pet," Sky shrugged. "You'll be in it, too, I expect."

"He asked about all the Winslow women who married," Rebekah commented, "and wants to know if we have heard of any of them. He listed quite a few names. Do you know if any of your people around here could be related?"

"I guess there are a few. The Perrys over in St. Francis County are some kin. My aunt Judith—she was Pa's sister, remember? She married a man named Les Perry—but I expect the old man knows about that. Wish you'd write and tell him about her, Rebekah." Then he remembered something and snapped his fingers. "You know that rich Yankee Rowena Barton took up with—or so the gossip went. I was told he had a friend in West Point by our name. Barton asked me about it. His name was Winslow. I *believe* he may be the son of Robert. Ask him when you write, will you, Rebekah?"

She stared at him. "It's getting more grim all the time, this war. Our sons might be killing this man—or he might shoot one of them. Brother against brother!"

The thought brought an oppressive atmosphere. Wishing to dispel the gloom Pet asked, "Papa, you said I could go on a hunt this year. Toby's going possum hunting tomorrow, and I want to go."

"That's not ladylike," Tom grinned. "You better stay home and play with your dolls."

"Mind your own business, Tom." Turning her eyes on her father, Pet implored, "You promised, Papa!"

"Did I?" Sky smiled. "Then, I guess that settles it. We Winslows are men of our word." He took another bite of steak and said, "Better tell Whitfield to put that in his book, Rebekah." He put his hand on her arm, adding, "And tell him to include the fact that we always marry gorgeous women!"

Tom grasped the opportunity for his bid and asked, "Are you going to let me join Mr. Barton's company?" Pet had gotten her own way so easily that he thought it was a good time to pursue the endless task of getting what he wanted most.

Tom's question brought the parents back to the frightening specter that loomed before them, and the gaiety vanished. But for Tom and others his age, the only fear was that the action would be over before they could get a taste of it. Sky said quietly, "I expect you'll get your fill of the war soon enough, Tom."

After the children had left, he sat there silently, his thoughts on the storm that would soon envelope them, and Rebekah came over to put her hands on his shoulders. "We must trust God more than ever, dear," she said quietly.

He rose and put his arms around her. After all their years together, he loved her as he had when she was his bride, and he kissed her tenderly. "I've always leaned on your faith in the Lord. I guess I always will." They stood there, holding each other, and he sighed deeply, then drew back. "This war will be hard on everyone—but for those of us who have children—it'll be worse."

"Jesus is the same—yesterday, today, and forever," she said. "No matter what happens to us, we'll have Him. But I do wish the children were safe, Sky. They all go to church—but I pray for them to really know the Lord as their Savior."

"I know. I've thought the same thing," he murmured. "I suppose all over this country, the North as well as the South, parents are talking like this. We'll have to believe it's in God's hands, Rebekah. We can only trust Him!"

Mr. Winslow was watching his blacksmith, a huge black man named Frank, shoe his new buckskin hunter when Dooley rode in accompanied by his little brother Acie and two other young fellows. "Dooley—come here!" Winslow called, and when Young slipped off his horse and came to stand before Sky, he said, "Pet pestered me into lettin' her go on this hunt. Would you and Toby keep a sharp eye out for her? I'm not sure that it's right for a young woman to go hunting with a bunch of wild characters like you, but she caught me in a weak moment, so I have to let her go."

"Why, shore, Mr. Winslow," Dooley nodded. "I'll be her guardian angel!"

"Never mind that—just don't let a bear get her. She's got enough food for a regiment, so you won't starve." He looked across the fields, and then said, "This war—it's going to make a lot of changes, Dooley. Think you'll go?"

"Guess so. All us Youngs have fought whenever we got the chance."

The words seemed to depress Winslow. "All right. Just watch out for Pet."

When the party got together at three in front of the Big House, Toby showed up accompanied by two young black boys. Soon Pet came out of the house and joined them. Thad drove the wagon up, having loaded it down with food and blankets, and she climbed up and sat beside him. "Thad, isn't this exciting!"

"Sure is," he nodded, then added, "I see you got your possum huntin' clothes on." Pet glanced down self-consciously at her outfit—a pair of overalls especially cut to fit her slim figure, custom-made leather boots with thick soles, a fine soft leather coat lined with wool, and a wool cap perched on her head. "You look real fine, Miss Pet," Thad commented.

She turned a little red. "Oh, they're warm enough, I guess. Are we about ready?"

Dooley rode up on his feisty little bay, calling out, "Let's git!" and led the procession out of the yard at a brisk gallop. Thad spoke to the team and they followed. Toby drove the second wagon with a mixture of young boys and yelping dogs bouncing wildly around. Dooley's brother Acie, aged thirteen, and the other two boys rode their horses in front of the last wagon.

For several miles they traveled along muddy roads. At first Thad had nothing to say. He could talk to Dooley and his people, or to the slaves, but the young woman beside him came from another world. Pet, however, was not quiet. She chatted happily, telling him about hunting, and Thad relaxed. "You sure do know a lot about farming and hunting," he said when he got a chance. "I thought girls were only interested in parties and dresses."

"Oh, most of them are, I guess. Why, it would take an act of Congress to get Belle out to watch a mare foal—or in this wagon, but I like it, don't you?"

He met her eyes and noticed that it was impossible to tell if they were blue or gray, and her nose had freckles sprinkled so lightly that they were almost invisible. She was going to be a very pretty girl when she grew up, he realized. Even now she made him a little nervous.

They left the wagon when the road ended, with Pet riding behind Dooley. By the time they got to the campsite, it was almost dark. The group stopped long enough to eat some sandwiches and drink a great deal of tea. "We'll build a big fire later," Dooley told them. "You boys start pickin' up wood, while the rest of us get on with the business at hand. Now—there's too many of us to go in one bunch, so Acie, you go with Laddie and Josh over to that place I showed you last week. Should be a passel of critters there. Take Rowley and Henry with you to bring the game back. I'll take Toby, Thad, and Miss Pet over to that ridge I tol' you about. Let's all try to git back 'fore dawn, and we'll have a good breakfast."

Acie and the other boys took off quickly, and Dooley said, "Let's git goin' our ownselves." He led them through the woods, with Pet right behind him, followed by Thad and Toby and one slave named Jim who carried a lantern. Dooley held three of the yapping dogs on long leashes, but their strength almost dragged him through the brush. Only a sliver of a moon gave light to the dark woods, so Thad found himself stumbling over logs and into holes constantly. Dooley and Pet pulled away, and he wondered how the girl could keep up. Finally the dogs began barking in a hysterical pitch and Toby said, "Dere! Dey done got one treed!" They continued on until they located the others standing under a massive oak. The dogs were trying to climb the tree, barking with all their might.

"What you got, Dooley?" Toby asked, peering up into the tree. "I cain't see nuffin'! Jim, gimme dat lantern!" In one quick motion he held the lantern high and they all stared into the dark recesses of the mighty limbs of the tree.

"I see his eyes!" Dooley shouted. "He's a big one!" He threw up his gun, then lowered it. "Shoot! He ducked around the tree."

"Let's spread out an' see if we can spot him," Toby suggested. But they couldn't get a glimpse of the animal, so finally Toby decided, "We gonna haf to go shake him out, Dooley."

"I can go up and blow him out with this here rifle gun!" Dooley exclaimed.

"No—don' you 'member how Jimmy Hope done shot his whole hand off climbin' a tree wif a loaded gun?"

Dooley started to argue, then his eyes fell on Thad with a gleam. "Thad, you go up and shake that critter out. I'll shoot 'im when he hits the ground."

"Cain't do dat, neither," Toby insisted. "He'll likely be spinnin' round like dey does—and you might shoot Miss Pet."

"Oh, all right!" Dooley said in disgust, then leaned his rifle against a sapling. "Go shake 'im down, Thad, and I'll git the sucker in this sack. *That* suit you, Toby?"

"Dat will answer. Up you go, Thad."

"But—I don't even know what a possum *looks* like!" Thad protested as Toby shoved him up to the first branch.

Pet broke out in a fit of laughter. "Just throw down the first thing you find, Thad—that'll be a possum."

"Well . . . all right." Thad moved easily up the tree. When he reached the middle, he heard a rustling of branches over his head, and shouted, "He's going up—I'll catch him, though!" The spirit of the hunt excited him, and he climbed higher until finally he saw that the animal had backed out on a branch. "I got him now, Dooley!" he yelled. "Get your sack ready!"

"Let 'im come, Thad!"

Thad walked out carefully, holding tightly to a branch overhead, but he stopped when he saw the bright sharp teeth of the possum. Then he began to jump up and down on the branch and yell "Here he comes" as the animal slipped and fell toward the ground. "Don't let him get away, Dooley!" In his excitement Thad started to scramble down when a blood curdling scream from below stopped him.

Dooley had been running around trying to get under the possum while Toby held the lantern.

Pet was screaming "Git him, Dooley!" while the dogs frantically tried to climb the tree.

The dark shadow had fallen squarely into Dooley's arms, and he clutched it, instinctively yelling, "I got 'im! I got 'im!" Then a red-hot pain struck his ear and he felt a set of razor-sharp claws raking him across the chest!

"THIS IS A PANTHER!" he screamed.

It wasn't a panther, but it was the closest thing to one—a full-grown bobcat weighing over thirty pounds! The angry beast was trying to get free, but Dooley fell to the ground and began rolling to get away from the animal. Toby and Pet could see what was happening, but the dogs jumped into the fray and instantly there was one whirling mass made up of Dooley, the bobcat, and the dogs—all screaming at full pitch. Sometimes the dogs got a grip on the bobcat, but sometimes it was Dooley they grabbed—and all the time Thad was scrambling down the tree, hollering, "Don't let him get away, Dooley!"

Pet, on hearing this, burst into gales of laughter, and Toby joined in. This infuriated Dooley, who finally kicked the bobcat away, and the animal raced off, followed by the dogs. Dooley staggered forward, his fists raised to fight Toby, but he was intercepted by Thad who yelled, "If you got that one in the sack, Dooley—I got another one ready!" Thad had found something overhead—a small animal with gray fur and a naked tail, looking like a large rat.

Dooley staggered back and wiped the blood from his ear. He looked up with horror, and screamed, "No—you crazy Yankee! Don't knock nothin' else outta that tree!"

Then the humor of it struck him, and he said to Toby and Pet, who could not stop laughing, "N-no tellin' what that kid will send down to be sacked up next! Probably a full-growed grizzly bear!"

Just then Thad reached the ground, demanding, "Where's the possum, Dooley? I think we've found a nest of 'em up in this tree—" He stopped and stared at the three still laughing, and he joined in, remarking, "This possum huntin' is sure fun, ain't it?"

They left that place, but it was midnight before they caught the dogs. Dooley decided to try a spot about five miles away. He had not been seriously hurt—just a few cuts in his earlobe and on his chest. "We'll build a fire for you, Miss Pet," he told her, "and you and Thad wait here while Toby and Jim and me go see if we can get a coon." After they got the fire going, they disappeared into the darkness.

"Cozy here by this fire, isn't it, Thad?" Pet asked. Her eyes were bright despite the late hour. Then she said, "You never say anything about yourself, Thad. Tell me about your family—and how you grew up."

"Why, I don't think it'd interest you much, Miss Pet. I can't remember my pa. He was killed in an explosion at the mill when I was four. I had one sister and two brothers. I was the youngest. After my pa died, it was sort of hard. We all had to work just to keep alive. Lived in a one-room shack in an alley."

"All of you?"

"Yep—and we all worked. Ma and my sister worked in a spinning mill and my two brothers worked in a steel mill. When I was eight years old I went to work in a factory where they made medicine. I tied little strings that kept the tops on. I remember I would eat a piece of bread for breakfast when it was still dark. Then I'd work all day until it was dark again. I'd come home and Ma would have some soup, maybe. I'd eat it and go right to bed."

He picked up a stick and poked at the fire, a bitter expression on his face. "Things got bad and there wasn't no work. They said it was because Jackson had closed the banks, but I don't know. We all lost our jobs, though. One day my oldest brother came home. He'd been out looking for work. Ma had his clothes tied up in a bundle. She met him at the door and gave him the bundle and a dollar—then said, 'I can't keep you no more.' She kissed him and sent him off. Two months later, with my other brother, she did the same thing. Gave him his clothes and a dollar. Kissed him and sent him off."

An owl hooted far off, and Thad lifted his head to listen. He said no more, so Pet asked, "What happened then?"

"I come home about a month after that, and Ma was waitin' for me. She had my clothes tied up in a bundle, but she didn't have no dollar for me. She said, 'I can't keep you no more, Thad.' I waited for her to kiss me—but she never done it. I went on down the street—and just before I turned the corner, I looked back. She was leaning against the door, and I waved to her—but she never waved back. So I left. I went back to see her a year later, but she had died of pneumonia and my sister was nowhere to be found."

His shoulders slumped and his voice dropped as he added, "Took me a long time to figure out why she didn't kiss me. She just couldn't stand no more. Now, when I see folks who think they've got trouble, I think about her."

He heard a small sound and looked up to see Pet's eyes brimming with tears, her fists tightly pressed against her lips. "Sorry," he muttered. "Shouldn't have said nothin'."

"No, it's all right." She wiped her eyes, and asked, "Where did you go then?"

"Went to Boston and got a job for a while unloading ships— but that didn't last long. So I went back to New York." He poked the fire again and watched the sparks whirl wildly upward. Finally he said, "I got in with a wild bunch—and into trouble with the law. Nearly starved before I slipped away on a freight wagon. When I got to the river, I stowed away on the *Dixie Queen*. They threw me off at Richmond. Guess you know the rest."

Pet could feel the hurt. "It's been awful, Thad—but Papa likes you—I can tell. He'll help you."

"I ain't fit for much," he replied bitterly.

"You are so!"

In a gesture of frustration Thad tossed the stick to the ground. "I can't even read or write!" He turned his back to hide the shame on his face.

Pet got up and went to sit beside him. "I can teach you to read and write, Thad!"

He turned to look at her, and she saw the tears of anger welling up in his eyes. But he refused. "Your father wouldn't like it."

She smiled and squeezed his arm. "It'll be our secret, Thad!" Then she giggled. "I never thought I'd be a schoolmarm!" She picked up the stick he had been prodding the fire with, and made a letter in the soft earth.

"That's an *A* . . ." she said firmly, and as the fire cast its flickering shadows over their faces, they continued their first lesson until they heard the dogs coming back.

CHAPTER EIGHT

THE RICHMOND BLADES

★ ★ ★ ★

"Thad, hitch up the buggy. We need to make a trip to Richmond."

"Yes, sir."

Sky Winslow watched as the young man wheeled and ran for the stables; then he turned to his wife. "I've had about all the chatter I can stand, Rebekah. My head's ringing like a bell." The young men and women of the county had made a rendezvous at Belle Maison for two days, getting ready for the military ball at Richmond, and Sky was weary of it.

Rebekah smiled at him, patting his arm. "I'm surprised you lasted this long. Just remember, you've got to lead off the dance with me at the ball tonight."

He gave a sour glance at the crowd of uniformed soldiers and pretty girls attired in all the colors of the rainbow, then snorted, "I thought this was a *war* we were getting into—not a blasted tea party!"

Rebekah bit her lip. "Let them have this time, dear," she said quietly. Her smooth brow creased and the light went out of her eyes. "Some of them won't be here for the next ball, I'm afraid."

He blinked in surprise. At her comment his keen eyes swept the yard, seeing it in a new light. The bright July sun beat down on the milling crowd, illuminating the scene with a brilliant intensity. Brass buttons, newly coined, flashed as the soldiers dressed in gray moved across the yard, and Winslow thought, *They're all as newly minted as the buttons they wear—and none of them have the slightest idea of the hell they're walking into!*

Winslow well knew the horror of violence, for he had grown up in a savage world. Although his father had been a missionary, Sky himself had been thrust into the bloody wars that flared up constantly between the Indians. He had endured the screaming charges of his enemies, and he had dealt the death blow more often than he liked to think about. Now the memories flooded him, and he wondered how this group of perfumed, barbered, and cultured young men would react when they waded over a field with men literally blown to raw meat.

There had never been any question about their conscription. They would have to go. Sky's mind raced over the events of the last months—events that had brought these young men to Belle Maison. It was like a series of steel doors slamming on the South. It had started when Lincoln had been elected in November of 1860. His election had set in motion a swift reaction from the South; in February of the next year, seven southern states had met in Montgomery, Alabama, and formed the Southern Confederacy. Another fated door clanging shut. Their first act was to take possession of federal property—forts, arsenals, offices—within their boundaries. These were all bloodless takeovers until on April 12, the Confederates attacked Fort Sumpter—the first shots of the war. Another door shut—and the sound of the guns triggered a reaction, causing four more states to join the Confederacy.

Even before Virginia withdrew from the Union, the patriots of the Old Dominion were being formed into a regiment. Sky looked around and saw that Colonel Barton was surrounded by his officers, which included Captain Shelby Lee of Company A, called the Richmond Blades, Beau Beauchamp, and his own son, Mark, wearing lieutenants' uniforms. He shifted his gaze and saw his son Tom wearing corporals' stripes, and then he looked quickly at Rebekah. Her face was still, but the pain in her eyes was not difficult to read. He put his arm around her protectively. "It's hard. They're so *young.*"

She sighed and forced a smile. "Go for your ride, dear." As

he climbed into the buggy, she watched, thankful to God that he was not going with the Company A. When Jefferson Davis had asked Sky to come to Richmond as part of the staff, Rebekah had listened patiently as her husband protested to the hilt that his place was with the company. Finally he had agreed—but she was well aware that it would take very little to make him forget Richmond and ride out with the others. *Thank God, he's not going—and maybe it'll be over before Dan has to go.* Her youngest son had been wild to enlist, and only a stern command from Sky had kept the boy from joining up. Even now he was standing to one side, his face rigid with disappointment. Dan had pointed out repeatedly that many of the volunteers were only seventeen, a year older than he—but Sky had said adamantly, "The best thing that could happen to you, Dan, would be to miss the whole blasted war!"

As Sky left later for the two-hour trip to Richmond, with Thad at his side in the buggy, he thought of how he himself would have reacted to such a statement when he had been Dan's age. A wry smile touched his lips as he recalled how he had ridden out with a Sioux war party for a raid on the Pawnees when he was a year younger than Dan. Then bringing his mind to the present, Sky noted with pleasure how well Thad had mastered the skill of driving a team. An ironic thought crossed his mind: *If the rest of the Yankees learn to ride and shoot as quickly as Thad, we're in real trouble!*

The trip to Richmond went quickly, for the two talked of the plantation work—Thad with enthusiasm and Sky answering with a quiet smile. Finally as they rode into the edge of town, the older man said, "I'm right proud of you, Thad. You've learned more about farming in a few months than most people do in a lifetime."

Thad flushed with pleasure, and ducked his head awkwardly as he always did when Winslow praised him, but Sky went on with a touch of sadness in his voice. "I'm going to count on you to keep things together, you know. Everybody else has gone loco over this war—but they don't understand that somebody's got to keep the farm going while the war's going on. The army can't eat moonbeams!"

"Lots of folks say the war's gonna be over in a few weeks,"

Thad remarked. "All your boys are scared to death they'll miss it—especially Dan."

Winslow shook his head and didn't answer for so long that Thad thought he had not heard. Finally Sky spoke. "They don't have to worry about that, Thad. There'll be enough battles to satisfy all of them before this thing's finished."

As they turned down Cherry Street, a shrill yelping cry made them both turn, and Dooley Young, mounted on his fine-boned mare, wheeled and raced toward them. "Hey, Thad—hidee, Mr. Winslow," he cried as he pulled the animal to a dead stop. "Come in to see the show?"

"What show's that, Dooley?" Sky asked.

"Why, look around." The banty-legged rider grinned, waving his hand at the milling crowd that pushed and shoved all along the crowded streets. "I been to three county fairs, six revival meetin's, and a couple of snake stompings—but I ain't never seen nothin' like this!"

"You two better stick together while I get my business done," Sky smiled. "One of you will be in bad company, but I couldn't swear which." He stepped out of the buggy and moved through the crowd, saying over his shoulder, "You go on to Oliver's and pick up the supplies, Thad. I'll be pretty busy, so you and Dooley try to keep each other out of trouble until about three. Pick me up in front of the bank."

Dooley stepped off the mare and tied her to the rear of the buggy, then leaped up to sit beside Thad, chattering like a squirrel. As they made their way toward the west end of town he remarked, "Looks like the whole town's gone crazy, don't it, Thad? I ain't seen this many folks in Richmond since they hanged Ramsey Tyler and his bunch."

Thad held the reins tightly, knowing the spirited matched set of blacks would bolt at any excuse. "Hold up there, Molly!" he commanded sharply as the sleek mare lowered her head and plunged forward, startled by the sudden cacophonic blast of a small band that was marching down the middle of the avenue. As he skillfully guided the team through the maze of horses, wagons, and a mass of careless pedestrians dressed in colorful garb, he shook his head. "Don't see that going to war is all that much to shout about."

Dooley twisted around to stare at Thad, his pale blue eyes bright in the July sunlight. He could not explain the friendship that had sprung up between the two of them, for like most hill-country people, he was slow to form lasting friendships with outsiders. His friends had ragged him for spending so much time with a Yankee, but Dooley ignored them, realizing that Thad had a solid quality that was rare—even among Southerners! He considered Thad's remark, then loosed a stream of tobacco juice over the side of the wagon, narrowly missing the boot of a dandy in fine array, who gave him an angry look. Then he replied, "Why, shoot, Thad, it's jest *natural* to get excited when they's a fight comin' up. 'Course, it's all new to you, but if you'd been here and had to put up with the way the Yankees been shovin' us around, tellin' us we can't own no slaves . . ." Dooley spat again, and nodded vigorously.

"But—Dooley, you don't *have* any slaves, and I heard you say once you never intended to own any."

"Mebby not, but there ain't no gorilla like Lincoln goin' to tell me I *can't!*"

Thad shook his head and gave up, for he had this argument often with his friend and knew it was hopeless. He could understand why the Winslows would go to war over slavery, but in his short sojourn in Virginia he had become aware that the majority of slaves were owned by a very small group of rich planters. Some small farmers owned one slave, but it was far different in their cases, for the owner and the slave had to work closely together because of economic necessity.

He guided the team down main street to a large store with a sign reading "Oliver's Mercantile Store" spanning the sidewalk high overhead. Thad led the way inside and stepped up to the counter. Len Oliver, the portly owner, gave him a quick look, then turned to wait on another customer. Dooley's sharp eyes took in the slight, but said nothing. Thad waited patiently, though there was a flush on his high cheekbones. Finally Oliver moved to where Thad was standing and asked briefly, "Something for you?"

"Mr. Winslow wants these things." He handed the list to Oliver, who stared at it.

"Ain't got no help to load all this stuff," Oliver said in a surly tone. "You'll have to do it yourself."

Thad straightened to his full height, and his words carried over the store. "I'll step on down to Miller's. If you don't need Mr. Winslow's business, I guess that man can use it."

Thad wheeled angrily and left the store, ignoring Oliver's sputtering "Now—just a minute there. . . !" As Thad and Dooley stepped into the buggy, the store owner rushed out, his face pale. Waving his finger in the air, he protested, "You won't get by with this. I'm telling Mr. Winslow about this—and I'm also telling him what a mistake he's making letting a Yankee run his business!"

Thad ignored him, released the brake, and drove off, leaving Oliver in the street shaking his fist and cursing. Dooley stole a glance at the boy, then grinned and struck him a sharp blow on the shoulder. "If that don't beat all!" he cackled. "It shore puts the hair in the butter, don't it now?"

"Guess I shouldn't have done that," Thad said unsteadily. He had taken Oliver's slights for weeks, saying nothing, and he was shaken at the fiery gust of rage that had so quickly exploded in him.

"Aw, don't fret none about Mr. Sky, Thad," Dooley grinned. "He knows ol' man Oliver's the tightest geezer in Richmond. He's so stingy he breathes through his nose to keep from wearing out his false teeth! Mr. Sky's had a round or two with Len Oliver his own self. I think he'd like an excuse to trade with Miller."

Thad drove the buggy over to Oak Street, where John Miller filled his order with alacrity. He was a small, fair-skinned man with bright blue eyes. "Appreciate the business, Thad," he said as he loaded the last of the supplies in the rear of the buggy.

"You get a lot of ragging, Thad?" Dooley asked as they walked down the board sidewalk. " 'Bout bein' a Yankee, I mean?"

"Oh, some people are pretty short with me, Dooley." He studied the street carefully, then added, "Guess it's going to get worse."

"Aw, we'll whip those Lincoln monkeys in no time, Thad," Dooley boasted. "Anyways, you ain't no Yankee no more. You're a good 'ol southern boy now."

The pair wandered down the street, and it seemed that

Dooley knew almost everybody in Richmond. He was constantly singled out, and by the time he had been pulled into half a dozen saloons to celebrate the war, his eyes were slightly glazed, and he said, "Thad, I'm gittin' a little drunk. You gotta promise me I won't enlist." His speech was slurred, and he put his hand on Thad's shoulder and gave it a shake. "These here recruiters got their eyes on me—but no matter what happens, don't let 'em git me! You promise?"

"But—how can I stop you, Dooley?"

Dooley's mouth turned up beneath the huge mustache. "Hit me over the head with a fence post and sling me over my hoss if you have to," he said. "This here liquor is makin' me downright patriotic—and I ain't made up my mind which bunch I wanna be in—so you stick close and keep me away from them recruiters!"

Dooley's request seemed absurd, but Thad discovered that the small man had been prophetic, for more than once he had to pull Dooley away from an avid recruiter—or what was even more difficult, from some of his friends who had signed up and wanted Dooley in their company. Finally, Dooley stared at Thad through glazed eyes and mumbled, "Good ol' Thad! Bes' friend I got—in the whole—world!" But an hour later, when Thad tried to pull him away from a burly sergeant, he got angry and began to curse. "Mind your own business!" he yelled, and took the pen and was about to write his name.

"Come on, Dooley." Thad was relieved to see Mack Young, Dooley's cousin, a huge man in his thirties, step up and remove the pen. Dooley cursed him, too, but Mack simply walked him off, saying, "Much obliged, Thad. I'll take keer of him now."

Thad wandered around the streets; it seemed that the frenzied excitement of the people increased as the shadows grew longer. He heard snatches of songs improvised for the emergency—"Maryland, My Maryland," "John Brown's Body," and a parody that ran:

> I want to be a soldier
>   And with the soldiers stand,
> A knapsack on my shoulder,
>   And musket in my hand;
> And there beside Jeff Davis,
>   So glorious and so brave,

> I'll whip the cussed Yankee
> And drive him to his grave.

He paused to watch some boys who were keeping their patriotism warm by playing "Yank" and "Reb" in mock battles. At one time one of these groups had grown so feisty that the city authorities had been forced to break up the game. Thad crossed over to Church Hill where some boys had scattered and reformed, beginning the battle again. Not to be outdone, a group of young girls showed their patriotism by filling their aprons with small chunks of coal from a coal house, then racing into the fray, shouting, "Kill them! Kill them!"

The whole thing depressed Thad, and he was glad when three o'clock finally arrived. But he was in for a surprise. Mr. Winslow was flushed and out of sorts. "Thad, I've got to stay in town. Take the supplies back and give this note to my wife—and I want you to drive her and the girls here for the ball."

"Yes, sir." Thad half turned, then stopped and wheeled back to face Mr. Winslow. "I got the supplies from Miller's store."

Winslow knew more about the situation than Thad thought. Sky had observed the manner in which Len Oliver treated the boy, but had said nothing. Now he waited for Novak to explain, but he stood there quietly. Finally Sky said, "If you think that's best, Thad, then that's what we'll do." His brow creased and he placed his hand on the boy's shoulder, saying, "I'm going to need all the help I can get, Thad."

Thad's shoulder seemed to glow under the pressure of Winslow's hand, and he said, "I—I'll try to please you, sir!"

———

As darkness fell on Richmond, the city glittered; thousands of lamps and lanterns seemed to reflect the brilliant stars overhead. By some sort of mystic communication, every patriotic citizen had his residence ablaze with a thousand lights, leaving the dark houses as suspect—those who lived in them being labeled "Yankees," "Abolitionists," and "Black Republicans," and virtually ostracized.

The Exchange Hotel and the Ballard House dominated Cherry Street. The Ballard House had a glass balcony stretching over the street, connecting the two hotels; and they lit up the darkness in a grand spectacle, glittering and reflecting the crystal lights. Both had large ballrooms, and on this night each was filled to capacity with newly minted officers, civilians with the weight of the new government of the Confederacy on them, and what appeared to be hundreds of women dressed in gorgeous gowns of every hue. Each ballroom had an orchestra, and music spilled out of the buildings, rising at times over the excited voices of the guests who spun about the dance floors and milled at the outer edges.

Belle was being whirled around in a fast waltz by Vance Wickham, who was wearing a new ash-gray uniform. A humorous light danced in his eyes, and he pulled her closer and whispered, "You really must choose me, Belle. After all, I'm the first lieutenant and Beau is second." He laughed as she threw her head back, adding, "Of course, by that logic you ought to marry Shelby Lee since he's the major."

"Oh, don't be silly, Vance," she said with a brilliant smile. She was wearing a light blue gown with a tight bodice, and two blue stones dangled from her ears. Her hoop skirt brushed against him, and the excitement of the evening made her eyes enormous. She leaned against him, whispering, "Vance, you look absolutely *handsome* in your uniform! The Richmond Blades just has to be the best company in the whole Confederate Army!"

After Sumpter, Seth Barton had begun at once to raise a regiment, The Third Virginia Infantry, of which one company was The Richmond Blades. Its ranks had been filled immediately by young men generally of wealth, education and refinement. Wickham was first lieutenant, Beau second, and Belle's brother Mark was third. None of them had the faintest idea what processes of thought had made those decisions since they had never served a day in the army. "I think they must have gone by intelligence," Vance had teased Beauchamp and Winslow when they were notified of their respective ranks. Both Mark and Beau had laughed, but it was evident to Wickham that Beau's laughter was forced. It had grated on Beauchamp's pride to be under his rival's shadow, and Wickham knew that every decision he made would be picked to pieces by the other.

As if in echo to Vance's thoughts, Beau appeared magically as the last notes of the waltz sounded. Vance smiled and handed

Belle over to Beau. "I hope you're as prompt in your military duties as you are in your ballroom ones, Beau," he commented.

Beau grinned rashly, and wheeled Belle away as the band struck up a new tune. She smiled up at him, thinking that the two men were as different in styles of dance as they were in everything else. Both were excellent dancers, but whereas Vance was smooth, polished and light with his direction, Beau went at the dance as he did everything else—with complete assurance and a forceful manner. At first she resisted his tight embrace and his domination, but as the dance went on she found herself enjoying it in a perverse fashion. She was a girl who had learned quickly that she could do what she liked with most men, and the strength of this one had been a challenge. Now with the martial spirit of the evening, the emotionally charged times of war, she shivered with excitement as he held her close, his light blue eyes shining in his strong masculine face.

"We don't have much time, Belle," he said. "I expect the regiment will be leaving in a week or even sooner."

"Now, Beau, I may be young and naive, but I know that kind of talk!" Her eyes were filled with laughter, and she smiled at his surprised expression. "All soldiers tell that to the girls: 'I'm going away and I may get killed—so you have to love me right now!' Isn't that the way it goes?"

He laughed down at her, captivated by her beauty, and grinned, "You're too smart for me, Belle. I'll have to find another way to get you." Then he sobered and said with a seriousness that was not characteristic, "But it's true, all the same. We'll beat the Yankees, but some of us will get a funeral out of it."

"Oh, Beau, don't talk like that!" she pouted. "I couldn't bear it if anything happened to you!"

He grinned more broadly, knowing that she had probably said the same thing to Wickham. He dominated her dances, keeping her away from the eager young officers who threatened him for being so greedy with the prettiest girl at the ball.

Pet had watched the competition for Belle, but it was an old story, so she walked over to Dan, who was sitting in a straight chair with a rebellious look on his face. He was her favorite, being close to her own age. Tom and Mark were grown men who treated her with a kind of condescension, but Dan and she had grown up roaming the Virginia woods together. She sat down beside him quietly, then reached over and put her hand over his, whispering, "Don't feel bad, Dan. Your turn will come."

"It's not fair, Pet!" he burst out. "What's a year or two when there's a war on?"

She knew the impatience that was gnawing at him, but could not ease the matter. Instead, she patted his hand and said, "Look over there at Father, Dan. He's getting mad about something."

Dan looked across the room to where a group of men were gathered around Oscar Toombs, the lieutenant governor. "You're right," Dan replied. "I know that look. Come on, let's see what's got his dander up."

They made their way to the small group and heard their father say, "It's well enough to talk, but talk won't keep the Yankees out of Virginia. We don't have a single steel mill, and not even one rifle factory. What are we supposed to fight with, Mr. Toombs—hoe handles?"

Oscar Toombs had not risen to power in the state without learning how to handle men. He knew when to crush a man, and had no compunction when that time came, but he knew also when to smile; and to alienate a man like Sky Winslow would be foolish and bad for his political future. He nodded and said smoothly, "I know how you feel, Sky, but we'll get the arms."

"From whom?" Sky demanded bluntly.

"From England, of course," Toombs quickly responded. "England is a country that lives on its looms. It supplies the world with cloth—and they *must* have our cotton! Without it, their mills would shut down in a month. Why, there'd be a civil war in England!"

A murmur of approval went around the room, and Sky realized he was talking to a group that had made up their minds. He tried one more attempt, however. "We're not the only country that grows cotton, Mr. Toombs. But even if what you say is true, how will we get our cotton to England? They'd be fools in Washington if they didn't blockade the coast."

"Oh, come now, Winslow," Milton Speers broke in impatiently. "They don't have enough ships to watch everywhere—and our schooners can outrun any warship afloat." Speers was a wealthy planter, and he spoke what most of them felt. "Come now, Sky, don't be so gloomy! We'll send these fine young fellows out, give the Yankees a sound thrashing, and then we can get back to our way of life." He waved his big hands expansively. "Actually, this war can be the best thing that's ever happened to the South, gentlemen. Once the North has learned it can't run roughshod over us, we can get something done in Congress!"

Sky stared at him, then shrugged and moved away, saying only, "You better be right, Speers. We're betting everything we have on it."

Dan and Pet slipped away and hurried toward him. When they called his name, he turned. There was a set, angry look on his face, but his expression softened as the two drew near.

Pet asked, "Papa, can I go down to see the fireworks?"

He stopped and looked at them, his face relaxing. "What? Oh, I suppose so." His eyes searched Dan, noting the rebellious set to his youngest son's face, and impulsively put his hand on the boy's shoulder. "You mustn't hate me, Son."

"Ah, Pa, you know I don't hate you—but it's not fair! I bet *you* didn't have to wait until you were eighteen before you were treated like a man!"

Sky thought back to his boyhood, the days he had spent with his mother, White Dove, and smiled at the memory. "Before a Sioux could be a man, a real warrior, he had to prove himself a thousand ways, Dan. They were just about as impatient as you, I guess. All boys want to grow up fast. I know you won't understand this, but missing out on this war would be the best thing you could have!" Then he grinned. "Well, nobody can teach anybody anything, I reckon. Take your sister down to see the fireworks."

"Yes, sir."

Dan and Pet left the crowded ballroom and had to practically force their way through the crowds that pushed and shoved their way along the streets. There was no hope of getting a horse or wagon down Cherry Street, for a river of humanity seemed to flow first one way, then the other. The air was full of singing, and the smell of cigar smoke and raw liquor floated on the warm spring air. They finally made it to the end of Cherry and found a large crowd gathered around the courthouse where the fireworks were to be set off.

"Let's get over by the statue. We can see better from there, Dan," Pet suggested, pulling him along.

"Might as well get a good look," he grumbled. "Probably be the closest thing to a battle *I'll* ever see." He pushed his way through one group and they came to an open space. Suddenly Dan paused so abruptly that she ran into him. "Hey, there's Thad over there. Looks like he's in trouble!"

Pet looked up swiftly to where Dan pointed, and saw Thad with his back to the base of the statue of Lafayette. "Come on, Dan!" she cried, and the two ran toward the group surrounding Thad.

There were at least six or seven young men, most of them in their teens—and they were town boys, the pair saw. One of them was standing directly in front of Thad, his fists doubled up, and he was saying, "You got a lot of gall coming into town tonight, Novak. But we're gonna fix you so you won't be comin' to no more parties, ain't that right, boys?"

"Sure is—fix him up, Studs!" A series of cries went around the group. Fear shot through Pet. She had seen an undersized coon once, trapped by the pack, and she still had nightmares of the raging dogs finally tearing the small animal to fragments.

Dan pushed his way forward to stand beside Thad. "What's going on here, Thad?" He recognized the larger young man as Studs Mellon, a local bruiser who did some prizefighting.

The one called Studs was taken aback for a moment. He was a hulking youth of eighteen, with a low brow and a broken nose. For one moment he regarded Dan, then sneered, "You another Yankee boy? We can take care of you, too."

"He's not a Yankee," one of the onlookers said. "That's Sky Winslow's boy."

Studs considered him, then smiled. "Well, Winslow, you probably don't know it, but this here fellow is a Yankee spy—and I aim to see to it that he don't do no more spying for a long time."

"You're crazy!" Dan snapped. "He's worked for my father for months. Come on, Thad, let's get out of here."

"Easy won't do it, Winslow," Studs said harshly. "You just move on and we'll take care of this bird!" He reached out to grab Thad, and at that moment the rebellious spirit that had been raging in Dan for weeks was unleashed. He drew back his fist and struck the bully square in the nose.

The blow caught Mellon off guard and he fell backward to the ground, but immediately jumped to his feet. Blood was streaming down his face, and an unholy joy shone in his eyes. "All right, you all saw it. Now I'm gonna have to bust you both up!"

He stalked forward with his left out and his right cocked. None of the spectators doubted the outcome. Lunging at Dan, Studs lashed out with a straight left that sent the boy reeling. Thad leaped at Mellon with arms flailing, striking the bully with a wild right that opened a cut over his eye, blinding him. Studs screamed in fury, swiped at his eyes and roared with a stream of curses as he dived straight at Thad, knocking him to the ground. Studs was so quick that Thad never saw the blow coming.

Mellon drew back his foot to kick Thad, but at that instant a pair of arms wrapped around his neck and a keen pain sliced through his left ear! He whirled around, but Pet, who had clamped herself onto his back, reached around and raked his face with her nails.

The crowd stared at the scene, for they knew that the Winslows were the children of a wealthy planter, but they knew as well that Studs Mellon had a wicked temper. Although some began shouting "Don't hurt that girl, Studs!" nobody dared to interfere.

Mellon reached over his head, pulled Pet off and threw her at the crowd, but just as he turned Dan and Thad were up and at him like a pair of terriers. For the next few minutes the wild fray continued, each pitching with all his might. Suddenly a small figure materialized from nowhere with a shrill cry. A hard object struck Mellon on the top of his head, knocking him flat. His head throbbed, but he was up at once—face-to-face with Dooley Young.

"You stay out of this, Young!" he snarled.

"Aw, you're not so mean as you like to make out, Studs," Dooley grinned. "I bet you go to church when nobody's lookin'." He gave the heavy revolver he had used on Mellon's head a twirl and said, "Now, you jest git along with your business, Studs."

Studs stared at the small figure, and he heard the laughter that ran through the crowd. Enraged, he shouted, "I'm gonna git me a Yankee, Dooley; and if I gotta chaw you up to git him, I'll do it!"

He was about to take a step when a shot rang out, and he stopped dead still. He raised his hand to his right ear, the one the girl hadn't bitten, and felt the warm blood. He stared at Dooley in unbelief. "You shot me!"

"Jest wanted you to have a matched set, Studs," Dooley grinned. Then he leveled the revolver and the humor dropped from his voice. "Now git your carcass outta here, Studs, or I'll ventilate you sure enough!"

Studs stared at the muzzle, then into Dooley's eyes. He whirled angrily. "You ain't heard the last of this, Young!"

"Come any time, Studs; we never close," Dooley called out as Mellon's hulking form disappeared. Then he turned around, his eyes merry. "You boys all right?"

"Sure, Dooley," Thad replied. "But I sure was glad to see you."

"Aw, he's jest the kind that gives us tough guys a bad name," Dooley said. Then he peered at both boys. "We better git you two patched up or you won't be fit to go to preachin' tomorrow."

Pet, who had stood by for the rest of the fight, asked Dooley as they all walked away from the crowd, "Would you really have shot him, Dooley, if he hadn't backed down?"

"I'm a pretty mean feller, Miss Pet," Dooley answered solemnly. "Never care to let myself find out jest how mean I be. Hey, looks like you got a little scrape in that fiasco!"

Pet felt her cheek and discovered blood from a cut. She stared in surprise at the stain on her hand, then laughed, "Well, Dan, looks like we got started on our war before Tom and Mark, after all."

"Pa will scalp that Studs Mellon!"

Dan was not far wrong, for when they finally faced their parents with their cuts patched up, Sky Winslow looked like one of his Sioux ancestors, his eyes blazing and his mouth a slit. They were standing in the lobby of the Ballard House with a small group, getting ready to leave. "Guess I'll have a talk with that fellow," he said quietly. Too quietly Rebekah knew. She had seen the explosive Winslow temper flair out of her husband only on a few occasions. "It's all over, Sky," she reminded him.

"Leave him to me, sir," Vance said with a knowing smile. "He's signed up in Company A. I imagine when he finds out that his third lieutenant is the brother of the young people he roughed, he'll quiet down a little."

Sky reluctantly conceded, and it might have been over, but Beau remarked, "This fellow Novak has put you in a bad light, Mr. Winslow. It's well known that he's a Yankee, and you ought to get rid of him."

"On the say-so of trash like Studs Mellon? Not likely, Beau."

"I know you're a loyal man, sir, but we're in a shooting war now, and anybody from the North had better declare themselves. Has Novak said anything about enlisting?"

"He's too young," Sky replied quickly, looking at Dan.

"We've got some his age in the Blades already," Beau insisted.

A curious silence fell over the group, and every eye rested on Sky. He bowed his head, studied the floor, then lifted his eyes to meet those of Beau. "I know something about men, I think. I trust Thad. This may not be his fight, but he's been loyal to me and I'll stick with him."

"It's like you, Mr. Winslow," Beau shrugged. "But before this is over, a lot of us may have to part with some we thought were friends."

On that note, the party broke up, and the next day the Richmond Blades marched out of Richmond in formation, headed for their training camp. Sky stood watching with the rest of the town. When Company A marched by he couldn't help the thrill of pride he felt at the sight of Mark and Tom. He shook his head and said quietly to Rebekah, "Beau was wrong about Thad, but it's going to be hard on a lot of people like him."

She put her arm around him, and they watched silently as the proud gray line disappeared into the distance, the shrill, martial music of the band fading like the last thin peep of birds as the sunset falls. And as the music faded, so did some of the hope that had always been strong in the hearts of Sky and Rebekah, for both of them knew somehow that the proud young men of Company A of the Richmond Blades would never be as whole and complete as at that moment.

PART TWO

THE FARMER

★ ★ ★ ★

(April '61 to '62)

CHAPTER NINE

YANKEE RELATIVES

★ ★ ★ ★

"I still say it's foolish," Robert Winslow declared testily. "Here we are in the midst of a war, and you want to go into the very heart of rebel territory. At your age, you ought to know better! And right in the middle of the July heat!"

The last of the speaker's words were drowned out by the shrill whistle from the steam engine, and he cast a look in its direction as if it were a personal affront. He was an impatient man and accustomed to obedience, having given orders all his life—as a naval officer, a lawyer, and now as a New York congressman in the House. But as the whistle sounded another warning, he shook his head in frustration, knowing that no matter how other men trembled at his temper, the old man who stood before him would not be moved. Yet Robert tried one more time, modifying his voice—even putting a hand on the man's thin shoulder.

"Father, just wait six months and I'll go with you. This rebellion will be over then. I'd like to work with you on the book, but I can't do it now."

At seventy-eight, Whitfield Winslow was not impressed with the effort. He grinned at Robert's words. "You've tried threats all week, Robert, and now as a last resort, you're attempting bribery—just like a good politician. But that won't work either, so you just run along and take care of the government while

Davis and I go mingle with our rebel kinfolk."

The third member of the trio was a young man, large in stature, with bright red cheeks and crisp curly brown hair. "He's got your number, Father," he grinned, looking at Robert Winslow. "There's no way you can bully Grandfather." There was a trace of an English accent in his voice, superimposed by three years at Oxford, and the English flavor was apparent in his dress as well. "Try to keep Mother calm, and we'll be back in a few weeks."

Robert shrugged and then laughed. "I knew it was hopeless the moment you decided to go, and I suppose you two *can* be trusted—but don't do anything foolish. If the tempers down there are as fiery as I hear, a pair of Yankees could get into trouble."

"Not with papers signed by Stephen Mallory," Whitfield reassured him. "We may have a little trouble with our kinfolk, but with a pass from the Confederate Secretary of the Navy, we won't be taken for spies." He had obtained the pass by simply writing to Mallory, who had served under him as first officer when Whitfield had commanded the frigate *Courage*. Mallory had sent a pass with the warning: *I am happy to be of service, Captain, but be sure that you do no more than work on the history of your family while you are in our country. Feelings are running very high, and I cannot answer for the hotheads among us who see every man from the North as a traitor.*

"All right, then, on with you," Robert conceded. He took charge of getting them aboard the train and settled in their seats, giving advice constantly. Then the whistle blew two sharp blasts, and the train lurched into motion. Hurrying off, Winslow stood near their window and waved until they were out of view.

"He's really worried about us, Davis," the older man remarked as the train picked up speed. "Thinks the rebels will eat our drumsticks or something worse."

Davis was looking out the window, taking in the sight of the unfinished Capitol on the small rise. Capitol Hill was a muddy, dreary, desolate spot—and the structure itself no less dilapidated, with a dome that looked as if it had been guillotined. Unlike the centuries-old buildings of England, everything in Washington appeared raw and unfinished to Davis. He shifted his gaze to his grandfather. "He may be right, you know. They're aching for a fight, if all we hear is true."

"So is the North," the old man returned grimly. "Both sides are demanding a battle, and neither one is ready."

"You don't think the South has a chance, do you, Grandfather?"

"In a war, Son, anything can happen. A lot of our people didn't want this confrontation in the first place; and if the South wins a decisive victory, we could see an anti-war movement that would be the end of the whole thing." A thought flashed into his mind, and he looked at his grandson with a strange expression. "You don't care much about all this, do you, Davis? I think your heart's still in England, and you resent having to come home."

Davis flushed, for that was exactly how he felt. "I guess you've hit right on, Grandfather—but I haven't said anything to Father."

"He's a pretty sharp man, and he's got Lowell on his mind, too."

Lowell was Davis's brother; at twenty-three he was three years younger. The two were very close, but Lowell had chosen to go to West Point, while Davis had insisted on an academic career. It was natural that Robert Winslow, active man of affairs that he was, would look down on the choice Davis had made; and the relations between the two had been strained.

Davis shifted uncomfortably. "There's a lot of sympathy for the South in England. If they support the southern cause, it'll be a hard war."

"So it would—just another reason why I believe it won't be over in ninety days like some of the fools in Congress think!" Whitfield snapped. Then he turned back to his grandson and asked directly, "What will you do? Fight—or not?"

Davis sat there, trying to frame an answer. Finally he replied, "No, I won't fight. I'm not political, as you know. I guess I'm just one of those 'fools' who think it'll be over quickly. Then I can go back to England and try to be a writer."

The noise of the train changed as they crossed a bridge, leaving a lazy trail of smoke. Some of the coal smoke seeped into the coach and burned the older man's eyes. He took out a snowy white handkerchief, wiped his face, then put it back into his breast pocket before speaking. There was a far-off look in his eye and he spoke so softly that Davis had to lean toward him to catch it.

"I pray you're right—but these are grand, yet awful times, Davis. There's some strange portent in the air—like a stillness before a gathering storm. This country's been on a collision course for a long time, and as Mr. Lincoln said, we can't endure half slave and half free. It'll be one or the other, and I think we're on the razor's edge. You'll probably have to make a decision sooner or later. There won't be any disinterested spectators in this war!"

"I hope you're wrong, sir," Davis replied finally. The trees flashed by as the train sped south. "Because I can't feel a part of it," he murmured.

"Well, don't fret, Son," the old man encouraged. "We Winslows have a habit of being pulled into things against our will. You just smile and be agreeable while we're in Richmond."

A strange thought struck Davis and he asked, "What if I got converted to the southern cause, Grandfather?" He shook his head and laughed, "No, I'm the family eccentric, but I'm not crazy!" He chuckled again, but did not see the startled look on his grandfather's face—a look of alarm.

They made the journey, changing trains twice, and got off at their destination at noon. Like Rome, Richmond sat on seven hills, a pleasant city on the James River. Its position as a railroad terminus and the industrial resource for the Confederacy made it the logical site for the capital in place of the earlier choice of Montgomery.

The Winslows departed from the train station and took a carriage through the city. They were impressed by the activity they saw. "It's like a beehive!" Davis exclaimed. It was grimy from the atmosphere of smoke, and the streets were filled with people jostling one another—all appearing to be on some mysterious business. Many of the buildings rumbled and hummed. Through windows Davis and his grandfather saw hundreds of women leaning over benches in the cartridge factories. Throughout the city there was a constant pounding and wheezing of foundries and lathes and wood-working plants.

"Looks more like one of our industrial cities than I expected," Whitfield grunted. "But I expect it's about the only manufacturing center they've got."

The shops were numerous, and the windows displayed an air of plenty, the two men noticed as they walked toward their hotel. There was a plethora of French perfumes and wines, the finest hams, ducks, partridge, oysters, and terrapin. The French and English prints were reminders that lanes to Europe were still open. The streets were filled with men in uniform; on every corner busy recruiting sergeants were doing a brisk business. "They really seem to be serious about this, don't they?" Davis remarked as they entered the Ballard House.

The older man only shook his head, saying as they approached the desk, "They won't be so lighthearted after they bury a few thousand of their boys." Then he turned to the clerk. "You have rooms for us?"

"Not very good ones, I'm afraid," replied the clerk, a tall, skinny man with a bushy head of black hair. "I can give you a small room on the third floor."

"That'll do," Winslow replied. "I need to find Mr. Sky Winslow. Do you know him?"

The clerk's eyes opened wider, and he nodded vigorously. "Why, yes, indeed! Mr. Winslow often stays here with his family—but they've taken a house now, I believe." He called to the other clerk who was sorting mail, "Harry, do you know where Mr. Winslow's house is?"

"The old Nelson place."

"Ah, yes, I can give you directions—but you'll no doubt find him at the capitol at the session. Let me have your bags taken up, and I'll get you a carriage to take you there when you're ready."

"Thank you."

The clerk's bright eyes fixed on the pair with an intense speculation, and he asked, "You are a relative of our Mr. Winslow, I take it?"

Whitfield nodded. "Yes—from Washington." He enjoyed the shock that touched the man's face, and said, "We'll wash up; then you can get that carriage for us."

They followed the black man who carried their bags upstairs;

then when they were inside the room, Davis grinned, "You did that on purpose, didn't you—told them we were from the North?"

"Save their detectives a lot of time," the older man nodded, his eyes sparkling. "Now, let's go find Mr. Sky Winslow. It's time we met some of our rebel kinfolk!"

———

With Richmond bursting at its seams, Sky had been fortunate to obtain the white frame house on the outskirts of town. It was an old structure, but sound, and the three bedrooms were adequate since Mark and Tom both billeted with the company. Sky and Rebekah used the largest one, Pet and Belle the next, and Dan slept in the smallest. Though Sky was gone a great deal, he tried to be home for the evening meal whenever possible.

This evening he came home earlier than usual, and found Rebekah preparing supper with Mary, the single house slave they'd brought with them from Belle Maison. "Put some more beans in the pot; we've got company tonight."

"From the President's office?" Rebekah asked.

"No, this is kinfolk." He smiled at her look of surprise. "You remember I told you about Whitfield Winslow?"

"Oh, the naval officer?" Rebekah tasted the cornbread dressing and then nodded.

"That's him. He's the one who is interested in the family— can trace the Winslows back to Adam, from what I hear. He came into the office today with his grandson. Says he's come here to pump us dry about our side of the family."

"It'll be nice to meet them," Rebekah replied, "and we have plenty to eat. Thad brought in a mountain of fresh vegetables from the farm—oh, by the way, I asked him to whitewash the servant's quarters. Was that all right?"

"Sure. I want to talk to him about the crops. May be best if he stays overnight." He turned to go, then hesitated. "You'd better say a word to the children. You know how they claim to hate the Yankees, and here I am dragging two of them home with me."

"I'll warn them," Rebekah smiled. "What time will they be here?"

"I told them seven. Will Tom and Mark be here?"

"No. They're on some kind of military exercise. You go get freshened up, and take a nap—if you can in this heat."

By the time the meal was ready to set on the table all the children were home and Rebekah cornered them to give a stern warning. When she mentioned that two relatives from Washington were coming, their reaction was typical. Dan glowered and muttered something about "traitors," Belle asked, "How old is Cousin Davis?" and Pet said, "I remember Papa telling about the captain. He sounded real nice!"

"Just you keep quiet about the war," Rebekah warned. "They're our kin and I won't have any of you hurting their feelings." Even as she spoke there was a knock at the door and she heard Sky's footsteps as he went to answer it. "Let's go meet our relations," she said rather nervously. Despite her talk, she was apprehensive about the visit. She had heard so much talk about the cruelty of northern people that she dreaded to think there would be trouble within the family. True enough, the communication between the two branches of the family had been little; still, she knew that Sky had an admiration for some of them, and she was fearful he might be hurt.

She and the children proceeded into the parlor where Sky was conversing with the two men. Sky introduced his family. "My wife, Rebekah, and this is my son Dan and my two daughters, Belle and Patience."

Rebekah nodded, but the fine-looking older man stepped forward and took her hand, saying warmly, "I've always heard that Sky married a prize—and now I can verify it, my dear."

"Why—thank you, Captain Winslow." Rebekah thought she saw something of her husband in the stately carriage and direct gaze of the man, and she smiled into his eyes.

"Oh, this is my grandson Davis." A twinkle glinted in his eyes. "If he talks funny, it's not because he's retarded. He just returned to America after three years in England."

Davis flushed as they all scrutinized him like a specimen under glass. He nodded slightly, saying only, "Good of you to have us."

Sky immediately asked, "What do they say about us there, Mr. Winslow? About our war, I mean?"

Rebekah put a warning hand on Sky's arm and said disdainfully, "None of your politics, Sky! The food is on the table and I'm sure our guests are hungry after their long trip."

Davis was relieved at her words, and although the distance from the parlor to the long dining room was only a few steps, he discovered somehow that the older girl, Belle, was at his side and that he had offered his arm to escort her. She was so beautiful that he was intimidated, for his experience with women was slight. Taking one glance at her flawless skin, sparkling teeth and raven hair drawn back from her brow, he could only answer her questions in short monosyllables as they entered the dining room. When she came to stand behind a chair, he did have sense enough to pull it out for her—then he went around the table to sit beside his grandfather across from her.

Sky bowed his head and without preamble prayed, "Our Father, we thank thee for this food. We thank thee for our guests, and we ask that you would prosper them with every blessing. Protect us from harm and cause us to love thee more every day. In the name of Jesus we pray."

The sudden blessing had caught Davis off guard, for although his grandfather was a Christian, none of the rest of the family were church people. His own father was a thorough skeptic, calling himself an agnostic and admiring only the transcendental views of Emerson in the religious field. Davis himself had unconsciously adopted this attitude, and the obvious simple Christianity of Sky Winslow shocked him.

He had been his grandfather's greatest ally in the matter of tracing the family history, and knew the story of Sky Winslow very well. Looking across the table, he saw the Indian ancestry that came to Sky through his Sioux mother—the wife of the famous mountain man, Christmas Winslow. His host, he remembered, had led Sioux war parties, been a guide for wagon trains across the Oregon trail, and had been something of a gun fighter in his youth. As a boy, Davis had loved to hear his grandfather tell those tales of the wild west, and now, looking at Sky himself, it was like a legend come to life.

The food was good, and both Davis and his grandfather realized that they were being studied openly by the family. The conversation stayed on matters of the family tree until the dessert came, and with the thick, bubbling blackberry pudding came a sudden shift.

"Captain Winslow," Dan asked abruptly, his eyes fixed on Davis, "do you have any other grandsons?"

They all knew instantly what the question implied, and Rebekah could have pinched his ears off. Her eyes met Sky's and he shrugged. But they need not have worried, for Captain Winslow leaned back and studied the young man with a calm gaze, a smile touching his lips.

"Yes, I have one more grandson, Mr. Winslow," he replied, and the use of the title made the boy flush with pleasure. "He's a graduate of West Point. His name is Lowell; he's Davis's only brother."

Belle asked quickly, "Mr. Winslow, you've been out of the country for three years—did you come home because of the war?"

"Well . . ." Davis hesitated, not knowing how to answer the question. The truth was that his parents had insisted on his return, but that made him sound like a weak sister. "I'd just finished up my work at Oxford and had always planned to come home after that."

"What did you study there, Mr. Winslow?" Rebekah asked.

Davis grinned. "Nothing important, Mrs. Winslow. Which is to say, I took a degree in literature."

"You want to be a professor?" Sky asked, his curiosity spilling over.

"No, he wants to be a writer," the captain interjected, looking fondly at Davis. "We've had horse thieves and governors in the family, but never a writer as far as I know."

The tense moment passed, and as they ate the cobbler and drank coffee, Pet noticed that Belle was studying Davis carefully. *She's got to size up a man—even if he is a Yankee!* she thought. She herself was much more impressed with the captain. Davis was overweight and looked soft, but his grandfather had the history of a hard life at sea written on his face. Those years had given him a mahogany complexion, and the lines around his eyes spoke of much time under the tropical sun.

After the meal they moved back to the parlor, and for two hours Captain Winslow told them the fascinating history of the

Winslow family and his dream of putting it all in a book. Finally, he looked at his watch and smiled. "Never let a man loose with his hobby horse! I must ask your pardon for holding you captive."

Belle said with a glow of intensity in her eyes, "Oh, Captain Winslow, I never knew we had such a family!"

"Well, I've told you mostly about the heroes, Miss Belle, but we've had our villains as well—but on the whole we've done very well."

"But with this war," Belle asked, "isn't our family going to be divided?"

"Not the family!" Dan burst out impetuously. "The *country* will have to be divided!"

An awkward silence fell across the room, and Captain Winslow looked directly at Dan, saying slowly, "It's been nip and tuck with this country, lad, from the beginning. I've seen the time, more than once, when it looked as if we'd be swallowed up by France or England." He paused and they could see that he was re-living the bygone days before they were born. Finally he said quietly, "I remember when Jefferson decided to cut back on the Navy. By the time he was done, there were only five light frigates and eight heavy ones. I had a berth as midshipman on the *Constitution*, a frigate 44, with Captain Edward Preble commanding. Well, the pasha of Tripoli decided that what he needed was a war with the United States, so he cut down the consul's flagpole and demanded a payment of $250,000 to set it up again. Jefferson decided that compromise with those barbarians was impossible, so he sent five ships to Tripoli."

Sky leaned forward. "How could five ships fight a war?"

"Why, nobody on board ever thought to ask, sir! We'd whipped the greatest nation on earth in the Revolution, and we thought we could do anything. But you must remember that no one had attacked the Barbary powers at home since the age of Charles V. The castle batteries held one hundred fifteen guns and were manned by twenty-five thousand men. Preble had the *Constitution* and six small ships. Sailing into Tripoli's harbor was like a mouse entering a cage full of hungry lions! I was on one of the small gunboats, with Stephen Decatur commanding, and on August third, we went in under a bright sun. The shore batteries opened up, and the shells fell around us like rain!"

The old man paused, the remembrance turning his eyes bright. "I can still smell the salt air mixed with gunpowder. My best friend went down beside me with his chest blown away— but we went in until we were close enough to open fire. Decatur yelled, 'We'll finish what they started at Lexington and Concord, men!' So we drove them out and the Navy was born again that day at Tripoli!"

"But that time the enemy was not Americans," Sky commented gently.

"No. That's what makes this time so tragic," the captain replied. Then he looked at Sky. "I remember your grandfather, Nathan. I met him only once, but I've never forgotten it. He told me about the day your father was born—December 25, 1777. At Valley Forge, wasn't it?"

"That's why he was named Christmas," Sky said quietly.

"Nathan told me about those days—when men were walking on snow, leaving crimson marks because they had no shoes. I asked him, 'How could they do it?' He said, 'They believed that God had given this land to mankind for a special reason and they were ready to pay the price.' "

"Yes, I heard that Grandfather Nathan used to say those very words," Sky nodded.

"Well, Dan Winslow, that's the only answer I can give you," the captain said, referring to Dan's statement about the country being divided. He looked pensively at the boy. "I believe God's hand is on America. If I'm right, somehow we won't destroy each other. We have other Winslows in the Midwest, too, who are fighting for the North. It's your father's brother, George—his family. He's dead now, but his grandson, Zacharias, is in the army of the Potomac. Lots of Winslow men have died for this country, and more of us may die yet." He stood up abruptly, saying, "My grandson Lowell has a very good friend. They went through West Point together, but just last month, his friend resigned and went to serve in the Confederate Army in South Carolina. What if Lowell and he meet on the field of battle? I can't say, but my heart tells me that we are in for a tribulation time." He shook his shoulders and moved toward the door. "We'd best be on our way, Davis."

"I'll have my man drive you to the hotel," Sky offered. Then while the others were saying farewell, he went to the kitchen where he found Thad half asleep at the table. "Thad, take the two gentlemen to the Ballard House."

"Carriage is all ready, sir," Thad told him. He got up and followed Mr. Winslow through the house.

"Thad will take you, Captain."

"Why, that's a kindness," the old man returned. He looked at the boy with a quizzical expression on his face. Pet noticed that he seemed to falter; then he asked, "Do I know you, young man?"

"I don't think so, sir," Thad replied.

"Well—you remind me of someone. It'll come to me later, perhaps. Thank you all for your hospitality. I've talked to many of our family, north and south, but none have shown the graciousness I have met tonight."

The two men left, and immediately the inevitable dissection began. They all agreed that the captain was an exceptional man. "But," Belle said, "something should be done about that young man."

Pet grinned. "You intend to convert him to the *cause*, Belle?"

"He's not much, is he?" Dan added with disdain. "Can't see how any grown man can stand on the outside and watch like he's planning."

"How long will they be here, Papa?" Belle inquired.

"Long enough for you to try to make a rebel out of him," Sky commented. "But it might not be as easy as you think."

"You know what, Sky?" Rebekah slipped her arm in his. "I've always loved your family, but tonight, after listening to Captain Winslow, I'm prouder than ever!"

Sky squeezed her, then looked at her soberly. "It's a good name, all right. But there are Winslows wearing blue uniforms."

He turned and left the room. After he had gone Pet spoke. "He's worried about the war."

Oblivious to what Pet had said, Belle murmured under her breath, "If Davis Winslow would lose some of that baby fat, he'd look wonderful in a gray uniform!"

CHAPTER TEN

THE VICTORS' RETURN

★ ★ ★ ★

The blazing August sun beat down on the fields with a scorching heat, but Thad took off his straw hat anyway, enjoying the faint breeze that gently moved the tiny cotton plants. An early morning rain had swept across the fields, transforming the dry, dusty soil into thick mud, and drops of moisture glittered like diamonds on the tiny green leaves.

Pet, walking beside him, leaned down and pulled up a stalk. "The rain will help the crop," she remarked. Tossing it down, she flashed Thad a smile. "A lot different out here than in Richmond, isn't it?"

Thad put his hat on and looked across the wide field for a moment. It was a way he had of thinking over questions before answering, and Pet liked it. Most young men she knew talked too much. He nodded finally. "Like a different world. Staying in that place would be like living in a lunatic asylum for me." He gave her a swift glance and added, "I know Miss Belle likes it, but I'll take Belle Maison any time."

"It's just a big party to Belle," Pet nodded, and then she laughed. "She's been keeping company with Cousin Davis the whole two weeks he and the captain have been here. She's determined to make a rebel out of him, but *she* does it to make her beaux jealous, too."

Thad also thought that, but feared saying anything critical of Belle, so he changed the subject. "Let's ride down to see how the corn is doing by the creek."

They walked to the end of the row, mounted their horses, and Pet cried out, "I'll race you!" Driving her heels into her mount's sides, she shot off before Thad was ready. He grinned, admiring the way she rode, then raised the reins and spurred his horse after her. They thundered down the muddy road. Slowly, slowly he gained, riding furiously until he pulled up beside her. She turned to see him coming alongside and began to cry out "Come on, Lucy!" as she urged her mare on. Thad kicked his heels against his horse's side and picked up speed, driving his mount hard. Soon he was side by side with Pet, but he pulled his mount back to keep from passing her. They rode together at a dead run, turning off the road to go crashing through the grove of large oak and pine that dotted a ridge. The trees whipped by and he allowed her to get ahead so that when they emerged from the trees she was leading by several lengths. She pulled up suddenly beside the small creek that marked one border of a huge corn field, and slipped to the ground.

"Beat you!" she laughed as he dismounted beside her. Her straw hat had slipped back on her head, held by the cotton cord, and her face was flushed from the ride. Her gray eyes sparkled, and the sun caught the glints of gold in her rich crown of auburn hair. She reached out and touched his face, saying, "You look as if you've got some kind of chicken pox!"

He pulled his bandanna from his pocket and wiped his face, but she took it away from him, laughing at the smears he made. "Now you look like a field hand! Come here, let me wash it off." Leading him to the creek, she made him sit down under a bull pine, then dipped his bandanna in the clear water. She sat beside him and began to clean off the mud.

He sat very still, listening to the water gurgle over the mossy stones, and noticed that she smelled of soap and lilac. She had a light touch, and her face was close to his, so close that he could count the freckles on her smooth cheeks. His thoughts made him uncomfortable and he was relieved when she drew back and said, "There!"

He leaned back and looked at the slender emerald stalks that stretched out in endless rows. Sighing with satisfaction, he murmured, "Looks good. Soon as the ears appear, the coons will be at 'em."

"We'll have to go on another possum hunt," she said, leaning back against the trunk of the tree. "Remember last time how you tossed the bobcat down to Dooley?" The thought amused her, and she laughed softly, giving him a punch in the side. "Were you ever green! Didn't know a possum from a bobcat!"

He smiled at her. "Sure, I remember that—but what I remember best is what happened after the hunt." He looked at her and there was a serious light in his black eyes. "You offered to teach me how to read. And you have, too."

His praise brought color to her cheeks, and she dropped her head. "Oh, that was nothing."

"Yes, it was." He reached over and put his hand on her shoulder, and the action was such a surprise she lifted her eyes. He had never touched her once in all the months he'd been at Belle Maison, and now the intense look on his angular face kept her silent. "I've never said thank you, but I say so now. Thank you, Patience."

"I . . . I had a good student, Thad," she murmured. "You learned to read so quickly!" She reached up impetuously and touched his face. "And you're the best friend I've ever had!"

He sat there, feeling the light pressure of her hand on his cheek. Then his dark face with its slavic cast broke into a smile. "Well, shoot, you're my best friend, too!" The comment made him feel embarrassed, and he removed his hand from her shoulder. Getting to his feet, he suggested, "We'd better get back. I'm taking some fresh garden stuff to the market this morning, and you have to go back to town."

"Oh, rats!" she snapped as she mounted her horse. "I wish I could stay here all the time! I'm going to ask Papa if I can come back with you. Those house servants are letting the house fall to pieces!"

"Maybe he will. Dooley's found a place to run a trotline, and we could get a few of those big river catfish that taste so good. Your mother mentioned our getting some because your father likes them."

As they approached the house they heard a horse coming at

a dead run, and Pet cried, "It's Dan—something must be wrong in town for him to ride like that!" They spurred their horses forward and intersected him as he turned down the road that led to Richmond. "Dan! What's wrong?"

"The regiment is back!" Dan shouted over his shoulder, then spurred off without another word.

"Oh, Thad, Mark and Tom will be there!" Pet said urgently. "Let me ride in and you can bring the vegetables later."

"No. Your father wouldn't want you to ride in alone," Thad said.

"He wouldn't care." She looked at him defiantly. "I'm going!" She kicked her horse into motion and took off after Dan. But Thad's powerful stallion caught up with the mare in fifty yards, and he leaned over and caught the bridle, then hauled back on the reins.

"Let me go!" she blazed, struggling to pull the bridle from his grasp.

"We'll go as soon as I get the wagon loaded," he promised firmly, and there was a determined set to his jaw. "It won't take but a few minutes."

"Oh, you don't care about the soldiers!" she countered, and instantly saw the hurt look in his eyes. Her face broke into shock. "Oh, Thad, I didn't mean that! I'm sorry!"

"It's all right," he replied quietly. "I know you want to see your brothers—but your father asked me to look out for you, and I have to do it."

"I know," she agreed quietly.

She helped him load the wagon with the vegetables from the huge garden, working in a subdued way unusual for her.

Finally they got into the wagon and headed for town but were stopped by Sut Franklin at the gate. "I'll take the wagon to town, Novak," he said gruffly, his face flushed.

Thad saw the red veins in the man's nose and noted the way he almost fell as he tried to get into the wagon. "You're drunk, Sut," he told him.

Franklin stared at him out of his pig-set eyes, then began to curse; but Thad simply slapped the reins and spoke briskly to the horses. The team plunged away from the overseer, who staggered and fell to the ground as he attempted to stop them.

"I don't know why Papa doesn't get rid of him!" Pet declared. "He stays drunk half the time and he treats our negroes awful!"

Thad agreed with her, but didn't voice it. "He behaves better around your father than he does with anyone else. And a good overseer is hard to find."

"Oh, fuzz!" Pet snapped in disgust. "You do most of the work he's paid for, Thad. And the negroes always come to you when they have a problem. I'm going to tell Papa to make you overseer and get rid of Franklin."

He laughed at her. "You're going to get a snub if you do, Pet. Your father realizes I don't know enough about farming to be an overseer. You have to be brought up here to know that."

"Oh, the negroes know about when to plant and all that! What we need is someone to *lead* them. All Sut Franklin does is whip the poor people—and they hate him for it. You know they do, Thad. They all work just as slowly as they can, 'cause he's so mean they don't want him to look good. But they try harder for you, because they know you care for them."

"Well, maybe; but all the same, you'd better not be running Mr. Winslow's business."

As they rode along at a fast clip, they talked about the Battle of Bull Run that had been fought on July 21, a month earlier. It had been an anxious time for those far from the battlefield, since most of them had sons or other relatives in the army. The battle had been brought on because of pressure, for North and South had been pushed into the skirmish before the troops were ready.

The two green armies had met at Manassas, a small town in Virginia, but in the South the battle was called "Bull Run," named after the small creek nearby. General Beauregard, the hero of Fort Sumpter, commanded the southern troops, while Brigadier General Irvin McDowell led the Union Army. There had been a great deal of confusion as the untrained troops blundered out of position, and at first reports, the Union was winning. Then Beauregard made a final effort and the Union troops faltered. What started as an orderly retreat by the Union became a disorganized throng as the retreating soldiers clogged the escape roads mingled with "sightseers" who, reportedly, had come from Washington to witness the Confederate Army smashed with one great blow. The newspapers reported that the congressmen with their ladies, the society leaders who had come from Washington to watch the battle, led the mad rush back to safety, never stopping until they reached the Capitol.

It was a stunning defeat for the Union, and the South was alive with hope. Now the troops were back in Richmond, and as Thad drove the wagon into the main district, he saw that it would be impossible to get the vegetables to the merchants. The streets were filled with riotous crowds, jamming the streets so densely that he said, "We'd better go to your house. They're not thinking about tomatoes and greens in Richmond today."

They found the house occupied only by Mary, who said, "Dey all done gone to town. Big doin's, wid all dem solgers back."

"Oh, Thad, let's go try to find Mark and Tom!" Pet pleaded, and he agreed at once. Leaving the wagon, they made their way on foot across the town, and when they got to Cherry Street, they were just in time to see the regiment parade between the screaming throngs that lined the streets.

The gray-clad troops marched by, and suddenly Pet cried out, "Oh! there's Mark," and before Thad could move she darted out to throw herself into the arms of her brother. Mark was caught off guard, and his dignity went with the wind as she glued herself to him. The crowd laughed, and Mark's face turned red, but then he, too, laughed. "Go give Tom a hug, Sis. He's right back there."

She found Tom, who was marching along with a wide grin, and Thad noted that Pet was not the only one breaking into the parade. He caught sight of Belle Winslow in a snowy white dress. She detached herself from the crowd and ran to where Vance Wickham was marching behind Captain Sloan. She had a flag in her hand and gave it to him, then marched along with him, clinging to his arm. Other girls did the same, and soon the military gray of the Third Virginia was dotted with the vivid reds and blues of taffeta dresses.

Thad pushed his way along with the crowd until they got to the park at the west end of town, where the regiment was formed in front of a platform often used for band concerts and special speakers. The platform was shaded by a group of stately elms and decorated with red and white streamers. Seated in place were a group of dignitaries.

Eventually the crowd quieted, and Jefferson Davis came forward. He was a thin man, straight as a ramrod, and his face seemed almost cadaverous as he faced the troops and the massed crowd of civilians. His wife, Varina, stood to his left. She was a striking young woman, dark-haired and attractive. The President began to speak, and despite his austere manner, he spoke well, ending his speech with a promise: "When the last line of bayonets is leveled, I will be with you!"

A shrill, yelping cry erupted, and then soldiers and civilians alike joined in, filling the air with cries of victory. Thad felt out of place, alienated, standing there quietly when seemingly every other person was jumping and screaming. He moved his eyes over the crowd to his left and was surprised to see Captain Winslow and his grandson standing at the edge. They, too, were marked by their lack of enthusiasm. Davis was listening intently to the President. But the sharp eyes of the older man were locked on Thad, and for one brief moment, the cries seemed to fade. It was almost as if the captain and Thad were alone. The two stood there in that strange manner until Thad dropped his head and moved back into the crowd, escaping the scrutiny of the other.

All day, the people milled around, but Thad made his way back to the house and sat in the swing on the front porch, listening to the sounds of laughter and joy that floated over Richmond. He was depressed. He wished he were back at Belle Maison. He longed for the silence of the woods, for the warm, dark laughter of the negroes as they worked in the fields.

Again and again, his mind went back to those eyes riveted on him. *I have to get away!* he thought. He got up and walked toward the fields lying west of town, going far enough to shut out the sounds of revelry floating over the city.

———

Every public room that would hold twenty people was packed that night, but the most prestigious celebration was in the large dining room of the Ballard House. Colonel Barton and his staff were the guests of President Davis, and the cream of the Confederate world was there.

Sky had pressed Davis and his grandfather into attending, and both of them felt out of place as speaker after speaker lauded the troops of the Confederate Army. Davis studied the cabinet members, especially the pale, emaciated Vice-President Alexander Stephens and the attorney general, a plump, seal-sleek Jew named Judah Philip Benjamin of Louisiana. He sat at the table next to Davis's, masking his thoughts with a perpetual smile held before himself like a silk-ribbed fan.

After a while Colonel Barton arose. "You have heard much about our brave men and the victory they won. I want you now to hear from one of our own officers concerning the death of our beloved General Bee." A hum went around the room, and Barton continued. "Lieutenant Winslow, I want you to tell our guests what happened at the Henry House."

Mark stood up slowly, his uniform gray as ash, his boots shining like well-rubbed wood, and the tassels on the colored sash gleaming in the candlelight. Rebekah gripped Sky's arm, for she could not stem the tears that spilled over. She thought how handsome he was—so vulnerable! One ball could bring this child of hers to a grave on some far battlefield! Yet, she was proud and hung on every word he said.

Mark spoke quietly and soberly, telling of the confusion that gripped both armies, and a hush fell over the room. Finally he got to the death of General Bee.

"General Bee's brigade was broken by Burnside, and moved back to the Henry House. I had been sent by Colonel Barton to find General Beauregard, but the air was so thick with lead, I couldn't get through. General Bee rode by, his loping black hair fluttering. There were about two thousand of our men trapped in a little ravine below the woods. Everything was in confusion. Nobody knew which way to go. I caught up to General Bee to ask if he knew where General Beauregard was, and he said he didn't."

Mark paused, then raised a hand to touch his forehead. When he looked out at the audience, his eyes were sad. "General Bee tried to stop the men from running. He stood up in his stirrups and waved his sword—then he saw Jackson's brigade at the top of the ravine. General Bee called out: 'Look, men, there's Jackson's brigade! It's standing like a stone wall. Rally behind the Virginians!' "

A burst of applause broke the silence, and most of the crowd jumped to their feet, faces aglow with pride and admiration. But when they sat down, Mark said, "Jackson's brigade saved the day, but right after that, a ball knocked General Bee out of the saddle. He died before we could move him off the battlefield."

Mark sat down, and Jefferson Davis stood to his feet and said, "I think we must now pray for our brave wounded—and for the families of those who paid the supreme sacrifice for their country. Chaplain Butler, will you lead us, please?"

A tall, strong-faced man with a shock of black hair prayed, and then the dignitaries at the head table left the room, while others stayed to talk. Davis would have left also if he had felt free, but he sat beside his grandfather, who was having an animated conversation with Stephen Mallory about their time of service together.

Soon only a very few remained. Davis fidgeted in his chair, bored and wishing to leave. His eyes swept the room and he saw Belle Winslow approaching with a group of officers around her. "You must meet my cousin Davis," she said with a smile, and as he rose she detached herself from the arms of two of the officers and introduced the men: "Major Lee, Lieutenant Wickham, Lieutenant Beauchamp, and my brother, Lieutenant Mark Winslow . . ." She named off others in the group; then she turned to her cousin. "Davis has just come back to this country after getting his degree at Oxford."

"I understand your home is in Washington, sir," Beau remarked, smiling slightly. "I would imagine you feel rather uncomfortable here with all us rebels."

"I must admit, it is a little thick for a Northerner, Lieutenant," Davis acknowledged.

"We are glad to have you, Mr. Winslow," Major Lee added, his manner indicating to his junior officers that they were to be courteous to the Yankee. "I know your brother Lowell. We were very close at the Point."

"He has spoken of you often, Major," Davis returned.

"I'm told you're a writer, sir," Wickham said. "Did you come here to gather local color?"

"No, sir. I came with my grandfather. He's the writer, actually."

Major Lee hesitated. "Would it be imposing on you, Mr.

Winslow, if I asked about England's feelings—concerning the South, I mean?"

Everyone was listening carefully, so Davis gave them as accurate a report as he could, ending by saying, "So there is much sympathy for your cause, Major Lee—but there are many who are opposed to slavery, and would not be in favor of coming to your aid."

"Ah, Captain Winslow," Lee said, turning to the older man, "we are putting your grandson through a painful interview. Perhaps we might have your views? How will our victory at Bull Run affect your people? Will they give up?"

Captain Winslow shook his head. "Would *you* give up, Major Lee, if you had been defeated? I think not." He paused. When he spoke again, his voice was gentle. "If I may be permitted one observation as an outsider, I think your victory may do you much harm."

"How so, sir?" Beauchamp demanded sharply.

"I have been a sailor for many years, some of them in hard battles at sea—and it always seemed to me that winning the first victory of a war tended to make us overconfident."

"Why, that's exactly what Stonewall Jackson said!" Mark exclaimed. "Others wanted to go on and take Washington, but Jackson said, 'This will be a costly victory for us. We will be overconfident.' "

Belle took Davis's arm and smiled sweetly at the others. "I have a few questions to ask my cousin, if you gentlemen will excuse us."

Davis followed her out of the main dining room into a small parlor used by guests. She sat down and patted the space beside her. "Sit down, Davis."

He followed her instructions, saying, "I think I saw a jealous fire in the eyes of several hot-headed young Confederate officers, Miss Belle. Are you trying to get me killed in a duel?"

"Oh, Davis, you are foolish!" she laughed, then arched her eyebrows and leaned against him. "Would *you* fight a duel for a little southern girl?"

"I couldn't hit that wall with a pistol," he answered. "Anyway, Grandfather and I are leaving day after tomorrow, so I won't have time to cut the lieutenants out of your favor."

"Do you have to go?" she pouted. "If you'd stay just a little longer, you'd learn the truth about this war."

"Don't try to make a Confederate out of me, Miss Belle," he replied quickly, his face suddenly sober. "I'm going back to England just as soon as Father permits it. My life is there."

She stared at him a moment, and when she spoke her voice was edged in anger. "But this is *your* country!"

"Not really." He saw the bewilderment in her eyes, and added, "I think after this war, there'll be nothing left of what I liked best about this country. No, I'll probably take citizenship in England as soon as possible."

Belle stared at him, then rose to her feet, her face set. "I don't understand a man who won't fight for his country." With that she spun on her heels and left the room. She was immediately met by the two lieutenants. *No doubt they were waiting in the wings for her!* Davis thought wryly.

He went directly to his room instead of returning to the table. When his grandfather came in, Davis asked, "How much more work do you have on the book?"

"Ready to go back home?" the captain responded quietly. "I guess the little rebel girl gave you a bad time."

"Oh yes, but it isn't that. I . . ." He hesitated. "I want to go back to England."

"Yes, I know. But are you sure that's what you really want, Davis?"

"I know what I *don't* want—and that's to get mixed up in this crazy war."

They said little more to each other, and two days later Sky accompanied them to the railway station, with Thad driving. As they stepped down from the carriage, Captain Winslow walked around to Thad's side. "Boy, where are you from?" he demanded, staring up into his face.

Thad's eyes shifted to Sky, who stood there waiting for the boy's answer, and finally said reluctantly, "New York."

"Oh?" The captain studied Thad's thin, dark face as a jeweler might study a stone he was about to cut. "I lived in New York once, after I retired from the Navy." He stood there so long that Davis nudged him. "We'd better get on the train, Grandfather."

"All right." The men moved away, and Thad waited for his

employer to return. As they made their way back to the hotel, Sky said, "Captain Winslow is a smart man, Thad. He thinks he recognizes you." When Thad remained silent, Sky added, "Anytime you want to tell me anything, Thad, I'll listen—and I mean *anything*."

Thad nodded glumly. "Yes, sir, I'll remember."

Sky knew he had come up against a locked door, so he changed the subject. "Tell me about the farm." As Thad spoke enthusiastically about crops and field hands, Sky half listened, for his mind kept drifting back to Thad's first appearance. Toby had said the boy was asking for "the Winslow place." Since then Sky had grown to love the boy, and the secrecy troubled him, but right now he could do no more.

It'll be up to Thad to tell me whatever it is.

CHAPTER ELEVEN

CAMP MEETING

★ ★ ★ ★

The year 1861 closed with a harvest that exceeded anything ever seen in Virginia. Cotton bales were stacked like fortress walls on every dock, waiting shipment to England, and the corn-cribs were overflowing. The ground had been a cornucopia, pouring forth its riches, and Sky Winslow should have been rejoicing. Instead, as he walked over the stripped fields with Sut Franklin and Thad, he was discouraged.

"Best we ever did!" Franklin nodded. "I never seen cotton grow like this—and the bugs musta gone somewhere else, 'cause they shore didn't hit us like usual."

Thad said little. He could tell by his employer's face that he was unhappy. Finally, Franklin got his orders from Winslow and left the two walking alone through the fields. The cotton stalks were like ghosts, with shreds of white clinging to their skeleton arms, stirring in the sharp breeze. The keening of the wind added to the illusion, for it sounded to Thad like the cry of tiny phantoms calling from the ground.

"I wish winter was over," he said, breaking the silence. "Seems like the earth is dead, don't it, Mr. Winslow. I like spring plowing and putting the seed in the ground—then waiting for the first little blades to come up." He kicked at a stalk, snapping it off, and added, "This is the part of farming I don't like."

"It's all part of it, Thad," Sky told him. "Land has to lie fallow and rest up for the next year."

"I can hardly wait. I'll be a lot more help than I was this year. I sure was ignorant, wasn't I? Didn't know one end of a mule from another!"

Winslow smiled and nodded. "You've learned more in a year than anyone I ever saw, Thad. I don't think there's a square foot on Belle Maison you don't know. You're just a natural-born farmer—which I'm not." The deep lines that had creased Sky Winslow's face deepened and he grunted, "I'm just a dumb Indian who should never have left the high country!"

Thad hesitated, for Winslow rarely revealed himself. Finally he asked, "Is something wrong, Mr. Winslow? Are your boys all right?"

"Oh, Mark and Tom are well. No action at all—which puzzles me. I thought this war would be in full swing by now, but it's almost like the Union's gone to sleep."

Since Bull Run there had been nearly no action inland, just a few skirmishes in Missouri. McCulloch had whipped Lyon at a place called Wilson's Creek, and later had been killed at Pea Ridge while leading a force that included Choctaw, Chickasaw, Cherokee, Creek, and Seminole Indians.

But there had been much action in coastal waters, for in April, as expected, Lincoln had ordered the blockade of the entire southern coast. At first it was almost totally ineffective, with blockade runners slipping through the thin lines almost at will, but as the U.S. Navy was built up by northern shipyards, the net had tightened. The blockade runners still got through, and one successful trip was enough to make the owner rich enough to retire, but it was getting more difficult all the time.

Sky had watched as the Confederate empire was built, but he was unhappy with what he saw. "Best year for cotton anyone ever saw," he said to Thad. "But what good does it do sitting on the wharf? We need *guns*, not cotton."

Thad had listened much to the speeches that flowed like wine on the streets of Richmond. Now he decided to share his thoughts with his employer. "Mr. Winslow, it looks to me like we ought to forget about cotton next year."

Winslow stopped in his tracks. "How's that, Thad?"

Embarrassed at his own audacity, Thad shrugged. "'Course I don't know anything about this war, and like you say, there's enough cotton to make shirts for the world! But what are the soldiers going to eat next year? Can't eat cotton—and neither can we. I mentioned to Sut that we ought to plant food crops, and he just said, 'This is cotton country.' Well, I guess it's corn country, too, far as that goes. And we could sell corn here in Virginia."

"And what would you do, Thad, if you had your way?"

"Aw, Mr. Winslow, you're funnin' me! But if it was me, I'd plant corn and buy up all the brood sows and yearlings I could find. Later I'd sell the corn, and the pigs, and the cattle. But that's just my Yankee ideas."

Sky snapped his jaws shut and said with some vehemence, "That's more sense than I heard from the Confederate Congress in a whole year—or from any of these planters! All they can think is *cotton!*" He mused over Thad's idea, and a smile split his dark face. "Thad, I've been trying to decide what to do, and everybody else around here will think I'm crazy; but you and I are going to have the biggest cornfields in Virginia come spring. You get Toby to teach you all he knows about pigs and cattle, because he knows more about critters than any man in this state, white or black!"

They had now reached the house, and Winslow grew more thoughtful. "There's another aspect of this plantation you ought to know about, Thad. I want you to learn to keep books."

"Why, I'm no scholar, Mr. Winslow!"

"Don't have to be a scholar to know that most of our troubles are tied up with slaves. I don't mean the right and wrong of that. I mean that it takes an army of slaves to raise cotton, and they're expensive. But you take corn—why, it won't take half as many field hands to raise enough corn to put us in the black."

Thad stared at him. "You'd sell your slaves?"

At that moment Sky Winslow let his guard down in a way he never had since moving from Oregon to Virginia. "Thad," he said soberly, "if I had my way, I'd set every last one of them *free*. Before God I would! Robert E. Lee said the same thing to me at the Chestnut House the other night." He noted the startled look on Thad's face, and snorted, "Why, boy, do you think I *like* slavery? I hate the idea, but I got caught in it when I bought this place. If I'd known then what I know now, I'd have gone into another line of work—but it's too late now."

"I didn't know you felt like that, sir," Thad said. "I feel the same way, only I don't own any slaves—and I'm from the North."

"You'd be surprised how many Southerners feel as I do, but this war exploded in our faces like a bomb, and now we've got to fight a war over a cause we don't really believe in." He shook his head and turned to go, saying, "Keep this under your hat, Thad. But keep on thinking about next year. I like the idea."

Thad left and stopped by his bunk to pick up the shotgun Winslow let him use. All the family loved quail, and with the older boys gone he was the hunter, along with Dan. He had taken to hunting, for he liked the outdoors, and had developed into the best shot on the place. He took the gun, stuffed his pockets with loads, and went outside to untie Rufus. The animal, the best bird dog on the place, was delighted. He knew at once what was ahead and took off, running with his nose to the ground, sweeping back and forth.

"Thad! I want to go with you!"

Pet came flying out the kitchen door and ran to join him. The whole family had come from Richmond for a two-week vacation at Belle Maison, and Pet had gone wild with relief. She had pestered Thad to death with requests to ride, to fish, to hunt—and since there was little work to do, the two had been in the woods constantly.

"You've got to let me have every other shot," she announced with a nod.

"It'll take too long to get enough birds!" he protested. But as usual she had her way. He knew where every covey on the plantation was located, and led her to the first one. Rufus found the place at once, and went on a point. When Thad and Pet advanced, the dog kept still as a rock, even when the covey left the earth with a miniature thunder of wings. Thad took his time and knocked two birds down with the two loads of the shotgun. "Wish this thing would shoot ten times!" he exclaimed as Rufus broke his point and went to retrieve the birds, one at a time.

The next covey was a quarter of a mile away. This time he let

Pet load the gun, and when she knocked down two birds, she squealed with joy and ran to get them herself, which insulted Rufus. Bringing them back, held gingerly in both hands, she was not so happy, for they were bloody and looked very frail. "I love to shoot, but I hate hunting," she moaned.

"You don't hate to eat what's shot," he remarked callously.

They took turns until they had enough to feed everyone, then walked silently back to the house. Thin skeins of clouds were racing low on the horizon, and the smell of cold weather was in the air.

"Know what today is?" Pet asked, breaking into Thad's thoughts.

"The fifteenth of November."

"And what day is that?"

He looked at her, puzzled. "Why, it's just another day to me."

"No, it's not." She stopped and he paused to face her as she smiled up at him. "It's your birthday."

"Why, my birthday is next month!"

"What day?"

"The twenty-fourth."

"What a rotten day for a birthday!" she grimaced. "Too close to Christmas. You'd never get much on either day."

"To tell the truth, Pet, I *never* got much on either day," Thad grinned. "What's this about today being my birthday?"

She looked up at him, her eyes wide. "It's your birthday, Thad! You're one year old today—because it was on this day a year ago that you first came to us."

He realized she was right, and shook his head in wonder. "You know, that's true, Pet! I hadn't really kept up with the days." He looked at her with a smile. "I remember the first time I saw you. I was burning up with fever, and I kept seeing this vision of an angel."

"And it was only me?" she teased. "I'll always remember my first look at you. You were thin as a rail and your eyes looked big as moons in your face. I don't think you weighed much more than I did! And Dr. Wright said he didn't think you'd live, and I remember sneaking off to my room and praying for you not to die."

"I never knew that!"

"Well, I did—and God must have heard me, because you obviously didn't die, did you?" She suddenly reached up and put her hands on his shoulders. "I never saw anybody grow as much as you have! How tall are you, Thad? Six feet?"

"I don't know."

"Stand still!" She suddenly moved forward, keeping her head down, and leaned against him. "You must be almost six feet, because Mark is six feet and I come up to his chin just like I do on you." Tilting her head back she smiled up at him. "You're almost seventeen, Thad, almost a man. Funny, I always thought of you as a boy."

Thad was thinking along the same lines, for he had looked on her as a companion, almost like another boy. She usually wore loose fitting overalls when they roamed the woods, but now she was wearing new ones, and he noticed with a shock that she had filled out over the year. When he first met her she had been leggy and awkward, like a young colt. But now he was acutely aware that the year had metamorphosed the angular shape into the swelling curves that marked the beginning of womanhood.

"You—you've grown up, too, Patience," he said nervously. She was still standing close, with her hand on his chin to measure her height, and he coughed and took a step backward. "Guess you won't be running coons with me much longer. Be party dresses and balls—like Miss Belle."

Pet had caught his look at her, and her cheeks turned pink. She knew he was seeing her for the first time as something other than a boyish companion. She put her hand to her cheeks, dropped her head, then quickly raised her eyes and murmured softly, "Thad, I don't care anything about things like that. I want us to go on like we are."

He bit his lip and shrugged his shoulders. "So do I—but things don't stay the same."

"Oh, let's not talk about what's coming tomorrow," she broke in. "There's a revival meeting tonight. I want you to go with us."

"I don't think—"

"It won't kill you," she interrupted.

As they made their way back to the house, she told him about the new preacher. "He's real good, Thad," she said earnestly. "The meeting's only been going on for a week and already over twenty people have been saved. And lots more are going to the anxious seat."

"Saved? Saved from what?"

Pet stopped and stared at him. "Why, saved from their sins, of course." She shook her head in amazement. "Didn't you ever hear of being saved?"

"No. I've heard of being baptized. And what's an anxious seat?"

Pet took a deep breath and said, "You be ready to go at noon. It's a camp meeting and all of us are going. I'll tell you all about it on the way over." She stared at him again. "I thought *everybody* knew what it was to be saved."

"Are you 'saved'?" he asked hesitantly.

"Sure! I was saved when I was ten years old. Old Rev. Hooper baptized me in the creek along with twenty-seven others. I'll tell you all about it on the way to the meeting."

Toby had been delighted to hear Thad was going to the meeting, for he himself was a firm believer and attended every meeting, black or white.

When Thad asked him what "being saved" meant, he reacted exactly as Pet had. "You don' know what dat means, Thad? My land, I figgered everybody knowed dat."

Thad grew irritated and snapped, "Well, I don't, and I wish you'd tell me!"

"Why, boy, it means bein' washed in de blood of de Lamb! It means gittin' yo' feet on de way to dat ol' pearly gate—an' sayin' goodbye to dat ol' debil!" The big man waxed eloquent, but when he was finished, Thad was no wiser.

"Well," he said, "I was christened when I was a baby, so I guess I'm all right."

"No, dat won't answer," Toby objected with a fierce shake of his head. "You got to git rid of all yo' sins, an' only Jesus can do dat little job! You jes' listen good to de parson tonight, and do what he says—he'll git you on de way!"

Thad was sorry he'd ever heard of a camp meeting, and decided not to go; but when Mr. Winslow passed him later that morning, he wasn't sure. "Pet told me you'd be going to the meeting this evening, Thad," Sky said. "I'm glad to hear it. Hitch up the big buggy and you can go with us. Tell Toby he can use any of the wagons to take the slaves who want to go."

The big carriage had three seats, and Dan crawled in the back and immediately went to sleep. Mr. and Mrs. Winslow took the middle seat, and Pet sat down beside Thad and said, "Let's hurry or we'll miss the exhorting."

He dared not ask what *that* was, but drove the matched blacks at a fast clip on the road north. The camp meeting, Pet informed him, was to be held in a brush arbor close to where the Youngs lived.

"Don't expect we'll see Dooley at a religious meeting," Thad ventured. The young man in question had stayed out of the army for a year, claiming that he was going to wait until the *real* fighting started and they stopped all the fooling around. In the meantime, if the reports about Young's activities were true, Thad knew the man was trying to cram all the parties and wild times he could into the intervening year.

"Oh, Dooley's been there every night," Pet told him. "Of course, he just comes looking for girls, but he'll get under conviction if he keeps on listening to Rev. Boone."

"Guess I won't be the only sinner there, then," Thad grinned. "Not with Dooley on hand."

"Let me tell you how I got saved," Pet said quickly. She told him about the terrible time she was going through when she was ten years old. She'd heard the gospel preached, and for the first time realized that she was a sinner.

"At ten you were a sinner?" Thad asked in amazement. "I thought sinners were drunks and—and worse!"

"All have sinned and come short of the glory of God," Pet replied. "That's in the book of Romans, chapter three, verse twenty-three." She began to quote scripture so fast he couldn't keep up with it. Finally, she said, "Well, anyway, Thad, I gave my heart to Jesus, and He saved me. And that's what it means to get saved."

"I see," he said, but he didn't—not in the least. It was all jargon to him, and he thought, *I'll just have to go through with it tonight, but no more for me!*

They heard the sound of singing long before they got to the

meeting. It came swelling on the air, and Thad was shocked when he pulled into the space reserved for wagons and buggies. There were at least two or three hundred. He had been expecting a crowd of fifty to a hundred people, but as they got out of the wagon and made their way toward where the singing seemed to come from, he realized there were close to a thousand.

Pet steered him to a spot packed with people, and he saw that a rough platform had been built for the preacher to stand on. Over part of the area was a roof of brush piled on a framework of poles. Many people spoke to the Winslows, and a few of the neighbors gave Thad a greeting as well. At the edge of the crowd he saw the huge mustache of Dooley Young, and the little man gave him a big smile and waved wildly.

For over an hour they stood there, singing songs, some of which he had heard the slaves sing, but most of which he didn't know. A leather-lunged man would sing the first line of a new song; then the congregation would repeat it, and this went on until the crowd knew the song. It didn't seem to bother them if they sang the same song ten times, it seemed, and Thad managed to join in, trying to look less conspicuous than he felt.

Finally there was an end to the singing, and a young man of medium height but powerful build came to the center of the platform, carrying a Bible. "That's Rev. Boone," Pet whispered. "He's a descendant of Daniel Boone."

Thad had heard stories about the old frontiersman, and now looked at the man with more interest. Boone began quietly enough, welcoming them to the meeting; but soon his clear tenor voice was raised, and he began to quote scriptures as he raced from one side of the platform to the other. Thad could not follow him, but he heard one phrase over and over: "Ye must be born again!"

As the sermon was well underway, a woman to his left gave a loud cry and fell to the ground, weeping. A man standing next to her helped her to her feet and led her off to one side. "She's under heavy conviction," Pet whispered. "She'll get saved pretty soon."

That meant little to Thad, but it was a scene repeated often during the course of the sermon; and at the end, many were gathered around the platform, weeping and crying loudly. Thad wanted to leave, for he felt a fear he had never known, and when Pet left his side to go pray with a young girl who had gone forward, he slipped away.

As he found the outer edge of the circle, he felt a hand grasp his arm, and looked around to see the gleaming eyes of Dooley. "Come to git religion, Thad?" he slurred, the smell of whiskey strong on his breath.

"I just came because the Winslows wanted me to."

Dooley nodded and said in a voice tinged with admiration, "Well, you couldn't have come to hear a better preacher. He's all sorts of a feller, ain't he now! I heard lots of preachin', but that Boone, he really lays it to us sinners, don't he now?"

Thad stared at him, and finally asked, "Are you saved, Dooley?"

"Naw, not yet. But I figger the good Lord's on my trail, Thad, and 'fore long I expect He'll tree me like a coon dawg trees a boar coon!" He smiled widely. "This is the real thing, boy. Not like that Rev. Tate you run afoul of at the Mission."

Thad shook his head. "I guess I'm just too dumb, Dooley. I don't know anything about all this. To tell the truth, Pet talked to me all the way here about being saved—and I don't even understand what *that* means."

Dooley laughed. "Well, don't fret, boy. I've noticed that when God gits after a man, the feller don't have to know much. Jest keep listenin' to that leetle ol' gal, and to preachers like Boone, and first thing you know, you'll find out what it means to git God on your trail."

Thad never knew how long the meeting lasted, for the Winslows left at ten, but Pet said as they made their way home, "Some of the people will stay all night, and start over at ten in the morning. It's a real revival, Thad! Did you like it?"

He shifted uncomfortably. "I'm mixed up, Pet. I've never been around things like this. My people didn't go to church, and this is the first time I ever heard of things like getting saved."

She sat there quietly. After they had ridden for a while, she put her hand on his arm, saying, "I tried to tell you too much, Thad. I'll show you some things in the Bible. It'll be good for you to read for yourself. And when you're ready, God will come to you."

"That's what Dooley said." He looked at Pet and added, "If your father is a Christian—and your mother and you—it's something I need to know about."

Pet didn't respond, and when she did speak he could barely make out her words over the sound of the horses' hooves tapping on the road.

"That's the nicest thing I've ever heard you say, Thad!"

CHAPTER TWELVE

TOBY

★ ★ ★ ★

Spring fell on the land in 1862 like a blow. The ground lay frozen into solid iron, sparsely covered with dead spikes of grass. But by the second day of March as Thad was walking across the field with his game bag packed with squirrels, he felt a sudden pocket of warm air touch his cheek, almost like a caress. He stopped, looked around, and was surprised to feel the earth soft under his feet. Looking around him he saw tiny emerald tongues piercing the rich brown crust. He knelt and picked up a handful of earth, feeling its warmth, marveling at the tiny white roots of the fledgling grass. Excited, he stood to his feet and walked rapidly north toward the house.

"Time to start spring plowing," he murmured to himself. A thrill ran through him at the realization that the long winter was over. He paused at a large tree arching over the creek, remembering the day he and Pet had sat under it; she had washed the mud from his face and Thad had thanked her for teaching him to read. "Seems like a long time ago," he mused, and his face sobered, thinking over the months that had passed.

The winter had not been a happy time for him. The war had dragged on, casting its shadow over the land. The parties still went on at Richmond, and twice there had been balls at Belle Maison when the men came home; but despite the gaiety, Richmond was a grim place. At Mr. Winslow's request, Thad had spent some time in the city, learning the rudiments of book-keeping, for it was evident that the owner wanted to make him an overseer.

It was the bookkeeping that let Thad know the troubling state of the small Winslow empire. There were large debts outstanding—enormous to Thad's thinking—but he quickly discovered that such things were common. Most planters borrowed money from the bank to make the cotton crop, which they paid off when the cotton was sold. But with the cotton still unsold for the most part, Belle Maison was plunged deeper into debt; and it was this situation that brought a crisis that darkened Thad's life.

It had first been mentioned by Mr. Winslow in a conversation with Thad in February. The two had been working on the books in the small study, and after two hours of trying to make things balance, Winslow threw his pen down and said, "Blast it all! There's no way to get out of this mess!"

"If the corn crop is good, and if the meat market holds up," Thad replied quickly, "you can get out of debt next fall."

"That's a lot of *ifs*," Winslow grunted. "And where's the money coming from to pay the interest on last year's debts? And it takes money to buy sows and yearlings." He leaned back, fatigue lining his face. Thad knew that he was not happy with the way things were going in Jefferson Davis's cabinet, and the burden of debt was another load that had aged him over the year.

"Could you sell some land, maybe, to take care of that?"

"No, not land," Winslow returned. "Never sell the land—that's the first rule." He took a deep breath and said, "I'll have to sell some slaves."

His words struck Thad like a blow, for although he was aware that slaves were property, this was his first taste of handling them like bales of cotton. It left an empty feeling in his stomach. "I hate to think of that," he said quietly.

Winslow shot him a sharp look. "I don't like it, either, Thad. But it's the only thing I've got to sell. And you won't like it any better when I tell you that Toby will probably have to go."

"Why him? He's the hardest working and the smartest slave on the place."

"Which means he's worth the most. Milton Speers needs some good hands, and if we're not going to raise cotton, we won't need so many. We've already talked about it."

"What about Jessie and Wash? Will they all go together?"

Winslow shifted uncomfortably. The boy's direct stare stirred the guilty streak that grew larger every time he sold slaves. "Speer's got plenty of women and young ones. He needs about ten prime field hands to handle his production this year."

Now as Thad walked slowly across the field, that scene came back to him like a fresh wound, and the first breath of spring and the green shoots of grass lost their appeal. He tried to blot out the idea of selling Toby, but failed. The huge black man had become his best friend, and he wondered how Toby would react if the sale went through. Thad was most afraid that the man would try to escape with Jessie and Wash by means of the underground railway. He had seen one slave who tried it and was caught. He had been beaten so badly that he died. Thad shivered at the thought of such a fate for his friend.

Rebekah was looking out the kitchen window, and smiled, saying, "Dan, there's Thad with our supper. Go help him clean it."

"Sure, Ma." Glad to get out of churning the milk, Dan ran out the back door and greeted Thad. "What'd you get for supper, Thad?"

"A few squirrels." Thad stopped under the big elm tree fifty feet from the house and upended the worn canvas bag. The top of the old oak table they used for cleaning game and fish seemed to be covered with the bodies of the animals.

"Good grief! How many did you get?"

"Dunno. Ought to be plenty, though."

Dan picked up a plump red squirrel, examined it closely, and threw it down. "Right through the head!" He shot an envious look at Thad. "It's not fair, Thad! I been shooting squirrels my whole life and the best I can do is hit 'em in the body. You never even shot a musket before last year, and now you can shoot the eye out of a gnat at a thousand yards."

"Not quite." Thad pulled out his knife and began dressing the squirrel. Dan joined him and in no time the naked corpses lay in a neat row, with the hides and entrails on the ground.

"Any news from your brothers?"

"Ah, same old thing, Thad. The scouts say that McClellan's raised the biggest army ever seen. Mark says all the generals think McClellan will put the men on ships and invade us by water—maybe even up the James River." He paused and his eyes were bright. "I wish those damn Yankees would come up the James—we'd show 'em!"

Thad smiled at the boastful air of the boy, and asked, "What would we do, Dan?"

"Why, we'd put a few sharpshooters in trees along the river!" Dan grinned and waved his bloody knife in a circle. "McClellan wouldn't have enough bluebellies to eat a whole chicken by the time the ships got to Richmond." A thought struck him, and he slanted a careful look across at the other. "Thad, you know there's been talk about you—about your bein' a Yankee sympathizer."

"I guess I heard about it."

"That ol' buzzard Len Oliver keeps it going! He got sore when you took our business over to Miller, so he gets even by telling everybody you're a spy or something." He eyed Thad carefully, then said with a casual tone, "'Course, if you'd join up with the Richmond Blades, that'd shut 'em all up." He waited for Thad to answer. When he saw none was forthcoming, he scowled. "Wish I could sign up! The whole dirty war will be over before I even get a shot at a Yankee."

Thad said only, "Take these in to your mother, will you, Dan?" He divided the squirrels into two piles and put the smaller ones back into the game bag. "I'm taking these to Toby."

Dan entered the kitchen, noting that Belle and Pet had just come in. "Look at these!" he said. "Won't they be good with dumplings and corn bread!"

"Where's Thad going?" his mother asked.

"Taking some squirrels to Toby."

"I want to send some rice to Matilda—and some of this chicken broth for Joseph. He's been poorly."

"I'll take it, Mother," Pet volunteered eagerly, picking up the iron pot.

"I'll take the rice," Belle offered. The two girls went out the back door, and Belle called, "Thad! Wait for us!"

They caught up with him, and as they walked to the slave quarters, Belle said, "I got a letter from Davis yesterday, Thad. He mentioned you."

"Thought he had his eyes so full of you he didn't see anything else, Miss Belle," Thad grinned.

"Oh, you!" Belle smiled, adding, "He says his grandfather is about to go crazy trying to remember where he met you."

"He got me mixed up with someone else."

"Davis said that the old man has a mind like glue—never forgets a face." Belle was intrigued by Thad's refusal to speak of his past, and she nudged him a little by asking, "You must remember Captain Winslow, Thad. He's not a man you can forget."

Thad shook his head, and both girls saw that he was not going to respond. He changed the subject, and they continued on to the white-washed buildings, where Thad found Toby outside splitting wood.

"Got some meat for you, Toby."

"Thank you kindly," the slave replied, but there was no smile on his lips as he took the sack.

"Let's deliver the rest of this food, Belle," Pet suggested, pulling her sister toward the cabin at the far end.

"Why are you rushing me so, Pet?" Belle demanded.

"Something's wrong with Toby. Didn't you notice?"

"Oh, you're always worrying about the slaves," Belle shrugged. "You and Thad would wrap them in satin if you had your way."

Pet had read the big slave correctly, and as soon as the girls were gone, Thad asked directly, "What's the matter, Toby?"

The muscles in the broad cheeks of the black man tensed, and his powerful hands clenched the sack of game. He said nothing, but ducked his head and stared at the ground. "Ain't nuthin' wrong," he muttered finally, and turned to leave.

"Wait a minute!" Thad exclaimed, grabbing Toby by the arm.

"Take yo' han' off me, white man!" The words flashed out, and quick as a coiled snake Toby jerked his arm free and drew back his fist to strike Thad. His eyes were bulging, making the whites stand out like those of a panic-stricken horse, and his thick lips were contorted with rage.

"Toby!" Thad cried out, and his voice seemed to drive the

wildness out of the slave. The clenched fist dropped, and his body trembled. "Toby, what *is* it?"

"I gonna be sold," he whispered. He swallowed hard. "One of de hands ovah at Speers place say Mistuh Speers done tol' him dat he has bought hisself a top hand—and he named me. But he ask and found out dat Jessie and Wash ain't gonna be sold wif me."

The black face was gray with tragedy, and Thad found himself speechless. He stood helplessly in the heavy silence. Finally, he could bear it no longer and urged, "Don't give up, Toby! We'll think of something!"

Toby lifted his head, tears filling his eyes. "Mistuh Winslow evah say anything 'bout dis to you, Thad?"

Thad had an impulse to lie, but he choked it back. He nodded slowly. "He . . . said once that he might have to sell some slaves. But he was trying to find a way out of it."

"I cain't stan' it, Thad!" The trembling increased in the powerful hands, and he whispered, "I gonna run off, Thad—me an' Jessie an' Wash!"

"No! They'll be watching you, Toby! They'll kill you for sure! Let me talk to Mr. Winslow. He thinks a lot of you, I know."

Toby stared blankly at him. "Guess it won't do no hurt to talk." He took a deep, ragged breath and said, "You talk fo' me, Thad, but if he say no, I don' think I can stan' it!" With that he turned slowly and entered the door to his cabin.

Numb at the news, Thad walked quickly back to the house. The last hundred yards he took off, running like a deer. Reaching the veranda, he leaped to the top step and knocked on the back door.

"Come in, Thad," Rebekah called. When he opened the door, she stared at his face and cried, "What's the matter? Is someone hurt?"

"No, Mrs. Winslow—but I have to see Mr. Winslow. May I use one of the horses? It's important!"

She saw he was tense with strain, and said gently, "Mr. Winslow isn't in Richmond, Thad. He's gone on a mission for President Davis." She could tell her words disturbed him, so taking his arm she urged, "Come in and sit down, Thad. You're shaking." She poured him a cup of hot coffee, then asked, "Now, what's wrong?"

He told her of Toby's plight, and as he talked, he could not know how her heart went out to him—and to Toby. But when he finally finished, she said, "I'll do what I can, Thad—but it may be too late. Mr. Winslow told me before he left that he'd signed some papers at the bank. He . . . he did say that some of the slaves would have to go, but I didn't think it would be Toby."

"Let me go find him, Mrs. Winslow!" Thad urged. "He can change his mind."

Rebekah drew in her lips and made a hopeless gesture. "Why, Thad, he wouldn't even tell *me* where the President was sending him. But even if you did find Mr. Winslow, if he's signed the papers, there's nothing he could do now!"

A dark expression crossed Thad's face, and a stubborn light touched his eyes. "It's not right, Mrs. Winslow!"

She bit her lips, then put her hand gently on his shoulder. "I know it's not right, Thad—none of it is. Everything about slavery is wrong!"

He looked at her, startled by her vehemence. He had not known she felt so strongly, and he pleaded, "Can't we do something?"

She said quietly, "We can pray, Thad."

He dropped his eyes, mumbling, "I don't think so. Not me."

She put her hand on his thick shock of black hair, just as she might have done with one of her own boys. "Nothing is impossible with God, Thad. You don't know that now—but you will someday. Until then, I'll pray for both of us."

He stared at her with a hopeless expression, then got up and left the kitchen without another word.

———

"Mistuh Speers, there's a young man wants to see you."

Milton Speers looked up from his book with an annoyed expression. "Who is it, Caesar?"

The tall black slave shrugged. "I don' know, suh. He sho' ain't no quality folk. He say his name is Thad Novak."

The name wasn't familiar to Speers. "Well," he said after a moment, "show him in."

"Yas, suh."

Speers went back to his book again. After reading a few lines of *Uncle Tom's Cabin*, he snorted and slapped the novel on the table. "Awfulest garbage I ever read!" He got to his feet, walked over to the walnut secretary, poured himself a generous portion of brandy, and downed it smoothly as the door opened and a young man entered. Putting the glass down, Speers stared at the rough dress and shaggy hair of his visitor. "Yes, what is it?" he snapped.

"My name is Thad Novak, Mr. Speers. I work for Mr. Winslow."

Speers' frown smoothed itself out, and he nodded. "Oh yes, I've heard of you, Novak. Mr. Winslow speaks highly of you. Is there a message from him?"

"No, sir. I . . . I came about Toby."

"Toby?" A puzzled look washed across the planter's face. "Which Toby is—oh, he's one of the slaves I'm buying."

"Yes, sir." Thad tried to go on, but the impulse that had brought him here had faded. He had come out of desperation, with a germ of an idea in his mind. Now, staring into the sharp features of Milton Speers, Thad could not find a way to say what had brought him.

"Well, out with it, Novak. Is the nigger sick—or had an accident?"

"No, Mr. Speers; he's fine. It's just that—well, I came to make you an offer."

Speers stared at him. "An offer? What kind of an offer?"

Thad twisted his cap in his hands, then blurted out the thought that had come to him after leaving Mrs. Winslow. "I want to work for you in place of Toby."

Speers looked puzzled, shook his head, and said, "Why, I couldn't hire you, boy. It wouldn't be right for me to hire you away from a friend." He paused and asked, "You're not satisfied with your job? I know for a fact that Mr. Winslow is satisfied with you. Don't want to give you the big head, young fellow, but he claims you'll be the best overseer in Virginia in a few years."

"I don't want to leave Belle Maison, sir. It's just that—well, Toby has helped me a lot. He's taught me just about all I know about farming and horses." Thad bit his lip, then added, "We've gotten to be real good friends, and I don't want to see his family broken up—so I thought I could work for you for nothing until you got the price for him back."

A silence filled the room, and Speer's eyes searched the young face. He was a man of little experience outside his own small world, and nothing of this nature had ever occurred. Suddenly his eyes fell on the novel he had tossed down, and he hardened. "You're a northern boy, aren't you, Novak?"

"Yes, sir."

"And you've probably got your head full of wild notions about slavery. That crazy woman who wrote *Uncle Tom's Cabin*—why, she ought to be locked up! The way she tells it, all our slaves are treated worse than dogs, and you know that's not so." Speers shook his head in anger and waved his finger in Thad's face. "A good field hand is worth a lot of money, boy, and I'd no more ruin a good hand by beating him to death than I would a good horse! You don't see Mr. Winslow mistreating his slaves, do you?"

"No, sir, but—"

"Well, I'm telling you that *I* don't, either! The slave will be just as well off here as he is there."

"But he's got a wife and son, Mr. Speers!"

Speers lifted his hand. "Novak, you said something that tells me you're all mixed up about slavery. You said about this Toby, 'We've gotten to be real good friends.' Now *that's* where you've gotten your harness tangled, boy. If you'd been raised in the South, you'd know that no white man can be a *friend* with a nigger. Why, they're not *like* us, Novak! Some of the finest theologians in the world have proven that they don't have souls!"

"But, Mr. Speers—!"

"Novak, I better tell you this," Speers said sternly. "I remember now what some folks are saying about you. There's a lot of talk about how you're a Yankee, pure and simple—and some even tell it that you're some kind of a spy! Now, I don't believe that, of course, but you better be more careful the way you handle yourself. You've got to keep these niggers in their places. No way you can be an overseer and be *friends* with them."

Thad stood there, his face pale, and he made another attempt. "Mr. Speers, what Mr. Winslow said about me being a good hand—do you believe that?"

"Why—certainly! Sky Winslow is a man of honor!"

"Well, if you'd let me take Toby's place—let him stay with his family, I'd work for you for nothing until he was paid off. All I'd want is just a place to sleep and a little food."

The planter's face reddened, and he raised his voice. "Are you stupid, Novak? Didn't you hear *anything* I just told you? Why, you'd have to work for ten years to pay off that slave—and if people heard about it, they'd think I was getting crazy ideas about slaves myself! You just get out of here, boy!" He took a step toward Thad and shoved him toward the door, shouting, "And after I tell your employer about this, I don't reckon you'll have any job at all! *Get out of here!*" As Thad stumbled from the room, Speers stuck his head out the door and screamed, "Go on back to the North where you belong! We don't need your kind around here!"

Blind with rage, Thad swung onto his horse, calling out loudly, "Go, Blackie!" The stallion reared, then plunged in a headlong gallop down the dark road. By the time Thad pulled him up at the stable, he was covered with lather. Thad leaped to the ground, stroked the nose of the exhausted animal, and began walking him to cool him down. After about an hour the stallion was calm and the madness had seeped from Thad.

He stabled Blackie, then walked toward the cabin but stopped abruptly when he noticed the light was on. Rather than face Franklin, Thad turned away into the darkness and did not return until dawn. He felt empty and helpless, and when he heard the sound of stirring in the Big House, he couldn't face the thought of talking to anyone, so he slipped into the cabin, picked up his gun, moving carefully to avoid waking Franklin, and left the farm.

All day he walked the fields, avoiding farms and all contact with the few hunters he saw, not caring that he had left no word of his whereabouts. He shot two rabbits and roasted them on a stick; when he was thirsty he drank from a spring. That night he lay looking at the million points of light overhead until he dozed off. He got up stiffly at dawn, and with a set jaw made his way back to Belle Maison.

He went directly to his cabin and was met by Franklin, who demanded angrily, "Where in the blazes have you been, Novak?"

He reached out and grabbed Thad's arm, cursing, but suddenly was knocked back against the wall as Thad struck him across the chest with a forearm.

"Don't put your hands on me, Franklin."

Thad waited for the overseer to challenge him, but something hard in the dark eyes of the young man silenced the other; and without a word, Thad turned and walked out of the cabin. He was crossing the yard when he heard his name called.

"Thad!" He raised his eyes and saw Mrs. Winslow and Pet come out of the house. They ran quickly to him, looking anxious. "Thad, we've been worried about you," Rebekah said.

"Where have you been?" Pet demanded.

Thad was weary to the bone, and too heartsick to care much about what he said. "I went to see Mr. Speers. Told him I'd work for him to pay for Toby."

Rebekah nodded, sadness in her fine eyes. "He came this morning, Thad. He told us about it."

"He said you wouldn't want me anymore—me bein' a Yankee spy!"

Rebekah shook her head. "He's a pigheaded, stupid man, Thad. I know you did what you thought best."

"It was noble, Thad!" Pet said, and her eyes glistened with tears.

Thad stood straight and asked directly in a harsh voice. "Did he take Toby?"

Rebekah nodded, unable to meet his gaze. She put her hand on his arm gently. "You'll hear about it, Thad. I'm sorry to be the one to tell you. Toby . . . fought them. I guess they expected it, because they sent four big men, and it took all of them to put the chains on Toby."

"They were beating him with a whip!" Pet cried angrily. "And Mama ran in and made them stop. She said she'd shoot them if they didn't quit!"

Thad blinked his eyes and glanced at the slave quarters. "But there won't be anyone to do that at Speers', will there?" He swallowed hard. "I thank you, Mrs. Winslow, for what you did. Excuse me, please. I'll need to talk to Jessie."

The two women watched him walk away, and Rebekah felt

her heart grow cold and weary. She knew that something dark and tragic had fallen over the young man she had learned to trust and admire—but there was nothing she could do. Nothing any of them could do.

CHAPTER THIRTEEN

THE CHOICE

★ ★ ★ ★

Although it was already the middle of April, everyone could still remember the last major happening in the war.

Twice during February that year the bells of victory had rung in every city in the North, and the name of Ulysses S. Grant had become known in the South. Spirits in Richmond plummeted when the first real victory for the North came with the fall of Fort Henry in Tennessee, just a few miles south of the Kentucky line. Two weeks later came the news that Fort Donelson had also fallen to General Grant. The people of the North shouted: "God bless old U.S. Grant—Unconditional Surrender Grant." Newspaper headlines screamed that the end of the war was in sight, and victory was celebrated in every city of the North.

"Do you think it's about over, sir?" Thad asked Mr. Winslow late one Saturday evening as the two worked on plans for the week. They were in the parlor of the Richmond house, and the silence after everyone else had gone to bed made the men's voices sound loud. Thad lowered his tone, adding, "Some people are saying the North has won."

Sky put down his pen, leaned back in his chair and rubbed his eyes wearily. "It was a big win for the North, Thad, but the war is a long way from over." He took a drink of water from the pitcher on his desk. "Look," he said, replacing the pitcher, "I'm going to show you something." Picking up a sheet of paper and dipping his pen in the inkwell, he motioned Thad closer. "Let's have a history lesson together."

He drew rapidly, sketching the outline of a block of states, adding lines to represent rivers and railroads and small squares for towns. "Now," he instructed Thad, "this is the Confederate line, beginning over here in eastern Kentucky." He studied his sketch and added a row of x's to represent the Confederates. "Here it comes across the Blue Grass country; then it crosses the Mississippi about here; on it stretches across Missouri and on over here into Indian Territory—a line several hundred miles long. Now, all of this is under the command of our best general, Albert Sidney Johnston—you've heard of him?"

"I think I've heard Lieutenant Mark talk about him."

"Well, here are two rivers, the Tennessee and the Cumberland. See how they run side by side and only a few miles apart as they come up toward the Ohio, and notice, too, that they are crossed by our line."

Thad stared at the drawing and asked, "What if they *did* threaten it? Their gunboats couldn't lick that long line of soldiers stretchin' across the map, could they?"

"No, but look what they *could* do—what, in fact, they've already done. Notice how the Cumberland dips down into Tennessee and flows past these towns—Clarksville here and Nashville here. It's from these towns that the Confederates have been getting their supplies; this line can't move far or fight the blue-bellies if it doesn't have food, guns, or ammunition. These items have been coming up the river to us and this"—Sky made a small square on the line representing the Cumberland and labelled it *Donelson*—"this is the fort that the Confederates thought would be enough to keep the Union gunboats from cutting our supply line."

"And was it the same on the other river?"

"Just about. See, this line represents a railroad; it comes up here from Memphis and crosses the Tennessee just below Fort Henry. Supplies have been coming up here by rail, probably every day, and reinforcements for General Johnston, too. As a matter of fact, that's the way the Richmond Blades made their trip up there. Now do you understand why Grant struck at these forts?"

"Yes, sir," Thad said, studying the map. "But the North says it's about over."

"That's just fool talk," Sky replied. Putting his pencil down, he began to walk around the room, stretching his cramped legs. "Think for yourself, Thad. If the Union gets control of the Mississippi, the Confederacy will be cut in two. That would mean that our army in the west would be powerless, so we'd pretty much lose the war in the west. The North is in control of Kentucky right now, so Johnston's men can't get supplies. But look at how the Mississippi stretches through the states of Tennessee, Mississippi, and Louisiana. The North will have to take all those. Remember how hard the fighting was at a little place like Donelson. No, the North has misjudged us. It'll be a bitter fight to the end, and the end won't be soon."

The two sat there, letting the silence run on, and as Thad studied the map, the older man took the occasion to study him. *He's grown up to be a man in just a year,* he thought, studying the shoulders that had thickened with muscle, and noting the mature planes of the angular face. *He was just a skinny boy when I saw him in that bed, all burning up with fever. Now he's doing a man's work—despite all that's happened.*

He stirred at the thought of the past month. "Thad," he asked, "I've never said much about Toby, but I hope you don't hate me for selling him."

"I could never hate you, Mr. Winslow!" The answer came back quickly, but there was pain in his eyes, and he added, "I know it's not your fault."

The boy's words only increased the guilt Sky Winslow felt over his part in the transaction. "I've wished a thousand times I could have found another way to survive, Thad, but you know from the books how tough it is just to keep the bank from taking Belle Maison. Aside from just walking away from the whole thing and letting them have it, there was no other way. Sometimes I think I'll just *do* that!" Winslow looked angrily at the books with their long lines of figures, and pushed away from the desk in frustration. "But a man likes to give his children something. It would mean that Belle and Pet would have nothing."

"I heard what you said to Mr. Speers—about being kind to

Toby," Thad replied, trying to ease the man's agony.

"Oh, I did the best I could, Thad, but it wasn't much. A man like Speers isn't going to let another man tell him what to do." He had gone to Speers immediately after learning of Thad's mission there and had tried to buy Toby back, but he had never told Thad that. Speers had said, *'Sky, once we start lettin' personalities get into this thing, slavery will be dead.'* He had, however, promised to be extra careful with Toby—for business reasons, Sky had realized.

Thad hesitated. "He's goin' to try to escape, Mr. Winslow," he informed him.

"He can't make it, Thad!" Winslow bit his lip and asked, "Did he tell you that?"

"Yes. Before they took him. I haven't talked to Toby since he left. They won't let me."

Winslow shook his head. "It would be suicide. It's almost impossible for a slave to get away under any conditions. And they're watching Toby like a hawk, you can be sure. And no matter how valuable a slave, he would be beaten to death when he was returned—if he hadn't already been killed when caught. Speers would see to that. He'd think that'd be the way to discourage others from running away."

Thad stared at the floor, worry creasing his brow. "I know—but Toby's not afraid of anything." A feeling of despair touched him, and he stood up. "Guess I'll be getting home if there's nothing else."

Winslow rose slowly and, in a rare gesture of affection, put his hand on the boy's shoulder. "I know how hard it is for you, Thad, but we're all in bad shape one way or another. In a couple years you'll probably be running Belle Maison. I'm counting on you."

The words stirred Thad, and he lifted his head and tried to smile. "It's all I want to do, sir." With that he turned and walked out, leaving Winslow staring after him. Finally Sky closed the books and went to bed, hoping that he could shake off the grim feeling that gripped him.

———

Thad returned to Belle Maison and for the next two weeks

buried himself in his work, trying not to think of Toby. Spring, he had discovered, was the critical time for a plantation because the quality of the crop rested on the planting. Choosing the time to plant, tilling the soil, judging the weather—all depended on a delicate balance hovering over the tiny grains of seed; for soil, weather, and seed had to come together in a catalyst that could not vary much if a good crop was to be produced.

Franklin was little help, for he was in a constant state of half-drunken rage. He was a man of no imagination, and planting cotton was the only thing he knew. He burned with resentment against Thad, being firmly convinced that the young man was somehow responsible for the new methods. He dared not challenge the owner, and he was sly about covering up his drinking; but day after day he abused the slaves and constantly harassed Thad with curses and predictions of failure.

Thad never retaliated in any way, but as Franklin became more and more abusive, the slaves inevitably turned to the young man. Thad knew little about corn farming, but the slaves did— especially old Jacob, a seventy-two-year-old whose knowledge of farming Thad cultivated. The old man had been relegated to small clean-up tasks, but had blossomed as Thad sought him out for advice about the corn crop. Jacob had been bought from a farm in Illinois and knew pigs as well, so he was doubly important. Thad took him all over the county to buy a crop of piglets and yearlings, and soon the two developed a system that worked well.

Thad would look at the animals and appear to be evaluating their worth; actually, he was waiting for a sign from the slave. A nod from the old man or a shake of his wooly head gave Thad a lead, and he would begin to bargain on the price. Soon Belle Maison was alive with pigpens, and newly fenced pastures held a crop of fine yearlings.

Pet came out often and spent all day with the young animals, which she loved. She knew them all, and had named them before they had been there three days. Thad laughed at her one morning as she fed the squealing piglets. "You're going to get too fond of these critters, Pet," he teased. "They're all headed for the frying pan, you know."

"Oh, don't talk about that!" Pet cried. She was wearing her

faded overalls with a checked shirt that Dan had outgrown, and she looked fresh and filled with health in the morning sunlight. She picked up a black and white porker and put her nose to his while he kicked and protested vehemently. "You little sweetheart," she cooed. "I could just kiss you!"

"Better save that for Tim Mason," Thad said with a straight face. The young man was the youngest son of a wealthy planter who had been riding over under the pretense of spending time with Dan, but actually was mooning over Pet.

"Oh, don't be silly!" she snapped, her face reddening.

"Well, he's better looking than that pig, isn't he?"

"Oh, you. . . ! Maybe he doesn't smell as good, though."

Thad was perched on the top rail of the fence watching her, and he appeared to be in deep thought. "I guess you'd know more about how Mr. Mason smells than I do, Patience. You were standing close enough together when I saw you over by—hey!"

Pet dropped the pig and in a swift motion lunged at Thad. He was caught off guard and went over backward, and she landed on his stomach, driving all the breath from his body.

"Well, how does this smell, Thad Novak?" She snatched a handful of bitterweed and crushed it into his face as he lay there trying to get his breath.

"Get—off me—!" he gasped, but she kept stuffing the ill-smelling weeds into his face; and when he rolled over, throwing her to one side, she yelled at him again and shoved him over, beating his chest with one fist. Wildly the two struggled in the dirt of the corral.

"Pet—stop it!" he protested. She was small but strong, and though he could have thrown her off, he didn't use his strength as he might have if she had been a boy. "Blast it—get off me!"

She was laughing now, and as they rolled over and over, she said viciously, "You don't smell too good yourself, do you?"

Thad suddenly reached out and captured her wrists, saying, "If you don't quit, I'm going to throw you in the trough."

"You wouldn't dare!"

"Wouldn't I?" he demanded. In one motion Thad heaved himself up, and with an easy strength he picked her up and took three quick steps to a horse trough made out of cypress. It was covered with a thin green scum, and he held her over it, saying with a wide grin, "You're the one who needs a bath—handling those pigs."

She looked down at the scummy water and screamed, throwing her arms around his neck and holding him with all her power. "Don't you dare!"

"Say *please,*" he ordered, and when she stubbornly refused, he pretended to drop her.

"No! *Please!*" she screamed, and held on tighter.

He laughed and stepped back, holding her. He was about to set her down when she drew her face back and yelled, "You're terrible!"

"I'm not the one who's going around smelling young men," he said with a broad grin.

She shut her eyes and whispered, "You are awful!"

At the same instant both of them became aware of the other. She was pressed so close to his chest he could feel her breathing. They looked at each other, speechless.

"You tryin' to guess her weight, Thad?"

The sound of Dooley's voice shocked Thad, and he dropped Pet so quickly she almost fell. He tried to speak, but the bright laughter in Dooley's eyes kept him mute. His face flamed and he snapped, "You're liable to get yourself hurt, Dooley, sneaking up on a man that way."

Dooley glanced back at the mare he held and said innocently, "Yeah, when I go sneakin' up on people, I always do it in broad daylight, out in the open and leading a twelve-hundred-pound horse—jest to be sure I ain't bein' noticed."

Pet's face was scarlet, and she whirled and ran blindly away. "Nice talkin' to you, Miss Patience," Dooley called after her.

Thad stared at the bandy-legged figure, but knew there was no way he could verbally get the better of Dooley Young. "We was just foolin' around," he said lamely.

Dooley took off his soft felt hat, picked an imaginary speck of dust from the crown, and remarked nonchalantly, "I wondered what it was you was doin', Thad. Now I know."

"Ah, you stupid fool! She's just a kid!"

"You tell me so," Dooley grinned. "Well, I didn't come on a

pleasure trip. If you're through with your girlin', I got a message for you."

"For me?"

"Yeah. I took a couple of hosses over to the Speers' place. He's buyin' 'em for his boys. After we made the deal, he looked kind of funny. Finally he asked me if I would stop by here and give you a message." He reached into his shirt pocket and fished out an envelope. "This is it."

Thad stared at it, then opened the note and read the single line: *If you will call on me, it may be I can be of help to you.*

He put the note in his pocket and said to Dooley, "I think he's changed his mind—remember I told you what I did. He wants to see me."

Dooley stared at him. "Thad, that man wouldn't go to the funeral unless he could be the corpse. Better watch out what you promise him." As Thad turned to leave, Young decided, "Reckon I better ride along with you—sort of advise you. Git yore hoss—we'll show that feller where the bear sat in the buckwheat!"

Thad saddled up, told Mrs. Winslow he had an errand, and the two rode out at a fast pace. Dooley told him about the war news as they moved along. "They was a big battle, over to Tennessee, Thad."

"That's where the Richmond Blades are!"

"Shore is."

"Who won?"

"Well, that's hard to say. Happened at a place they call Pittsburg Landing—somewhere on the Tennessee River. Our fellers caught Grant off guard, they say, and we whupped 'em good the first day, but Grant come back and them Yankees held out." Dooley hesitated before delivering the bad news. "General Albert Sidney Johnston, he got hisself kilt—and they say 'bout ten thousand Yankees bought the farm—and 'bout the same number of our boys."

Thad stared at him. "Twenty thousand men killed!"

"Well, killed or wounded," Dooley said soberly. He added in an off-hand tone, "Guess I'll jine up, Thad. Been waitin' till I got the farm in shape—but looks like the general's gonna need me."

Thad stared at him. "It's a bad thing, Dooley. I bet the Winslows are near sick worryin' about their boys."

"Guess people all over the country are prayin'—North and South," Dooley nodded.

The two of them said little more, and when they got to the Speers' plantation, Dooley warned, "Don't you sign nothin' till you talk to me, Thad. With a feller as crafty as Speers, you gotta be cautious as a monkey on a barbwire fence!"

"All right."

Leaving Dooley beneath the big chestnut tree, Thad walked to the front door, and was surprised when he was shown directly to the same room he'd been thrown out of a few weeks earlier.

"Come in, Novak." Speers was sitting at his desk as Thad entered. Getting up he came across the room and said, "I was a little rough on you the last time you were here."

It was as close to an apology as the planter would ever come, and Thad responded, "I know you were upset, Mr. Speers."

"Yes, caught me off guard—that proposition of yours." He started to speak, but halted uncertainly before going on. "Well, I sent for you to find out if you still want to help that slave."

"Yes, sir! I sure do. I'll work for you until you get your money back."

"Well—that's not what I have in mind." Speers gave Thad a peculiar look. "Have you heard of the Conscription Act?"

"No, sir."

"Well, our Congress passed a law three days ago. It says that a man can be drafted—that is, he can be made to serve in the Confederate Army."

Thad stared at him. "Even if he don't want to?"

"That's right. The North passed the same law about a month ago." Speers added quickly, "You may not know it, but I have a son. James has got another two years before he gets his law degree. I want him to finish, and then he'll do his duty to the Confederacy."

"Well . . ." Thad couldn't see what that had to do with him, so he just shrugged and waited.

"Now, there's only one way I can be sure James gets to finish his schooling. The law says that if a man wants to, he can send what they call a 'substitute.' "

Thad looked up sharply. "And you want me to do that? Go in place of your son?"

"That's it, Novak." Speers looked uncomfortable and added, "It won't be too easy for either of us. A man who employs a substitute will be criticized for not serving in person—and the substitute himself will be looked down on by the man he serves with."

"I can see that," Thad nodded. Looking sharply at Speers, he asked abruptly, "If I go for your son, you'll let Toby go free?"

"Well, not quite. He's a valuable piece of property, Novak. I can get a man to go for James for a thousand dollars, but Toby is worth twice that." He gave Thad a bland glance. "I'll do this— I'll sign the slave over to you on two conditions. First, you'll only have a fifty percent interest in him. Then, when you pay me the other thousand, I'll sign the other fifty percent over to you."

"But Toby will still be away from his family."

"No, I'll let him go back to work for Mr. Winslow. His pay can go on the thousand."

Thad's head was reeling. The idea had caught him off guard, and he asked, "What if I get killed?"

"In that case, Toby will work out the other five hundred at Belle Maison. When I have it, he's free. Until then, he's back with his family—and that's what you wanted, isn't it?"

"I—I guess so." Thad tried to sort it all out, but could not think clearly. Finally he said, "But . . . I'm not a Southerner, Mr. Speers. You might as well know that I don't believe in slavery. They wouldn't take me in the army, would they?"

"If you keep quiet about it, they will," Speers shot back. "That's another reason why I'm retaining an interest in the slave. It'll keep you from getting your hands on him—then deserting as soon as he's clear."

Anger flared in Thad's eyes. "If I do it, you can bet your life I'd stay with it!"

Speers retreated quickly, "Well, I—I just have to be sure." He stared at the boy and asked, "How old are you?"

"How old do you have to be to enlist?"

"Eighteen."

"That's what I am, then."

"Will you do it?"

Time seemed to stop for Thad, and the room grew dim. He remembered the first time he'd seen Toby, as Thad lay freezing in the snow. He thought of the many kindnesses the black man had shown him—and what his friend would look like if he were caught trying to escape.

Speers stood there silently, not trying to rush the young man. He *had* told the truth when he said he could hire another substitute, but his plan was shady. He would say, *Both James and I were against hiring a substitute. James is anxious to go—but this young fellow, well, he begged so hard, we just couldn't say no.*

Finally Thad looked up and his eyes were hooded, but there was a set look on his dark face.

"All right, I'll do it. But you'll have to get Mr. Winslow to fix up the paper so I'll know for sure Toby is all right."

Speers agreed quickly. "That will be fine with me. When do you want to do it?"

"Today."

The answer took Speers by surprise, but he stood up quickly. "Let me get my hat, and we'll ride over to see Mr. Winslow."

"I'll meet you there." Thad turned and walked out of the house.

When he reached Dooley, he told him simply, "I'm going to be a substitute in the army for Mr. Speers' son. It'll be enough to get Toby free." He held up his hand as Dooley started to protest, "Don't argue with me, Dooley. My mind's made up!"

Dooley scanned the boy's face and knew by his set jaw that there was no use to argue. "All right, it's your say, Thad—at least we get to soldier together."

The two got on their horses and rode back to the Big House. That day was never very clear in Thad's mind. He could remember Sky Winslow's look of shock, and how his wife had protested his decision. He could remember going into Richmond with Winslow and Speers, to an office where he signed many papers. He remembered Winslow saying, "Toby is safe, Thad. My word on it."

Finally it was over, and he went back to Belle Maison in the carriage with Mr. Winslow. They said almost nothing, and the next morning, Thad went with Dooley to Richmond where they took their oath of allegiance to the Confederacy.

The two were given uniforms, and that afternoon they boarded a train with other men to be rushed to Tennessee where the army was still struggling with Grant's troops.

Thad would never forget the sight of all the Winslows at the station. Mrs. Winslow cried as she hugged him. Pet could not say a word, but clung to him fiercely for one brief moment, leaving his new uniform moist with tears.

As the train pulled out, Sky turned to his wife. "Rebekah, I feel as if another one of our sons has gone to war—but it'll be harder for Thad because of this substitute business." Then he put his arm around her and suggested, "Lets go by the church and have a time of prayer for all of them, Rebekah. Only God can help us now."

PART THREE

THE SOLDIER

★ ★ ★ ★

(April '62—August '62)

CHAPTER FOURTEEN

THE RECRUIT

★　★　★　★

The Third Virginia had been in the thick of the battle at Pittsburgh Landing. Their baptism in fire had left gaps in their ranks, and the carnage had driven all romanticism about the glory of war from their heads. They had been part of the force that attacked the center of the Union line after the flanks had been rolled up—but General Prentiss rallied the Yankee troops by placing them in an old sunken road, which proved to be the center of the battle.

Mark Winslow had stared into that furnace of shot and shell, his heart beating. When Captain Lafcadio Sloan cried out, "Company A—let's get the Yankees!" Mark had joined the charge; and after the first few seconds, he forgot his fears. Minie balls filled the air, and the sound of their own cannon was deafening. He had not gone fifty yards before Corporal Daily, the color-bearer, fell with several balls in his breast. A private he didn't know picked up the standard, only to fall before he had gone ten steps. Mark learned later that six color-bearers died in the blazing fire which exploded in their faces.

The Third Virginia was never able to take the position, being forced to retreat after all efforts to take it by assault failed. Afterward Pittsburg Landing was called "The Hornet's Nest," and many veterans remembered it as the hottest, most deadly single battle of the war. Mark had led the remnants of the company back to a refuge after retreat was sounded, a place which came to be known as "Bloody Pond." So many of the wounded on both sides died that the water was stained red by their blood. When Mark got back to the main body, he heard that General Albert Sidney Johnston was down. Later they learned that his wound had not been mortal, but because he had insisted on staying on his feet, he literally bled to death.

The brigade was pulled back to care for the wounded, and for several days after the battle the gruesome task of burying the dead went on. The bodies swelled and their faces turned black under the April sun. The Third Virginia was composed almost entirely of men from the same county, and many of them were relatives. To Mark and Tom, who helped bury the dead, it was worse than the battle. Time after time a man would find the body of a brother, and twice men found the bodies of their sons on the bloody field. Tom, his face pale, said in a shaky voice to Mark, "I can't take much more of this. I keep thinking what it would be like if I found you out there!"

Mark was hollow-eyed and every movement was an effort. The sight of his men going down like stalks of wheat under the scythe seemed to be etched on the inside of his eyelids; he could not close his eyes without seeing the carnage. Though groggy with fatigue, he urged his brother on. "We've got to do it, Tom. Thank God you didn't get hit!"

Colonel Barton called a meeting of his officers that night, and it was a sober-faced group he addressed. Barton was not the same self-assured man he had been a year earlier. He had discovered that, unlike most officers, he was almost chronically afraid of battle, and his monumental struggle to keep this from his men had drained him dry. Now he said as cheerfully as he could, "I want to tell you how proud I am of you, gentlemen. The Third Virginia proved its metal."

Vance Wickham, his left arm in a sling, commented ironically, "What's left of it, Colonel. If we prove ourselves in another fight like that one, we won't have enough men to mount a guard."

Beau Beauchamp grunted his agreement. "Whoever sent us in against that fire ought to be court-martialed!"

Mark added, "Well, I guess it was our only hope, Beau. If

we'd made it, we could have cut the Yankees off—and I still think we could have done it if Buell's forces hadn't got there just when they did."

An argument broke out, and Shelby Lee, noting that the younger men were almost blind with fatigue, urged calmly, "Gentlemen, we mustn't show any disagreement to the men. They're in poor shape. Most of them have lost relatives, and they feel as if it was a defeat." He went on talking to them in that vein and finally said, "We'll be receiving reinforcements soon—and we'll need them, for if McClellan's army is half as big as our reports say, we'll need every man we can get to whip him. Therefore, it's important that we work hard to build morale. When these new men come, they need to find the Third in fighting trim."

Colonel Barton agreed quickly, "That's very true, Major. Now, for replacements, we lost Captain Sloan. Lieutenant Wickham, you will be appointed to his place, and Mr. Beauchamp, you will be first lieutenant of Company A . . ." He continued doing what he did best: making appointments and plans.

"Congratulations, Vance," Beau said after they left the tent. "Any orders from the new captain?"

"Bring me an easy chair and a mint julep, will you, old boy?" Wickham grinned. Then he sobered. "Lee is right, isn't he? I reckon we'll be sent back to face McClellan straight off. And he's right about the men. They're in a bad frame of mind. We've got to work on that."

When the first replacements came marching in, Company A got the first pick, but the company was *not* in a happy frame of mind. As the officers had indicated, the men were angry at their defeat and grieved over the loss of close friends and relatives.

The men of Milton Calhoun's mess had a fire going, fueled by rails from a farmer's fence—which was strictly forbidden. Colonel Barton had ordered the troops to do no damage to local property. At one end of the group, Calhoun was frying ham on Sharp's skillet; and at the other, Lafe Sharp was baking flour bread. The dough had been shaped into a loaf around the ramrod of Sharp's Springfield rifle, like a fleece on a distaff. As he turned the mixture in his hamlike hands, he sang in a whiskey tenor, "Oh, Lord, Gals One Friday."

None of the men appreciated Sharp or his singing, but they needed his skillet. Milton himself had owned one once, but it had been stolen. He'd been carrying it on a march, its handle down the barrel of his rifle, sticking out like a huge black sunflower, and a cavalryman had simply lifted it and carried the pan off. Now four men depended on that skillet: Sharp, Calhoun, Peyton Law, a twenty-two-year-old schoolteacher, and Lew Avery, a dark-faced man of thirty who had been a gambler on a riverboat. All four looked half starved, for they had lived on short rations for months—eating everything from green apples to unripe corn. It had made havoc out of their digestive systems, all of them suffering from dysentery to some degree.

When the food was cooked, the soldiers sat around and ate hungrily, washing the meal down with sips of river water from their canteens. They had finished and lit up their pipes or taken a chaw, as the case was, when Captain Wickham approached and spoke loudly enough for most of the men of Company A to hear. "All right, boys, you can rest easy. Our reinforcements from Richmond are here. You may have heard that the Confederate Congress passed a conscription law. Well, the conscripts are at the gate, and I expect you will go and *exchange* your old equipment for their new, but let me give you a word of warning. Some of them are substitutes. Some wealthy boy was drafted and rather than join our party himself, he paid another fellow to take his place. Now, there's just one thing about these substitutes— *we need them bad!* So you can use a sharp tongue on them, but you are *not* to harm them bodily, nor after this first day humiliate them—and you had better heed what I say. Now, let your eyes feast upon them, for they come through yonder gates."

Wickham waved his hat toward a group of fifteen men who were marched like harried chickens to the camp. The third lieutenant stopped and yelled: "These fifteen are for you, Lieutenant Wilson!" Then cutting out the assigned group, he herded the rest of his flock to the next brigade.

"Mind what I said," Captain Wickham warned his men, and walked off. As soon as the captain disappeared around a clump of trees, the volunteers of Company A descended like vultures on the wide-eyed and helpless recruits. One conscript would be surrounded by four or five of the company, and in no time he would be stripped of his new uniform and forced to put on the lice-infested rags of his tormentors. The veterans went through the conscript's haversacks and took coffee, tobacco, food, and anything else they fancied.

Some of the conscripts resisted, but it was no fair contest. They had already been derided as latecomers to the fight, and there was little spirit left in them—except for a few.

Lafe Sharp had swooped upon the conscripts like a whirlwind, depriving several of choice items, at last coming to a small man with a huge mustache. The newcomer looked innocently at Sharp and said, "Hidee."

He was carrying a full haversack, and Lafe reached down to snatch it, but somehow found himself on the ground looking up. His head throbbed and the sky whirled. He crawled to his feet and looked around to find the Regulars laughing at him. He turned to look at the recruit, and realized that the fellow had used the musket in his hand, leaving a deep cut in Sharp's skull.

"You didn't say *please*," the little man remarked.

"I'll *kill* you!" Lafe yelled, but as he reached for the throat of the smaller man, Sharp's bare toes were smashed by the butt of the recruit's rifle, and he fell to the ground cursing and holding his foot.

"My name's Dooley Young," the recruit said. "Come to help you fellers fight the Yankees."

"Hey, Dooley!" Les Satterfield, a tall, thin boy with stringy yellow hair, came up to thrust out his hand. "We was wonderin' when you'd get here." He laughed at Sharp, who was glaring at the man. "Lafe, this here is my cousin. Don't reckon it'd profit you none to mess with him. He's so ornery a rattlesnake bit him five times and died!"

Just at that moment a harsh voice drew every eye to where a hulking recruit stood, holding a tall young man by the arm. "And this here," he rasped, "is one of them paid substitutes—of which there ain't nothin' lower—'ceptin' the yellow dog who paid him!"

Tom Winslow had been alerted by Captain Wickham to keep close to the men to see that none of the new recruits were abused. He had kept still while the veterans had helped themselves to the newcomers' fresh supplies, but now he started to move forward, for he recognized the speaker as Studs Mellon—and the pug was holding Thad Novak by the arm! Tom was brought to a stop, however, when Dooley blocked his way and whispered, "Better let it go jest now, Tom."

The others moved to surround the pair, and Dooley quickly explained the circumstances to Tom. "He done it for Toby. You know them two is great friends. But they ain't no way that you nor me can fight the boy's battles, Tom. He'll have to prove hisself to the men."

Tom realized that truth, and stood with the rest, listening to Mellon. "And this here Yankee boy ain't jest no ordinary paid-for substitute—oh, no! Tell these fellers what you done with the bounty money, Novak!"

Thad's face was pale as he faced them all, held in place by a massive hand. The burly Mellon had tormented him ever since the group had been assembled at Richmond. Somehow the bully had discovered the details of Thad's enlistment, probably through Sut Franklin, a crony of his, and he had never let the matter rest.

"Why, he took that money and bought a slave loose with it!" Mellon bellowed. "Reckon he couldn't steal him and git him up North, so he done jined up jest to git the job done."

A mutter ran through the group, and Thad saw distrust, even hatred, in the eyes of some of the veterans. He lifted his head and stared back at them, determined not to give them the satisfaction of seeing him show any fear. Will Henry, one of the few aristocrats who had entered the army as a private, recognized Novak at once. He was now second sergeant, and spent much of his time with Tom. He had been at the New Year's party when Wickham had made his bet with Beau Beauchamp. Henry, still hopelessly in love with Belle, had followed the history of the young Yankee who had nearly won the shooting match. He knew that Sky Winslow valued the young man, and he knew as well that if something didn't happen, Novak would have a wretched time in the army. A thought occurred to him.

"Wait a minute, boys," Henry said; and winking at Tom and Dooley, he stepped forward. "Before you start in on any of these recruits, I think we better check them out. If they can shoot, I don't give a hoot why they came. McClellan is headed for Virginia with the biggest army anybody ever saw, and we lost some good men at Shiloh—and I want all the firepower we can get in Company A."

"Aw, I can outshoot any Yankee that ever lived!" Lafe snarled. He was, as a matter of fact, a deadly shot, and Will Henry saw his chance.

"Wouldn't be so quick to brag, Lafe, especially about a man you never shot against," Sergeant Henry replied mildly.

Lafe Sharp had always hated Will Henry, as he hated all aristocrats, so he looked at him and grunted, "That wouldn't take long to prove."

Tom Winslow added quickly, "Might not be a bad idea, Corporal. Let's have these recruits fire off a few rounds. Need to see how good they are, anyway."

Lafe grinned at his friends, and then saw that Novak was carrying a new Whitworth rifle, a parting gift from Sky Winslow, and he snarled, "Hey, nigger-lover, that rifle gun's too good fer you. How 'bout a little bet—my gun agin' yours?"

Dooley interrupted. "Why his gun is worth five of that old musket you got! Make him throw in some boot, Thad."

Thad had an idea, and said, "I'll put up my gun against yours—and the only boot you have to anti-up is to give me back all my things."

"It's a bet!" Lafe shouted gleefully. "Come on, boys, I'm gonna have me a new rifle gun!" Tom and Dooley followed the group to the shooting range, an open field with several huge oak stumps, some as far as half a mile away. Sergeant Henry sent Peyton Law to set up some empty cans, waving him back to a distance of two hundred yards. "Take your shot, Lafe," he said.

Sharp took a steady rest, knocked the can off, then turned and bragged, "Beat that, nigger-lover!"

Thad stared at him and shook his head in disgust. "We've got twelve-year-olds that can make that shot. I thought this was a grown-up shootin' match." He whirled around and shouted, "Move that can back!"

Peyton moved another fifty yards and paused.

"Move back!" Thad yelled. Three times he had Peyton set the mark back until the distance was well over five hundred yards.

The can was a mere speck, and a murmur of doubt rose from the soldiers.

"He's bluffin', boys!" Lafe laughed.

Thad knew that Sharp was half right, for it was a difficult shot. He had hit harder ones, but he had also missed easier ones. He loaded the Whitworth so quickly that a gasp went up from the men, and Milton Calhoun remarked, "If he shoots as good as he loads, he's a wonder!"

Nothing short of a great shot will do me any good, Thad thought. So he did what he had often done—took a snapshot of the target. He was fairly certain of hitting the mark if he took a steady rest, bracing his rifle against a tree or a stump, but there was no tree nearby. He decided to gamble. He had long ago discovered that it did little good to try to hold a rifle steady for any long period of time. The weight of the heavy weapon inevitably pulled his arms down, causing the rifle to waver. But for one split second, he could hold the rifle as steadily as if it were encased in rock—and that was what he did.

Sweeping the Whitworth up, he caught the dim vision of the distant can, froze the motion of the rifle, and instantly pulled the trigger. The explosion and sudden firing caught the men off guard, for they were waiting for a careful shot. A cry from the lips of Dooley rang out: "He done 'er!" and a spontaneous cheer went up.

"It's gonna be all right, Tom," Dooley remarked after the men had dispersed. The two had watched carefully as the men of the company had gathered around Thad, marveling at the Whitworth and demanding to try it. Thad had surrendered the rifle, and watched while the veterans took turns firing shots, like children with a new toy. Lafe had thrown Thad's uniform and haversack at him, along with his promised rifle, but Thad had tossed the rifle back.

Tom nodded, and gave a hard glance at Studs Mellon. "There'll be some trouble from that one." A thought flashed through Tom's mind. "I wonder if Beau will remember Thad."

He found out very quickly, for that afternoon the new captain and his two lieutenants held an inspection of the new men. And as soon as Beauchamp saw Thad, the first lieutenant's face reddened. He shot a look at Wickham, who had also seen the new conscript but gave no sign of recognition. Tom had informed his brother of Novak's presence, so Mark was watching Beauchamp carefully. *Got to be sure he doesn't abuse the boy,* he thought, seeing the anger in Beauchamp's face.

Captain Wickham addressed the company in his off-hand fashion, standing loosely in front of them. He was still uncomfortable with his promotion, but he said with an authority that was unusual for him, "Men, I have some good news for you—we're going back home. Our brigade is being sent to reinforce General Joe Johnston." He waited until the cheers died down, and added, "It would be foolish for me to give you any speeches. You proved at The Hornet's Nest that you're fighting men. But we've got our work cut out for us! All I will say is, you're the best company in the army, so learn to live together. We have a long way to go in this war, and the man standing next to you is the one who'll be at your side when we go against the Yankees. They've got more men than we have, but I think we're *better* than they are—so let's make Company A a smooth fighting machine!"

"That was a good speech, Captain," Beau remarked as the officers walked off. "I didn't know you were so eloquent. Good thing you're not as smooth where the ladies are concerned."

Vance looked at him sharply, and noted that Beauchamp was in a good humor. "Who knows, maybe this practice will help me, Beau."

Beauchamp changed the subject, saying casually, "I see that Dooley Young finally made it—and that young fellow your father's so high on—Novak, is it? That was quite a sample of his shooting at that party, wasn't it?" He saw that the other two were relieved at his mention of the affair, and grinned, "I was upset with that match, Vance, but we need all the marksmen we can get."

Later, after Beau left, Captain Wickham commented to Mark, "Now, that's a relief! I was afraid Beau would take it wrong—Novak's coming, I mean."

"If Thad takes to soldiering as quickly as he did to farming, he'll show them all the way, Captain!"

The brigade pulled out two days later, beginning a slow march back to Virginia. The wounded were transported in wagons, which moved slowly because of the muddy roads. And it was on this long march that Thad learned what it was to be a soldier in the Army of Northern Virginia.

He and Dooley soon got rid of all excess equipment. They discovered that the heavy boots they had been issued were not conducive to long marches, and both soon obtained strong brogans with broad bottoms and big flat heels. They also got rid of the heavy overcoats, exchanging them for short-waisted gray jackets. In addition, they were now wearing broad-brimmed soft hats that protected them from the hot summer sun. By the time the two arrived in Virginia, they were reduced to the minimum—one hat, one jacket, one shirt, one pair of pants, one pair of drawers, one pair of shoes, and one pair of socks. Their baggage included one blanket, one rubber blanket, and one haversack. The haversack contained smoking tobacco and a pipe (for Dooley), a small piece of soap, with temporary additions of apples, persimmons, blackberries and other commodities they picked up along the way. No soldiers ever marched with less to encumber them, and none ever marched faster or held out longer!

As the days passed, Thad found himself becoming accustomed to the new lifestyle. Somehow he and Dooley joined with Milton Calhoun's mess, and after weeks on the road, the routine had become so regular that Thad felt a part of it. There were still those who despised him for being a substitute, but there was no time for them to do much about it.

Finally they got back to Virginia, and Captain Wickham was ordered to report with Company A to Richmond. When they marched into the city, Thad felt peculiar as he saw Cherry Street lined with cheering citizens. He remembered the first time he'd seen Richmond, covered with snow, when he'd fled the city looking for Belle Maison. He thought of the farewells he'd received from Mrs. Winslow and Pet. He had not dreamed that he'd be back so soon, thinking rather that he would never see it again.

Then, as the company passed the courthouse, he spied a huge black man, his face split in a wide grin, with tears flowing down the cheeks. Toby! Thad could not break his march, but their eyes met, and for one fleeting instant, he felt that in all his life, he had done one thing that was good! As Toby passed out of Thad's sight, he thought, *No matter what else I've done, for once I was right!*

CHAPTER FIFTEEN

"I'M AFRAID FOR THEM!"

★ ★ ★ ★

The officers of the Third Virginia had little spare time the first two days in Richmond. Under the urgent commands of Colonel Stone and Major Lee, the men worked feverishly to get the regiment in first-class condition. Mark was responsible for the wounded, getting them into the huge Chimborazo Hospital. Beau scurried from office to office, trying to obtain signatures that would free replacements for their depleted supplies. Wickham and Major Lee scoured the country for new recruits, while Barton campaigned among his friends in Congress for both men and arms for the Third Virginia. All the officers were well aware that their unit would be rushed to join General Joe Johnston's forces very soon, so they worked day and night to bring the regiment to full strength.

In addition to the intense preparation by the Third Virginia, someone else was working just as hard—Belle Winslow. "It would be a shame to let our men get away to fight without some sort of celebration for what they did at Shiloh," she protested to her father.

"Guess you'll take care of that, won't you, Belle?" Sky teased. "But it might be difficult to do. Major Lee knows that most of his staff is on the verge of a duel over you, so he may not want to take any risks."

Belle had laughed, but as Sky guessed, on Wednesday evening he found himself dressing for a ball that Belle had organized on short notice. As he changed into his evening clothes, he asked Rebekah, "Which one do you think she will take? Wickham or Beau?"

"I don't think she herself knows, Sky," Rebekah replied soberly. "I'm afraid she'll make a decision too fast. It's hard on young people, this war. Remember how Rose Howland married that young Tarrent boy just before Bull Run? They were afraid to wait, and look what happened—he was killed, and she's a widow."

"I guess there's really nothing we can do, is there?" Sky said. He came over and put his arms around her, saying fondly, "If any old fogey had tried to keep me from marrying you, I'd have either shot him, or eloped with you." He kissed her soundly, then took her arm. "Let's go to the show."

When they entered the ballroom, it was filled with officers and guests. "I didn't know there were so many young women in Richmond," Sky commented. "I think they come out of the woodwork every time there's a ball." He nodded toward a group. "I see the moths have already swarmed around the candle."

"Let's hope they don't burn up in the flame," Rebekah smiled. "Belle *is* lovely, isn't she?"

"Second best-looking woman in the room," Sky said, giving her a squeeze. "Come, let's find a spot to sit down. My feet hurt." The group of officers clustered around Belle was composed largely of young men who had been on duty in Richmond, and they listened avidly as Captain Wickham and Lieutenant Beauchamp told of the battle at Shiloh. Mark stood back with Rowena Barton. They listened awhile, then drifted over to the refreshment table. As they ate, Rowena asked, "Remember the New Year's Ball at Belle Maison a year ago?"

"Yes." Mark looked around, observing. "Seems like a long time ago. But Beau and Vance are still right where they were with Belle."

"I don't think she loves either one, Mark. She's in love with love."

Mark stared at her, for it was as if she had read his mind. "You're a perceptive woman, Rowena," he commented, sipping his punch. "That was the night you told me about your rich Yankee suitor. You still seeing him?"

"No, he got away," Rowena laughed. "But remember I told you about his friend, your relative, Lowell Winslow? He's still a good prospect. Rich and handsome—but a Yankee officer, of course."

"I remember. His grandfather came down not long ago."

"I met him," Rowena nodded. "And you met Davis—but he's nothing like his brother."

Mark shot her a straight look. "What about us?"

"Oh, Mark, you were never in love with me!" She touched his arm gently and murmured in a soft tone, "You're much like Belle, I think. You're young, and everybody else is thinking of love and courtship. I was just the closest one, that's all."

His face flushed, and he laughed at her perception. "I guess that's right, isn't it? Well, you deserve someone better."

She shook her head and her eyes were kind. "No, I only hope my man will be half as fine as you are, Mark." She smiled up at him and said quickly, "Let's dance before we get maudlin! It may be a long time before the next ball."

Belle was at her best that night. She danced every dance, her dark beauty drawing the young men's eyes, and was cordially hated by most of the young women.

It was a contest between Wickham and Beauchamp, each trying to maneuver her away from the crowd; but it was almost midnight before Wickham's ploy worked. Beau was dancing with another girl, and Vance deftly moved Belle outside onto the wide porch that by some miracle was not occupied.

"Now, I've captured you!" he exulted, pulling her into a tight embrace, his cheek against her hair.

"Why—Vance! You mustn't hold me like this!" Belle protested.

"I can't play games any longer, Belle," he murmured, kissing her hard. His lips sent a shock through her, and she found herself responding, her arms creeping behind his neck. He held her tighter, then finally drew back and looked into her eyes, saying huskily, "Belle, it's got to be yes or no. Which will it be?"

This was not the Vance Wickham Belle had known, and her hands fluttered to her heart as she studied his handsome face.

"Why—Vance, you've changed!"

"I've seen what this war is like, Belle," he replied quietly. "Men die and life is over. It may or may not happen to me—but in any case, I can't dangle on a string any longer. I've told you for months now that I love you and I want to marry you. You've shuttled back and forth between me and Beau—and that's been all right. It's the way a beautiful young woman will do. But I won't play anymore. I love you and want you to marry me. Will you?"

She caught her breath, realizing he was deadly serious. The suddenness of his words and the enormity of the decision she must make frightened her. She stood there, thinking of life without him, and found it unbearable. "Yes, Vance—I'll marry you," she whispered.

He gave a glad cry, kissed her and held her close. "I'm a lucky man, Belle! I'll make you happy!" After a while he asked gently, "What about Beau?"

She leaned against his chest, saying, "He's a very attractive man, Vance. But he's . . . he's very *demanding*. I was drawn to him, yet I think I've known all along that he and I would fight all the time if we were married. Both of us want our own way too much."

He laughed and asked lightly, "Is that your feminine way of informing me that I'm too well mannered to cross you, Miss Winslow? Well, we'll see about that!" Then he sobered and said, "It's going to make things harder—with Beau and me. We've got to get along, and I'm just not sure how Beau will handle it. I'm not even sure how *I* could handle it if you had chosen him. But we've got to get it out in the open, Belle."

"Yes. I'll go tell Mama and Papa."

"No. Go tell Beau. He deserves to hear it from you, not in a public announcement."

He led her back to the dance floor, and she went immediately to Beau. The two disappeared, and within five minutes Belle returned. Her face was pale and her eyes teary. She whispered, "I hate myself, Vance."

He shook his head sadly. "You're just paying the price for being a beautiful woman. Come on, I'll speak to your parents."

Thad and some men from his unit were digging on the end-less lines of fortification around Richmond when Mark rode up. He pulled his horse to a stop and called, "Corporal Winslow, I need a man to drive a wagon out to Belle Maison. The owner there has a wagon load of fresh vegetables for the company." He added solemnly, "Detail a man for the job."

Corporal Tom Winslow caught the slight droop of his broth-er's eye, and looked over the line of men, all of whom would rather drive a wagon than dig a ditch. Then he said, "Novak, you drive the wagon for the lieutenant—and take Young with you to help with the loading."

Thad and Dooley followed Lieutenant Winslow back to the supply station where a spring wagon was waiting for them. "It's getting pretty late in the day," Mark commented with a wise look at the afternoon sun. "Wouldn't be too surprised if dark didn't catch you fellows. You might not make it back before tomorrow."

Dooley's mouth twitched behind his mustache as he recog-nized the ploy to give him time to go see his people, but he only said, "Time do go by, don't it, Lieutenant?" He watched as Wins-low turned his horse and left. "See, Thad," Young remarked, "prayer does work, like I always tol' you."

Thad laughed. "You mean you've been praying for a chance to get home?"

"Hare, no! I mean that leetle ol' Julie gal's been praying to git me back, and she's a foot-washin' Baptist gal. Come on, boy, let's stir some dust!"

They made record time on the trip to the plantation, and as soon as they pulled through the front gate, Dooley jumped out of the wagon, saying, "Thad, don't let them count the hosses too close tonight. I'm gonna borrow one to go see my Julie gal."

"Take Blackie, Dooley," Thad called as the soldier scooted toward the barn. "And you better get your courtin' done by noon tomorrow. I think that's about as far as we can stretch the lieu-tenant's patience."

He drove the wagon around to the back of the house, and as he wrapped the lines around the seat and got down, the front door slammed, and he saw Pet come sailing out of the house. "Thad!" she cried out, and he thought for one instant that she was going to throw herself into his arms, but she halted abruptly, and said awkwardly, "Well, you made it back, didn't you?"

She was wearing a blue dress he had never seen before, and he thought she looked prettier than ever. The late afternoon rays washed over her hair, bringing out the reddish tints, and her gray eyes were bright and clear as she smiled. "I—I didn't know you'd be coming out here," she added.

Thad felt a little uncomfortable in her presence. He had been gone only a matter of a few weeks, but she seemed different. Then he realized that *he* was the one who was different. His life had been rooted deeply in the cycles of Belle Maison, and his sudden baptism into army life had already begun to shape him. Everything in the army was rough, so her youthful beauty, her soft skin and feminine air moved him greatly.

"You look fine," he commented uncertainly, then added, as a horse tore out of the barn and disappeared into the woods, "That's Dooley. He's going to see his girl."

"What's her name?" Pet asked.

"Oh, Julie something." He licked his lips and said, "I sure am thirsty, Pet. We burned up the road getting here."

"I'll fix you some lemonade," Pet offered and led the way into the house. As he was sipping the refreshing drink, he told her how Mark and Tom had arranged for him and Dooley to come for the supplies. "The other men sure were mad," he remarked. "We'll get it when we get back."

"Has it been hard—I mean—"

"You mean me being a substitute?" He completed the sentence for her, seeing she was embarrassed. "Not as bad as I'd thought it would be. 'Course having your brothers in the company hasn't hurt any—and Dooley, he'll get by anywhere, and he's stuck real close."

He lingered a little longer as she urged him to tell about his experiences. Suddenly he stopped. "I nearly forgot! Your brother sent this."

She opened the note he gave her, and looked up with a strange expression. "It says that Belle is engaged to Vance Wickham."

"Is that right? Well, she picked a good one."

"Yes—but Beau, he's going to be unhappy. He loves Belle so much." Then changing the subject, she said, "Come on, there's one chore you've got to do right now."

"What's that?" he demanded, but she grabbed his hand and pulled him out of the door. "Come on, I'll race you!" she cried, and ran lightly down the path leading toward the east. She ran like a deer, but in his heavy brogans he was no match for her. She didn't stop until they came in sight of the slave cabins, where she called loudly, "Toby! Toby! Look who's here!"

Thad pulled up beside her, wondering what she was up to. He looked around and saw some of the slaves either puttering in their little gardens or sitting in front of their cabins waiting for supper.

"Thad! It's Mistuh Thad!" Jessie cried as she threw open the door. Soon it seemed that from every cabin the entire population of black people—young and old, big and small—descended upon him. He shot a bewildered look at Pet, but she smiled and stepped back. Then he was engulfed—hands patting him, everyone crowding to get near him, laughing and crying. The rich black drawls of their speech, calling out his name, brought tears to his eyes.

As quickly as the joyous cries had filled the air, silence fell, and a path opened up in the black sea of faces. There coming toward him Thad saw Toby! He walked slowly up to where Thad stood, and as the tall man looked down on the white boy, the black face was contorted with suppressed emotion. Toby stood there, weaving slightly in the fading light; and then a single tear made a silver track down his cheek, and he said hoarsely, "My friend—is come home!"

Thad stuck out his hand blindly, but it was ignored. Toby wrapped his mighty arms around Thad and lifted him clear from the ground, crying over and over from the depths of his heart, "Thank yuh! Thank yuh!"

Thad had never felt so weak and helpless. The adulation staggered him and he spoke in a shaky voice, trying to cover his emotions. "Well, shoot! You don't have to kill a fellow, do you?" And when Toby let him go and stepped back, Thad cleared his throat, saying hoarsely, "If you all are through with your carryin' on, I sure would like to have something to eat! Been thinkin' about your fried chicken ever since I left, Jessie."

He and Pet were guests of honor that night—the guests of

slaves. Everyone insisted that the two try something from every cabin, and by the time it was over, Thad groaned, "If this don't kill me, reckon the Yankees have no chance at all!" He stood up and Pet followed. "Toby, I'll see you at dawn. Like to see what you've been doing since I left."

"You'll see, sho' nuff!" Toby nodded.

As the two left the quarters, Pet said, "You made them so happy, Thad! They love you more than anyone else in the world—all of them do, not just Toby and Jessie."

He could not answer, for he was happier than he had ever been. Finally he spoke, his voice choked, "If I don't make it, Pet—I mean, if I get killed—you'll look out for Toby and Jessie, won't you?" He waited but she didn't answer. When he looked up he saw that she had turned her face away. Surprised, he stopped. They were standing beside the huge hedge that was filled with honeysuckle, the fragrance sweet in the warm air.

He hesitated uncertainly, then asked, "Is anything wrong, Pet?"

She whirled and buried her face in his chest and began sobbing as if her heart would break. Not knowing what else to do, he put his arms around her and just held her. When the long, racking sobs began to cease, he asked again, "What's wrong? Did I do something?"

She did not move out of the circle of his arms, but looked up, the tears in her large eyes glistening like diamonds. Her full young lips trembled as she whispered, "I'm so *proud* of you, Thad! So very *proud!*" A shudder swept through her firm body so close to his. "I'm afraid for you . . . if anything happened to you, Thad—!"

She didn't finish, for when she turned her face up to him, he was captivated by her youth. He bent down and kissed her. It was a kiss of innocence—he had never kissed anyone, nor had she. Both were caught by surprise, and his hands trembled. Then she drew back and whispered, "Don't talk anymore about getting killed, Thad!"

He stepped away, flustered. "I—I didn't mean to do that."

She smiled and said softly, "It wasn't only you, Thad—it takes two to kiss." She took his arm and they continued toward the house. When they reached the steps, Pet suggested, "Let's sit on the porch awhile."

He sat beside her, and she asked, "How long can you stay?"
"Till tomorrow."

They talked for hours, getting up several times to walk around the house. Finally Thad said goodnight and went to his room. He was glad Franklin was not there. He lay down on his bunk fully dressed and stared up at the ceiling, wondering what the future held. Pet's kiss had shaken—and saddened—him, for he knew that nothing could ever come of it. The barriers between the aristocracy and the poor whites were too solid. Eventually he fell asleep and dreamed of a time when there was no war and no slaves.

The next morning Thad went over the plantation with Toby, who was proud of his work. Little was said about the overseer, and Thad accurately guessed that Franklin left most of the work to Toby. Soon it was time to say goodbye, and Toby smiled. "I ain't gonna blubber all ovah you agin', Thad—but jes' once let me tell you I ain't nevah gonna fo'git what you done fo' Jessie and Wash and me! Now you be keerful in dis heah war, and don' let them Yankees do you no hurt, heah me?"

"Do my best to oblige," Thad promised, and the two shook hands. "Next thing is to buy Jessie and Wash, Toby."

At noon Dooley rode in on Blackie, and the two men loaded the wagon with an abundance of fresh fruits and vegetables. When they finished and were ready to leave, Pet got in between them, saying, "You're not leaving me here. I wouldn't trust the two of you with all these goodies." Then she turned to study Dooley's face, which was a fascinating collection of purple bruises and assorted cuts and scratches. "I see you weren't the only one who was interested in Julie," she remarked sweetly. "Did you win?"

"Does a cat have climbing gear?" he demanded. "It was Buck Hollins that was tryin' to beat my time," he confided to them, "But I educated him."

"Looks like he objected some," Thad grinned.

"Oh, it wasn't nothin' special as fights go," Dooley shrugged. "He was sittin' in Julie's front room, and when I walked in he didn't say nothin', jest whupped out his pistol and snapped the hammer down on an empty chamber.

"I said, 'I don't want no trouble,' but all he done was pull the hammer down on another empty chamber. By that time I was gittin' kinda nervous, so I yanked out my knife and sliced him acrost the top of his stomach. Then he pulled down on me agin, but he missed, so I picked up a chair and parted his hair with it—and that's when the trouble started."

As they laughed, Dooley glared at them and said gloomily, "It taught me never to let no man get the edge on me again."

"What about Julie?" Pet asked curiously.

"Oh, she sided with Buck. I reckon he's been makin' time while I been gone—but that's all right. She's got three sisters that's jest as good-lookin'; an' so long as they hold out, I'm all right." His face crinkled in a sly grin and he added, "The youngest one is named Sue. She's the one who patched me up. Always did long to have a gal named Sue!"

He kept them laughing all the way to Richmond. But when they arrived they saw instantly that something was up. They pulled into the supply depot and looked around, startled. Men were running and officers were frantically driving squads. Dooley spotted Sergeant Henry and yelled, "Sarge! What's goin' on?"

"Order to advance down the Peninsula, Dooley," Henry answered. "McClellan has made his move—and we're on our way to stop 'im! Get that stuff into our wagons!"

Thad and Dooley drove to where one of the army wagons was waiting, and jumped down. They had plenty of help, and as soon as the produce was transferred, Thad hopped in beside Pet, saying, "I'll take you to your father's house."

He drove at a rapid pace, then got out and helped her down. "Have to leave you here, Pet." He reached out and touched her hair softly. "I—I'll think of you."

He whirled and drove down the street. She waved, but he didn't see her, and she turned and went slowly into the house, her heart heavy with fear. When her mother asked what had happened, she said, "They've gone to fight the Yankees, Mama—and I'm afraid for them."

There was such sorrow mirrored in Pet's eyes that Rebekah wanted to say something comforting, but she couldn't. Her own spirit was heavy. She reached out and took the girl in her arms and held her tight.

CHAPTER SIXTEEN

TRIAL BY COMBAT

★ ★ ★ ★

The first battle of the Peninsula Campaign took place at Williamsburg on May 3, 1862, and the Third Virginia arrived just in time for the shooting. They had come at a rapid pace from Richmond, and on the night of May 2 were led into the line of battle by Colonel Seth Barton. Later that night, Major Shelby Lee spoke to Lieutenant Wickham and his officers, giving them the battle plan.

When the meeting was over and most of the troops were asleep, Mark stopped to see his brother Tom, as was his custom. Dooley and Thad were also huddled around the small fire. Mark sat down nearby and announced, "We'll be having company first thing in the morning, I reckon."

"Mr. McClellan is coming for breakfast?" Tom grinned, his white teeth gleaming in the darkness.

"I guess we're his breakfast," Mark countered.

"Has he got the hull Yank army with him, Lieutenant?" Dooley asked. "I ain't never rightly asked how he got all them bluebellies this far from Washington."

Mark took a bite of the beef from the spit over the fire, chewed it thoughtfully, then gave a little lecture—as if to get the whole picture in his own mind. He made quite an impression on Thad, who admired the way the lieutenant was able to express himself.

"McClellan's built up the Army of the Potomac—that's what he's good at, they say. Our spies tell us that he's bringing five corps to take Richmond. They loaded 400 boats at the Potomac docks—more than 100,000 men, and 14,500 animals, they say—not to mention 350 guns. Well, they landed at Fort Monroe on the second of April, and moved out. It was Magruder that stopped 'em at Yorktown."

"Old General John B. Magruder?" Tom asked.

"Yes. Magruder had only 13,000 men, but he held back McClellan's whole army for a month. He marched his troops back and forth to make them seem like more, and set up logs as fake artillery—Quaker Cannons, he called them."

"This here General McClellan," Dooley put in; "sounds like he's a mite overcautious."

"Lincoln said the man's got a case of the slows," Mark smiled. "Anyway, McClellan was fooled, and when he *did* move, Magruder evacuated Yorktown and pulled back here. He yielded his command to General Joe Johnston." Mark thought about the host of soldiers in blue that waited for the dawn, then stood up and said, "It'll be lively, but we've got to slow 'em down. You fellows take care of each other."

After Mark left, Tom rolled into his blankets and left Dooley and Thad to stare into the darkness. Finally Dooley yawned and said, "Guess I'll catch some sleep."

For a long time Thad sat beside the fire, thinking of the precarious future—of what the dawn would bring. He got up and walked toward the outer limits of the camp. As he reached the edge, he was startled by a voice warning, "Better be careful, soldier."

He wheeled and whispered hoarsely, "Who's there?"

A tall man with a blanket over his shoulders stepped out of the darkness. "Just a poor old Baptist preacher, son—Chaplain Boone."

Thad had seen the chaplain several times, and had gone to the services twice. "You're up late, sir," he commented.

"Can't ever sleep when something big's coming up in the morning. What's your name, soldier?"

"Thad Novak, Reverend." Thad hesitated, then added, "I went to a meeting once where you were preaching. Over at

Shady Grove just west of Belle Maison."

"Oh, yes," Boone nodded. "We had a good meeting there. God moved mightily! Are you a Christian, Thad?"

"Well, not rightly, sir."

"It might be well to think of it at this time," Boone suggested. Thad felt uncomfortable. "Yes, sir, I guess you're right." Then he asked, "Reverend, I—I've never killed a man before—and it looks like I may have to in the morning. I guess I'm more afraid of that than I am of being killed myself." He thought long and the minister waited patiently, for Boone had heard this fear expressed many times. "How can I do it, sir? I don't hate those men over there."

Chaplain Boone shook his head, and there was a deep note of regret in his voice as he spoke. "There are thousands of boys on our side, and thousands on the other—all asking that question, Thad. And I can't help you much. You see, we're living in a world that's gone awry—it's not the kind of world God intended. What He purposed was a paradise where all people would live in perfect peace. But something went wrong. Adam sinned, and we all trace our family back to him. The Bible says that the whole *world* fell, and that someday we'll see a new heaven and a new earth—a world without sickness and wars. But until that happens, we have to do what we can to find God."

"Some of the men in my company are Christians, and they've killed the enemy—but they believe in the Confederacy."

"And you don't?"

For a moment Thad struggled. Pretty soon he found himself telling the chaplain how he had come to Belle Maison, and how he'd gotten into the army. He ended by saying, "So I'm in the army, but I think slavery is wrong. How can I fight for something I think is wrong?"

"You have sworn an oath, Thad," Chaplain Boone replied quietly. "That's one reason for doing your duty. And you have comrades who are depending on you; that's another. Your oath and your comrades—are they important to you?"

"Why *sure* they are!"

"Then until you know God, I'd say that you have no other recourse than to do your duty. It's a grim duty, and it will no doubt involve shooting at the enemy." He felt a keen pity for the young man and said, "I pray that God will keep you safe, Thad. And I pray that as He does, you will open your heart to His grace. Goodnight, my boy—and God be with you."

He faded back into the darkness, and Thad stood there silently, thinking of the man's words. It was too much. He sighed and went to roll up in his blanket, dreading the morning.

Well before daylight he was awakened by the sound of other men stirring, and Dooley poked him. "Git up, Thad. We're movin' to the line."

He sprang up, and soon the company had marched until they heard the first crackle of rifle fire. It did something to Thad's whole body; the crackle sounded so much like a bunch of firecrackers going off in the distance. The hair on the back of his neck stood up, and he began to perspire.

"We're in for it now!" Lafe Sharp groaned. "Oh, Lord, we're in for it now!"

"Close up! Close up those ranks!" The sergeants all ranged back and forth like hunting dogs, and once Shelby Lee rode down the line on a beautiful brown horse, shouting, "The line is breaking up there. Go in and support them."

"Load muskets!" At the call, the men all stopped and loaded their pieces. From the right Captain Wickham approached them, a fixed grin on his face. He cried out, "Well, boys, let's show the Yankees what Virginia men can do. Keep low and don't break rank."

They passed over some little fields in an oak forest. Suddenly Thad froze. Spread over grass and in among the tree trunks, he could see knots and waving lines of bluebellies who were firing as they ran.

Thad floundered down a bank, his hands trembling. His comrades, too, were scared. Their eyes were wide and white, like those of frightened horses. They paused at the top of the bank to re-form, then started across a wide field thinly lined with scrub timber. They almost stepped on the body of a dead soldier, a Confederate with the top of his head blown off. The line parted to avoid the corpse, and Thad saw the wind lift the tawny beard, as if a hand were stroking it. He quickly looked away, sick to his stomach.

The line, broken into moving fragments by the terrain, moved as fast as possible—all of a sudden ahead of them they saw the battle line! Their unit had crested a small ridge, and Lieutenant Winslow ordered, "Get into the line, boys!" They ran down the hill to fall in place beside the men who were rapidly loading and firing into the blue line of soldiers running across an open field. Thad heard a deafening roar from some guns over to his left, and then he saw Dooley lift his rifle and fire. As soon as he had shot, he rolled over and began to reload. He caught Thad's eye and shouted, "Got one of 'em, Thad!"

Thad lay still, and then he thought of the chaplain's words: *You have comrades who are depending on you.* He jerked around and saw that many of the shapes in the line were lying motionless in peculiar positions—some with one arm lifted high as if in prayer, and others flat on their backs with vacant eyes staring up at the smoke-scored sky. Then he looked at his comrades who were desperately loading and firing as fast as they could—and he knew he had no choice.

With a sob he threw his musket up and fired at the first Yankee in his view. He tried to avoid the sight, but saw the figure flailing wildly, then tumble down and lie still. Tears blinded Thad's eyes, but he forced himself to reload his musket and fire. Then it seemed as if he became not a man but a member. He was no longer Thad Novak—he was just a part of Company A, Third Virginia Infantry. He was working at a task, like a carpenter who had made many boxes and was now making another one.

Some of the battle rage that infested the others touched him, and he looked around, noticing that there was an absence of heroic poses. He had seen pictures of armies going into battle, all in perfectly formed lines, but there was none to be seen in this battle. The men were bending and surging in their haste, and the steel ramrods clanked and clanged incessantly as the men pounded them into the hot rifle barrels. The rifles, once loaded, were jerked to the shoulder and fired into the smoke without apparent aim, or at one of the blurred and shifting forms that appeared through the battle haze.

Here and there, men in the line with him dropped like bundles. Milton Calhoun had been killed almost at once, and his body lay stretched out in the position of a tired man resting.

Farther down the line Peyton Law, the schoolteacher, had his knee joint shattered by a ball. He dropped his rifle and gripped a small tree with both arms, clinging to it desperately and crying for help.

Finally a yell went along the line, and Dooley screamed, "They're runnin'! The Yanks are runnin' away."

Thad looked up and saw the blue line falling back, and he took a deep breath. The guns stopped abruptly as a strange silence fell over the field. Now for the first time he could hear the crying of the wounded. There was a rush to help those who were still alive, and before long, two ambulance wagons lumbered to the line and Thad helped to get the injured into them. He assisted Peyton in tying a sash around his leg to stem the flow of blood, while the man kept asking, "Do you think they'll cut it off? Do you?"

As soon as the stricken man was taken away, Dooley remarked, "He'll lose that leg, Thad. Knee was plumb busted." They both discovered they were extremely thirsty, and drank what little water they had in their canteens. "We crossed a creek back aways," Dooley said. "Let's see if the officers will let us git some water."

They approached Lieutenant Beauchamp for permission. At first he hesitated, then nodded. "You better go in small groups, Young. The Yankees might come at us again, and we're pretty thin."

They called to Lew Avery and Les Satterfield, and the four took as many canteens as they could carry. The creek was small, but seemed clear, and they filled the canteens and started back. "That was almost too much of a good thing," Lew remarked. He was a dark-faced man with the expressionless features of a professional gambler. "I hope they don't try it again until we get more of our guns in place."

Even as he spoke there was a clatter of rifle fire, and Les cried out, "They're startin' in again!" and the four raced back just in time to see that the regiment was falling back.

"We can't hold this position," Major Lee shouted to Mark and Beauchamp. "Pull back into that gully; then you'll have to hold them back. Cover the retreat. Hold as long as you can!"

He galloped off, and both officers began running down the

line, shouting, "We'll retreat to that gully. Keep firing as you go!"

It was about three hundred yards to the gully. The rest of the brigade went first, followed by Company A. As they all dropped into place, they quickly formed a thin battle line. "Gosh, there's a million of them bluebellies!" someone shouted, and it didn't seem far wrong to Thad and the others either.

Mark Winslow knew they were in a vulnerable position, and voiced his concern to Beau. "We're going to get slaughtered here. There're too few of us."

"Orders are to stay," Beau replied. He wiped his face and asked, "You got any ideas?"

Mark had been surveying the ground behind them, and his eyes focused on a series of steep ridges to their rear. "Look, Beau—see that gap in those ridges? If we can get behind them, the Yanks will have to break up their lines. They can't climb those ridges, so they'll have to come at us right through that gap."

Beauchamp immediately saw the advantage and cried out, "You're a young Napoleon, Mark! Let's try it!"

It took little urging to get the company to fall back, for they saw a massive line of bluecoats starting across the field toward them. The Virginians raced through the thin line of trees, dashed across the gap, which was no more than thirty feet wide, and regrouped behind a series of low mounds about five hundred yards from the gap.

"We got to stop 'em, boys!" Mark called out.

"Lieutenant," Beauchamp said, "I think we better let our best shots do the shooting. The rest can load."

Mark stared at him, then at the open space between their position and the gap. "That's a long shot, Beau. But we've got enough sharpshooters to do the job. Sharp and Young for sure . . ." He named off several more of the best shots.

"You left out Novak," Beau said with a wry grin. "I know for sure he can shoot! Let's position them quickly—I think the Yankees are about ready to charge."

Thad and the others were named, and Mark shouted out, "The rest of you load up. Don't take a shot yourself. Sharpshooters, drop the Yanks as soon as they come through that gap!" The men broke up around the twelve others chosen, with rifles loaded and ready.

"HERE THEY COME!" somebody roared, and instantly Thad saw the gap turn blue as the enemy crowded through. He lifted his Whitworth and knew he could not miss that thick mass. At the same instant he heard the other sharpshooters firing. A hand snatched at his rifle and replaced it with a loaded musket. He threw it up, fired, and at once another musket was thrust into his hands. There was no letup. The muskets down the small line were exploding like the gatling gun he'd heard about, and with every shot a blue-clad soldier fell.

Thad didn't know how long it went on, but he fired what seemed like hundreds of times, never having to wait for a loaded gun. The gap was filled at least four deep with the dead, and as soon as others staggered and crawled over the bodies of their dead and dying, they were shot down at once.

Finally someone shouted, "That's retreat! Hear it?" Far off over the ridge, a bugle was sounding.

"They're quitting!" Mark cried.

A ragged cheer went up, and everyone pounded Thad's back for the tremendous job he'd done. With jubilation the group returned to the main body, where Major Lee greeted them. He jumped lightly off his horse and said to the officers, "My congratulations to you both! I never saw a finer holding action!"

"Well, we had some pretty fair shooters, Major," Mark grinned.

"Yes, I've seen *one* of them shoot before, I believe." Lee smiled at Beau, who returned it, then came over to where Thad was standing. "You did well, soldier. I wish we had 100,000 soldiers just like you."

They pulled back that day, and the next morning were in full retreat. "Going to Richmond," Tom told the squad. "Officers say we'll be waitin' there with our whole army when McClellan arrives."

"Whooee!" Dooley yelped. "Won't we give them Yankees particular fits!"

McClellan moved his forces north of the Chickahominy in a position to make contact with McDowell's I Corps, which Lincoln had promised to send. The remaining Federal forces were deployed south of the Chickahominy, facing Richmond—only five miles away. In the evening the Yankee soldiers could hear bells from the churches and see their spires through the haze.

But the total might of the Federal Army was now poised to strike at the very heart of the Confederacy. McClellan with his vast army of over 100,000 men was ready to overrun the thin ranks of the Army of Northern Virginia. One determined push, and the whole thing would be over. The North would have crushed the rebellion.

CHAPTER SEVENTEEN

THE SEVEN DAYS

★ ★ ★ ★

"How would you ladies like to go to a camp meeting tonight?"
Sky's words evoked a different reaction from each of the three women sitting at tables wrapping bandages for the hospital. Rebekah exclaimed, "Oh yes, that would be refreshing, Sky!"

Pet asked cautiously, "Who is the preacher, Papa?" She was somewhat choosy about preachers, and did not want to commit herself to a boring sermon.

Belle responded, "Oh, I'm too tired to go tonight."

Sky's eyes twinkled. "Well, you girls stay at home then. Rebekah, put on your best dress so the soldiers will have something nice to look at."

"The soldiers?" Belle asked quickly.

"Why, yes." Sky winked at Rebekah, keeping his face turned. "Chaplain Boone is having a real good meeting with our men, so I thought we'd go visit. Mark and Tom will be there—and Vance and Thad, of course. I'll tell them you were too tired, Belle."

"Papa! You are *awful!*" Belle jumped up and ran to her father, throwing her arms around his neck. Whirling around, she cried, "I must get something beautiful to wear! We can't go looking like a bunch of beggars!"

She flew out and Sky asked, "You think you might like to go, Pet?"

"Oh . . . I guess so," she replied casually. "I always liked Brother Boone's preaching." She got up and followed Belle, adding, "I'll make a cake for the boys."

Sky laughed at them, then sobered. He sat down beside Rebekah and watched as she continued her task. Finally, he broached the subject neither one wanted to face. "It may be our last chance to visit the boys. I talked to Colonel Chestnut today. General Lee thinks that McClellan is ready to move."

"Will they get to Richmond, Sky?"

He put his chin in his hands and thought about the situation. "Well," he began, "Chestnut said that on June twelfth, Jeb Stuart went on a scouting mission. He was just supposed to feel McClellan out, but you know how Jeb is—he rode around the whole Yankee Army! Chestnut said the generals got their heads together, and Lee decided to send most of the army against the force that's north of the Chickahominy." He paused, awe in his voice. "That Robert E. Lee is a natural-born gambler! He's leaving Richmond with not much more than a thin screen, but he knows there's no other way to stop the big force that McClellan's got right at our front gate."

"What if the Yankees attack while most of the army is gone?"

"Well, that might be the end of it all," Sky shrugged. "Chestnut told me that Lee sent Stonewall Jackson to the Shenandoah Valley to make trouble so that the reinforcements the North is sending to McClellan will have to go there, take them off our back."

Rebekah put the bandage down and rose to stretch her aching back. "Guess it's a good time for us to go to church. What time will we leave?"

"Soon as we can get Belle dressed and Pet's cake made."

They left at three o'clock, but the short distance took them longer than usual. The roads were crowded with troops and guns—all headed for the front. Sky had to pull over and wait several times. It didn't matter, though; they were impressed with the fortifications that had been built. When the family did get to the army camp, they found a madhouse of activity. Sky asked a harried sergeant where the camp meeting would be held, and soon they were on their way. They arrived in time to share their supper and Pet's cake with Mark and Tom. Belle captured Vance as soon as he appeared and the two vanished.

"I'll be surprised if they hear much of Boone's preaching," Sky whispered to Rebekah. Then he said, "Look, there's Thad."

Pet had been watching the soldiers file in, most of them going at once to stand before a wagon that was used as a platform for the preacher. She saw Thad look toward her, nod, and look away. She knew he was too shy to come to her, so she said, "Papa, may I go down front where I can hear better?"

"Of course," Sky replied soberly. "I've been real concerned about this hearing problem of yours. Go right on down."

She flushed, knowing that he was teasing her. Without delay she made her way through the crowd seated on the ground. Since there were no civilians at the meeting, the sight of the young woman drew the eyes of most of the men. "Hello, Thad," she said breathlessly when she reached his side.

He turned at once, and was embarrassed by the attention she had drawn. "Why, hello, Miss Patience." Every ear immediately around them was tuned to their words, and he asked, "Come to hear the preaching?"

She nodded and would have spoken, but a corporal had stepped up on the wagon and begun singing a hymn. The two seated themselves quickly. The men sang lustily, so there was no opportunity for Pet and Thad to talk. After many songs, Chaplain Boone got up on the wagon and began his sermon. He was preaching to men who might not outlive the week, as they well knew, so he preached a simple message, speaking of the need of forgiveness, and the love of Jesus. He spoke mostly about Jesus as the Lamb of God, and to Thad it was all new. He did not know the Bible, so when Boone began to tell them how every Jewish family on Passover would take a lamb and kill it, he listened intently.

"For hundreds of years," Boone said, "thousands of lambs died. They were offered as a sacrifice for sin, representative of the perfect Lamb to come. The lambs in themselves could not forgive sin, for the Bible says, 'It is impossible that the blood of bulls and goats could take away sin.' Those innocent lambs were a *picture* of what was to come, and one day it all came true." He opened his Bible and lifted his voice like a trumpet: "The next day John seeth Jesus coming unto him, and saith, 'Behold the Lamb of God which taketh away the sin of the world.' "

The words pierced Thad like a sword, and he was aware that many of his fellow soldiers were also touched. He felt Pet's hand grasp his arm, holding it tightly. As the preacher went on, telling of how the blood of Jesus did what the blood of animals could not, Thad felt as he had at the camp meeting in earlier days when Boone had preached on "Ye must be born again."

The sermon finally ended, and many soldiers were on their knees, some of them weeping and crying to God. He saw Les Satterfield, Dooley's rawboned cousin, weeping. At the same moment he noticed that Chaplain Boone had spotted Les. The chaplain came down and put his arm around the boy and began to pray. Thad watched as Les finally lifted his tear-stained face and nodded.

"He's been saved, Thad!" Pet whispered, and waited for him to speak, but he sat there silently. Then she whispered, "Wouldn't you like to be saved, too?"

Thad was shaking physically, his legs weak and his hands trembling, but that was nothing to compare with what was going on in his heart. He had always thought of God as someone far off, but he was now totally aware that God was in the meeting— a sudden consciousness that in Thad's own heart there was a Presence. He could not put it into words, but as he sat there, he suddenly felt terribly unclean. Something in him knew that he needed forgiveness.

But he could not yield.

Despite the desire to give in, to throw himself on his knees and beg for mercy, he could not force himself to do it. Instead, he tore his arm from Pet's grasp, wheeled, and shoved his way through the crowd, his face set and his eyes burning.

Chaplain Boone had been watching the two, and now he came to stand beside the girl. "Don't give up hope," he encouraged quietly. "That young fellow is running from God—but your prayers will bring him to the cross."

Pet's face was wet with tears, and she could not speak; but in the days to follow, she would recall the preacher's words again and again. Slowly she went back to her family, her heart heavy and filled with dread, for she knew that Thad had rejected the thing he needed most in all the world. All she could do that night and for weeks thereafter was to pray, "Oh, God, keep him safe—until he finds you!"

————

On June 26 Lee's troops struck the V Corps at Mechanicsville—the first battle in what became known as The Seven Days' Battles. The Third Virginia was in the forefront of that battle, and in the following days, Thad and the others in Company A grew so weary they could not distinguish one battle from another. Gaines' Mill, Savage's Station, Glendale—they followed one after another, but at some point McClellan's nerve failed and he began to call for a retreat. The final battle was an elevation called Malvern Hill, and it was in this final struggle that General Robert E. Lee made one of his rare tactical errors—and Thad Novak paid part of the price for it.

It all began when McClellan and his Union Army stopped their retreat long enough to fight the Confederate force, and he could not have picked a better spot. His defensive position was ideal. He had the military advantage of height. Swampy ground below forced Lee's men to concentrate in a single area for attack. There were siege cannon behind McClellan and river gunboats on the James to back him up. And he had an army that had been beaten back but not defeated.

Captain Wickham found his company flat on their backs, gasping for breath. They had been rushed from another part of the battlefield at a dead run. Wickham paused before he spoke, for he thought this last move was a mistake. He could see what the generals could not see from their position in the rear—a charge up the hill would be suicide for the men. He had argued fiercely with Colonel Barton, but Barton was in the grip of such a mindless fear that he could only follow orders blindly.

It was four o'clock, Wickham saw by a glance at his watch, and the attack was set for five. He forced himself to smile, and walked quickly toward the exhausted troops, saying, "Get your breath, men. We're going to shove Little Mac all the way back to Washington!"

Beau had been standing to one side, studying the terrain with a jaundiced eye. He came over to say quietly to the captain, "We'll never get up that hill, Vance."

"It's orders, Beau," Wickham replied. "We'll have to do it." He nodded toward the right of the slow rise of hill and said, "If we could swing right instead of charging straight up that hill, I think we could use those trees for a shield—maybe come at them on the flank."

"You don't know what's behind those trees," Beau said. "I'll take a look."

"No, you stay with the men," Wickham ordered instantly. "But we'll send a scouting party." He thought about it, then said, "Send Sergeant Henry, Mellon and Novak. Tell them that all I want to know is what's on the other side of those trees."

Beau nodded and hurried to find Will Henry, telling him briefly what the captain wanted. He looked at Henry's pale face and thought, *Wish I didn't have to order him out.* Will and he had something in common—both of them had loved Belle Winslow. The lieutenant thought back over the years and realized that Henry had suffered quietly, never hoping for success with Belle, and Beau felt a quick pang of remorse at the way he'd always had a mild contempt for the little fellow. He impulsively put his hand on the thin shoulder and said with a smile, "Now you be careful, Will. Don't go getting yourself killed, you hear me?"

Will Henry looked up with surprise, for Beau Beauchamp had never shown any concern or respect for him. "Why, I'll do that, Lieutenant. You just wait till we get back before you start the ball."

Will left and called out, "Mellon, you and Novak come with me."

"What's up?" Mellon demanded. He had turned out to be a good enough soldier, tough as boot leather, though he was lazy and shiftless in many ways. He had never gotten over his hatred for Thad, and it showed as he glared at him.

"Got to find out what's over behind those trees," Henry told him. "Let's go—we don't have much time." They left immediately, and soon were encased in the thick growth of oak and pine that lined the bottom of the slope and meandered up the hill in a desultory fashion. As the hill grew steeper, the men began to pant for breath, once stopping for a breather. "Shouldn't be too far to the edge of those woods!" Henry gasped. "Be careful now—the Yankees ought to be right where the woods leave off."

They cautiously pushed their way through the scrubby growth, and found themselves at the edge of a clearing. "We'll go as far as that thicket," Henry whispered. "We'll be able to get a good view of the whole back side of the hill from there."

They ran at a half crouch across the clearing. *Just a little farther,* thought Thad. *We're almost*—"Hold up!" a voice split the air. Thad whirled to see a troop of mounted men emerge from the trees to his left.

"Cavalry!" Will Henry shouted. "Run for it!"

Thad turned and sprinted for the woods they had just left, but a shot rang out and he saw Will go down. Out of the corner of his eye he saw Mellon make it back to cover, bullets kicking up dust at every step. Thad threw his rifle down and stooped to help the sergeant up, but Novak could see it was too late. The bullet had struck Will in the throat. When he opened his mouth to speak, he said in a throaty gurgle: "Tell—Belle—always loved—her—!" and then he slumped and his head fell back.

Thad leaped to his feet and made two steps toward cover, but a massive form blocked his way, and a blow struck his head. He fell to the ground, losing consciousness. He came to some time later and looked up to see blue uniforms all around him, and he heard someone say, "He's coming around."

Thad felt arms pulling him to his feet, and an officer's face swam into focus. It was a thin face, and the eyes were the bluest he'd ever seen. "Well, Reb, you're a lucky man. Usually when I hit a man in the head with my saber, he doesn't live to tell about it."

"Guess he caught the flat of it, Captain," a short lieutenant said. "He's got a knot big as a goose egg!"

Thad's head was clearing, and he looked around to see the body of Will Henry over to one side. Twenty or so cavalrymen were waiting on their mounts to his right, and the two officers were staring at him curiously. The captain began peppering him for information. "You men were scouts, I take it. What's your name and unit?"

Thad had no idea what he was or was not allowed to tell, so he answered, "Thad Novak, Third Virginia Infantry, Company A."

The lieutenant said, "That's part of Longstreet's division, isn't it, Captain Winslow?"

"I don't think so, Madison." He looked at Thad and asked, "You're from which corps, soldier?"

Thad stared at the officer, for he had caught the name *Winslow*. However, he shook his head, saying, "We been shifted so much, I don't rightly know, sir."

Lieutenant Madison demanded, "What units are down there? We know they're getting ready for a charge."

Thad shook his head stubbornly. Captain Winslow turned. "Masters, bring up that extra mount." A corporal rode forward leading a horse, and Winslow asked, "Can you ride?" At Thad's nod, the captain barked, "Get mounted, then."

"We're taking him with us, Captain?" the lieutenant asked in amazement.

"We can't spare a man to take him back, we can't turn him loose, and we've got to scout the rebs," Winslow countered. "Nothing else to do. Besides, I want to ask him a few questions when we get back."

Thad mounted the horse, and Winslow ordered, "Forward." Then he began to ask Thad about things other than military. "How is the spirit of your folks? You said your name is Novak. Where're you from?"

As they walked the horses slowly down a dim trail, the captain's eyes were constantly searching the terrain. He paused once to set out flankers, but he listened carefully to Thad's reply.

Thad had one idea—escape, but he knew that such a thing was impossible unless something changed. At his back were twenty cavalrymen with carbines, so he waited for a break. He spoke freely to the captain, for he saw no harm in talking about conditions as long as he did not reveal any information about the army.

He noted that the troop was winding around a set of low hills, and he knew that if they continued, they would soon make contact with Lee's troops lying ready to make the charge. He hoped they would run into them; maybe in the action he could slip away.

He saw that the captain was about to end their conversation, and he wanted to keep him occupied, so he asked quickly, "Are you any kin to Mr. Davis Winslow and his grandpa?"

As he had known it would, the question brought the captain's head around sharply, his bright blue eyes fixed on him. "How do you know *them*?" Winslow demanded. He listened intently as Thad explained, as slowly as he could, how that he worked for some people named Winslow, and the two he'd mentioned had come for a visit.

Captain Winslow laughed incredulously and said in a strange tone, "Well, I'll never doubt coincidence again, Lieutenant. Here we capture a reb and out of the whole rebel army, we get the one who knows my family."

"Hard to believe, Captain," Lieutenant Madison agreed. "Are the Winslows this fellow works for your kin, sure enough?"

"Oh, yes. Grandfather digs them up—a real buff on our family tree." He began to question Thad about his relations on the rebel side, and in doing so he did exactly what Thad hoped—he led the troop around the bend of the woods and right into the Confederate battle line!

"Captain!" Lieutenant Madison yelled, "there they are—and they've spotted us!"

"Make for that gap in the trees!" Captain Winslow yelled, and Thad was caught up in the sudden charge. There were troopers to the rear and on each side, but he began to guide his horse to the outside of the mass. Rifle fire crackled and he heard the shrill rebel cry. A trooper to his left fell from his horse, and then another.

Winslow saw at a glance they'd be cut to pieces if they didn't change direction, so he shouted, "This way—right through the middle, men!" He yanked his revolver from his belt and led the troop right into the center of the rebel line. And as they dashed through, Thad spotted his own company just to his right!

He jerked at the horse's bit, but the animal was wild with fear and began running away, caught up in the mass of horses that plowed through the thin line of soldiers. The cavalrymen were hit hard, but they left a trail of Confederate dead as the Union cleared the enemy line.

In the flurry of activity, Thad looked to his right—there was Lieutenant Beau Beauchamp staring at him! He tried again to pull his horse to the outside, but he couldn't budge against the mass of horseflesh around him. To slip to the ground would mean being trampled to death by the troop behind.

In the end, the charge carried the cavalry troop clear of the Confederates, and Winslow ordered sharply, "Take the prisoner to the rear of our lines, Lieutenant. I'll get our information to headquarters. They're forming for another charge, and the colonel needs to know."

He spurred off at a dead run, and the lieutenant commanded, "Private Johnson, take this prisoner to the rear. He's the only reb we've got now, but we'll have plenty more after they try to take that hill!"

His words were prophetic. Brigade after brigade of riflemen came up that hill into a blanket of shrapnel, grape and canister. Those who survived the Union guns were cut down by musket fire from the 14th New York, which received the brunt of the rebel charge.

A few isolated rebels survived the charge, but when they were brought to where Thad was held under strong guard, only one of them seemed to have any knowledge of the Third Virginia. "I think they got cut up bad," he said.

The Union Army finally moved out, and Thad's mind was filled with fear as he recalled all the stories he had heard of the prison camps in the North. When they stopped, he and the other prisoners were put in an old barn, and all night long he kept thinking of the company, wondering if Dooley were alive—and wishing that he'd been with them when they charged up that hill!

CHAPTER EIGHTEEN

A MATTER OF BLOOD

★ ★ ★ ★

The day after the battle of Malvern Hill, General Lee withdrew to Richmond, and Thad was taken with the other prisoners to Harrison's Landing by McClellan's army. As the prisoners were herded onto a gunboat to be taken to prison, Thad heard the lieutenant in charge argue with the sergeant, who claimed they had beat the rebels.

"Beat 'em? No! We're running for Washington just like the Army of the Potomac always does—like a yellow cur with its tail between its legs."

"But—we must of kilt half the rebs in Lee's army yesterday!"

"I heard the general say that we lost 15,000 and the rebs lost 20,000—but the thing is—now we got to do it all over again." The lieutenant cursed and added, "We got the right *cause*, but the rebs got the right generals. If we had *one* man like Jackson or Lee, we'd be in Richmond right now—but we don't, so now we'll go back and McClellan will build up another army for the rebs to bluff again!" He saw that Thad was listening and said, "Don't get proud, Reb. You'll probably be rotting in a prison for the rest of the war."

As they made their journey north, Thad heard more about the terrible conditions in the prisons. A middle-aged private named Jake Hill had been a prisoner in Elmira, and he gloomily shared his memories with Thad and the others.

"Nothin' but swill to eat,—and sometimes not even that," he complained as they huddled in the tiny room on the gunboat, suffering from the suffocating heat. "And talk about vermin— you ain't seen nothin' yet! It got so bad they had to make a daily haul to get the bodies of those of us that died in the night."

"They've fed us pretty well so far," Thad mentioned.

"Ah, these is Regulars," Hill stated. "The prisons are run by civilians or else them that just signed up for prison duty service to git out of fightin'. Scum of the earth, most of 'em!"

They were on the gunboat for three days, learning on the way that they were headed for The Old Capitol, a Yankee prison in Washington. From the gunboat they were transferred to a train and packed like sardines into boxcars. They were forced to stand up, but it was a short ride, lasting only three hours. Falling out, and put in a rough marching order, they shuffled their way down the streets of Washington. Their ragged appearance was a spectacle many citizens stopped to peer at as the unkempt group made its way through the burning July sun.

Someone said, "There it is," and Thad looked up at a tall, faded red hulk of a building, rambling in several directions, with a series of connected structures. He discovered later that after the British burned Washington, the prison had housed Congress, and afterward it had become a boardinghouse. As they marched into the main gate, a handsomely arched entranceway, he saw many boarded-over openings, and a line of barred windows with gray faces staring out and clenched hands against the barriers.

The prisoners were shoved inside one of the largest buildings, and Jake Hill commented, "This sure weren't built for no prison, but it beats Elmira all hollow!"

They filed down a short passage, then up a stairway to a dark hall. The warm, fetid air struck them with smothering force, and the sheer size of the place was staggering. Everywhere there were prisoners crowded into the frame of crumbling brick, broken walls, and worm-eaten wood. Rough boarding had been nailed across many doors and windows; from other creaking doors hung large piles of rancid clothing, mingled with an all-pervading odor of bad drainage. The building was incredibly dirty—spider webs in the corners, unswept floors and accumulated piles of filthy cloth, paper and other debris.

As they entered a large room, the armed guards yelled, "Hold up!" They stopped abruptly, nearly fifty men, and waited. Finally a door opened and a short, thick-bodied man emerged and stood before them. He had the red face of a drinker, and small piglike eyes set deep in his skull.

"I am Superintendent Josiah Dickens," he announced in a hoarse voice. "I want to give you some good advice on your first day at Capitol." He paused and let his eyes run over the prisoners, then began to pace back and forth as he spoke. He had very short legs, and rolled from side to side, in a bearlike manner. He had large yellowish teeth, and bared them in what he evidently thought was a smile as he continued. "You will make life easy for yourself if you keep *The Rules*." When he said *The Rules*, it was as if he had changed to another language. They were soon to learn that Superintendent Dickens thought *The Rules* were handed down by Moses along with the Ten Commandments.

"There are some among you who, no doubt, are troublemakers, but we have ways of dealing with those. I am a fair man"—he bared his yellowish fangs again—"and so long as you keep *The Rules*, you will find me most understanding." Then he jerked to his full, though stunted, size and aimed a blunt forefinger at them, his voice rising to an incredible roar. *"But if you break one of The Rules, you will wish you had died on the battlefield!"*

For the next thirty minutes, he continued pacing back and forth, threatening them, and at the same time yelling that he was a fair man. Having finished, he abruptly wheeled and left the room.

"All right, down the hall," the guard commanded, and they filed down a narrow hall until the guard stopped, consulted a piece of paper, and called out four names: "Adkins, Simms, Alberts, and Rosner—number 12." Another guard opened a door and the four men entered; then the door was shut and bolted. The rest moved slowly down the hall, and the guard read out: "Peterson, Novak, Willis, Brown—number 18!" Thad followed the other three into the room, and the door slammed behind them.

The room was about twelve feet square, with four double-

decked bunks on either side. In the center of the outer wall was
a barred window with no glass. The furniture was sparse—a
battered table and three chairs in the center of the room; another
smaller table braced on the outer wall with a small mirror fastened to the wall just above the table.

Two men were lying on their bunks, and one of them got up,
saying, "Welcome to The Capitol, boys. I'm Sam Little." He was
a tall, thin man with a cadaverous face and not a tooth in his
head. "That's Beans Melton—but he's ailin' a mite, so just excuse
him."

The newcomers introduced themselves: Roger Willis, a
thirty-two-year-old blacksmith from Tennessee; L. C. Brown, a
young farmer from the same state; Giles Peterson, a forty-five-
year-old musician from Helena, Arkansas; and Thad.

Peterson asked immediately, "What time is dinner served at
this hotel? I'm plumb hollow!"

"Sorry, you missed the main meal," Sam Little grinned. "That
comes near noon. They'll be around with something 'bout dark."
He waved his hand around the room. "Take your pick, gents.
You git all the livestock that comes with any bunk you chooses."

Thad was exhausted and flopped on one of the bunks. He
closed his eyes and fell asleep instantly. He woke up some time
later when the door slammed and somebody called, "Novak—
suppertime." He rolled out of the bunk and saw that a large black
pot had been placed in the middle of the table. Sam Little grinned
at him. "Here's your plate and hardware. Come and git it!"

A deep tin plate and a pewter spoon had been issued to each
man, and Little picked up the pot and poured some of the contents into each of the bowls that were on the table. Thad picked
up one of them, and Little said, "Break yourself off a piece of
that loaf, you fellers." They all got their food and three of them
sat down in the chairs while the others sat on their bunks. Thad
tasted the stew, which was mostly rice with a few pieces of
strong-tasting fish. It was not as bad as he had expected, and he
wolfed it down, ate the bread, then took a long drink out of the
single bucket, using the dipper attached to the pail with a cotton
cord.

"I've had worse," Giles Peterson stated, licking his spoon.
"When I was with the Stonewall Brigade we would have thought

we were eating at the Planter's House in New Orleans if we'd
gotten grub this good."

"Well, this is a little better than the usual," Little replied. "But
on the whole, I guess we git better than the fellers at Fort Del-
aware. Friend of mine was there. Said they had to eat rats."

After the meal the men sat around while Little told them
about the prison.

"How about the escape?" L. C. Brown asked.

Small shook his head vigorously. "You might get through the
pearly gates, boy, but you ain't gonna get through the gates of
The Capitol. Why, there's guards here that'll shoot you on a
whim! It's Superintendent Dickens' boast that no man ever got
away from him. That's right enough in a way—but he don't tell
'bout them that die in here—and the twenty-two that's been shot
down tryin' to run off."

"Guess we're here for the rest of the war," Willis grumbled.
He looked down at his huge hands. "Sure hope it don't last long.
I ain't never been locked up before."

Thad felt the same way, but Little said gloomily, "Since
McClellan got run out of the Peninsula, I don't figure it's gonna
be over no time soon." He took a plug out of his pocket, bit off
a small bite, then waved his hand at the sick man in the bunk.
"They's a lot of men gonna die like Beans there." He saw them
look quickly at the still figure, and added, "Oh, he can't hear me
none. He give up two days ago. Won't eat nothin', won't even
answer. I seen it happen before. Man jest can't take this place
and plain gives up. He'll go pretty soon—maybe tonight, but in
a week for sure."

"Isn't there any hospital?" Peterson asked.

"Oh, they's a hospital, all right, but they don't take men who's
got what Beans has," Little answered. "Guess there ain't nothin'
they could do for him, anyways."

"Men don't die from just wanting to," Peterson argued.

"Oh yes, they do!" Little countered, nodding emphatically.
"You'll see it enough in here. Thing to do is don't think 'bout
tomorrow. That's what pulls a feller down. If you git to thinkin'
'bout bein' here for five years, why it ain't cheerful. Thing to do
is jest think 'bout *right now*."

Thad thought about Little's words a great deal the next two

days. The food was the same at every meal, and he grew tired of it, and knew that he would despise it in a week. They were taken out once a day to the exercise yard—which was nothing but a narrow alley and packed with so many men they saw nothing but brick walls and a patch of sky.

Beans Melton was slowly dying, and there wasn't much anyone could do. He refused to eat, even if Thad and Willis did their best to get some of the stew down the man. He never spoke, though L.C. tried to talk to him about the Lord. "He shouldn't be let to die without gettin' ready to meet God," he said to Thad. For many hours Brown read to the dying man from the grubby New Testament L.C. carried, praying over him several times. Once Brown asked the others to pray, but only Willis responded. Peterson, Little, and Thad all stood back while the two men prayed.

On the third morning, after the new prisoners had arrived, when Thad woke up, Little said, "Poor old Beans—he was took last night. I guess he's at rest now." He informed the guards, and a pair of them came with a stretcher and removed the body. They left his things, and Little said, "He's got a wife and baby in Georgia. Guess we ort to write an' tell 'em 'bout Beans. I don't write so good myself."

"I'll do it," Thad offered when nobody else volunteered. He found it harder to write than he had thought, however. He tried to be as gentle as he could, and added a line that was not quite honest, but which he hoped would give some comfort. *He went easy, and he died hearing the Bible read and with men praying over him.*

After Melton's death the monotony of life bore down. For the next three weeks, nothing varied for Thad. He read the two books in the cell that had been worn thin by many readings until he knew them by heart. One was an American history book designed for children; the other, a British novel *The Royal Slave*, a strange book about a slave who had been captured in Africa but rose to become a part of English aristocracy. It was a foolish book, but he found himself reading it out of sheer boredom.

He also read Brown's New Testament all the way through during those weeks, then started over. Most of it was a mystery to him, especially the book called Revelation. He loved the Gospels, and spent many hours dwelling on the life and activities of Jesus.

But he was tormented by dreams of Belle Maison; and by the end of the third week, he was fearful that he would lose his mind. He was often seized with the impulse to throw himself at the guards when the prisoners were taken to the yard, although Thad knew that a bullet in the brain was the inevitable end of that.

He lost weight on the skimpy diet, and saw in the mirror that his eyes were larger in his thinning face, and held a glassy look he didn't recognize. Once Little said to him, "Thad, you've got to settle down. You ain't been here a month, and you're already crackin' up. If you don't jest block out thinkin' 'bout gittin' out, you'll be took out of here like poor ol' Beans."

But Thad found it impossible to think positively, and by the time August came he was worse. He had fits of trembling that he could not control, and once during the night he had suffered an uncontrollable crying spell. He was sure the others heard, but they said nothing about it. After that he prayed to die, for he could not endure the place any longer.

He was lying on his bunk staring at the ceiling when the door opened and the guard called out, "Novak! You got a visitor!"

He got up quickly and followed the guard, his mind in a whirl. None of them had had a visitor, and he couldn't think of anyone who would visit him. Following the guard down the narrow corridor, he was led down the stairs to another hallway, and finally the guard opened a door, saying, "In here."

He went through the door and saw two men sitting at a table. He did not recognize them at first, for the bright sunlight from the high windows slanted into his eyes. Then he heard one of them say, "Well, Thad, we meet again."

Both men got up, and Thad moved his head to avoid the sunlight. He stared at them blankly, unable to recognize either one. Then the older of the two stepped forward and Thad cried, "Why, Captain Winslow, it's you!"

"Yes—and you remember my grandson, Davis?"

"How are you, Thad?" Davis asked and extended his hand. "Have a seat here—and we've got some fresh coffee. You might like it."

Thad sat down, unable to speak. He took the cup of coffee in his trembling hands and drank it quickly. "That's real good, sir," he murmured.

The two looked at him, hardly recognizing the thin youth. He had been strong and brown with sleek muscles when they had seen him in Richmond, but prison had pared him down until there was an unnatural brightness in his eyes.

Captain Winslow said quietly, "Thad, I received a letter from my grandson—Captain Winslow of the Federal Army. He was quite surprised that you knew me, so he told me about your capture."

"I—I was real surprised when I heard the other officer call his name," Thad replied.

"Have some more coffee, Thad," the older Winslow urged, and he poured a stream of strong coffee into the cup, then considered the face of the young man. Finally he said, "You remember the first time I saw you, Thad?"

"Y-yes, sir."

"I thought I recognized you." The old man's eyes searched Thad's features and nodded, "And I wasn't wrong." He put his hand on Thad's arm and asked gently, "We *had* met before that, hadn't we, Thad?"

Thad dropped his eyes, and his voice cracked as he answered, "Yes, sir."

"Your mother was Elizabeth Winslow—before she married your father; isn't that right?"

Thad swallowed and nodded.

"Why are you hiding your past, Thad?" Davis broke in.

When the boy only shook his head, Captain Winslow said, "I found your mother when I was tracing the descendants of the Winslows, Thad. I remember coming to your house and talking to her several times. You must have been ten or eleven, but as soon as I saw you at Belle Maison, I recognized you." He pulled a sheet of paper from his pocket and put it on the table. "This is the Winslow family tree, Thad. Our line in this country began with Gilbert Winslow who came over on the *Mayflower*. Now, you see, he had a son named Matthew born in 1642—and he had a son named Miles. Miles Winslow had three sons. One of them was named Charles. He was my grandfather. One of the other sons was named Adam, and he's the ancestor of Mr. Sky Winslow. But the other son, whose name was William, moved to England—and he was your mother's great-great grandfather.

Her own father came to this country when your mother was only six, and then, of course, she married your father Stefan Novak. But you're just as much Winslow as I am, or Sky Winslow."

Thad looked up quickly. "I remembered everything you'd said about the Winslows. That's why I went south when my folks died. You'd talked about Belle Maison and about Mr. Sky Winslow being part Indian." He seemed embarrassed and then added, "I hated working in the factory, and I got into trouble."

"So you decided to go see your southern relatives?" Davis prompted when Thad ceased talking.

"I—I dunno, Mr. Winslow," Thad replied slowly. "I guess I was just runnin' away from trouble. But it sounded like what I'd always dreamed of. Being outside—and hunting and fishing. And I always liked to grow things. Used to grow tomatoes in the alley, in cans, you know. And when I got to Belle Maison and Mr. Sky gave me a job working on the farm, why it was all I wanted!"

"Why didn't you tell Sky you were kin to him?" the captain asked gently, though he thought he knew the reason.

"Oh, I couldn't do that!" Thad shook his head vigorously. "It wouldn't be right. He'd think I was trying to—to bum him out of something."

"I see." The old man shot a look at Davis, who nodded at him with approval. "Well, I admire you for that, Thad. And if you want to keep your secret, Davis and I won't violate your confidence." After a moment he cleared his throat and continued. "But that's not the only reason we've come." He paused, then said, "I've arranged for you to be exchanged, Thad."

"Exchanged?"

"Yes. You'll be traded to the rebels for one of our men they've captured."

Thad sat as if transfixed. He tried to understand what the old man was saying, but it did not seem possible. "I—I'll be leaving here?" he asked faintly.

"That's right, my boy," Captain Winslow replied. "And it's all arranged. I have some small influence with the War Department, and when I found that an exchange was planned for this date, I made up my mind that you'd be one of the men to go."

Thad stared at him and finally wiped his hand across his eyes in a hasty gesture. "I—I can't ever thank you enough, sir!"

"Nonsense!" the captain snorted. "We Winslows have to stick together—even if we happen to be on different sides in this war." He got to his feet and the other two rose with him. "You'll be leaving this afternoon, Thad. Give my best wishes to Mr. Sky Winslow."

"Thank you, sir!" Thad said, shaking his hand fervently. "Thank you!"

"Oh, now," the captain said, somewhat embarrassed at the boy's gratitude. "It's a matter of blood—and I'll put my faith in the Winslow line every time. You go all the way back to Gilbert Winslow, boy, and he came to this country with nothing but a sword and a dream." The two men turned to leave, and when Captain Whitfield Winslow reached the door, he turned and said almost reverently: "That's about what you've got—so be true to both!"

CHAPTER NINETEEN

BITTER HOMECOMING

★　★　★　★

Thad felt the envy of his fellow prisoners as he left the cell for the last time, and knew that he would have felt exactly the same way if he had been in their place. He shook hands with all of them and said, "Sure wish we were all going out together."

"Go kill all the Yankees, Thad!" Little grinned. "Then we'll all be outta The Capitol."

He left hurriedly, and was marched down the same street he'd come in on just over a month earlier. The August sun was hot, but the whole world seemed different—the sky bluer, the trees greener, and the fresh air like wine after the stale odors of the prison. There were twenty other men who were also being released. This time they rode in a regular coach instead of the cattle car. They still carried the stench of the prison, and the brakeman who came through the car took one look and held his nose, saying loudly, "Phew! I always knowed rebels stunk—but these is worse than skunks!"

A tall soldier sitting beside Thad glared at the man and snapped angrily, "You yellow-livered son of nobody! I'd like to get you in my sights—but you're the kind that lets other men do his fightin' for him, ain't you?"

The brakeman flushed angrily and started to curse the lot of them, but the guard, a stocky young man with a full set of black whiskers, shoved him from behind, saying, "Get on with your business, brakie." He watched the fuming man disappear at the far door, then grinned. "You rebs still got the starch, ain't you now? Musta been one of you that put a ball in my leg at Manassas."

The men saw that he was friendly, and the tall soldier replied, "Wasn't me, Yank. But I'll be glad to oblige if you git back in the fightin'—if you can stop Little Mac from backin' up after the whippin' we give you at the Peninsula."

The guard was not offended. He grinned broadly and nodded. "You shore put the skids under us, didn't you, Reb? But we'll get a bunch together and be back to call after a spell. Which general you boys work for?"

"I work for Stonewall Jackson."

The guard's eyes opened wide, and he shook his head. "By golly, you boys work for Stonewall Jackson?" He shook his head and asked plaintively, "I wonder what it feels like to work for a winning general?"

"I thought you boys all loved Pope and McClellan," Thad said.

"Well, Mac, he looks after us boys—but where's the success they promised us? We got good mounts, fine boots, clean drawers, and them fancy new Spencer guns—and we can't even whip a bunch of ragged beggars like you boys."

The guard talked about the war for most of the trip, and when they all disembarked, he said with a wave of his hand, "Reckon I'll be meetin' up with you again. Keep your heads down."

"You know," the tall soldier mused as they filed toward the crowd of Yankee prisoners that stood waiting behind the station under Confederate guards, "that's not a bad fellow, him. Didn't know they was any human bein's in that Yankee bunch."

"Guess they're pretty much like us," Thad answered.

They waited for a couple of hours until the two lieutenants in charge of the respective prisoners got their lists checked; then the Yankees headed for the train, and the Confederate lieutenant said, "All right, men, you're back in the Confederate Army." A ragged cheer went up, and some of the ex-prisoners did a little victory dance.

"Most of you are going back to Richmond," the officer told

them, "but I reckon you'll all get a little furlough before you go back to your units. You could use a little fattening up." He slapped his hand against his thigh, saying, "We've got a mess over yonder. Let's eat."

They were fed a good meal prepared by the ladies of the town, and given some clothes that, though worn, were better than the rags they had on. After the meal, they started for Richmond, marching down the road; but the pace was slowed to a few miles at a time because most of them were so weak.

The lieutenant left them in charge of a sergeant. "Do the best you can," Thad heard him say as he left. "They'll all be going home, I suppose, so if any of them are close to where they live, you might as well let them go."

The next day it became apparent to Thad that it would take days to get to Richmond, so he went to the sergeant with a proposition. "I'm in fair shape—why don't I go on ahead?"

"Suits me," the sergeant grunted. "I ain't got no papers to give you, but you can tell them to check with the lieutenant at the courthouse in Richmond. Like he says, most of you will probably be goin' home on furlough. Wisht I was!"

Thad headed out and caught a ride almost at once with a freighter who clipped along at a rapid speed. He even shared his food, and when the man turned off the main road to Richmond, Thad told him, "You just about saved my life."

"Got to take keer of you solger boys," the teamster said. He reached into his pocket and gave Thad a bill, adding, "Buy yoreself a steak when you git to Richmond!"

The next two days he spent walking, but he managed to catch a ride with a liquor salesman named Plunkett on his way to Richmond. He was a jovial man and tried the entire journey to press his samples on Thad. When that failed, he commented, "Well, boy, you're probably better off. Demon rum gets lots of folks in trouble."

They pulled into the city limits at three in the afternoon, and Thad got down and thanked the man, then headed for the courthouse where the sergeant told him he could check in. Richmond was as busy as ever and he had to step quickly to avoid the wagons of supplies that rolled down the streets.

The courthouse was crowded with a mass of soldiers and

civilians, and it took him until almost dark to find the right office. When he did, there was a line waiting, and by the time he got inside, he was dog-tired.

"Name?" the civilian clerk demanded when he told his errand.

"Thad Novak." He thought there was a sudden jerk in the clerk's neck when he heard Thad's name, and then the man said, "Wait here, Novak."

Thad slumped down in the chair wearily, and thought of going to Belle Maison. The clerk was gone a long time, and Thad had almost dozed off when the door opened and the man walked in followed by a captain and a corporal in uniform.

"That's him, Captain," the clerk said, indicating Thad with a wave.

"Your name is Thad Novak?"

"Why, yes, sir."

The captain gave him a careful look. "I'm placing you under arrest, Novak. Come with me."

Thad jumped up quickly, the drowsiness gone in a flash. "Arrest? What for?"

"Desertion to the enemy and treason," the captain replied.

Thad stared at him blankly. "Why—there's got to be some mistake."

"You're Private Thad Novak, Company A, Third Virginia Infantry?"

"Yes, but—!"

"I wouldn't say anything more, Novak. It might be held against you. Come along now."

Thad felt numb, as if he had been struck by a minie ball. He mechanically followed the officer, the corporal falling into step behind him. They went down the hall and out a side door, then took a path that led to a red brick building with barred windows. Thad followed the officer into a room at one end of the hall and stood there as the captain said, "Got a man for you, Laurence. Write him up as Thad Novak. Charged with desertion and treason."

The man at the desk, a thin, close-shaven individual, looked up quickly at Thad, then nodded. "Guess he'll be tried by court-martial."

"Yes, but you keep him close until the court can be convened."

He turned to go, and Thad said in a tight voice, "But—I've been in a Yankee war prison."

The captain gave him a sharp look, and shrugged. "You'll have your day in court, Novak—but you'll find out pretty soon that the witnesses are pretty strong."

"Witnesses? What witnesses?"

"Why, just about every man in your outfit—including the first lieutenant." He studied the pale face of the young man who stood before him and added, "They all saw you clear as day guiding a Yankee cavalry patrol against our troops at Malvern Hill."

Thad began to protest, but was cut off sharply. "You can save your story for the court, Novak—but unless you can convince about a hundred Confederate soldiers and at least two officers that it was somebody else riding with that Yank cavalry, you're going to be shot dead in a week!"

Then he left the room, and Thad was put in a cell with no windows and no other prisoners. After the door closed, he sat down shakily on the single cot and tried to think; but as the hours passed he could only lie with his face pressed against the rough blanket and try to keep from losing control. He had been afraid of getting killed on the battlefield, and he had been terrified at losing his mind at The Old Capitol. But nothing he had ever known was like the thought of being shot like a dog for a crime he had never committed, and he cried out in a choking sob, "Oh, God, don't let me die like this!"

But there was no answer—only silence and darkness.

PART FOUR

THE PRISONER

★ ★ ★

(August '62—September '62)

CHAPTER TWENTY

THE LAWYER

★ ★ ★ ★

"I—I can't believe it, Sky! There has to be a mistake!"

Rebekah stood in the middle of the kitchen, staring at the set face of her husband, knowing that he would not have brought such news unless he was certain. Her knees felt wobbly, and she dropped down on the stool beside the table. She had been peeling potatoes for supper when Sky burst in, crying, "Rebekah! Thad's come back—but he's in jail—arrested on charges of treason!"

He began to pace the floor, his eyes electric with anger as he related the story. "Mark called me outside during the meeting with the secretary of war. Mark had just come from the jail. Said Major Lee had informed him and thought I ought to be told."

"But how can Thad be a traitor?" Rebekah demanded.

Sky hesitated. "Well, we didn't let it get out, but the soldier that was with Thad and Will Henry on that last scout came back telling the story that Thad had gone over to the Yankees. Claimed that he'd bragged about how he'd desert and get back to 'the right side' as soon as he got the chance."

"They didn't *believe* him, did they, Sky?"

"Well, some did and some didn't. On the one hand, Thad was a marked man from the start—his being from the North.

There's been talk around the town about his being a Yankee at heart."

"Most of that started with Len Oliver!" Rebekah snapped, her eyes bright with anger. "He was mad because he lost our business!"

"Sure, and some of the officers knew that. But Thad was a paid substitute, and word's gotten around about how he joined up to get a bounty so he could buy Toby's freedom. Now, that may be admirable to us—but lots of the men didn't like it. Sounds too much like something an abolitionist might do." Sky stopped pacing and lifted his hands in a helpless gesture. "So the officers couldn't make up their mind who to believe. I think Colonel Barton wanted to drop it, but the fellow who was with Thad has been stirring up the men. He got a bunch of them to bring a petition, and Barton didn't have much choice but to declare Thad a deserter. He told me that it seemed likely Thad wouldn't ever come back anyway, so he had to make the gesture to preserve the morale in the regiment."

"But what does Thad say?"

"Don't know." Sky slapped his hands together angrily. "It's not a civil case, Rebekah, and you have to have permission from an officer of the court to see him. Mark said the court would probably be appointed today or tomorrow—then we can get permission."

"What about a lawyer?"

"Has to be someone in the army," Sky replied. "I know quite a few lawyers in uniform, but right now I can't think of one I'd trust with this trial. It's Thad's life!"

She rose and came to him, her eyes filled with fear. "What—what if he's found guilty?"

"Rebekah, we've had a desertion problem since this war began," Sky answered grimly. "Every general I know, including Stonewall Jackson, has had men shot—and that's for plain *desertion*. Thad's in even more trouble; he's charged with treason—giving aid to the enemy. If he's found guilty, they'd shoot him out of hand!"

"Sky—no!"

He took her in his arms, and they clung to each other silently. When he drew back, he said heavily, "You better tell the children—if they haven't heard already. They'll take it hard—especially Pet. I'm going to see Major Lee." He rushed out the door and she watched him leave, her heart heavy. The tragic news had left her shaken and weak; now she let the tears roll freely for a time. Finally she stepped outside and looked across the yard where Pet and Dan were sitting under the big elm shelling peas. "Children, come inside," she called. "I—I have some bad news for you."

———————

Sky spent two hours with the officers of the regiment, then talked with several of the men. The last man he spoke with was Dooley, who had a sorrowful light in his eyes, but could only confirm what Sky had already heard.

"I don't believe none of it!" Dooley protested, and spat on the ground emphatically. "That Studs Mellon—he lies so bad he hires somebody to call his dawgs—and he ain't got no more sense than last year's bird nest!"

Sky calmed him down and demanded, "Now, Dooley—did you see Thad riding at the head of that Yankee cavalry?"

"Well—yeah," he replied grudgingly. "'Course that don't mean he's joined up with 'em!"

"But it would have been unusual for a prisoner to ride at the head of a column, wouldn't it, Dooley? Most of the eyewitnesses say he kept right up with the officers in the lead—that he didn't make any attempt to escape."

Dooley struggled to find an answer. He had gone over it many times—and he had to admit that it *looked* as if Thad had led the Yankees to their position, but he ended by swearing, "I don't give a hoot what anybody says! Thad ain't no traitor, an' that's all there is to it!"

Winslow agreed, though he realized that the members of the court would make their decision based on the evidence—and even Thad's best friends could not change the hard facts. Sky rode slowly back to his office and sat staring at the wall most of the afternoon. Finally, he got up and walked down the hall and turned into a room where three men sat at desks. "Major Rogers—would you have a few minutes?"

"Of course." Rogers was a tall, bulky man with a sour face.

He followed Winslow to his office, and took the chair that was offered. He pulled out a cigar, lit it, and asked through the blue smoke, "What's up, Sky?"

"Dave, who's the meanest, smartest lawyer wearing a Confederate uniform?"

Dave Rogers had been the most successful lawyer in South Carolina before joining the army. He looked at Winslow, intrigued by the question. "I'm the smartest. Won't that do?"

"Not this time, Dave." He gave the lawyer a sharp glance and said, "I've got a friend in trouble who looks guilty. Every bit of evidence is against him—but I know he's innocent. I don't care what it takes, I want him off."

Rogers puffed at the cigar, regarded a perfect smoke ring slowly disintegrate, then said quietly, "Novak."

"You know about him?"

"Sure. It's all over town, Sky." He leaned back and studied Winslow. "He's a gone coon," he added. "I hear he's sort of a protegee of yours. But talk is that the court's not going to have much choice. Been lots of talk in town about his being a Yankee, but that doesn't count for much. What does matter is that about a hundred eyewitnesses, including his commanding officer, saw him leading an enemy patrol to the position of our troops."

"I haven't talked to him, Dave, but I know he can explain how that happened." He held up his hand, adding quickly, "Yes, I know that won't carry any weight in court. That's why I want someone who'll use every trick in the book to get the boy off. I don't care if the lawyer is the most ornery person who ever drew breath!"

Rogers stared at him, leaned back in his chair and slowly smoked the cigar. Finally he looked at the inch of gray ash as if it had the answer. "You better get Harrison Duke, or Harry, as some call him," he suggested, and a smile curled the edges of his lips. "He's almost as smart as I am—and mean enough to suit you."

"Who is he, Dave? I don't recognize the name."

"You would if you came from Chicago. He made a name for himself as a criminal lawyer. Never had a client hanged, which was quite a feat since he handled the really hard ones—those who were caught with a smoking gun in their hands standing over the body." Rogers shook his head in admiration, adding, "Got elected as prosecuting attorney, and had the same kind of record. They say when a defendant heard that he was up against Duke, why, he made his will and got religion!"

"I'll take him!" Winslow shot back.

"You can try," Rogers replied slowly. "He's so contrary that if you threw him in the river, he'd float upstream. Let me give you a note. He's working for the secretary of state right now." He rose and asked for a sheet of paper, then sat down and wrote a brief note. Handing it to Winslow, he commented, "You got one thing going for you, Sky. Harry Duke is a low cur—but he likes to tackle impossible cases. This one fits that category!"

———

Thad had been moved to the third floor of the jail, where he spent most of his waking hours looking out the window at the bustling crowds that passed like ants in and out of the courthouse. He knew it was the tenth of August, and *that* morning some official had made a speech or some sort of announcement from the steps of the courthouse that had resulted in a rousing cheer. He had asked the guard who brought his dinner what the speech was about. "Why, Jackson whipped up on Banks yesterday—that was the ninth, wasn't it? Anyway, he gave the Yankees a good thumpin'!"

Thad ate the food listlessly, more to have something to do than to satisfy his hunger. The despair he'd felt at The Old Capitol seemed to return, and after he finished he lay down and tried to sleep. He had drifted off into a half sleep when he heard voices, and then the door opened and a man wearing the uniform and insignia of a captain in the Confederate Army walked in.

Thad got up, for he had seen only one official in the two days he'd been there. A major had stopped by to tell him briefly that a court was being called, and as soon as it was appointed he would be allowed visitors. He was thinking of this when he asked, "Has the court been appointed yet, sir?"

"Yes."

The officer stood there staring at Thad, saying nothing. He

was, Thad saw, a youngish man in his late twenties. He was of average height and very slight of build. His face was narrow, but he had a broad forehead under thinning blond hair. The eyes were deep set and seemed to be greenish blue; it was difficult to tell under his heavy, drooping eyelids. His prominent nose overshadowed a wide mouth wearing a short mustache. His uniform was rumpled and he needed a shave.

He appeared to have finished his inspection and plumped down in the single chair, seeming to collapse with fatigue. He pulled a plug of tobacco from his pocket, bit off a plug, stored it in his left cheek, then said, "I'm your lawyer, Novak. Name's Harrison Duke."

Thad was confused. "My lawyer?"

"Yes."

"I—I thought I might talk to Mr. Winslow—ask him to find me a lawyer."

"He's the one who sent me." Duke looked at Thad with sleepy eyes and asked, "You do it, or not?"

"Sir?"

"Bygad, don't fool around with me, Novak!" The lawyer rose, went to the window and sent an amber stream out. He turned and commanded, "Now, you listen to me, son, just like I was your daddy. You are looking at your only chance in this world to live, so you answer me, and don't lie. Did you do it?"

Thad stared back at him, angered by the callous tone. He didn't like the captain and snapped back, "No, sir!"

Duke waited for Thad to protest his innocence, but when that didn't come, he went to the chair and sat down. "Two years ago I defended a man who was accused of slitting the throats of his parents. First thing I asked him, too, was 'Did you do it?' " Duke allowed a small smile to touch his wide lips, then added, "He looked me right in the eye and said, 'Yes, I did it—and I'd do it again if I got the chance!' "

Thad blinked at that, and Duke said, "I don't like folks who murder their parents, and I don't like traitors. But when I take a case, I'll spit in the devil's face to win. I'll let the preachers decide what's right and wrong; but in a court of law, the only thing I give a hang about is getting my client off."

"Did you get *him* off—the man who killed his parents?"

"Yes. He walked out of the courtroom a free man." Duke went

to the window and spat again. When he came back, there was an odd light in his eyes. "A year later he used the same knife to murder his only brother."

Thad was revolted by the story. "Didn't that—bother you, sir?"

"Bother me? Why, it was none of my business!" Duke leaned back. "I need to know if you're guilty so I can plan a way to gut the prosecuting officer. But most people don't want to confess—even to their lawyers." He waited again for Thad to protest his innocence, and when that didn't happen, the man opened his eyes a little. "Well, Novak, guilty or not, I can't say—but if you want me, I'll do my best for you. May not be enough."

Thad studied the thin face and the sleepy eyes. Harrison Duke was not the sort of man he'd have picked, but an instinct told him that the lawyer was just what he needed for this crisis. "I'd appreciate it if you'd do what you can, Captain Duke."

"You know you can refuse—choose another lawyer? Won't hurt my feelings a bit."

"No, sir."

Duke showed no pleasure, but grunted and scrunched up in the seat, closed his eyes, and said, "Tell me everything. All of it. If you leave out one detail that you think's not important, that's the very detail I might need to keep you from getting shot. Don't stop—tell it all right from the beginning to this minute."

Thad nodded and began by saying, "I guess you ought to know that I'm kin to Mr. Winslow—but he don't know it . . ." Duke tilted his chair back against the wall, closed his eyes and didn't move. He seemed to be asleep, but several times during the recital he rose, went to spit out the window, then returned to his chair and resumed the same somnambulant posture.

Thad finished by saying, "So after I was arrested, they brought me here—and I haven't talked to anyone about all this until just now."

Duke didn't move for a full minute, and Thad thought Harrison was asleep. Then he asked, not opening his eyes, "Is that all?"

"Yes, sir. It's all I can think of." He hesitated. "Aren't you going to write anything down?" he asked.

Duke slowly opened his eyes, got to his feet, and replied,

"No." He stood there, an unimpressive figure, studying Thad. He walked to the door, knocked, and said over his shoulder, "I'll be back tomorrow." He left as soon as the guard opened the door—no backward look, no farewell.

Thad stood there, wondering if he had done the right thing; but it was done, and he thought, *I'm glad somehow that seedy-looking captain's on my side.*

Two hours later the door opened again, and Thad bounded to his feet as he saw Sky Winslow with Rebekah and Pet.

"Thad!" Rebekah rushed to him and put her arms around the boy just as if he were her own.

Thad's eyes blurred, and he couldn't say a word. When she stepped back, he saw that Pet's eyes were red, and she pressed her handkerchief to her lips to keep from crying.

"Well, now, Thad," Sky apologized, "I'm sorry we couldn't come earlier—but we had to wait for permission."

"It's all right, Mr. Winslow. I—I'm glad you're here." He dropped his head and struggled to keep from crying. "And I thank you for sending Captain Duke to help me."

Winslow shook his head with some doubt. "He's a strange man, Thad. If you want another lawyer, I'll find one."

"No, sir. I'd like to have him."

An awkward silence fell across the room, and Rebekah said, "I brought you some of the food you like."

"The guard was going to search her," Winslow chuckled. "Thought she might have a hacksaw or a file in her clothes."

"The very idea!" Rebekah sputtered indignantly. "Search *me*—a respectable married woman!"

That broke the ice, and they all sat down; and while Thad ate some caramel cake, they talked about the case. Thad went over the whole story again—until he got to the part about Captain Whitfield Winslow coming to The Old Capitol.

"What's the matter, Thad," Pet asked, noticing his hesitancy.

"Well, I guess I've got to tell you." Thad looked at all three of them. "You know how I was asking for the Winslow place when I first came to Richmond?"

"I've wondered about that," Winslow replied gravely.

"I didn't want to tell you—but the thing is, I'm—I'm a Winslow, too!"

"You're what?"

Thad nodded and went on to tell how his mother had been a Winslow, and how he'd come to Belle Maison as a result of the captain's tales about plantation life.

Overcome by the news, Pet squealed and threw herself into his arms, taking him completely off guard. "Why—we're *cousins!*"

Sky stared at Thad's red face over Pet's shoulder, and then a smile broadened his lips. "If that doesn't beat all. You sure knocked the wind out of us. But why did you have to make such a mystery of it?"

"I just didn't want you to think I was come to mooch off you—like a poor relation."

"You can let go of him now, Pet," Sky laughed. "Though he *is* what we call 'a kissing cousin' around here, so help yourself."

"Papa!" Pet rebuked, her face red, but she stuck her tongue out and whirled to give Thad a peck on the cheek.

"I'll have a kiss, too, Thad, if you don't mind," Rebekah smiled, and he kissed her awkwardly.

"No kisses, Thad," Winslow commented with a grin. "Just welcome to the family!" Then he shook Thad's hand, and as he drew back he said suddenly, "Why, we've got to get word to Captain Winslow's son—what's his name?"

"Lowell," Thad said.

"That'll be the thing to do—but, wait a minute. . . !"

"What's wrong, dear?" Rebekah asked.

"It might not be so easy. The news is that after Banks got stomped by Jackson, most of McClellan's army is on the way to reinforce him. If Captain Lowell Winslow is with them—and that's a pretty safe bet!—it's going to be hard to get word to him."

"But—the court-martial will have to wait, won't it, Papa?" Pet asked.

"Ordinarily, yes, but I think our troops are pulling out right away. They may rush the trial through just to get it over with. I'd better find the lawyer!"

He banged on the door, and as they left, Pet turned. "I'm glad you're my cousin, Thad. It makes it a lot easier!"

After they were gone, Thad thought about Pet's remark but

could not decide what she had meant by *it*. Their visit, however, had raised his spirits and given him a sense of freedom, for he felt that a door had opened. He looked up and gratefully whispered, "Thank you, God!"

CHAPTER TWENTY-ONE

THE COURT-MARTIAL OF THAD NOVAK

★ ★ ★ ★

Two days after Duke visited Thad, the lawyer came back again just after noon, looking even more rumpled and unkempt than before. He threw himself down in the same chair, took a huge bite from his plug of tobacco, then said without preamble, "We go before the court in three days—August fifteenth."

"So soon?" Thad exclaimed. "I thought it took a long time to get ready to try a case."

"That's for civilians," Duke answered. "Military ways are different. Try 'em—then either shoot 'em or let 'em go." He opened his eyes to stare at Thad. "We don't have a lot of time, boy. Tell me your story one more time."

"But—you heard it all."

"Sometimes clients change their stories. That's one of the things a court looks for. They'll hear the tale two or three times at least, and if you change your account one iota, it makes them think you're lying—which you probably will be." He didn't bother to go to the window, but spat on the wall. "That's one advantage of telling the truth, Novak. You don't have to *remember* what you said the last time as you do when you lie. Tell it all again."

Thad repeated his story and, as before, it seemed that Harry Duke slept through it all; but when Novak finished, he was surprised to see approval on the lawyer's face. "Good! Just the same as last time—almost word for word. Bygad, Novak, keep that up and you'll even convince *me* you're innocent!" Then he leaned forward and placed his elbows on the table. "Listen to me. I'm going to tell you how to behave in court. First thing is, don't get mad—and you'll probably want to. When somebody lies on you, don't let a thing show in your face. Second thing is, don't whine. You won't get any sympathy by tears. The men who'll be judging you have sat in on many court-martials, and they'll put stock in their knowledge of men. So you just sit there, hold your head up, answer any questions put to you—by me or anybody else— and leave the rest up to me. You got that?"

"Yes, sir."

Duke got up, his eyes probing Thad's, and allowed an edge of concern to touch his sleepy eyes. "You a praying man, Novak?"

Thad shook his head slowly. "I don't figure I got much right to claim anything from God, Captain. Seems like poor doin's to ignore Him all my life, and come cryin' like a baby when I get hurt."

Duke stared at him for a long moment, then nodded. "That's about my own sentiments, I guess." A thought brought a glint of humor into his eyes, and a trace of a smile curled the edges of his mouth: "May be proper for you to delegate that job to someone else—like that girl—what's her name? Patience, isn't it?"

"Why. . . !" Thad was startled, and his face reddened. "If anyone could do it, I reckon she'd be the one, Captain."

Duke turned, then wheeled back, saying, "Try to sleep. Shave close and look as good as you can." He left abruptly, and Thad went to the window to watch him walk from the jail, cross the street, and enter a saloon. As the doors swung behind the man, Thad wondered again if he'd been right to allow the eccentric lawyer to defend him, but it was too late to think of that.

Harrison Duke spent an hour in the saloon, sitting alone at a table and slowly consuming the two drinks he allowed himself. He had the facility of listening to people with part of his mind, and sending the rest of his razor-sharp mind off into a maze of possibilities. He had a photographic memory, and could repeat entire conversations months after everyone else had forgotten them. His firmest theory of law was that there was always a way to win—*always*. The trick was to find the single key that would pull the props out from under your adversary.

He sat there alone, and from time to time someone would mention the Novak matter. A bearded sergeant snarled loudly, "That Novak! A dirty rotten traitor! Shootin's too good for him. I seen him myself, leadin' the Yank cavalry right on top of us!"

Duke gauged the weight of the mutter of assent that went over the room, but said nothing. Finally he got up and left the saloon, walked around the courthouse and the jail twice, stopping once to stare up at the barred window where his client was kept. His mind sifted through a dozen plans that had surfaced. As he stood there, he saw Sky Winslow with his wife and daughter walking across the grassy plot that surrounded the jail, and something clicked. He walked rapidly toward the trio, catching them just as they were about to mount the steps of the landing.

"Mr. Winslow." They turned, and he said, "I need a word with you."

Sky asked, "Should we go back to my office?"

"No, let's go over to the shade of that tree." He led the way, and as soon as the four of them reached the shade, Duke broke the silence, saying urgently, "We've got to get that Union officer's testimony."

"You mean the one who captured Thad?" Sky asked.

"Yes. He's the key to this thing—the only key."

"I've already tried to wire his father, but the wires have been cut. I suspect Jeb Stuart and his boys did it."

Harrison Duke was not a man of great tact, and he put the matter bluntly: "Either we get that testimony, or Novak will be shot."

"Mr. Duke—no!" Rebekah exclaimed. "Surely there's some other way!"

"May be—but I can't think of it."

"But we don't even know which regiment that captain was in!" Sky protested.

"Yes, we do, Papa!" Pet's face was pale, and she added, "He

was with General Sherman's command."

Duke stared at her, thinking hard. "That's right, the boy did mention that. Of course, Sherman has several brigades, but not all that many troops of cavalry. Wouldn't be much of a trick to find out the unit—if somebody would go in person."

Sky stared at him. "That would be pretty difficult. The news is that Lincoln has replaced McClellan with Pope—and it sounds like General Pope is anxious to show more drive and spirit than Little Mac. He's headed for a big push, the generals all think, and we're rushing our men up to the Manassas area as quick as they can be mobilized." His face took on a determined look. "I'll go myself!"

"The President would never let you go, dear," Rebekah said.

"You can't go, Winslow," Duke agreed immediately. "I'll need you here to testify before the court."

"I know who can find them, Papa!" Pet cried eagerly. "Dooley Young! He's got fast horses and he's smart."

Sky thought it over a moment. "That's not a bad idea, Pet." His mind raced as he formulated plans. "I'll get a pass from the President for Lowell Winslow." He shook his head, saying, "It'd take that to get a Yankee officer into Richmond these days."

"Get it now, Papa, and I'll take it out to Dooley. He's at his parents' house until the company leaves."

"Do it quick," Duke advised. "The trial will start on the fifteenth. I can stall the jury for maybe a couple of days—three, I'd say." His mouth puckered and he added, "Got to point out that if they find him guilty, they won't waste time carrying out the sentence—probably the next day."

"Come with me, Pet!" Sky said hastily. "Rebekah, you go to Thad. I'll be there as soon as I can get the pass from the President."

He left immediately with Pet, and as they made their way to the Congress where the President's office was located, Pet suggested, "Papa, why don't you write a note to Major Lee, and I'll stop off at the camp and get him to give Dooley a pass—or maybe two passes. Dooley can take his cousin Les Satterfield with him. It might be better if the two of them went—just in case one got sick or hurt."

"I'd forgotten that," Sky muttered. He gave his daughter a

hug, saying huskily, "It'll be all right, Pet. God won't let us down."

They entered the building, and Winslow was admitted almost at once to see the President. Pet waited in the outer office, and was relieved when her father came out in less than ten minutes with an envelope in his hand. "Here it is, Pet. You know what to tell Dooley?"

"Find Sherman's command, ask for Captain Winslow in the cavalry, then tell him what's happened to Thad."

Sky nodded, and his face clouded. "It's asking a lot of a Yankee officer to come and testify for a Confederate soldier charged with treason." He pondered that, then said, "I'd better put it in writing." He led her to his own office, and she waited impatiently as he sat down and wrote for twenty minutes. Finally he got up, blew the ink dry, and put the note in an envelope. He reached into a drawer and took out a leather dispatch case, put both documents inside, and handed them to her. "I wish I could go myself!" he said in exasperation. "Well, get these to Dooley as quickly as you can. Take the buggy. Your mother and I will hire a ride home."

"All right, Papa." They walked outside to where his buggy was waiting, and she stopped and impulsively pulled his head down. Kissing him on the cheek, she asked, "Is it all right if I stay at the farm for a while?"

He thought he understood her desire to be alone, and nodded. "Yes. I'll tell your mother."

She got into the buggy, spoke to the mare, and raced down the street, soon disappearing around a corner at the end of the block. Sky took a deep breath and headed for the jail, wondering how he would keep a cheerful countenance before Thad.

Thad was surprised to see the full waiting room—much more crowded than the room where the court-martial was held. He had been brought out of his cell at nine o'clock by an armed guard of four privates, commanded by a lieutenant, and marched across the open space that separated the jail and the courthouse. He had a hard time when some of the observers called out insults at him, but he kept his head high and did not look at them. Inside, they passed through a large room with chairs all around the walls, and in that swift moment, he saw Mr. and Mrs. Winslow, Major Lee, and Captain Wickham in one group, and beyond them his two lieutenants, Mark Winslow and Beau Beauchamp. He caught a brief glimpse of several privates across the room, but did not have time to identify them.

He passed into a smaller room, perhaps fifteen by twenty, with a long table at one end. Seated at it were five officers, none of whom he knew. On the left was a small table, where a corporal sat with his writing materials in front of him. Across from him another table, somewhat larger, was turned to face the court. It was occupied by a fat captain. Thad understood at once that he was the officer who would try to convict him. Halfway down the room he saw Captain Duke standing beside another table with two chairs behind it. Then the lieutenant said, "Take that chair," indicating the one beside Duke.

As Thad walked across the room, three of the four guards left; the other took up his station in front of the door, with the lieutenant on his right.

The officer in the center of the long table was a thick-set colonel with direct black eyes. He spoke in a brisk, businesslike manner: "Private Thaddeus Novak, you have been brought to this place of court-martial to be tried on the charges of desertion and treason. I am Colonel L. C. Andrews. From left to right, the members of the court are Colonel Anderson Briggs, Major Jason Stillwell, Captain Otis Clark, and Major Donald McClain."

As the colonel went on to describe the procedures of the court, Thad studied each man. Briggs was an older man, in his late sixties. He stared across the room with obvious hostility. Major Stillwell, on the other hand, was extremely young, not over twenty-five, and he had a pink youthful face. He was examining Thad in a curious manner, but did not seem to be hostile. The captain to the judge's left, Otis Clark, was a hard-faced man of thirty. He was staring down at the table, apparently ignoring the proceedings. Major McClain was, Thad judged, in his early fifties. He had an ugly scar on his left cheek that drew his mouth up into a leer, so that it was impossible to tell what he was thinking.

"That's the enemy, Novak," Duke whispered to Thad, pointing to the captain seated at the small table facing the court. "Captain Aaron Abraham—a real hot lawyer."

Thad felt fear rising up in his chest as he stared at the man. Abraham was overweight, spilling out of his uniform like a ruptured sausage, but there was none of the jolly air of a fat man about him. He had a pair of inky eyes and a mouth like a shark.

"This court will presume the accused is innocent until proven guilty," Colonel Andrews stated. "You gentlemen both understand that?" He paused and stared at the prosecutor. "It is not up to Private Novak to prove his innocence. If you cannot prove that he is guilty, this court will set him free."

Abraham gave a nod, smiled toothily at the court, and said in a powerful bass voice, "Yes, sir. I understand that very well."

"Then call your first witness."

Abraham said, "I call Major Shelby Lee."

At the command of the court, the lieutenant beside the door left, and came back shortly with Major Lee behind him.

"Would you take that chair, Major Lee?" the judge requested. "Swear him in, Lieutenant." After this ceremony, Colonel Andrews said, "You may examine the witness."

Abraham did not rise from his chair, and his voice was gentle as he began. "Major Lee, I will ask you a few questions about the action that took place at Malvern Hill on the day of July first of this year."

Lee carried the magnetism of the family, and the court listened with respect as he related the action of that day. Even Captain Clark raised his eyes as the major reiated the step-by-step account. He came to the charge up the hill by the Third Virginia, and Abraham interrupted gently, "Ah—Major Lee, I believe you observed the attack by the Union cavalry that took place just before the charge. Could you describe that—and if you can, give us your views of how such an attack could have caught your men off guard."

"Objection." Harry Duke stood to his feet and said tolerantly, "Captain Abraham is too fine a counsel to expect the court to admit such 'opinions' as evidence. It is my belief that Thad Novak is innocent, but if I were to state my opinion, I feel certain that Captain Abraham would object—just as I am doing now."

"Objection sustained. Captain Abraham, you will rephrase the question."

"I stand rebuked by my worthy opponent," Abraham nodded, and turned again to his witness. "Major Lee, I will ask you, not for an opinion, but for a fact—did you see the defendant, Thad Novak, at the head of the Union cavalry that attacked the Third Virginia on the day of July first?"

Lee hesitated, then answered, "Yes, I did."

"No more questions," Abraham stated. "Your witness, sir."

Duke stood to his feet and asked almost idly, "How far down the line were you from the point where the cavalry hit the line, Major Lee?"

"About two hundred yards."

"And had our men started firing when you first saw the cavalry?"

"Yes."

"Was the Confederate you saw wearing a hat?"

"Yes, he was."

"Describe it, if you would."

Major Lee frowned as he thought. "Well, it was a black hat with a large brim. Most of our men wear hats like that."

Duke had been asking the questions in a manner that seemed almost boring, but now he straightened up and said in a voice that rasped across the ears of everyone in the room: "So what you are saying, Major, is that at the distance of two hundred yards, with the air filled with smoke, you recognized, *without any chance of error*, a man with a hat pulled down over his face, who was riding at right angles to you at a dead run—is that what you are saying?"

Lee hesitated, and Duke demanded, "You are telling this court that you have no doubt at all that Thad Novak was that man. I suggest, Major Lee, that you *do* have some doubt. I ask you to tell this court on your honor as an officer and a gentleman that you have *absolutely no doubt whatsoever* that the man you saw was the defendant!"

For once in his life, Shelby Lee was caught without his air of total assurance. He flushed, and replied, "Well, I cannot say that—but . . ."

"I have no further questions for this witness," Duke stated brusquely. "He has disqualified himself."

Abraham half rose and said smoothly, "I concede the point.

Thank you, Major Lee." As the officer left the room, with a rather thankful look, Thad thought, Abraham said with a shark-like grin at Duke, "Thank you, Captain Duke, for your astute perception. Call Lieutenant Beauregard Beauchamp."

Thad's heart beat faster as Beauchamp came in. Duke whispered, "Blast it! I wish I could have gotten Abraham to argue about Lee's testimony—but he's too sharp for that!"

After Beauchamp was sworn in, Abraham asked him for the same testimony of the Malvern Hill battle, and when he got to the cavalry charge, the prosecutor interrupted Beauchamp. "Lieutenant, is the Confederate soldier you saw riding with the Federals in this courtroom?"

"Yes, sir."

"Point him out—and name him, if you will."

Beauchamp lifted his head to look across the room at Thad, then said steadily, "Thad Novak was the man I saw."

Abraham paused, waiting for Duke to object, and when he did not, the fat lawyer raised his voice a trifle, adding, "How far away was the defendant from you?"

"Not more than fifty feet."

"But the defendant had on a hat that was partly over his eyes—and there was some gunsmoke in the air. Can you swear that there is absolutely no possibility of an error? Could it not have been a man who *looked* like Thaddeus Novak?"

Beauchamp shifted in his chair, but shook his head solidly. "The man I saw was Thad Novak."

"No further questions. Your witness, Captain."

Harry Duke rose to his feet, came to stand directly before Beauchamp, and when he spoke his voice cracked like a whip, and his eyes were piercing, not sleepy. "You have known the defendant how long, Lieutenant?"

"He's been in my command—"

"I didn't ask you how long he's been in your command," Duke rapped out. "Will the court instruct this witness to answer the questions as they are asked?"

Colonel Andrews looked up with a startled expression, for Duke's attack on the witness was unexpected. He said mildly, "The witness is so instructed—but I will instruct *you*, Captain Duke, not to bully a witness."

Duke stared at the judge, seemed to weigh the matter, then turned back to Beauchamp. "You were present at a New Year's Eve party at the home of Mr. Sky Winslow on January 1, 1861, were you not?"

"Why, I—I think I was."

"Would you like me to bring in witnesses who will swear that you were at that party? I will be glad to do so."

Beauchamp's brow began to show a fine line of perspiration, and he said, "That—won't be necessary. I was at that party."

"Oh, so you *do* remember it, Lieutenant? I'm glad that you can remember a few things!"

"Objection!" Abraham shouted. "He is badgering the witness."

"I will sustain that objection," Andrews said, then gave a direct look at the unkempt figure of the defender. "You will show more restraint in your remarks, sir. I will not warn you again."

"Yes, Colonel," Duke responded. Turning to the witness, he presented another question. "Lieutenant, on that occasion, you were humiliated by Thad Novak in a shooting contest, were you not?"

"Objection!" Abraham was on his feet, the suave manner now gone. He snarled, "Such a thing has no bearing on this case."

"How do *you* know, Captain?" Duke shot back. "You don't even know *why* I'm asking the question! How can you possibly know if it's relevant?"

"I know you'll do anything short of murder to win a case!" Abraham raged. "I've seen your scurvy—!"

"Gentlemen!"

Colonel Andrews' voice rose above the shouts of the two lawyers, and when they calmed down, he warned, "I may as well establish one thing right now—this court is not interested in the antics of two fancy big city lawyers. You can save that for the civil courts. This is a military court, and we are interested in one thing: Did the defendant commit treason? We will arrive at that decision when we have the facts. I will expel either or both of you if you persist in making a circus out of this court-martial. Do you understand me?"

Abraham nodded "Yes, Colonel!" and dropped into his chair.

Harry Duke made a sorry figure as he stood there in his wrinkled uniform, but there was something indomitable in his pale face. He said quietly, "Colonel, I suggest that you order me out of this court right now."

A shock swept through the room, and Thad saw that every officer was staring at Duke. There was something audacious in his words, and they were all caught with his determined air.

"Why do you say that, Captain?" Andrews asked with a look on his face that was half anger and half curiosity.

"Because I do not intend to defend my client with half measures," Duke responded in a ringing voice. He lifted his hand in a fierce gesture and cried out, "You call my actions 'antics,' sir. That is your privilege. I think, however, that you would not look with favor on any officer under you who failed to fight with every means at his command—and I suggest that if another officer ventured to call such fighting 'antics,' you would be offended. I will defend my client with every means at my command. That is my duty as a defender—just as it is the duty of a soldier to fight with whatever weapons he can lay his hands on—a sledge hammer if there is nothing else."

Thad had been watching the faces of the officers, and saw that they were evenly divided over Duke's blunt words. Colonel Briggs and Otis Clark showed anger in their eyes, but the other two, Major Stillwell and Major McClain, were almost smiling.

Finally Colonel Andrews, after staring at the brazen defender for a long moment, nodded, and Thad thought he could see just a glint of admiration in the colonel's black eyes.

"You are to be commended for your zeal, Captain—this time. But I will not be bullied, any more than I will allow the witnesses to be bullied. The objection is denied. Continue with your examination of Lieutenant Beauchamp."

Duke nodded, then proceeded to lay bare the circumstances of the shooting match. Beau had long been ashamed of that incident, and the longer the questioning went on, the worse he looked to the court. He could not avoid Duke's probing, and admitted that he had formed a bad opinion of Novak. Perspiration ran down his cheeks, and his hands trembled with anger and humiliation as he was forced to admit that he had spoken against Novak time after time, trying to make Mark Winslow get rid of him.

Abraham longed to get rid of the witness, for he was wise enough to recognize that Beauchamp's testimony was worthless, but it was out of Abraham's hands. He sat there sullenly as time ran on, and was totally out of patience by the time Duke concluded, "I don't believe I have any more questions. The court can judge the value of Lieutenant Beauchamp's testimony."

Beau stumbled from the room, his face pale, and did not even stop in the outer room, but left at once, relieved to get outside.

Lieutenant Mark Winslow was the next witness called by the prosecution, but he was of no help to Abraham. "I was beside Major Lee when the attack came, and I saw the cavalrymen come riding up from the flank."

"Could you identify the Confederate with them?" the prosecutor demanded. "Was it Thaddeus Novak?"

Mark gave an agonizing glance at Thad, then said, "Yes, it was."

"Thank you, Lieutenant. Your witness."

Duke asked, without getting up, "You were with Major Lee when the attack came, I believe?"

"Yes, I was. He was giving me some final orders before the charge."

"Major Lee refused to identify the defendant. He said the distance was too far, the smoke was too thick, and the hat was over the rider's face."

"Objection! Objection!" Captain Abraham's face was purple, and he shouted, "He is putting words in the mouth of the witness, Judge!"

"Objection sustained!" Andrews snapped. "You know better than to pull such a stunt, Captain Duke! This is one of those 'antics' I mentioned, and I am strongly tempted to put you out of this courtroom!"

His anger was real, and Thad was terrified. He expected Duke to challenge him, but instead the lawyer dropped his head. He stood there looking crushed, and his voice was husky as he lifted his eyes to the judge and said, "Colonel, I should not blame you. I can only apologize to the court and ask for your leniency. I was quite wrong."

Colonel Andrews had the words on his lips that would send Duke out of the room and off the case, but he was swayed by the sudden act of humility, so out of character for such a man. He looked swiftly at his fellow officers, then said gruffly, "Very well, sir. Very well! I will be very alert to see if your behavior is in line with your repentance."

Duke replied, "I thank the court." Then he turned to Mark Winslow and asked quietly, "Can you swear before God that the man you saw was the defendant, Thad Novak?"

"No, I can't."

The answer pulled Captain Abraham out of his seat, his face contorted, but he knew full well that he would get nothing out of Winslow. He cursed himself for a fool, but said nothing.

The morning dragged on endlessly. When they broke for lunch, and during the interim, Major Stillwell, with a twinkle in his blue eyes and creases of laughter in his pink face, commented, "McClain, that Jewish lawyer is fit to be tied. He never had a doubt about proving Novak's identity as the soldier who came riding in with that Yank cavalry. Now Duke's made him look like a fool!"

"That's right," McClain nodded. "But the waiting room's full of witnesses who'll identify the man. After all, Jason, the entire Third Virginia saw him."

"Maybe so, but we'll be here until the war's over if Duke keeps wiping the witnesses out."

The afternoon went on much as the morning, with Duke coming as close to badgering the witnesses as safety would permit. Abraham fumed, but he said to his assistant, "He's good, that *goy*! We'll get him in the end, but he is a real *mensch*!"

Finally the day ended, and when Duke emerged from the court, he saw Mr. and Mrs. Winslow still waiting. Going over to them, he said, "Well, I stretched it out as long as I could. It's going to be harder tomorrow, though."

"How does it look?" Sky asked.

"It looks like that Yankee relative of yours had better get here soon."

Winslow questioned him, but there was nothing of substance for Duke to say, and he got away from them as quickly as he decently could.

Sky and Rebekah rode back to the house in silence, for they had said all there was to say.

As they approached the house, Sky exclaimed, "There's Toby!"

He pulled up the horse, and Toby came running to meet them. "Heah's a letter from Miss Pet, suh."

Sky opened it, scanned the contents, then said, "Rebekah—she's gone with Dooley!"

"Oh no, Sky!"

"Toby—why didn't you bring this before?"

"Suh, Miss Pet tol' me not to bring it till today." He looked worried, and asked, "Did I do somethin' wrong, Mistuh Winslow?"

Sky shook his head, then sighed heavily, "No, Toby." He got out of the buggy, helped Rebekah down, and gave her the note.

Papa,

I am going with Dooley to find Captain Winslow. I don't really think the note you wrote will be enough to make him come, but I can convince him. Don't worry about me. And don't hate me, please, Papa!

Your loving daughter,
Pet

Rebekah read the note, lifted her head, and broke into smiles. "I'm glad she went! If she gets her hands on the captain, he'll *have* to come!"

CHAPTER TWENTY-TWO

PET'S RIDE

★ ★ ★ ★

By the end of their first day of travel, Pet realized that she could never have made the ride to the lines alone. She'd collected the passes from Major Lee, found Dooley at his home, and as soon as Young found out what she wanted, his eyes had brightened. He had produced three fast horses and stopped by Belle Maison long enough for her to change clothes and get Blackie. As dawn broke, they rode out, each leading a horse with a long tether.

It was her clothes, Pet discovered, that caused the trouble. She wore a well-worn pair of light tan overalls, a light blue cotton shirt and a pair of fine riding boots. She had another outfit much the same in the bedroll slung behind her saddle. It was the sort of clothing she had worn when riding around Belle Maison, but her slim figure had blossomed in the past year, so that the first two men they passed on the road gave her some bold looks, and one of them called out a crude remark. Dooley had wanted to go back and teach them proper manners, but she had urged, "We don't have time, Dooley."

All day long they kept up a hard pace, and by night they were camped beside the York River, west of Williamsburg. They cooked a supper of bacon, making sandwiches with thick slices of homemade bread, then washed it down with river water.

When they had finished, Dooley leaned back against a tree, lit his pipe, and commented, "We made good time today." He considered Pet as she sat across the fire, finally asking, "I guess this here ride is for all the marbles, ain't it, Miss Patience?"

She nodded, and hugged her knees to her chest. The stars were covered by low-flying clouds, and the trees beside the river moaned as the night wind stirred and shifted their branches. "The lawyer said so." She raised her head and the yellow flames of the small fire made her eyes look golden as she stared at him. "We've *got* to do it, Dooley! We've just *got* to!"

Dooley nodded. "Guess you better be sayin' an extra good prayer. We ain't really got no show in the natural." Then he added, "Best git to sleep. I aim to half kill them hosses tomorrow—and mebby us, too."

He was not joking, for they rose at dawn, and stopped to rest the horses and snatch a quick meal at noon. By night they camped by a small spring, and Pet asked, "Where are we, Dooley?"

He picked up a stick and drew several lines. "This here is the York River where we was last night. Over here"—he drew a set of wavy lines to the left of the river—"is the Shenandoah Valley. We're comin' up to the top of it." He poked a dot at the top, saying, "This here is Fredericksberg, and we'll pass that tomorrow sometimes."

"How much farther to the Union Army?"

"Well, as we don't rightly know where they are, I can't say," Dooley replied and threw the stick down. "But from what the officers was sayin', it looks like Pope will be linin' up somewhere west of Washington—jest 'bout where we whupped the Yanks the first time—at Bull Run."

They slept hard that night, but started out at dawn. At noon they stopped at a farmhouse, and Dooley arranged to leave the horses they'd be riding back so the animals would be rested on the return trip. "We'll be back in mebby three days or less to pick 'em up," he told the farmer. "Grain 'em and let 'em rest."

They continued at a rapid clip, but were passing troops now, all headed toward the north. "Them's our boys headed to meet Mr. Pope," Dooley said. Here again, Pet's face burned as the soldiers called her "honey" and "sweetheart," and a few things she didn't understand. Dooley had been philosophical about it. "Can't stop a bunch of lonesome soldiers from starin' at a good-lookin' gal, Miss Pet. Jest shut your ears and don't pay 'em no mind."

They made good time that day, but it rained that night and they were forced to find shelter in an abandoned barn. The next day as they rode out, Dooley said, "I reckon we might git some idees 'bout where the Yanks is linin' up. Can't be too far away now." They came up to a line of infantry, and Dooley asked the sergeant, "Hey, Sarge, where'bouts you reckon I could find me a piece of Mister General Johnny Pope?"

The sergeant spat on the ground, nodded his head toward the north, and said, "Word is he's over to the Warrenton Pike. We figure to catch up with him there and give his nose a pull."

"What outfit?" Dooley asked.

"Stonewall Brigade," the sergeant answered proudly.

"Whoopee!" Dooley yelped, then said, "Let's git, Missy. If Ol' Blue Light is on the march, we'll find the Yankees not far off."

They rode hard for the rest of the day and ran into a Confederate cavalry patrol at dusk. "You can't go any farther this way," the lieutenant said, staring at Pet. "The Yankees are building up just past that timber."

"Who is your officer?" Pet asked.

"Why, General Sheridan."

"Take us to him."

"I can't do that, miss!"

"I have a message here from President Davis. Do you want to explain to him why you refused to honor his signature?"

The lieutenant gulped, stammered, "Well—I guess maybe the general might want to see that."

He led them past rows of campfires until they came to a tent on a low rise. An adjutant challenged them and took the lieutenant aside for a brief conference. When it was over, the lieutenant rode rapidly away, and the adjutant said, "I'll get General Sheridan."

"Ain't never met no generals," Dooley remarked. "But I heard they wasn't too fond of bein' told what to do."

He cut his words off, for a slight man with a general's insignia emerged from the tent and came to stand before them. "I hear you have a paper with President Davis's signature on it?"

"Yes, sir." Pet opened the leather case, took the larger envelope, and handed it to Sheridan.

The general studied it by the light of his small fire. "Who is this Captain Winslow?" he asked, putting the letter back into the envelope.

Pet told him the whole story, shortening it as much as possible. He stood there, a small shape with a blunt face, and when she had finished, he slowly pulled a cigar from his breast pocket, lit it, then studied the pair through the haze of blue smoke. "This Novak, he's your sweetheart?"

"Oh . . . I don't . . ." Pet faltered, then lifted her head and said, "He's a good friend, General, and my cousin."

"I see." Sheridan smiled and shrugged. "Well, if the President of the Confederacy says to do it, I'm not going to say no. But you'll have to wait till morning. You'd get shot if you tried to go through their lines tonight. Tomorrow I'll send you through with a white flag."

The irrepressible Dooley said, "Well, if you don't think it'll give 'em funny idees 'bout us givin' up, General."

Sheridan smiled at the bandy-legged Dooley and responded, "I guess they'll not make that mistake." He puffed on his cigar for a minute. Finally he turned and said brusquely, "Be here at dawn. I'll have you taken over."

Dooley and Pet rolled up in their blankets far enough away from the soldiers so that they could not hear their talk. Dooley went to sleep at once, but Pet rolled on the hard ground for most of the night, wondering how she could convince her distant relation to come to Richmond. Finally she prayed for a while, and as the stars came out overhead, she slept.

––––––––

"A rebel and a woman?" General Phil Kearny stared at the captain who had come to the table where he sat looking at a map. "What in blazes are you talking about?"

"Well, sir, they just came in down the line under a white flag. They had an escort from General Sheridan." The captain grinned. "They're looking for one of Sherman's men, a Captain Winslow, 6th Cavalry."

Kearny got up and grinned unexpectedly. "Show them in, Captain. It ought to be more entertaining than anything else I've got to do."

He stood waiting, and when the captain returned, the general looked at the pair as the introductions were made. "Private Dooley Young, Third Virginia Infantry, and Miss Patience Winslow."

The girl smiled at him, revealing a dimple, and despite the fatigue that had drawn her face, the general saw she was a beauty. "I'm looking for Captain Lowell Winslow, General Kearny," she said. "Could I tell you about it?"

Kearny nodded, and said, "Sit down, young lady." He pointed at two canvas chairs and after she was seated, he took the other. "Go right ahead."

Pet told the story, weariness revealing the tiring three days. Her reserves had weakened and her voice trembled slightly as she spoke of the young man who was in trouble. She dropped her eyes, trying to hide the sudden tears. "So, the time is almost gone, General," she concluded. "Will you help me?"

Kearny studied the pale face. "Miss Winslow, I don't think you know what you're asking. I don't know Captain Winslow, but it seems to me he would not be likely to go to Richmond—on any errand."

She looked at him with steady gray eyes and whispered, "I have to try, General."

Kearny looked down, then lifted his head. "I'll give you an escort to Captain's Winslow's brigade. He may be out on patrol, or he may have been sent back to Washington. I'll give him leave to go with you. That's the best I can do."

"Oh, General!" she exclaimed, and before she could catch herself, she had risen and taken his arm, her eyes alive and her curved lips smiling. "God bless you!"

"Ah, well, now. . . !" Kearny sputtered, retreating quickly to his desk, where he made a brief note, folded it and gave it to her. "My dear, I hope it works out." He lifted his voice, "Captain Mitchell! See that this young woman and her—ah—escort are taken to the 6th Cavalry."

As the captain was getting his escort mounted, Kearny gave Dooley a sharp look. "You're in the Confederate Army?"

"Shore am, sir. Third Virginia."

The general studied the thin, short, bandy-legged soldier, and wondered for the hundredth time how such ragamuffins could whip the well-fed Union troops with such annoying regularity. "You'll miss this fight that's shaping up, Private."

"Aw, well, General," Dooley shrugged, "I guess I had enough fun running you fellers off the Peninsula to do me for a spell." He pulled at his mustache and added philosophically, "Feller can't expect to have fun all the time, can he now?"

General Kearny grinned ruefully, shook his head, and said, "You take care of that young lady, soldier, and get my captain back to me in one piece."

"Yessir," Dooley nodded. "I'll take care of both them chores." He turned to where Pet was mounting her horse. "Well, General, when Marse Bobbie Lee comes a'callin, you tell 'im I was here to visit."

Kearny watched as the pair were escorted down the line, and muttered to himself, "I must be gettin' senile—turning my officers over to rebel hillbillies and romantic girls!"

———

Captain Lowell Winslow was taking a nap after an all-night patrol. When Corporal Simmons had to shake his shoulder to waken him from the deep sleep, he pulled away and grumbled, "Go 'way!"

"Captain, please get up!" the corporal said. "It's important!"

Winslow sat up, looked around wildly and saw that there was no movement among the troopers. "What's the matter, Simmons?"

"You've got visitors, sir. A man and a woman, and they say they have to see you right away!"

Lurching to his feet, Winslow staggered to the washbasin and splashed his face with cold water. He ran his fingers through his hair, pulled on his blouse and jacket, then said roughly, "Did you say a woman, Corporal?"

"Yes, sir." Simmons' broad face broke into a sly smile. "And a rebel soldier."

"Are you drunk, Corporal? No, you wouldn't be that crazy."

"They're over here, sir. They came in with an escort from General Kearny."

Winslow gave him an unbelieving scowl as he followed the tall corporal past the picket line. Then they passed around a line of thick-bodied oaks, and there standing beside two mounted Union soldiers were a man and a woman. Winslow straightened his back at the sight, and walked up to them, saying, "I'm Captain Winslow. You wanted to see me?"

"Yes, Captain. Could I talk with you, please?"

He sized up, first of all, the small Confederate private who stood to one side regarding him with a pair of bright blue eyes. Next he shifted his gaze to the young woman, noting the smooth oval face with the largest, most compelling gray eyes he'd ever seen—and he didn't miss the youthful rounded figure that was attracting the gaze of every man in the troop. With an irritated glance toward the crowd that had gathered to observe the pair, he said, "I think we'd better go back to my tent, Miss—what's your name?"

"The same as yours—Winslow. Patience Winslow."

"Oh." He stopped, then noticing with some annoyance that several men had overheard her answer and were passing the information to those farther off, he suggested, "Let's get away from our audience, Miss Winslow."

"I'll jest wait here, Miss Pet," Dooley offered. "Mebby I can git some of these here bluebellies to engage in a little game of poker." As Pet turned to walk back toward the line of trees with the captain, she heard Dooley say, "Hey, why don't some of you fellers come on to Richmond? We been waitin' a long spell for you to come in."

Pet heard a dozen voices cry out, "You just wait, Reb! We'll get there soon enough!"

At Winslow's direction, she turned the corner and walked beside him to his tent.

"Sorry I don't have a chair to offer you," he apologized as they entered the tent. "Can I have the corporal fix you some coffee?"

"No, Captain Winslow," she replied. "I know you're wondering why I've come. It must seem strange to see a Confederate soldier and a rebel lady come into the Union camp."

"Doesn't happen every day," Winslow agreed, smiling. "You are a Winslow. Are we relatives?"

"Your grandfather says so."

"Oh, I see." He smiled again and shook his head. "The captain sent you, I take it? He's always finding Winslows—but not usually such attractive ones. Once he found a genuine descendant of our family who'd been sentenced to life for some crime. I remember he went all the way to Pennsylvania to see the man— and the fellow wouldn't even talk to him."

She returned his smile, the dimple in her cheek deepening as she did so, and said ruefully, "You may not be inclined to claim kinship, Captain, when I tell you why I've come."

He was intrigued by the situation, and replied quickly, "I can't imagine such a thing, Miss Patience. Just try me."

"All right. Do you remember capturing a Confederate soldier at the battle of Malvern Hill?"

"Why, of course!"

"His name was Thad Novak, wasn't it?"

"Yes." He let his direct blue eyes rest on her for a moment. "I take it you and Thad are—acquainted?"

"You don't have to be so delicate, Captain." Pet smiled, her cheeks dimpling. "Several people have asked if he's my lover."

The frank words from the soft lips of the innocent-looking girl took Winslow by surprise, and he colored slightly. "I'm sorry. Didn't mean to pry."

"Oh, don't apologize," Pet urged. "Thad has worked for my father ever since he came south. He's been my best friend—and now unless a miracle takes place, he's going to die."

"He's in a prison camp, isn't he?"

"No, he was exchanged. But when he got home, he was arrested—for desertion and treason."

"But—how can that be if he was a prisoner of war?" Winslow demanded.

Pet lifted tragic eyes and her lips trembled. "They say he deserted so he could lead your troop to attack our men. That's not the way it was, is it, Captain?"

"Certainly not! We killed one of his patrol, the other escaped, and we were taking the young man in when we accidentally ran into the Confederate line." He gave a chagrined laugh, adding, "*Led* us to the Confederate line! I reckon *not*! We were almost wiped out in that encounter!"

"That's what Thad has said—but nobody believes him." She bit her lip. "His court-martial has started, Captain. His lawyer says Thad doesn't have a chance! He'll be"—the word came hard, and she struggled over it—"he'll be shot unless—"

"Unless what?" he interrupted.

"Unless you come to Richmond and testify to his innocence."

"What!" Winslow literally leaped at her words, raising his voice in protest. "Go to Richmond! That's impossible!"

She stood there—so helpless, so forlorn in the yellow sunlight that pierced the foliage over their heads, falling on her face. It transformed the dark hair into auburn, highlighting the red glints. She seemed somehow very small and vulnerable as her gray eyes held his. She let the silence run on, then whispered, "No, it's not impossible, Captain. All things are possible with God."

"I'm not God!" he protested.

"No, you're a Winslow!" she challenged. "And your grandfather told me about the Winslows—about Gilbert and Adam and your own great-grandfather, Paul. And he said *they all were men of honor*. I have to ask you, Captain, because a boy I love very much may lose his life: Are you a man of honor—like the other Winslow men?"

He flushed angrily, for her words stung, and he said with asperity in his tone, "I believe I am—however, Miss Patience, I'm a soldier. There are many lives at stake here."

"But this one life you *know* is in your hands. General Kearny has given his permission—and this young man is of your blood." Lowell's face registered shock. Spurred by the urgency of the situation, she put her hand on his sleeve and whispered, "Oh, Captain Winslow, please save him—you're his only hope! It may be too late already, but God has brought me this far. Don't let him die!"

It would have taken a harder man than Lowell Winslow to refuse such a plea. She could see he was wavering, and she pressed in. "It will be dangerous for you to go to Richmond in the midst of your enemies. No one can guarantee your safety."

She could not have said a better thing, she realized. His eyes brightened, and his jaw tensed. "Dangerous? You think I'm *afraid* to go with you? Well, I may not be as 'noble' as some of my fabulous ancestors, but I can face a bunch of rebels any day!" He strode outside and yelled for the corporal, who appeared instantly. "Corporal, have my horse saddled—at once!" He whirled and plunged back into the tent, almost knocking Pet down as she was leaving. After a brief absence he emerged with a pair of heavy saddlebags in his hands. "Have to wear my best uniform when I ride into the den of lions," he remarked.

The two walked back where Dooley was circled by a group of grinning Yankee soldiers, who were fascinated by the little rebel. Pet ran to him and cried, "He's going with us, Dooley!"

"'Course he is, honey!" Dooley grinned. "Wasn't never no doubt in my mind 'bout that." He turned to the blue-clad troops, and waved a hand. "Well, we gotta skedaddle, Yanks. Ya'll better go on back to Washington 'fore Marse Bob and ol' Blue Light Jackson gobbles you up."

A yell went up, but Dooley swung into the saddle and followed Pet and the captain out of the camp.

"You better have that pass from the President handy, Miss Pet," Young remarked as they cleared the camp and set off at a fast pace, headed toward the south. "They'll shore be shocked in Richmond to see this here Yankee captain comin' in like he owned the place." The thought tickled him, and he laughed, "Whooee! Here General McClellan couldn't git to Richmond with 100,000 men—and one leetle ol' rebel gal takes one in all by herself! Whoooee!"

CHAPTER TWENTY-THREE

"I HATE TO LOSE!"

★　★　★　★

Monday morning Thad's cell was flooded with a bright shaft of yellow sunlight falling through the window. The warmth of the beam touched his face, begging him to shake off his fitful sleep and open his eyes. Every morning since he had been imprisoned, he had resisted consciousness, trying to slip back into the world of sleep. But the brightness of the sun intensified, and slowly he rolled his head over to one side and opened his eyes. As the room swam into view, he felt the same cancerous hopelessness that had deepened every day, draining his spirit of all vitality. The crowded cell he'd shared with other prisoners at The Old Capitol had been far worse physically, but there he'd been imprisoned for a just cause. There he had deteriorated physically, but had clung to his hope; now as he lay on the bunk staring across the room, a heaviness in his spirit seemed to suck him dry, leaving him in a deathlike state.

Slowly he pulled himself out of the bed, took a sip of tepid water from the jug on the table, then went to stare listlessly out the window. Although it could not have been later than five o'clock, the streets were already occupied—women going to ammunition factories, soldiers beginning to stir, and here and there a farmer in a wagon rumbling into Richmond with a load of produce.

As he stood motionless watching the city awaken, Thad thought wearily of the days in court, and the bitter memory drew his lips into a compressed slit. Every day had been like the first, and though at first he had been hopeful that Harrison Duke could sway the court—battling witness after witness who swore that the accused had ridden at the head of the Yankee cavalry— slowly he had given up. The faces of his judges had hardened, so that by the late Saturday afternoon session, when Colonel Andrews had dismissed the court until the following Monday, Thad seemed to see a prophecy of doom in every countenance.

Harrison Duke may have given up, but there was no evidence of it in his face or voice as he'd said Saturday afternoon, "We'll start all over again Monday, Thad." Then noting the despair in his client's dark eyes, he'd added, "It looks bad to you—but you can't ever tell with a jury. When you think you haven't got a prayer, a jury will bring in a *not guilty* verdict. Never give up, Thad! Never give up!" He had added with a grin, "Lord, I hate to lose!"

The Winslows had visited Thad after church on Sunday and left a basket filled with fruit. They had sat beside him, talking of the sermon and of Belle Maison, trying to instill some hope. He remembered Rebekah's words concerning the sermon: "Brother Lowery preached about Abraham this morning, Thad. Did you know that God promised Abraham he'd have a son when he was ninety years old—and his wife Sarah was almost that?"

She had opened her worn black Bible and read a verse. "It says in Romans four that Abraham believed God's promise even when all hope was gone. Let me read it to you:

God . . . quickeneth the dead, and calleth those things which be not as though they were. Who against hope believed in hope (and the pastor said that means when hope was gone he kept on hoping), that he might become the father of many nations, according to that which was spoken, So shall thy seed be. And being not weak in faith, he considered not his own body now dead, when he was about an hundred years old, neither yet the deadness of Sarah's womb: he staggered not at the promise of God through unbelief; but was strong in faith, giving glory to God.

She had put her Bible to her breast and said, "Don't turn away from God, Thad! He loves you!"

Thad thought about the words of the scripture as he stared down on the town, wondering how anyone could force himself to hope. *A man can't hope just because he wants to, can he?* he thought. But as he stood there trying to free himself from the fear that rose up in him like a creeping tide, he remembered Sky Winslow's last words the previous day. He had paused at the door, and with an intense stare in his penetrating eyes, he had said, "I guess we're putting our hope in God—and in Pet, Thad."

He was trying to think of that when the lock rattled and the guard stepped in. Another guard brought a plate of food, and behind him stood Harrison Duke. He waited until the guards were gone, then nodded at the food. "Try to eat some, Thad—and spruce up the best you can."

"You think it'll be over today?" Thad sat down and tried to nibble at the plate of cornmeal mush, but pushed the food away as it refused to go down.

"Could go that way. After a jury's had a day off, they sometimes come back bound and determined to finish up so they can get on with their business. And I reckon they've got their minds on what Johnny Pope is up to over at Manassas." Harrison talked for about an hour, most of it having nothing to do with the trial. He always did that with his clients before a critical hour, and he felt in his bones that the court would make up its mind before the day was over. *No way I can help him much,* he thought sadly. He had grown fond of the boy over the few days, and despite Duke's firm habit of refusing to get emotionally involved with his clients, he had done so. *If this were a civil case, I could do it— but these officers have seen so much death, they're more liable to hand out a death sentence than civilians would.*

He glanced at his watch and said casually, "I expect they'll put their star witness on the stand today. Abraham has been saving him for the cherry on the cake."

"Studs Mellon?"

"Yes. He's been making his brag about how he'll nail us to the wall."

"What if the court believes him?"

"We'll see." Duke rose to his feet, saying as the guard opened the door, "Keep your head, Thad—and remember, you got one thing going for you—I hate to lose worse than anybody in the courtroom!"

Thad shaved carefully, brushed his black hair into place, then put on the new uniform Rebekah had brought. It was still an hour before the court convened, and he wished it were over. His nerves began to creep, and he had to grip his hands with effort to keep them from trembling.

"Mistuh Thad! Mistuh Thad! Come to da winder!"

Leaping up, Thad dashed to the window and looked out to see Toby standing on the sidewalk beneath his cell. "Dere you is!" Toby's white teeth flashed in his coal-black face, and he waved at his friend. "Jes' come in from da farm. Thought I bettah fill you in on all da doin's!"

Thad listened as Toby rambled on in his powerful voice, giving all the minute details of the livestock and the crops. This was the first time since Thad's arrest that he'd seen Toby, and the sight of him lifted the boy's gloom. He realized that Toby was doing more than giving a report on conditions at Belle Maison; he had come to bring what cheer he could to his friend.

Once while they were talking, a short, burly man in a white coat and hat came marching along the sidewalk. Finding his way blocked, he snapped roughly, "Get outta my way, Nigger!" He reached out and pushed at Toby's shoulder, and found that it was like pushing at the courthouse building. He cursed and drew back his fist, ready to strike. "You slaves think Lincoln's already set you free!" But he never completed the blow. Toby caught the fist in his massive paw—just as he would have palmed a walnut. Though he exerted only a fragment of his power, Toby saw the man's face turn pale and he flinched, staring up at the black immobile countenance.

"You see dat man up dere?" He gestured at Thad; and when the burly planter followed Toby's directions, he said slowly and with a steady look, "He done paid fo' me, suh! He bought me—and set me free! So I'm as free as any man in dis world!" He released the hand, and the thick-set man threw a quick look at the small crowd of spectators that had gathered. With a withering glance at Toby, he scurried off, muttering under his breath.

Two of the spectators had been Major Stillwell and Major McClain. They waited until Toby turned back to finish his conversation with Thad; then the pair resumed their walk toward the courthouse. McClain broke the short silence as they went up the steps. "I wish I were at Manassas, Jason. Everything about Novak makes me want to turn him loose—except the evidence."

"Know what you mean, Mac," Major Stillwell agreed soberly. "If there were just one gap in the evidence in the boy's favor, I'd vote him innocent like a shot."

"How do you think the vote will go?"

Stillwell was a keen judge of men, and the shrewd eyes in the boyish face conveyed his answer: "Guilty as charged." Aloud he said gloomily, "If we had any real doubt about the evidence, he'd go free. You and I and Colonel Andrews would vote innocent."

"That's the way I see it, Jason—but we can't vote on our feelings," McClain replied as they entered the courtroom door.

The morning dragged by as Harrison Duke threw every possible measure of delay into the proceedings, and everyone in the room knew that he was fighting for time. The court dismissed for lunch, and during the interval Captain Clark said to Colonel Briggs, "Duke is the man I'd want defending me if I were up for murder—but he can't drag this thing out forever."

"It'll be today, I think," Briggs said.

At one o'clock the trial resumed, and Abraham announced, "I have one more witness—Private Leonard Mellon."

"Call Private Mellon, Sergeant," Andrews ordered. After the swearing in, Abraham began immediately.

"You are a private in the Third Virginia Infantry?"

"Yes, sir." Mellon looked better than Thad had ever seen him. He was clean shaven and his eyes were clear. His uniform was spotless and pressed. Thad knew instinctively that Abraham had seen to that.

"You have known the defendant, Thaddeus Novak, for how long?"

"About two years, sir."

"How did you meet him?"

"We got into a fight."

"Blast him!" Duke whispered bitterly. "Abraham is smart! He knew I'd dig that out and make that pug look bad!"

"Into a fight?" The thick-set prosecutor looked surprised, and inquired, "How did that happen?"

"Well, it was my fault, sir," Mellon admitted. "It was the night we celebrated the fall of Fort Sumpter. The whole county was there—and I'd been celebrating too much."

"Very regrettable—but quite understandable," Abraham nodded. "What was the fight about, Private?"

"Well, sir, a lot of people had been saying that Novak was a Yankee sympathizer—"

"Objection!"

"Objection sustained," Colonel Andrews nodded. "Hearsay is not evidence."

"I apologize for the witness, sir," Abraham said instantly. "He's only a simple soldier fighting for his country, not a lawyer."

"He's spent enough time in courtrooms to know quite a bit about the law," Duke spoke up loudly.

"That will do, sir!" Andrews reprimanded angrily before Abraham could object.

"I apologize to the court," Duke replied, but there was no regret on his pale face.

Abraham obviously wanted to make a sharp remark to Duke, but after a quick glance at Colonel Andrews' face, he turned back to Mellon. "You have been a member of the same company as the defendant?"

"Yes, sir. Company A. We both got to camp the same day. I was a volunteer, and he was a paid substitute."

"Objection!" Duke called.

"On what ground, Captain?" Abraham looked puzzled, but a sly grin tugged at the edges of his lips.

"The implication is that my client is not a good soldier, and your witness is."

"Is the witness mistaken?" Abraham asked. "Was Thad Novak a volunteer rather than a paid substitute?"

Duke knew that every word he said would simply allow his opponent to harp on the fact that Thad was a substitute, so he said, "Oh, very well. I am sure these gentlemen are aware that the Congress of the Congressional States passed the Act of Substitution. I am equally certain that they accept the acts of our Congress as wise—therefore, I withdraw my objection."

Abraham was disappointed, hoping to draw the matter out, but he turned back to the witness. "You were captured at Malvern Hill while on a patrol with the defendant and one other soldier?"

"Yes, sir."

"Tell the court every detail of that mission."

"Well—Sergeant Henry called for me and Novak to go with him."

Mellon made a good witness. He told the story of the action simply, though he sounded as if he were reciting a piece rather than telling a story—which was exactly the case in Duke's opinion. Finally he got to the incident of the capture.

"We was creeping across this open ground, and I heard Sergeant Henry shout, 'Yankees! Run for it!' I started to run, and then I heard the sergeant holler, and when I turned, I seen he was down."

"What did you do?"

"Well, I ran to him, and tried to pick him up, but it was too late. The Yankees was all around us."

"Did you see what Novak did when the sergeant gave the warning?"

"Well—" Mellon looked down and mumbled, "I don't like to say."

"Speak up, Private!" Colonel Andrews rapped out. "You are required to tell what you saw. Never mind what you 'like'!"

"Y-yes, sir!" Mellon lifted his head and stared across the room at Thad; then said clearly, "He threw his rifle down and put his hands up in the air, and he was yellin', 'I surrender'!"

"That's a lie!" Thad burst out, leaping to his feet.

"Be quiet, Private Novak!" Colonel Andrews commanded instantly. "You will have your turn to speak."

Thad sat down, his face pale, as Duke pulled at him, whispering, "Sit still! That won't help!"

"What happened then, Private Mellon?" Abraham asked. He had been pleased with the outburst. Novak had been impressing the court with his quiet behavior, and Abraham was disappointed when Duke pulled Thad up short—but Duke knew how to handle witnesses!

"They started asking us questions—like which company we was in and how to get to 'em. But I knew that all we had to tell was what outfit we was in—and that's all I told 'em." He shifted his glance toward Thad and said, "But then they started asking us where we was from—what state, I mean."

"What state? That's not what captured prisoners usually are asked. Did they say why they wanted to know?"

"The Yankee captain did. He kept listening to us, and found out I was from here, from Virginia, and then he asked Novak, 'Where you from, soldier?' "

"Did Novak tell him?"

"Oh yes, sir. He said he was from New York."

"What did the captain do then?"

"Why, he told one of the soldiers to take me back through their lines where the other prisoners was bein' held."

"Just you?"

"Yes, sir."

"What about the defendant?"

"He said not to take him. Said he wanted to talk to him some more."

"Did he say what about?"

"Well, I heard him say jest as they was takin' me off, 'You're not a real rebel, young man. Not like this other trash! A New Yorker, you say? I'll bet you just got mixed up with the wrong crowd, isn't that right?' "

"And what did the defendant say to that?"

"He said, 'That's the way it was, sir'—or something like that."

Abraham waited for an objection from Duke, but none came, and he said, "How did you escape, Private?"

"Oh, it was easy! Soon as we was out of sight of the troop, I made to stumble, and when that Yankee stopped, I made a grab at him and beat his head in with his own rifle. Then I headed back to our lines."

"Did you see the defendant after that?"

"Sure! I got back in time to see him leading that bunch of Yankees in a charge against our line!"

Abraham went over the story several times, trying to get Duke to object, but the unkempt lawyer seemed to be asleep, staring at the ceiling. Finally the prosecutor said, "No more questions. Your witness, Captain Duke."

Duke slowly lowered his head and stared at Mellon, but did not rise. He asked lazily, "Are you a patriot, Private Mellon?"

"Sir?"

"I asked if you are a patriot."

"Objection! The witness is not on trial!" Abraham protested.

"The prosecution has put great stress on the fact that he was a volunteer," Duke remarked. "Ordinarily I would not press this point, but the prosecutor has made much of it. May I ask just one or two simple questions?"

"I will allow that," Andrews nodded.

Duke rose, picked up a piece of paper, and walked to the witness stand. Thad could see that the paper had nothing but a series of drawings—mostly of ill-drawn birds—but Duke studied it carefully as he stood before Mellon. He lifted his eyes from the paper and asked in a loud voice, "Were you tried on a charge of attempted murder in Lynchburg, Virginia?"

Mellon's face went pale, and he seemed unable to speak.

"Answer the question!" Duke snapped.

"I—I was, but it—!"

"And what was the verdict of the jury?" Duke barked, then shouted, "Don't look at the prosecutor! He can't tell you what to say this time! What was the verdict?"

"Found guilty," Mellon mumbled. His jaunty assurance was gone, and his shoulders began to droop.

"And what was the sentence?"

"Ten years hard."

"I see," Duke said, and then asked, as if it were an afterthought, "But why aren't you in jail?"

"They said—they said I had my choice—either jail or join the army."

"So you aren't a patriot?" Duke smiled, and his sleepy eyes played over the officers at the table. "You didn't join the army because you believe in our *cause*? It was just to stay out of jail?"

Mellon looked down and nodded his head.

"Well, we need not press this matter—unless my worthy opponent would like a witness called to testify to the character of *this* witness? No? I thought not, Captain Abraham."

There was a smile on the sour face of Colonel Briggs. He leaned over and cupped his hand to whisper to Captain Clark: "That is one mean cuss! He's my kind of lawyer!"

For the next hour Duke proved that Briggs was right. He

dissected the hulking Mellon until the man was practically dissolved into a lump, shapeless and wet with perspiration. By the time Duke got to the end, not a man in the room would have trusted Mellon to hold his horse!

". . . so you just stumbled, and when the Yankee guard stopped, you beat him with his own rifle—is that the way you made your escape?"

Mellon was afraid of Duke, and it showed in the way he hunched in his chair and said faintly, "I-I guess so."

"You *guess* so?" Duke asked sharply. "You didn't tell this court you were *guessing* when you gave your testimony under the prosecution! These officers aren't interested in guessing games, Mellon!"

"Objection! Defense is badgering the witness!" Abraham was trying desperately to think of a way to get Mellon off the stand before Duke totally destroyed the man's credibility, but could think of none.

"Objection denied. Witness will answer the question."

"Yes, that was the way it happened," Mellon answered.

"Let me see if I can picture that little scene," Duke jeered. "If I were a cavalryman and had to take a prisoner to the rear, I believe I'd put a gun on him and force him to go ahead of my horse. The Yankees are wrong about slavery, but they're not completely stupid! So here we go—with you in front of me on the ground. I'm on my horse with my five-shot repeating carbine aimed at your back. Now, how does it go? You are seven or eight feet in front of me, and you pretend to stumble. I keep on riding and when I pass by, you leap to your feet, grab my rifle, pull me off my horse, and beat me with my own gun. Is that the way it happened?"

Not a man in the room believes that story! Abraham thought dismally. *I don't believe it myself! What a corker that Duke is! I'll have him in my law firm when this stupid war is over or die trying!*

Each of the officers waited for Mellon to answer, but there was no way for the burly private to say anything right. If he said "No," he branded himself a liar, while if he said "Yes," there was no way his story would stand.

"It happened like I said," Mellon whispered.

Duke had exquisite timing. He always knew the exact second

when he had milked the last drop from a hostile witness, never making the mistake of lesser lawyers who kept pounding the witness until he became an object of sympathy.

He said quietly, "I have no further questions." But as Mellon half rose, Duke said, as if a new thought had hit him, "Oh, just one perhaps. Private Mellon, are you aware of the penalty of the court for perjury—lying under oath?"

"I object!" Abraham leaped to his feet with a scream. "You've gone too far this time, Duke! Sir—I demand that remark be stricken from the record!"

Before the colonel could answer, Duke raised his hand and said mildly, "Oh, I withdraw the remark, Captain Abraham— and I certainly trust that the officers of this court will give my remark no heed."

The officers might not have paid heed, but they all noticed that the words had struck Mellon a hard blow. He gave an agonized look at Abraham, who ignored him, and when dismissed scurried from the room like a sheep-killing dog.

"Do you have other witnesses, Captain Abraham?"

"No, sir." Abraham took a deep breath and said slowly, "The prosecution rests."

"Very well. You may make your opening statement, Captain Duke."

Duke walked back and forth, slowly pointing out the inconsistencies in the testimonies from many witnesses. His phenomenal ability to remember word for word everything that had taken place during the week kept the court spellbound. As he spoke, he had one of those flashes of insight that came to him sometimes when he was fighting for a client. He had planned to call a long string of witnesses testifying to Thad's character, including the Winslows—but suddenly he realized that Abraham would only make the point that it was not a question of whether or not Thad Novak was a respectable young man, but whether he deserted and led the enemy to his unit.

Thad is his own best witness, he thought, and jettisoned his original plan. If he had one ounce of hope that the girl Patience would get back with the Yankee captain, he would not have chanced it; but he knew that he could not hold out for long, and Mellon's testimony had been Abraham's best shot. *Got to try it— it's the boy's last chance!*

When he finished his statement, he caught them all off guard by saying, "I will call only one witness—Thaddeus Novak."

The officers stared at him, but McClain thought, *Always catches people off guard—like Robert E. Lee!*

Thad was sworn in, and for almost an hour Duke skillfully led him to tell his story, including how he came from New York and why. The boy spoke well, he saw, and he let him choose his own words. When Thad related how Toby had saved him from freezing, Duke saw a light of sympathy on the face of Colonel Andrews. Then later Harrison asked, "How much money did you get for joining the army, Thad?"

"A thousand dollars."

"I see," Duke replied, then asked mildly, "What did you do with all that money? Put it in the bank?"

"Why, no, sir. I never actually *got* any money."

"Who did?"

"Well, I guess nobody, sir. Mr. Speers owned Toby—and he needed somebody to go to the army in his boy's place. So I said I'd do it if he'd give Toby his freedom."

"Why did you do that?"

"Why?" Thad stared at him in surprise. "Toby was my friend," he answered simply. "He saved my life, like I've already told about, but he helped me in lots of ways. Taught me how to farm and how to fish—everything."

There was a simple dignity in Thad's face, and finally he told his version of the escape, adding nothing to it.

"You've heard what Private Mellon says, Thad. How do you answer it?"

Thad said evenly, "It's not true." He did not protest or argue.

McClain nodded slightly, thinking, *Much better than arguing and probing. We either believe him or not.*

Finally Duke turned Thad over to Abraham, and the swarthy lawyer rose. And for the rest of the afternoon he tried to make Thad lose his temper, but by four o'clock, he saw that he was not going to get the job done. He ended his interrogation in frustration: "No more questions."

"The defense rests," Duke stated.

"The prosecution has nothing more," Abraham added.

Colonel Andrews looked around at the other officers and said slowly, "It's very late. I propose that we adjourn until tomorrow. Would that be acceptable to you gentlemen?" Taking their nods he rose, saying, "This court will reconvene at eight tomorrow morning."

They'll talk it over tonight—bring the verdict first thing in the morning, Duke thought; but as the guard came to escort Thad to his cell, he only voiced, "I'll stop by for a while tonight. You play chess?"

"No."

"Good—I hate to lose!"

CHAPTER TWENTY-FOUR

A MINOR MIRACLE

★ ★ ★ ★

Harrison Duke's guess that the verdict would come early the next morning was off by four hours. Two of the officers, Major McClain and Major Jason Stillwell, asked for several witnesses to be recalled, and as they repeated their testimonies, Duke thought he understood the reason for the recall. "Those two are trying to find some way to make your case look better," he whispered to Thad.

But by eleven-thirty, however, the two fell silent, and Colonel Andrews said, "I believe we have no more witnesses. The courtroom will be cleared. You will all be recalled when the decision is reached."

The next two hours were the longest of Thad's life as he sat alone in his cell—waiting. He paced the floor the entire time, unable to sit or lie down on his bunk. Finally the guards returned, saying, "It's time, Thad. Court is ready."

When he entered the courtroom, everyone else was already in place. Harrison Duke touched Thad's arm as he came to stand at the table. Colonel Andrews nodded, "You may be seated." His face was void of all expression as he spoke. "This court has heard a great deal of testimony concerning the actions of the defendant, Private Thaddeus Novak. We hope that we have given every opportunity for a proper defense. . . ."

As he droned on Duke could not look at Thad. Duke knew the signs. A verdict of "not guilty" would not have called for a long preamble such as the colonel was giving.

And he was correct. Colonel Andrews paused, cleared his throat, and said, "It is the unanimous decision of every man at this table that the defendant, Thaddeus Novak, is—guilty as charged."

A silence fell on the room, and Captain Aaron Abraham stared at the youthful face of the defendant—and felt a shock of admiration. *By the Lord, the boy didn't bat an eye!* It was Abraham's job to prosecute to the best of his ability, but as he had felt on several other occasions, he now experienced a sudden poignant sadness. He discovered, to his surprise, that he had wanted to lose this one—a rare thing indeed for Aaron Abraham!

"The prisoner will rise," Andrews said quietly. And when Thad rose, with Duke at his side, the colonel declared: "It is the sentence of this court that you will be taken from this place tomorrow morning at ten o'clock and be shot to death."

The words hung in the air, a palpable presence, and every man felt the chill of them. Every member of the court had seen men die in action. Most of them had ordered troops to their death. But it was one thing to fight in the heat of battle, another thing altogether to take a man out to a wall and shoot him to death as he stood there helplessly.

Andrews announced abruptly, "This court is adjourned!" He rose and left the room quickly without a look at Thad. The others followed, with one exception. Major Jason Stillwell came directly to where Thad stood, and tried to speak. There were tears rising in his eyes, Thad and Duke saw, and he said huskily, "I'm sorry!" Then he wheeled and left the room.

Thad stared straight ahead. He had expected the verdict, but when it came, it was as if everything in the world had jerked to a halt. He had been conscious of the activities in the room, of the officers leaving, and of Stillwell coming to speak to him—but it was as if he were in a huge bottle of some sort, a silent place, and everything else was far off.

Duke stood beside him, feeling worse than he had ever felt in his entire life. Putting his hand on Thad's arm, he choked, swallowed. "I'm sorry, boy. I—I should have done better!"

Thad turned and said evenly, "No, Captain. You did better than anyone else could have done. Don't you ever have any regrets about this."

Then the guard came up quietly and said apologetically, "Time to go, Thad."

"I'll be by later, Thad," Duke promised, and watched while they filed out. Thad had his head high, and his back was straight. "By the good Lord!" Duke groaned, "I hate to lose!"

———

Duke did not come by. Instead, he got drunk. For several hours he tried to screw up his courage so that he could make the visit, but he drank so much in the process that he passed out in a chair in his room.

Sky and Rebekah came at dusk, and they sat beside him silently for several hours. At midnight, Thad broke the silence. "I want you to go now."

They looked at him, both startled, and Rebekah asked, "Why, Thad?"

"I . . . guess I just want to be alone for a while. And . . . I don't like to see you tearing yourself apart."

"Thad!" she cried out, but he shook his head.

"I want to say something, and as soon as I finish—please go. Will you do that?" He waited until they both nodded, then he said quietly, "I hate to die. I'd like to be around to learn more about farming at Belle Maison. But I can't, so I want to tell you how much I—love you both." He stumbled over the words, for he had never said them to anyone in his whole life. He felt love, but things like that were not said in the world in which he grew up. Even as he spoke them out, it seemed to release something inside him, and he took a deep breath and smiled. "I never told anyone that before."

"Oh, Thad, we love you too—as if you were our own!" Rebekah whispered. Sky found his lips were trembling, so he only nodded, unable to say anything.

"Anyway," Thad went on, "I want you to know that being with you and the whole family has been—more wonderful than I could ever put into words. I felt like it was my family, in a way." He stood up and said, "Tell them all how much I appreciate the way you all took me in—Mark and Tom and Dan. And Belle, too. And . . ." His voice suddenly grew husky, and he could not seem to say the name. Finally he cleared his throat and said, "Tell Pet—tell her she's been more than a best friend. Tell her— I love her!"

He got up and whispered, "Please go now!"

Rebekah threw her arms around him, and he held her as she wept deep sobs that racked her body. Finally he released her, and Sky Winslow, his face contorted, held out his arms and embraced the boy. He whispered, "My boy! My boy! My dear boy!"

Then Thad pulled back. "Goodbye—thank you for everything."

He turned his back and went to stare out the window into the darkness. He heard the rap on the door, then the sound of it opening and the final slam, but did not move. The lock was thrown noisily into place, and he turned and fell on the bed, his face buried in the pillow, his shoulders heaving.

Much later a guard called out, "Chaplain to see you, Thad."

"No! I don't want to see him," he answered.

"A real hard one, Chaplain," the guard said. "Most men would be ready to listen to a preacher. Must be a real bad sinner."

Chaplain Boone stared at the guard wordlessly, shook his head, and took a chair in the hall. He waited until the rosy traces of dawn began to show in the east through the window at the end of the hall—but there was not a single sound from the cell of Thad Novak.

———

The morning guard brought a big breakfast tray, and while the night man was opening the door, he said to the chaplain, "He ready to go, Brother Boone?"

Boone did not answer, and the guard walked in and set the tray down. He looked at Novak, who was standing quietly at the window. Thad was wearing his uniform and did not look around until the guard said, "Nice breakfast for you, Thad."

Thad turned and gave a brief smile, saying, "I hear eggs are hard to get in Richmond these days, Henry. Guess I better not waste these."

Henry stood there and watched him sit down and begin to eat. "Let me know if you want more, Thad—and—good luck to you."

"Thanks, Henry." Thad looked up and put out his hand. "You've treated me real good. Thanks a lot."

"Why—sure!" The guard swallowed as he took the hand, then turned hastily and left the room. He said to the night man and the chaplain, "He ain't got no nerves! In there eatin' like he was going on a vacation." He wiped his forehead with a trembling hand. "Look at that! I'm worse off than he is!"

"Henry, ask if he'll see me," the chaplain said urgently.

"Sure, Parson." Henry threw the bolt, stuck his head in, and said, "Thad, Chaplain Boone—he'd like to see you."

"Let him come in, Henry." Thad stood up as Boone came in hurriedly, saying, "Thanks for coming by, Chaplain. Have a seat."

"Thank you, my boy." He sat down and found himself speechless. It was a little after eight, and he knew the execution was scheduled for ten. All night long he had prayed for a chance to see Thad, and for wisdom to use the right words to bring him to God. Now he sat there, helplessly unable to say a word.

Thad said, "I know you want me to pray, Chaplain, but I can't do it."

"Why not, Thad?"

"I just can't." Thad's dark eyes were large in the thin face, and there was fear in them—but he spoke firmly. "I can't abide a man who'll ignore God all his life; then when he's about to die, he goes running to Him."

Boone had thought this might be the problem, and he said, "My boy, you've not got this thing right. Let me help you." He began reading scripture, trying to get the young man to see that God was anxious to show mercy. After about ten minutes, they were interrupted by a commotion. Thad rose up and went to stare out the window.

"What's going on?" Boone asked.

"Don't know. A crowd of people over at the courthouse. Must be news of the war. Maybe we've won at Manassas." He watched for a time, and finally came and sat down. "Do you think the South will win this war?" he asked.

"In all honesty, Thad—I don't." He shook his head sadly. "We've lost the best of our young men. The bravest and the best. They all went at the first call, and many of them are in graves on the battlefields." Then he said quietly, "Thad, it's almost nine o'clock. Only an hour left. Please, my boy! Let me pray for you!"

But Thad shook his head, and Boone was reduced to desperation. He talked steadily for thirty minutes, and suddenly jumped as the door bar was opened with a loud bang. Henry came in, followed by the rest of the guards.

"Is it time?" Thad asked.

"No." Henry replied. "The lieutenant here says you've got to go back to the courtroom."

"Hurry up, Novak," the officer snapped impatiently. "I don't know what's up, but my orders are to get you there quick."

Thad rose instantly and followed the lieutenant out of the building and across the yard. A huge crowd was there and quite a few of them yelled, "There he is!"

A large man with a red face blocked the way of the lieutenant. He screamed, "I wish they could kill you twenty times, Yankee!"

The lieutenant shoved him out of the way, saying, "Form on the prisoner!" At the command the guards stepped up to march on each side of Thad and they proceeded to the steps, then went inside.

Thad saw nobody in the waiting room, but when he went inside the courtroom, he immediately noted that the entire court was assembled, including the prosecutor and Harry Duke. He was directed to Duke's side, and stared at the face of the lawyer. The sleepy eyes were crackling with energy, and he said, "Hello, Thad. I—"

Then Colonel Andrews arose, irritation on his face. "We have been summoned to re-convene this court-martial by the order of the Vice President of the Confederate States." He had been practically snatched out of his home an hour earlier by a pair of lieutenants with a note from Alex Stevens, ordering him to re-convene the court. The others, he had discovered, had been pulled in with no more ceremony. "I presume that you know something about this, Captain Duke?" Colonel Andrews remarked with heavy sarcasm.

"I am indeed guilty, sir," Duke replied. "One more 'antic' for you to go through, I'm afraid."

"Well, what is it?"

"I request that the court hear the testimony of one more witness."

"Why was he not heard earlier?" Andrews demanded.

"He was on the field of battle, Colonel—at Manassas, to be more specific. It was no small accomplishment to get him here, I can assure you. At least two major generals had to sign his orders."

"Well, bring him in," Andrews growled.

"Call Captain Lowell Winslow," Duke said, and stood there with a small smile on his face. He heard a gasp from Thad and whispered, "Here's your miracle, Thad. A minor one, perhaps, in this large war—but it makes this sinner believe there's a God looking out for you!"

The door opened, and as the guard came back, an audible gasp went up from several members of the court. For the witness wore the dress uniform of a captain in the Army of the United States.

"By heaven! A Yankee!" Major Jason Stillwell exclaimed in a loud whisper.

"Yes, sir, I am a Yankee," the tall captain confirmed. "And proud of it!"

Colonel Andrews stared at him, then said abruptly, "Swear Captain Winslow in." He carefully searched the face of the officer for a moment before saying, "Your witness, Captain Duke."

"Thank you, Colonel." Never had Harry Duke enjoyed a moment in court more. *I've got all the aces*, he thought as he walked forward to stand before Winslow. *Poor old Aaron—looks like he's swallowed a dozen lemons!*

"Captain Winslow, will you relate to the court the incident that took place on Malvern Hill in which you took a Confederate soldier prisoner?"

Lowell Winslow was enjoying himself immensely. He looked across the courtroom at Novak, taking in the raven-black hair, the strong face, tapering from a broad forehead to a firm jaw. The steady black eyes, deep and wide set.

The events of the past few days flashed through his mind. He had relished his ride with Patience and Dooley. They had been stopped by Union soldiers at the sight of Dooley's rebel garb, but had been speechless when presented a paper signed by *two* major generals—Sheridan and Kearny. But that had been *nothing* compared with the events that occurred when they crossed the line into Confederate territory. Winslow's blue uniform had drawn almost half the patrols in the country. It had been almost comic to see their tough faces and harsh manner dissolve when they read the pass—and saw the name of Jefferson Davis at the bottom!

And he had been intrigued by the pair of rebels. He had never spoken to a Confederate before, except a few sullen prisoners, and Dooley Young had been a source of endless fascination to him. The little rider was tough as a boot, could ride like a centaur, and shoot like Daniel Boone! He could live on a cup of boiled grits for a day, and if there was any fear in the man, it never showed itself. Winslow had wondered how the Union troops could be beaten again and again by beggars with poor arms; well, now he *knew*!

And the girl was a wonder! She was more girl than woman, perhaps; but the entire journey, which was hard and demanding—and the second half for her!—never seemed to bother her. At nights she would sit around the fire talking with the two men. He would never forget her—he was sure of that! The sight of her large eyes regarding him across the campfire as she told him of her family and her life left a strong mark on him. He had never thought much of the citizens of the South as individuals. His vague notion of them was formed by lurid novels such as *Uncle Tom's Cabin* and scurrilous articles in the eastern newspapers. By the time they made their last camp, he had heard of Belle and her two suitors; Mark, a lieutenant; Tom, a corporal in the infantry; and Dan, who was dying to get into it. Most of all, he thought he knew something about Thad Novak—for the girl was obviously in love with him.

Yes, he thought as he looked at Thad, *he looks as if he might be worth her trouble!*

Then Winslow began his story, and as he related the events, he saw that every officer at the table seemed relieved. Two of them were smiling broadly, and the others looked highly satisfied.

Winslow concluded by saying, "And when we got back from

the patrol, I turned the prisoner over to the officer in charge of all our prisoners. Because of his connection with Sky Winslow, I intended to see him after the battle—but I was slightly wounded in the battle, and he was gone before I had the opportunity. I did write to my father and ask him to visit Novak, but he, too, was ill at that time and unable to do so."

He stopped and looked at the court with a smile. "I hope my testimony has been of some use."

"I think you may be assured it has," Colonel Andrews responded instantly. Then he gave a hard look at Abraham, asking in a challenging tone, "Do you wish to question this witness, sir?"

Aaron Abraham smiled easily and replied, "I have no questions."

Colonel Andrews said, "I will ask the members of this court to step outside." They filed out, and Thad watched Harry Duke draw small animals on a sheet of paper for five minutes. Then the door opened, and the officers took their places. "We have reached a unanimous decision," Andrews announced. "We have—"

"Colonel," Lowell Winslow interrupted. "May I make one request?"

"Why, I suppose so," Colonel Andrews replied. Then he smiled broadly, adding, "Any man that will wear that uniform on the streets of Richmond deserves some consideration."

"Thank you, sir." Winslow smiled. "I look forward to the day when it will be a common sight—but as to my request, there is one person who deserves to be in this courtroom to hear your decision."

"And that is?"

"The most dedicated rebel I've met in this whole war, Colonel—Miss Patience Winslow." He saw the eyes of Novak lift, and he told them how he had been practically kidnapped from the army of General Sheridan. "Anyone who can do that has my total admiration. I know she's outside—and it would mean a great deal to her if she could hear your verdict."

"Well, certainly!" Andrews responded at once. "Soldier, bring Miss Winslow into the courtroom."

Every eye was on the door, and when Patience stepped inside, a murmur of admiration went up from at least some of the officers at the table. She was still dressed in her riding clothes, and her face was a little wan; but when she saw Thad, her eyes sparkled like diamonds, and her lips framed his name—*Thad!*

"Miss Winslow, we are about to give our decision on this man—and since you have played a major part in it, we think it well that you should hear it." There was just a trace of dramatics in Andrews, and he drew the moment out. Finally he said, "We are in total harmony in our decision—we find the defendant, Thaddeus Novak—not guilty!"

No military strictness of the court-martial could keep Patience Winslow from dashing across the room and throwing her arms around Thad's neck. The court smiled and the avowed agnostic lawyer, Harrison Duke, tossed his papers into the air and hollered "Glory to God" with all the fervor of a Methodist evangelist. The Jewish lawyer, Aaron Abraham, joined Duke with equal enthusiasm, crying loudly, "Amen!" One by one the members of the court came down and shook hands with Private Thad Novak—at least *two* of them giving Patience a tender kiss on the cheek!

Later as the two lawyers celebrated the decision, Abraham said, "You are not a bad lawyer—for a *goyim*. But I feel sorry for you, so I will offer you a job in my law firm after the war!"

Duke stared at the fat man and retorted, "I wouldn't be a member of any law firm that would have *me* on its staff! However," he conceded, "I will permit you to join *my* firm. You can handle the unimportant cases while I do the big stuff."

Their sentiments became maudlin after a time, and both wept openly for the young couple.

Thad and Pet had left the building as soon as Thad was released. A covered buggy had been brought to the back door, and the two jumped in and drove rapidly down the side street, coming soon to the outskirts of Richmond, and then to the open country.

Dark clouds were rolling up from the north, and a brisk wind began tossing them around. Thad stared at the sky. "Looks like a bad storm coming."

"Yes."

Both were stunned by the recent events and found it difficult to talk. The silence grew heavy as they sped down the road. Soon they came to Cedar Creek, where Thad stopped the horses under the overhanging branches near the small bridge.

He sat quietly for a moment, then turned and murmured, "There's nobody like you, Pet." He took her hand and studied it. Holding it tightly in his hand, he looked up and smiled. "I heard once about a country where if you saved somebody's life, that person belonged to you forever. So I guess you own at least one lowly private."

"Oh . . . I don't want to . . . own you," she whispered. She lifted her eyes to his, her lips trembling and tears welling up again. She brushed them away, saying, "I can't seem to stop crying, Thad!"

He looked down at her—so close, so sweet; then he bent his head and kissed her. It was a man's kiss, not a boy's, and all the tension and weight that he had labored under suddenly found expression as he pulled her to his chest roughly. She was shocked at the intensity of her own response, for her arms were around his neck, pulling him closer—and when he finally released her, she was throbbing from head to foot.

Her eyes sparkled and a smile curved her full lips. "I saw Mama this morning. She told me what you said to tell me—last night when she talked to you."

Thad's face flushed. "I was sure I wasn't going to make it when I said all that."

"I want to hear you say it again—to *me*, not to Mama and Papa."

Thad swallowed hard—wanting her, yet not daring. "Pet— I'm nobody. You come from a good family and—"

"We're talking about what you said about me last night," Pet reminded him. She lifted her hand and grabbed his thick black hair, forcing his head around. Her gray eyes were soft, but there was a determined set to her mouth. "We're going to sit here until you tell me, Thad Novak!"

A smile crept over his face and he reached up and stroked her cheek tenderly, his eyes caressing her. "I told your folks— that I love you—and now I tell it to you, Pet. I've always loved you—and I guess I always will!"

Nodding slowly, she took a deep breath, and then pulled his

head down for another kiss. When she drew back, her dimples appeared as she grinned playfully, "If you hadn't said that, Thad Novak—I'd have gone back to the court and told them to shoot you, after all!"

They burst out laughing for pure joy, and all the way to Belle Maison they talked and giggled—exactly like a couple in love!

CHAPTER TWENTY-FIVE

BELLE OF THE BALL

★ ★ ★ ★

Belle Winslow's answer to most problems was very simple—
have a dress ball. Therefore, after Thad's miraculous escape,
everyone expected that Belle would arrange for a celebration.
She did so by simply putting her arms around her father's neck,
looking up with pleading eyes, and whispering, "Please, Papa!
Shelby will be taking the Richmond Blades to whip the Yankees
any day—and Vance and I haven't had much time together.
Please!"

Sky had caved in, lamenting to Rebekah, "I wish I could handle politicians as well as that girl handles me!" Then he grinned
and added, "But she's right about it. Lee is rushing every man
he can get to meet Pope. Nothing left in Richmond but a skeleton
crew. Anyway, it will be a nice celebration for Thad."

Sky's motive was good, but at the ball, which took place at
Belle Maison on the evening of August 22, Thad had never felt
more uncomfortable in his whole life. The ball was in full swing
when he arrived, and after greeting Rebekah and Sky, he sought
out the most obscure place he could find—an off-set space cre-
ated by the massive fireplace and a large china cabinet. Thad
picked up a cup of punch and squeezed himself back against the
wall, but he did not remain hidden for long. Pet spotted the
recluse and came to stand before him.

"Oh, Thad, you look wonderful in your uniform!" she exclaimed. She was wearing a new dress, but not a ball gown. It was a simple light blue frock with a high neck and a skirt that fell to the floor. Her only jewelry was a single sparkling diamond on a gold chain around her neck, which highlighted the simplicity of her attire. Her hair was not braided as she usually wore it, but fell like a shining waterfall down her back. Her wide gray eyes and curved lips were the frosting on the cake

"You look great, Pet," Thad murmured, admiration shading his face. Then he frowned. "But I feel like Dooley said *he* felt once—like a bullfrog on a busy street with his hopper busted!"

Pet laughed. "Oh, don't be silly. You're the hero of the hour. Everybody in Richmond's talking about you."

"Nope, they're talking about you and that Yankee captain," Thad retorted. "See that crowd around him?"

Pet looked across the room to where Captain Lowell Winslow was surrounded by an admiring group. "Every girl here wants to grab him," Pet smiled. "I don't know what they'd do with him if they caught him. Keep him in a glass cage? Become a Yankee bride?" Then she exclaimed, "Well, of all the nerve!"

"What is it, Pet?"

"Why, that sister of mine!" Pet's eyes flashed with anger, and she said impatiently, "She's stealing him away—and with her own fiancée standing there! I declare, I'm going to have Papa whip that girl!"

"It's too late for that, I reckon," Thad grinned. "Have to catch a child young to do any good. Now, if your father would just take a stick to you—!" He caught her hand as she raised it to strike him playfully. "But I think you're right," he said soberly as he glanced to where Belle was smiling enticingly up at the young Yankee. "Miss Belle shouldn't treat Captain Wickham that way. She'll be sorry for it."

"Belle's a flirt—always has been," Pet said, irritation lacing her voice. "But it's time to stop."

She would have been even more concerned had she been able to read Lowell Winslow's thoughts. As he led Belle to the dance floor, he was struck momentarily silent by the perfection of her face and figure. Many women look fine at twenty feet—but as he looked at her flawless creamy skin, he could see no fault. Her complexion was not quite olive, but there was just a faint trace of her Indian heritage to give her face a translucent glow that brought out the flush to her cheeks. Her eyes, he saw, were her best feature—large, almond shaped, with dark pupils, almost purple, surrounded by clear, bright white. This night she was wearing a daring low-cut silver gown that accentuated her exotic coloring—her figure was exciting, to say the least! She had a tiny waist, nipped in as far as possible, and her full bodice and curving body dazzled Lowell.

As they moved across the floor, he said, "I expect that your fiancée will challenge me to a duel as soon as this dance is over. Isn't that how you do it in the South?"

"Why, Captain Winslow, why would he do a thing like that?" Belle laughed up at him, adding, "You're a perfect gentleman, sir—which I thought no Yankee could ever be! You haven't done a thing to be challenged to a duel."

"He'd shoot me if he could read what I'm thinking," Winslow grinned. He was tall with slim flanks and trim shoulders, and a smile that revealed milky white teeth as he peered down at her.

"And what is that, sir?" she demanded.

"Why, that you are the loveliest woman I've ever seen—and I'd like to get you away from here and give you a mad, passionate kiss." He laughed at her startled expression. "See, I'm just an uncouth Yankee, after all."

Belle allowed herself to be pulled closer, saying, "If you hold me any closer, Vance *may* call you out, Captain Winslow!" She tilted her head back and pursed her lips, well aware that doing so made them into a tempting morsel. "I spent a great deal of time with your brother Davis when he came to Richmond. You aren't at *all* like him, are you?"

"No. He has all the brains. I expect he'll be a rich, famous writer one day, while I will be a humble soldier—if you rebels don't put me down."

"Don't say that!" A shiver ran over Belle, and she frowned. "I can't bear to think of such things!"

"Even for us Yankees?"

"Oh, why did you people ever start this horrible war?" Belle shook her head, and as was customary, put the grim realities of the war out of her mind. "Your brother—I can't understand how he can stand by and just *watch*! I didn't like him—but I adored your grandfather!"

"So do I. He's been my idol since I was a boy. I almost joined the navy to be like him, but I get seasick." He grinned and commented, "He liked you, too. I got a letter from him telling me all about his visit. He called you—let's see, how did he put it? Oh, yes—'the most toothsome wench I ever set eyes on.' "

"He didn't say that!"

"Oh, he did!—but he also said, 'Beneath all that raw beauty there is a woman who would satisfy any man.' " Lowell swung her around and leaned so close that his lips brushed her cheek. "My grandfather and I agree on that!" he whispered, and saw the delicate flush that rose to her cheeks at his compliment. *Vain as a peacock*, he thought as they moved gracefully around the floor. *But Grandfather is pretty sharp. Guess he sees something real in her.*

Sky was standing beside Vance Wickham, and he noted that his future son-in-law was watching the visitor dancing with Belle. He grinned. "You want your ring back, Vance?"

Wickham turned to smile at him. "No, sir. Let her torment the poor fellow. She's done it to all of us poor rebels; now let her wipe up on the Yankees."

Shelby Lee was standing to Sky's left and he added a comment lightly, "You'll have to be tougher on the men than you are with your fiancée, Captain Wickham, or they'll take advantage of your easy temper."

"They aren't as pretty as Belle, Major," Wickham grinned. "It's not hard to be tough on a bunch of hard-nosed soldiers." Then he changed the subject, asking, "You think we'll be pulling out in a day or two for Manassas?"

"I was talking to General Lee this morning, and from what I gather the Third Virginia will be left here to protect the Capitol. Plans haven't been finalized yet, so don't say anything to the men."

"We'll miss it then," Mark said, disappointment showing in his face.

"You bloody fire-eater!" Vance laughed. "Don't be so anxious to get us all killed. There'll be plenty of action for us here. Why don't you get yourself engaged to Rowena? Think how quickly you could rise in the army, being the colonel's son-in-law!"

Mark flushed, and then laughed at himself. "I guess I'll wait to see how you and Belle make it, Vance. If you can tame my sister, I may be willing to take on a high-flying southern girl myself." Then he asked Major Lee, "What does the general think of Pope?"

"Not much," Lee replied. "The man is a talker, and my uncle doesn't like that. Did you hear what he said when he took command from McClellan? 'I have come to you from the west where we have always seen the backs of our enemies. Let us study the probable line of retreat of our opponents, and leave our own to take care of itself.' "

"Sounds like a pompous fool," Sky nodded, then added, "I heard he said that his headquarters would be in the saddle."

"Yes, and do you know what Stonewall Jackson replied to that?" Lee smiled. " 'I don't expect to have much trouble from someone who doesn't know his headquarters from his hindquarters.' "

A burst of laughter went up from the small group. Major Lee continued. "Pope has ordered his soldiers to live off the Virginia countryside, which gives a license to every man who wants to steal. He also told his men that anyone who communicates with the 'rebels' in any way—including any mother or wife writing to a soldier—would be treated as a spy: shot by a firing squad." He stared at the angry faces and added, "I heard General Lee say, 'That miscreant Pope must be suppressed.' Strong words for him."

"Better not discuss any more strategy," Mark suggested. "Here comes our Yankee."

"I've pumped this Yankee dry of all his secrets!" Belle exclaimed as she pulled Lowell to where they stood. "If you'll get me an interview with your uncle, Major Lee, I will give him General Pope's plan and Robert E. Lee can run the Army of the Potomac back to Washington again!"

Belle's comment drew laughter, but the Yankee held up his hand, saying solemnly, "No need to do that. I am so captivated by this rebel spy that I am ready to divulge General Pope's battle plan to all of you."

"I'd be glad to hear it, Captain," Wickham remarked.

"Very simple. We intend to move all our troops from Washington by ship to Manassas." He spoke with a straight face, but the humor shone out of his blue eyes.

"Ah, yes, but there are no bodies of water in that area that would permit those tactics," Major Lee smiled.

"We Yankees are not bothered by such minor obstacles. General McClellan is an engineer, as you know. Well, sir, his plan is to dig huge canals, reaching all the way from Washington to the battlefield. It will take a long time, but General McClellan is a patient man."

"That is well known, Captain," Wickham agreed with a smile. "He moved at the terrific pace of two miles a day during the Peninsula campaign."

"Of course! But you have not grasped the heart of our strategy, Captain Wickham! It will take between fifteen to twenty years to complete the canals, and by that time you rebels will have become enlightened to the evils of slavery and will have freed them all!"

They were all amused by the Yankee's willingness to poke fun at himself, but Sky, who had been listening to the amiable conversation, now said solemnly, "I wish such a plan would work, Captain. It would save thousands of lives—rebel and Yankee alike."

Lowell stared at his relative with interest. Like Davis, he knew the history of Sky Winslow well, and admired him. He commented quietly, "It's sad, Mr. Winslow, that we are separated by this war. I doubt if Gilbert Winslow ever thought of such a thing when he came over on the *Mayflower* to find a place of freedom."

Sky shook his head slowly. "Every generation of Americans, it seems, has had to buy freedom with its own blood. But always before it's been a struggle with the British or the French—another nation. Now—it's brother against brother."

Belle frowned and interrupted the solemn exchange. "Come, Vance, you've ignored me." She pulled him away, and soon he was smiling at her as usual. "Were you jealous of Captain Winslow?" she asked, arching her eyebrows.

"Didn't notice he was paying any attention to you, Belle."

"Oh, you are a liar! I saw you watching us. I told him you'd probably send him a challenge if he didn't stop!"

"Well, then, I was. But if I'm going to fight a duel with every man who flirts with you, I'd better stock up on ammunition." He held her close and said, "You are lovely! I've never seen you look so beautiful!"

"Don't try to make up to me, you old stick!" She pouted and tried to draw back. "I declare I'm going to make you jealous, Vance Wickham, if I have to elope with that handsome Yankee!"

Later, when they went back to find Lowell still surrounded by the officers, she claimed him audaciously, saying, "Captain Winslow, come dance with me. This fiancée of mine is too self-assured. I propose that we make him turn green with jealousy."

"No need of that," Wickham protested and smiled at Winslow. "I hereby challenge you, sir, and demand satisfaction. You may choose the weapons."

Lowell Winslow instantly countered, "I choose cornstalks, Captain!" and led Belle away amid the laughter.

"The fellow has great wit," Sky said. "And even if he *is* my kin, I'd make a calculated guess he's a pretty good soldier."

A mutter of confirmation went up, and Mark remarked, "It's hard to think that in a few days we may be killing each other. He's a fine fellow. Don't see why he can't be on our side."

The hours rolled by and soon the candles were half their original length. The refreshments had been replaced over and over, and the musicians had played every tune they knew at least a dozen times.

Thad had steadfastly refused to dance with Pet, so she had remained at his side. But he had spoken to almost everyone, shyly at first, but with more freedom when he saw that no shadow of guilt remained on him after the court-martial pronounced him innocent.

But when the end of the evening came, he got caught in a trap that Pet had carefully laid for him. While Thad was watching the dancers, Mr. Sky Winslow stepped up beside the musicians and called for quiet.

The music stopped abruptly and everyone turned toward Sky. "We have welcomed you all," he said, "and we want to pay special appreciation to our kinsman from the North, Captain Lowell Winslow!" He waited until the applause died down, then continued. "But there is another person here from the North who has chosen to make the South his home—Private Thad Novak. Will you please come forward—and you too, Patience."

Thad was stunned and wanted to run from the room, but Pet discerned his intention and grabbed his arm, whispering fiercely, "Come on!" He realized he had no choice but to follow her as she passed through the crowd to stand beside her father.

"You know the story of this young man, so I need not repeat it, but I will say that I am as proud of him as I am of my own sons! He will soon be back with his company, and I want us to give him a hand for his courage and his selflessness!"

The room exploded with wild applause, and Thad found himself surrounded by well-wishing Confederate officers.

When order was restored, Sky said, "I think a speech is in order."

"Oh no!" Thad protested. "I can't, Mr. Winslow!"

"No speech?" Sky's eyes twinkled. "Well, my daughter Patience *did* say you would refuse—but she also said you have a fine singing voice, so we demand a song, do we not?"

A cry of approval went up, and Thad shot a stricken look at Pet. "You told!" he whispered hoarsely. "I'll get you for this, Patience Winslow!"

"Come now, Thad; what will it be?"

Thad had always been a singer, but not for others. Pet had discovered he had a gift, and had made him sing on the creek banks while they were fishing or in the woods hunting coons. But to sing before this group of rich people who had heard professional singers—it made the fear course down his back. Then Pet slipped her hand in his and urged, "You can do it, Thad! Sing the one I like so much."

He swallowed and said, "Well, all of you officers have heard this one, but maybe some of you ladies haven't. I guess, aside from 'Dixie,' it's the song our men like best—and I've heard that the Yankee soldiers sing it a lot, too." He took a breath and began to sing a cappella, but a French musician named Jacques DePont began to weave music from his violin as Thad sang. He had a clear tenor voice, and the words floated over the room easily:

"The years creep slowly by, Lorena,
The snow is on the grass again;
The sun's low down the sky, Lorena,

The forest gleams where the flowers have been,
But the heart throbs on as warmly now,
As when the summer days were nigh;
Oh, the sun can never dip so low
Adown affection's cloudless sky."

The audience stood motionless, for the young man's dusky handsome face and his clear melodious voice seemed to represent the whole war. The sadness of the lyrics brought the brevity of life close, and all of them were thinking of friends and relatives who lay in unmarked graves on distant fields. Vance felt a tremor run through Belle, and put an arm around her, drawing her close as Thad sang on:

"We loved each other then, Lorena,
More than we ever dared to tell;
And what we might have been, Lorena,
Had but our loving prospered well—
But then 'tis past, the years are gone,
I'll not call up their shadowy forms;
I'll say to them, 'Lost years, sleep on!
Sleep on! nor heed life's pelting storms.'

"It matters little now, Lorena,
The past is in the eternal Past;
Our heads will soon lie low, Lorena,
Life's tide is ebbing out so fast.
There is a future! O thank God!
Life, this is so small a part!
'Tis dust to dust beneath the sod;
But there, up there, 'tis heart to heart."

As the last strains of the song ended, Belle sobbed and left the room, followed by Vance. He caught up with her on the veranda, pulled her around and asked, "Belle—what's wrong?"

"I don't know, Vance!" She fell against him and began sobbing, her body shaken by a storm of weeping. He held her, confused by her reaction, for she was not prone to weeping.

Belle herself was confused. She had been a happy, carefree person all her life, wanting nothing. But lately, being the prettiest girl at the dance had become stale to her, and she had suffered fits of depression ever since her engagement to Vance. A vague dissatisfaction had crept upon her, and she had wept several times at night, not knowing why—just as she did now.

As the words of the song Thad sang came to her, she was struck with how little she had done in life—little that *counted*. And now as she composed herself, she drew back and looked up at Vance with tears running down her cheeks. "Vance, I want us to be married."

"Why, so we will, sweetheart," he said, somewhat astonished at her urgency. "We've talked about it—how it will be better to wait—"

"No. *You* talked about it—and my parents. Nobody asked *me* what I wanted."

"Belle!" he groaned, "you don't know what it can mean, being married to a soldier. I could be killed tomorrow—or even worse, I could be maimed and you'd have a cripple to take care of the rest of your life!"

"Am I a hot-house plant, Vance?" she cried out vehemently. "Are you supposed to make all the sacrifices—bear all the risks?"

"You're a child!"

"No!" She was suddenly in his arms, and pulling his head down, she kissed him with an urgency that she had never shown. "I'm not a child, Vance—I'm a woman! And I want to be your wife!"

He was overwhelmed by her passion. He himself, despite his casual airs, wanted to marry Belle more than anything in the world, but had not thought she was ready. Now he said, "Are you sure, Belle?"

She pulled him to her, kissed him with a long lingering caress, then whispered, "I want to marry you now, Vance! Let's not wait!"

The following Monday they were married in a hastily prepared wedding at the church—despite protests from all directions. But Belle had her way, and the newlyweds left in a carriage for a brief honeymoon, overjoyed and happily waving goodbye to everyone.

Sky stood with his arm around his wife, watching their daughter leave. "Well, Rebekah," he said, "it's done. What do you think?"

"They'll need our prayers, Sky," she replied quietly. "Even in ordinary times, Belle would be a difficult girl to make into a wife.

And in the middle of a war. . . !"

"He's got his hands full," Sky agreed. Then he smiled and gave her a hug. "But so did I—and we're still at it. Here I am, an old man and still in love with the girl I married!" He stared after the carriage, saying prayerfully, "God be with them!"

Thad and Pet also watched the couple leave. "I feel so happy for them!" Pet murmured.

Thad nodded and said cautiously, "Me, too, but—they sure are takin' a chance."

"You *have* to take chances!" Pet retorted rebelliously. "What do you want to do, go live in a cave and not think beyond the walls?"

He grinned at her. "A man sure wouldn't have to worry about bein' bored if he was married to you, Patience Winslow!"

CHAPTER TWENTY-SIX

INVASION

★ ★ ★ ★

"I wish you didn't ever have to go back!"

Pet had been lying on her back staring up at the thick, leafy foliage overhead. A combination of fatigue, the cool air beside the brook, and the singing of choirs of insects had almost lulled her to sleep. But a disturbing thought intruded into her mind as she dozed; she had rolled over to look at Thad, who was lying beside her, his mouth slightly open as he slept.

A smiled curved her lips as she lay there quietly thinking of the six days that had sped by since the court-martial. She and Thad had been out at dawn every day, and there was not a square foot of Belle Maison they had not covered. She had shown him the bumper crop of pigs and yearlings that had prospered under Jacob's expert care. The names she had given some of them had amused Thad—such as the stubborn boar she had named "U.S. Grant," and the prize yearling she called "General Lee." Toby had joined Thad and Pet at times to point out with pride the huge fields of vegetables that grew luxuriously, and which would be spilling over in a few weeks.

Pet picked up a straw and drew it lightly across Thad's lip, giggling when he slapped at it, taking it for a fly. She continued to torment him, thinking of the cool nights spent at the river fishing for blue channel catfish, and the nights they had sat around a fire listening to the dogs chase a fox. Dooley had always kept foxhounds, and Thad had been surprised to learn that the object was not to catch the fox—but to sit around and listen as different dogs struck trails. They all sounded pretty much alike to Thad and Pet, but Dooley knew each voice as if it were human. "That there's ol' Choklate," he'd nod as a low, moaning cry had come floating to them. He'd told them what a Yankee had said once about fox hunting as he'd watched the poor farmers at it: "The unspeakable in pursuit of the inedible!"

Thad slapped again at the straw, jerked himself awake with a grunt, then sat up, yawning widely. "Nearly dozed off."

"You've been asleep for about an hour," she said with a trace of tartness. "Fine way to treat a girl."

"Gosh! Guess I must be behind on my sleep." He stretched and asked, "Did you say something to me—or were you just talking?"

She pulled his ear playfully. "I said I wish you never had to go back."

He blinked quickly, then shrugged. "I guess everybody in the whole army wishes that—and all their families." He didn't like to think of going back either, and stood up, pulling her to her feet. "We have to get back," he said. "I got a chore to do in town."

She mounted the mare reluctantly and said as they walked their horses beside the brook, "I want to go to the meeting tonight." A new preacher had come to pastor the small church in their neighborhood, and word had gotten around that he was a fine evangelist.

"Reckon I'll be back in time, but Mark sent word that Major Lee wanted to see me, so I have to go." He swung his gaze over the panorama of fresh country, savoring the lush fields broken by low rolling hills. Fall stood on tiptoe, flavoring the late summer air with a sharp tang, and he took a deep breath, letting it out slowly. "Reckon it's something about going back on duty. The regiment's been expecting to go at any time."

"I feel sorry for Belle. She and Vance haven't had much time." Pet thought about her sister and shook her head in wonder. "Can't ever get over how much she's changed, Thad! Why, it's almost embarrassing to watch her, she's so took up with her new husband!"

"Love does funny things to people," Thad nodded sagely.

Pet giggled explosively, then rolled from side to side in the saddle, laughing helplessly.

"What's so funny?" Thad demanded.

"You are!" she gasped. Her eyes were filled with laughter. Finally she took a deep breath and asked, "Where did you get all this vast knowledge about love, Thaddeus?"

He reddened and ignored her. Kicking Blackie in the sides he shot ahead, calling out, "Let's get moving!" They raced madly alongside the brook, then cut across the fields. When they came to a rail fence, Thad turned toward the gate some fifty yards to his left, but Pet spoke to her horse and went sailing over the fence. Thad hollered, "You crazy girl! You'll break your neck!"

She was standing beside her horse laughing at him when he pulled up into the yard. "Let's go to town in the buggy, Thad—you can tell me some more about love and all that stuff!"

Belle and Vance came out of the house just in time to hear that, and both of them laughed. "We better go along, Belle," he suggested, holding on to her waist. "I may need a few pointers myself."

She turned and kissed him, whispering, "No, you don't. But I need some things."

As the women ran to get ready, Vance said, "I'll help you hitch up the team, Thad."

"Well—maybe you better not, sir," Thad answered uncomfortably. "Captains don't help privates, do they?"

"Not when anyone else is around," Wickham grinned. "But we're in the family now, and nobody's looking. Come on."

As they hitched up a set of matched bays, Thad asked, "Mark says Major Lee wants to see me. Would you be knowing why?"

"Don't know a thing about it, Thad." He slipped the collar over the mare's head and laughed. "I guess I don't know much about anything. Didn't know getting married addled a man's brain so." Threading the lines through the guides, he gave Thad a wry grin, adding, "Better keep an eye on me, Thad. If I start calling some of the men 'honey' or 'sweetheart' slap me alongside the head, will you?"

"Miss Belle is sure changed—and so are you, sir. Never seen two people so happy." As they finished and walked the team

out of the corral onto the drive, Thad asked hesitantly, "Do you—
I mean, have you all talked about what would happen if you
were . . ."

"If I were killed?" Vance finished for him. "No," he said,
shaking his head. "I tried to, but it upsets Belle so much, I had
to give up. Guess I'll just have to keep the Yankees from killing
me," he ended lightly, then said quickly, "There're the women.
Don't mention anything about this to Belle."

They made the trip into town, with Belle and Vance in the
back. Their amorous behavior embarrassed Thad, but amused
Pet highly. Finally they reached Richmond, letting the women
out on Cherry Street near the shops. "You go spend all my
money, sweet," Vance said. "I'll go on down to the camp with
Thad. Maybe there's some news of the battle."

They drove through the streets to the large encampment area
where the regiment waited. When Thad pulled up, Vance
jumped to the ground, saying, "Be here in one hour sharp, Private Novak!" winking slyly at Thad as a notice that they were
on official status now.

Thad found that Company A had gone into town almost to
a man, but Tom rose up from where he was reading a book. "Hi,
Thad. See you made it." He nodded toward the large tent hous-
ing the officer command quarters and said, "Mark told me to
send you in as soon as you arrived."

"What's it about, Tom?"

"No idea. Stop and tell me before you leave."

"All right." Thad walked across the line of small tents to larger
ones, and came to attention and saluted as Lieutenant Beauchamp suddenly stepped outside.

"Oh . . ." Beauchamp was caught off guard, but he returned
the salute. "Come in, Private."

He stepped back inside, and Thad followed. Major Lee and
Lieutenant Winslow were examining a map on a folding table.
"Private Novak is here, Major," Beauchamp announced.

Both men looked up, and Major Lee smiled. "Well, Private,
you are prompt." He examined Thad's face more closely and
added, "You're looking much better. Lost some of that prison
pallor. Feeling better, too, I'd wager."

"Oh yes, Major," Thad returned quickly.

"Well, I'll be brief," Lee replied crisply. "There are two matters my officers and I need to discuss with you, both of them having to do with building up our strength. We are down by thirty percent since the Peninsula Campaign, and before we move out, we need every man we can get. Now, I know that you were weakened by your prison experience, but Lieutenant Winslow here says that you've recovered marvelously well. I'll leave it with you, Private—do you feel able to march with your company?"

Thad had been expecting this, so he nodded at once. "Yes, sir."

"Fine!" Lee replied, then smiled and said, "As of right now, you are promoted to corporal."

Thad was startled and opened his mouth to protest, but Major Lee held up his hand. "It was by common consent in your company—and among the three of us, I might add."

"I'll do my best, sir!"

"I know you will. Now, there is one other matter, and I hardly know how to put it." He paused and looked down at the ground, then lifted his head as he spoke. "Private Mellon is being held on charges of perjury. It is, of course, a military court, so the matter is still in the hands of the court-martial. If things go according to tradition, he will be tried and sentenced. Since he is patently guilty, he will spend several years in a military prison." Major Lee gave Thad a curious look. "How would that seem to you, Corporal?"

Thad shifted uncomfortably for a second. "Why," he said, "I don't like to see anybody go to jail, Major."

Lee exchanged a glance with his lieutenants and nodded. "That was exactly what Lieutenant Winslow told me you would say. Now, here is what can be done. If I recommend it—with your agreement—the court will release Mellon for active duty. He will be on probation, but with the understanding that if he proves himself to be a good soldier, the charges will be dropped. What would you say to such a procedure?"

"I say let him join the regiment, sir," Thad answered at once. "He won't do us any good in a cell."

Major Lee smiled broadly and his dark blue eyes gleamed with approval. "I am happy you see it that way, Corporal Novak.

Now, I will ask you to join your company no later than eight in the morning. Lieutenant Winslow, will you draft the document for the court and take it at once to Colonel Andrews? I have— ah, *hinted* to him of this possibility, so you'll find him agreeable. Come with me, Lieutenant Beauchamp, and we'll visit that blackguard of a quartermaster again."

The two officers left, and Mark beamed at Thad. "Good! I knew what you'd do." He pulled a sheet of paper from the sheaf on the small desk and placed it on the map, preparing to write. He looked up, saying, "We just got word that Jackson and Lee have done Pope in, Thad."

"They won?"

"Sure did—but now Lee is calling for every man he can get, ready to march at once." Mark's eyes shone and he lowered his voice. "Don't breathe a word of this—but I think we're going to invade the North!" He turned back to his chore, saying, "Better get your goodbyes said, Thad. We may be gone for a long time!"

The camp meeting was in full swing when Thad and Pet arrived. They had come alone, and after hitching the buggy, they made their way to the outer circle of the congregation. The singing rose from hundreds of throats:

"How firm a foundation,
Ye saints of the Lord,
Is laid for your faith
In his excellent word!"

Then as soon as the sound of that died down, another rose, one that Thad had heard before:

"Am I a soldier of the cross,
A follower of the Lamb?
And shall I fear to own His cause
Or blush to speak His name?"

The words had a peculiar effect on Thad, especially the reference to a "lamb." He shifted uneasily and tried to shake off the feeling, but then the next song arose:

"Have you been to Jesus
For the saving power?
Are you washed in the blood of the Lamb?"

The song leader sang this over and over, and with each repetition, Thad felt more and more strange. Finally, the singing stopped, and the preacher, a short, muscular young man with a full beard and a rich bass voice, stood up and announced, "I will preach tonight from the gospel of John, chapter one, verse twenty-nine." He looked up, and Thad felt the drawing power of the man's gaze as he read, "Behold the Lamb of God which taketh away the sin of the world."

Thad sat there for an hour and a half, riveted by the words of the preacher. He had heard one sermon on this text, but it had only stirred his mind. Now, as the preacher spoke of the blood of Jesus, of His death on the cross, something began to break up inside Thad—something he had never felt before. It was like the breakup of the ice on the river that he had seen the previous spring. The solid river had melted under the heat of the sun, and broken up—first one large fragment of ice, then another, until the mass of frozen crust was swept away in a roaring torrent. So it seemed to be with him, his resolves and resistance leaving him empty and afraid.

Pet sat beside him, keenly aware of the turmoil in him, for he was trembling, and his eyes were so fixed on the preacher that he seemed almost hypnotized. As the sermon went on, he unconsciously gripped her hand when she put her own in his, and soon her arm was numb to the elbow, so tightly did he grip her! She did not complain, however, but closed her eyes and prayed harder than she had ever prayed in her life.

Finally the sermon ended, and as dozens began to go down to the front for prayer, Pet whispered, "Thad, will you let Jesus save you?" When he hesitated, she urged, "You wouldn't let Him in when you thought you were going to die—but now it wouldn't be a cowardly thing."

He turned to face her, and his eyes were filled with tears. "I—I never felt like this, Pet! I feel so bad!"

Pet was weeping as she put her hands up to cup his face. "Oh, Thad, that's because you know you've been a sinner! But you heard the sermon. All you have to do is look to Jesus—He'll forgive you! Oh, Thad, He loves you so!"

Then Thad Novak gave up. He suddenly fell to his knees and lifted his hands, crying out, "Oh, God! I have been such a sinner!

Please—forgive me, and save me—for Jesus' sake!"

He was never able to tell what happened next. He had no words to describe the sudden rush of peace that fell on him. It was a little like the calm after a storm, or like waking up from a bad dream with a tremendous feeling of joy that all the horror was only a dream. Yet it was more than any of that, so when he rose from his knees and found Pet crying her heart out, he could only hold her and say, "It's all right—it's all right, Pet! Everything's all right now."

As they made their way home under the full moon, they said little. He was too full of wonder at the peace that had fallen on him, and she was too happy to say much without weeping. Finally, when he pulled up in front of the house, he told her, "I'll be leaving in the morning, Pet. So will your brothers and Captain Wickham."

"I—knew it would be soon, Thad," she whispered. "Oh, be careful!"

He nodded, then looked down at her; the tears in her eyes overflowed, making silver rivulets from the reflection of the full moon. "I'd like to say a lot of things to you, but there's just no time." He dropped his head, and the silence hung for what seemed an eternity to her. Then he turned to face her, the angular planes of his face sharp with shadows. "When I come back, maybe we'll have more time to talk—about a lot of things."

She waited for him to continue, but he seemed to be far away. Finally she said, "Thad, I'll be here—when you get back." Impulsively she threw her arms around him, her body trembling violently as he held her close. When she pulled away, she whispered, "I'll always be here—for you!" She reached up and kissed him and then dashed into the house.

Thad slept little that night, and the next day at noon the entire regiment was loaded onto a train for the urgent journey. They disembarked, gathered into marching order, and for two days marched westward, where they joined the main body of the Army of Northern Virginia. Three days later, on September 4, Robert E. Lee led his troops across the Potomac into Maryland to carry the war north. On both shores stood Confederate bands playing "Maryland, My Maryland" and "Dixie" over and over again. The evening sun burnished the rifles and bayonets, making them glitter and blaze, but Thad could only wonder, *How many of us will come back from this?*

CHAPTER TWENTY-SEVEN

THE BLOODIEST DAY

★ ★ ★ ★

On September 17, 1862, General George McClellan with nearly 100,000 men in his Army of the Potomac met General Robert E. Lee with his Army of Northern Virginia, which had at the beginning of the battle no more than 19,000 men. If Ulysses S. Grant had been in command, he would have thrown his entire force against the tiny army that lay across Antietam Creek just outside of Sharpsburg, for he was a man who believed in total war.

George McClellan, however, lacked that streak of ruthlessness. The suffering of his men haunted him, and he spent sleepless nights thinking of his dead and wounded soldiers. So instead of throwing his magnificent force in one overwhelming assault, he committed his units one at a time.

In effect, he did what he had done on the Peninsula; that is, he built up massive bodies of troops, moved them toward battle as slowly as he possibly could, and only when forced to do so did he attack. As always, he bombarded Washington with demands for reinforcements.

Lincoln understood the general's temperament. If the President was able to fill McClellan's request for 100,000 more troops, he would promise to be in Richmond the following day—but then the general would discover reasons why he could not fight unless Lincoln gave him an additional 400,000. The President once said, "If I gave McClellan all the men he asks for, they could not find room to lie down. They'd have to sleep standing up."

Thus, in his attempt to spare his men, McClellan squandered them, and as Dooley Young later related it, "General McClellan was like my Uncle Seedy who had to cut off his dawg's tail, but he was too tenderhearted to do it all at one time—so he jest cut off an inch or so a day until the hull job got done."

Dooley pulled out a dirty sheet of paper with a rough map sketched on it, pointing out the stages of battle as he talked.

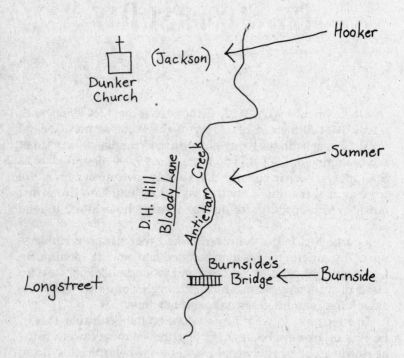

"Little Mac made three stabs at gettin' us, and any one would have worked, 'cause they was enough of them bluebellies to run over us. All three times they come at us across Antietam Creek. First, Hooker come acrost and hit Stonewall Jackson—right here at the top," he'd point. "The Yanks come through a cornfield right up to an old Dunker church; and I tell you, time we druv 'em back, they wasn't a stalk standing, and you could have walked acrost that field on the bodies! They had us—but General McLaw come jest in time—and they was 2,000 Yanks died in half an hour!

"Then right here in the middle"—Dooley would poke another mark on his map—"was Bloody Lane. It was a sunken road, and we got in it and the Yanks come at us like I never seen 'em fight! General Gordon was shot five times, and they wore us out. Right at that time if McClellan had made a push, they could of walked through us—and the hull shootin' match would of been over. But they never done it.

"Then—right here at the bottom"—Young placed another mark at the extreme southern point of the creek—"the Yankee General Burnside, he tried all day to get acrost a bridge—which was stupid, 'cause we shot them as fast as they crowded onto it! And when we finally pulled out, jest when they could of come acrost the bridge, they found a spot where the creek was only waist deep—and waded acrost it—but we'd done hightailed it!"

Thad did not have this clear picture in his mind during the battle. He moved into the center of the line at dusk on the night before the battle and waited with the others for dawn. Tom Winslow came along the line, whispering, "They'll hit us at first light, most likely. Try to get some sleep."

Thad put his cartridge case beside him, loaded his rifle and curled up, but as he did so, a form emerged from the darkness on his left. "Novak?" someone whispered.

"Here." Thad sat up and strained his eyes to make out the features of the man who came to crouch beside him. There was only a sliver of a moon, and he could not identify him.

"It's me—Studs Mellon." The big man moved closer, saying, "I gotta talk to you."

Thad had seen Mellon on the trip to Sharpsburg, of course, but had not spoken to him. Now he said, "What's up, Studs?"

"Well . . ." Mellon whispered huskily, "I been tryin' to figger you out, Novak, but I can't get no sense out of what you done. Captain Wickham, he told me 'bout how I'd still be in jail if you hadn't said for them to turn me loose." He shifted uncomfortably, trying to put his feelings into words, but seemed unable to do so. He was an inarticulate brute, choosing rather to speak with his fists than with words, but he had brooded over this action ever since he had been released from jail at Richmond and returned to his company.

With a puzzled tone he asked, "Why'd you do it—after I lied on you? I tried to get you shot—and then you get me outta jail."

"May not have done you a favor, Studs," Thad replied. "You'd be a lot safer there than here. There's about a million Yankees over across that creek."

"Aw, that ain't no bother! But I never seen nobody give a break to a mug who tried to do him in. Why for did you do it? You got religion or somethin'?"

Thad paused, thought about it, then said, "I didn't have religion when I did it, Studs. I just don't like to see anybody in jail." He added quickly, "But I got saved just before we left Richmond—at a camp meeting."

Studs thought about that, shifting his bulk so that he could get a better look at Thad's face by the pale moonlight. "I'm on my way straight to hell, I reckon—'least, that's what the preachers all say. Never gave it much thought before, but I get a funny feeling looking across that creek, thinkin' maybe there's a bluebelly there with a bullet that's got my name on it. But I guess it's too late for me to get religion now."

Thad didn't have the faintest idea of how to speak to the man, but he told him, "I don't reckon that's so—'cause that's what I thought once. Let me tell you how I got saved."

They sat there in the moonlight, with the sound of many men sleeping fitfully and occasionally a night bird giving a lonely cry and a monstrous bullfrog bellowing from the creek. Thad used no theological terms, for he knew none; but he told of his struggle to get away from God, then related how he had simply called on God.

"It sure wasn't a fancy prayer, Studs," he ended his story. "I just said, 'God, save me!' or something like that. And ever since that minute, I've been all right."

Mellon sat still, breathing heavily in the darkness, saying nothing. Thad said quietly, "I'd like to see you do that before the Yanks come calling, Studs—and not just because we're liable to get killed. It's just that the best and happiest people I know are

Christians. Seems like Jesus just does that to folks."

When Studs did not reply, Thad decided to leave him alone. "Reckon I'll get a little sleep. Wish you'd think on it, Studs." He lay down and the big man sat there, not moving. Finally Thad drifted off, and when he awoke at dawn he saw Mellon in his place twenty yards down the line. Thad was about to go and ask him if he had called on God, but cannon and musket fire broke out to his left.

"That's Hood over there," Dooley said wisely. He had come to take his place beside Thad, and spat emphatically. "Sounds like the hull Yankee Army's pilin' in on him, don't it, Thad?"

The roar of gunfire reached a crescendo, and seemed to go on endlessly. Thad saw a horseman gallop madly out of the smoke, ride up and yell, "Major Lee, General Jackson says give him support!"

Lee shouted at once, "Captain Wickham, take your company and engage the enemy with General Jackson!" He called out three other companies, and Thad stumbled along, keeping his head down as Wickham led the way through the curtain of smoke.

"There's Jackson!" Thad heard Mark Winslow cry out, and looked up to see a small church, the ground about it littered with bodies of both Confederate and Union dead and wounded. "They're coming across that cornfield, Captain!" Mark shouted, and then waved the men forward, "Company A—come on!"

Thad ran across the broken field until he heard Captain Wickham shout, "Form line of battle!"

Thad fell into the line not ten feet from where a Confederate officer stood watching the Yankees threading their way through the green field of corn. The man seemed as calm as if he had nothing to do with the affair. Then he turned and his pale blue eyes fell on Wickham, who identified himself. "Captain Wickham, Third Virginia, General Jackson."

Jackson nodded and waved toward the cornfield. Thad was amazed to see that he held a lemon in his hand! "Have your men stop those people, Captain."

Thad stared at the legendary leader, but there was no time to waste, for Wickham, along with Beauchamp and Winslow, was urging the men to action. Thad lifted his rifle, fired, and saw a blue coat drop like a bundle in the midst of the corn. As he reloaded, he heard the whine of minie balls in the air, and flinched. Then he fired again, but just as he stopped to reload, he saw Captain Wickham fall to the ground. "Keep firing!" Wickham shouted. "I'm all right!" He got to his feet and limped along the line, favoring his left leg, where a ball had cut through the flesh of his calf.

The Yankees faced a terrible fire, leaning against it as men will do against a hard, driving wind. As the men in front fell to the ground, those in the rear stepped over them and pressed on toward the church. The barrel of Thad's musket grew hot, and Dooley shook his head, shouting above the din, "Ain't they no end to them boys, Thad! Never seen so many Yankees."

The Confederates were not untouched, for the approaching Yankees fired as they came. Thad saw Les Satterfield, Dooley's cousin, take a ball in the face, destroying his features. Dooley paused to stare at him, then resumed firing with a new fury. Gaps began to appear in the line, and Wickham walked among the company, calmly directing their fire. Thad saw that the captain's left arm was dripping blood, and he held it away to keep his uniform clean. He stopped beside Thad and said, "Hot work!"

"Sir, let me tie up that arm."

"No! Let's get those Yankees back on the other side of the creek and then we'll take care of that. Keep firing! Keep firing!" he called out as he walked away to Thad's left.

The roar of battle swelled, and McLaw and Early arrived with reinforcements for Jackson and Hood's thin line of defense, but fresh Union troops poured across the field; and there was no letup until nine o'clock, when the Union troops slowly retreated, leaving a bloody harvest of dead and wounded in the cornfield.

In the momentary lull, Thad and his comrades crowded around the well beside the church to assuage their parching thirst. Novak filled his canteen and went back to the line, where he discovered one of his friends, Leroy Johnson, lying with a shattered leg. He knelt down and gave him a drink, saying, "I'll get you to the ambulance, Leroy."

"Oh, good God!" Johnson burst out weeping. "They've killed me!" Thad was struggling to lift him up when Mellon appeared.

"Let me have him," Studs said. He picked up the man easily and Thad went with him, finding the ambulance behind a grove of trees. Mellon put the injured man into the covered vehicle, and the two went back toward the line.

"Glad you made it all right, Studs," Thad told him. "We must have lost a fourth of the company."

"Well—I'm glad you didn't catch one, Thad," Mellon replied. He seemed to be struggling with something. After a moment he said with some embarrassment, "I done it."

Thad glanced at him puzzled. "You did *what*?"

"I—I asked God to save me—just like you did." He grinned self-consciously. "And He done it, too!"

"Hey, that's great!" Thad cried, giving Mellon a hard blow to his shoulder. "I sure am glad for you, Studs."

"You reckon I could get baptized, Thad?" Mellon asked. "In the creek. My ma, she always prayed for me to be baptized."

"Well, it might be pretty hard to find a chaplain—but we'll see."

They got back to the line, and just as they did, a crackle of musket fire broke out to their right. Captain Wickham yelled, "Come on, men!" They followed him back over the ground they had traversed earlier, and found General D. H. Hill and his group of Confederates in a sunken road under a furious attack. "We'll make a line behind that sunken road!" Wickham shouted. He raised his bandaged arm and waved them into position, and for the next two hours the most savage fighting of the entire war took place. Again and again the blue-clad soldiers charged the trench, falling by entire rows as the Confederates raked them from their well-protected position. But slowly the weight of the heavy Union divisions enfiladed the lane, enabling them to pour a deadly barrage on Hill's embattled troops from each end of the lane.

The toll was costly. Finally, Major Lee said, "There're not enough men in Hill's command to take another charge, Captain Wickham—and we don't have enough here to stand it, either."

"We've lost it all if the Yankees come at our position now," Wickham agreed, and the two men stood there braced for the attack that would wipe them out—and perhaps the Southern Confederacy as well—but it never came. Once again, McClellan was unable to give the order to send his main force into action.

Slowly the crisis passed, and Thad looked around, saying to Dooley, "I don't reckon we lost any of the boys in our company—but those poor fellows in that trench sure took it on the chin."

Wickham called his lieutenants aside. "We'd better move back to help defend the bridge. I have a feeling things are going to get hot there." His thin face was pale and his voice weak as he added, "The Yankees have tried the left flank and the center—I've got a feeling Burnside will make a big move to cross that bridge."

"If he does," Beauchamp replied gloomily, "he can sweep to his right and have us flanked." Then he studied Wickham's face and said with concern, "You'd better get those wounds taken care of, sir. You've lost a lot of blood."

"Later. Take the men back to their position."

"Yes, sir."

Beauchamp walked away with Mark. "I don't like Vance's look," Beau remarked. "Remember how General Johnston died at Shiloh from a wound in his leg just like Vance has?"

"You're right, Beau," Mark frowned. "I'll get Major Lee to order him to the rear."

But such was not to be, for as they made their way back to the bridge, a spattering of firing broke out, increasing in such volume that it nearly broke their eardrums. "It's started!" Beau yelled. "Double time, men!"

They stumbled back with lungs on fire, and as they reached Lieutenant Winslow's line he called out, "Sergeant! Take five men and scout the riverbanks! They may be trying to cross here!"

Tom yelled, "Thad, you and Dooley come with me—and Taylor and French!"

Thad joined the small group, plunging recklessly through scrub oak and tall willows until they reached the river. "Careful!" Tom whispered. "You can bet they have sharpshooters posted just for folks like us."

They moved more cautiously along the bank, searching the opposite shore and the ridge behind it for signs of the enemy, but saw none.

"What's that up ahead?' Thad whispered.

"Looks like a cabin of some kind," Tom answered, peering

through the brush. "Walk carefully—and don't shoot any civilians."

They found a half-built log cabin right on the bank of the Antietam with a number of huge freshly cut logs lying beside it, ready to be lifted. "Nobody here," Dooley said, and they advanced along the bank to where it made a wide bend. Tom was leading the way, then stopped abruptly and moved back. "Bridge is just around the bend—and it looks as if there're about ten thousand men trying to cross it."

"Could you see our bunch?" Thad asked.

"No. But we'll get to 'em if we cut through these woods to the right."

They fought their way through the thickets, emerging a hundred yards to the left of the main Confederate force. "Keep your heads down!" Tom warned. "We've got to get back in the middle of the line. I see a big gap there."

They ran across the broken ground, falling into place behind some logs, and began firing. The bridge was crowded, as Tom Winslow had said. Blue-clad men jostled each other and were cut down before they could get off. Thad wondered what kind of an officer would send men across to certain death from the blistering fire they ran into, but he had no time to speculate, for the gray ranks were thin and every gun was needed. He continued firing, and for the next half hour a gargantuan struggle took place, with terrific losses on both sides.

Thad discovered he was out of ammunition, and moved forward to the body of a dead infantryman. The air seemed to be full of lead, and he felt a sudden stinging sensation on the right side of his neck, then a warmth as blood trickled down under his collar. He gathered a small supply of powder and balls, and from that point sent his fire across the creek, but he soon had to find more ammunition.

He kept his head down and moved to his left, where a small cluster of bodies provided more powder and balls. The dust at his feet exploded as several balls thudded into the ground, and he threw himself behind a small mound, gasping with the effort. He loaded while lying down, poked his head up, and flung up his rifle for a quick shot.

As he reloaded, he looked around for Dooley, but could not

'find him. After ten more minutes, he heard a shrill cry from a soldier in front of him, "They're backin' off!" Thad looked quickly at the bridge and saw that it was true—for the third time that day the Yankees were routed. He joined in the fierce rebel cry and sent a final shot at the retreating enemy.

But there was still a continuous fire raking the Confederates from the determined Yankees who had taken station in a grove of trees a hundred yards from the creek. The Union men could not advance any closer, for the ground was open and it was certain death to cross it. The situation on his side of the river was about the same, Thad saw—the open field was littered with bodies of Confederates.

The firing slowed down, but never stopped. Most of his company was out of ammunition, and Thad called out to Lew Avery, "Hey, Lew, you got any powder?"

"No. And we better get some quick," the ex-gambler said grimly. "If they come at us again, we'll have nothing but bayonets."

Thad snaked his way along to his left until he came to Lieutenant Beauchamp. "Lieutenant, most of us are out of ammunition."

Beauchamp stared at Thad, his lips contorted. "I just sent Tom for some—but the word is that we're to move out as soon as we can do it."

"Let them have the bridge?"

"No choice." His face was red with anger, and he waved his arm in an abrupt gesture. "Am I supposed to leave Major Lee down there? I *won't* do it!"

"Major Lee?" Thad asked, and then as he looked down toward the stream, he saw through the smoke a dead horse not ten feet from the bank. Straining his eyes, Thad recognized a gray uniform—an officer's. "Is—is he dead, sir?"

"No!" Beauchamp exclaimed. "He's hit, but he's alive. Even if he weren't wounded, he couldn't move. No man could cross that open space without taking a dozen balls."

Thad stood there, struck dumb, but finally asked, "How'd he get down there, Lieutenant?"

"The Yankees broke through and Lee led a group down to repulse them. I tried to pull him back, but he spurred away.

They broke the Yankee's charge—but most of our soldiers didn't make it back."

"We can't leave him, can we, Lieutenant?"

Beauchamp's face was dark with anger. "How can we get him, Novak? We've lost half our company—and if we tried to send a force down, the men would be cut to shreds before they even reached him—much less got him back." He gritted his teeth in determination, then ordered, "Move down the line and have the men get all the ammunition they can from the dead. Maybe the Yankees will move off and we can try it."

Thad could see that Lieutenant Beauchamp entertained no real hope of success, but the corporal did as he was ordered. He stealthily moved to the end of the line where the creek curved sharply, giving Beauchamp's order, then made his way back.

As he returned, a thought flashed through his mind, which he dismissed as fanatical. But by the time he reached Beauchamp, with Captain Wickham beside him, Thad made a decision.

"I passed the word along, sir," he informed him.

"We're pulling out in half an hour," Wickham spoke up. "Orders from General Longstreet."

Anger flashed in their eyes, and as they turned away, Thad swallowed hard, then said, "Sir, I think I know a way we might get Major Lee off that beach."

Both men swung back instantly. "How?" Captain Wickham asked.

"Well, when I was with the patrol under Tom Winslow that scouted the riverbanks, I saw something I think might work."

"Speak up, Corporal!" Beauchamp snapped. "What was it?"

"There's a log cabin half built, sir, right beside the bank." He took a deep breath and plunged ahead, feeling foolish trying to tell these officers anything. "And I was thinking, if we could float one of the logs, a couple of us could keep behind it. We could move the log downstream and bring it up to where Major Lee is pinned down on the bank. Then we could jump out, bring him to the log—and, then we could keep down and let the current take us around the bend down there."

The two officers looked at Thad with disbelief. "That's the craziest thing I ever heard, Corporal!" Beauchamp exploded.

"Why, every marksman over there will be shooting at that log!"

"They can't shoot *through* a log, though, can they, Lieutenant?"

"But—you'd never get Lee from behind that horse into the water," the Captain protested. "They'd pick you off in a second!"

Thad dropped his head for a moment, and when he raised up, his eyes glowed with pride. "We can try, sir!"

His answer silenced both men, and Captain Wickham burst out, "By heavens, it's the only chance we've got! What do you say, Lieutenant?"

Beauchamp stared at Thad, then said slowly, "If I were the one down there, I'd like to think somebody here was doing something to get me out!"

"We'll try it," Captain Wickham decided. "Thad, get anybody you need to go with you. When we see the log touch the shore and you make a run for Major Lee, we'll have every rifle we can find loaded. We'll blast those Yankees with all we've got!"

Thad nodded, whirled, and ran down the line, calling out but keeping his voice low, "I'm going to get Major Lee back from the Yankees—anybody want to go with me?"

Several men laughed, but Dooley was at his side instantly. "Let's git on with our rat-killin', Thad. How you plan to work this here miracle?"

Studs Mellon appeared at Thad's left, said nothing, but nodded.

"Can you both swim?"

"Swim? Shore!" Dooley snapped, and Mellon nodded again.

"You won't need your rifles," Thad told them, placing his own on the ground. "Let's go!"

He led the two toward the rear at a run, and then swung right, plunging into the thickets that sheltered the creek. He made no attempt to explain his plan until he arrived at the cabin. There he paused and while the two listened, he told them what they were going to do.

Dooley just grinned. "Well, I wish to my never! It'd take a scudder like you to think of a thing like that!"

"It'll probably get us all killed," Thad said slowly.

"Naw, it's just nutty enough to work!" Dooley retorted. "Let's get this show on the road."

Mellon had been studying the logs carefully. Now he said, "They've left a bunch of ropes here, Thad. I think we ought to tie two logs together. If we have just one, it'll roll over and over and we'll never hang on to it. But two will ride better."

"Hey, that's good, Studs!" Thad exclaimed. "Let's do it!"

They chose two logs fourteen inches in diameter, pulled them near the water, then secured them together at several spots, using the ropes Mellon had noticed. "Ought to do 'er!" Dooley said with satisfaction.

"Gonna be hard to hang on to this thing," Studs said thoughtfully. "Why don't we tie some more rope to the ones that are on and pull 'em to the end so we can hold on without exposing our hands."

"Well, Studs, you do beat all!" Dooley exclaimed. "They'd have shot our hands off if we'd tried to hold on any other way."

Thad said, "Sure am glad you came along, Studs." He gave Mellon a look of appreciation that seemed to embarrass him.

"Another thing," Mellon suggested. "You two midgets stay with the logs when we get there. Ain't neither one of you could lug the major. You just don't let that log raft run off whilst I'm a'fetchin' him. Sure would feel foolish if I got back with him and the raft was already gone."

Thad and Dooley exchanged glances. "But, Studs," Thad said, "that's the hardest part. I figured to do that part myself."

"Well, just readjust yore thinkin'," Mellon grinned. Then he sobered. "I—I wouldn't have done this yesterday, Thad, but I feel different today. You know what I mean?"

"I know, Studs," Thad replied. He turned to Dooley and explained, "Studs got saved last night."

Dooley's eyes fixed on Mellon, but he said only, "We better git at it, then. The company's gonna pull out pretty soon."

They moved into the water, leaving their shoes behind and pushing the makeshift raft ahead of them. The water was cool, and Studs said, "You remember what I told you my ma always wanted me to do, Thad?"

"Be baptized? But—there's no chaplain to do it, Studs."

"Couldn't you? I mean, we're already in the water—and it don't take long, do it now?"

Thad was speechless. He had been at only one baptism, and

could not remember clearly what the words were, but the pleading look in Mellon's eyes persuaded him. He moved through the water and said, "I baptize you, Studs, in the name of Jesus Christ—and of the Holy Ghost, and of the Father, too." Then he pushed Studs' head under.

Studs came up, shook his face clear of water, and there was a smile on his battered lips. "Ma shore would be proud of me, wouldn't she, Thad?"

"Sure, she would, Studs!"

Then they took hold of the ropes, Thad wondering all the time how long he had to live. He was not afraid to die, but he hated the thought of failure. *God, let us get that man out of there,* he prayed as the current took them.

"Don't let this thing get too far in the middle," Dooley warned. "Mebby the Yanks will think it's jest a loose log."

But as soon as they floated within range of the Union line, they all heard a cry, and several slugs thunked into the logs, while others sent up small geysers of water around them. "Keep her steady," Thad said. He had taken the front position and looked back to see the heads of Dooley and Mellon bobbing steadily beside the logs away from the Union side. Then he turned and instructed, "When I call out, try to pull this thing into shore. We can't let it swing out, or they'll have a clear shot at us."

The firing from the Confederate line had ceased, and Thad knew they were saving up for a volley. He saw the dead horse lying on the bank not more than fifty feet downstream from them, and despaired to see that it was closer to twenty yards from the creek than ten. "Major Lee!" he called out in a low voice. "Major Lee, can you hear me?"

"Yes!"

Thad felt better then, and called again, "Get ready to leave. We're coming down behind some floating logs."

"I can't walk" was the calm answer. "Don't risk yourselves for me."

"You just be ready, sir," Studs Mellon said. "I'll have to handle you rough, but it's better than you'd get in a Yankee prison."

"Do what you have to, soldier," Lee answered.

They were only fifteen feet away when Thad said, "Now!"

and they all three kicked frantically. *It's not going to work!* Thad thought, for the logs did not seem to budge—then they moved toward the shore, and he managed to position the front of the raft about five feet ahead of where the dead horse lay on the bank. "Ready, Major?"

"Ready!"

Mellon slowly moved forward to the bank, gathered his legs under him, then in one terrific burst cleared the creek and in short bounds covered the distance to the horse. A startled cry went up from the Yankees, and a single shot slapped into the dead horse. Mellon snatched the officer up in his huge arms and plunged toward the logs, his face contorted with the strain. As he cleared the horse, a fusillade of shots from the Confederates broke out, and dirt flew all along the Yankee line. Most of the enemy ducked—but not all—as the balls shredded the thickets that covered them.

Mellon reached the bank, but just as he did, a shot hit him in the chest, stopping him as though he had run into a wall. "Studs—!" Thad shouted, but could do nothing. Mellon moved forward and managed to let Major Lee fall in behind the raft—and then two more shots struck him in the body. He fell backward but Thad reached out and grabbed his clothing, pulling him into the water

"Hang on to that rope, Major!" Thad cried. "Dooley—shove off!"

Both of them shoved with their legs, and now every man in the Yankee line knew what had been done, and the shots fell thick as raindrops. The current moved very slowly, and Thad felt the logs jump as hundreds of slugs tore into them—but the raft begin to move along the stream.

"We're gonna make it!" Dooley screamed. "Major—can you hang on to that rope for a few minutes?"

"Yes—I'm all right. It's just my leg that's hurt."

There was nothing to do but drift and endure the hail of lead that the angered Yankees poured into the craft. Thad had his right wrist secured with the rope, and with the other hand he pulled Mellon close, keeping his head above the water. He felt the shattered body give a lurch. Then Mellon opened his eyes, and for one moment, he saw Thad.

"I done—good! Didn't I?"

"You did fine, Studs!" Thad replied. "Hang on, now. We'll be out of this soon."

"Shore am—glad—you helped me—find—Jesus!" he gasped, and with his last breath, "Jesus!" his body slumped and he was gone.

Major Lee had been watching and now said, "A brave man. God have mercy on him."

"He will, sir!" Thad whispered, and he felt the hot tears scald his face as the raft drifted on. He raised his eyes to the bank and instantly cried, "Oh, no!"

"What is it, soldier?" Lee asked. Thad pointed.

Lee followed Thad's direction and saw Captain Vance Wickham come charging across the open ground, followed by a small band of men. "Go back, Captain!" the major shouted. He turned his head and saw that a party of Yankees had taken advantage of the Confederates attention on the raft. About a dozen Yankees had crossed the bridge and were running down the bank, one of them a lieutenant, opening fire with his pistol.

The helpless men in the water watched as the Yankees charged, and then Wickham and his men met them head on. Neither side could fire from the banks because the two parties were engaged in a wild melee. Thad saw Captain Wickham knock down the lieutenant with one shot, then, as calmly as if he were shooting at a target, two more on the ground. That broke the core of the Yankees' strength, and Wickham shouted, "Throw down your arms or we'll kill you all!"

The blue-clad soldiers obeyed promptly, which enabled Wickham to take the Yankees up the hill, using them as a shield. They were almost to the crest, and Major Lee exclaimed, "He did it! By the living God—he did it!"

But even as he spoke, a single shot rang out, and Wickham fell to the ground. He was instantly pulled to cover and the Yankees opened fire on the raft.

Thad hung on to Mellon's body until the raft drifted around the bend in the stream. Soon they were hidden, and were quickly pulled out of the water by waiting hands. Beauchamp was there with two stretcher bearers, but he paused long enough to look at Thad and ask, "You all right, Thad?"

"Yes, sir."

"You were magnificent!" Beauchamp's admiration stirred in his eyes. "But we've got to get out of here."

He turned and Thad struggled to pull Mellon's body ashore. Dooley came to help, but said, "Thad—we'll have to leave him."

"I know." Thad straightened up and paused long enough to give the burly shoulder a final pat. "I'll see you, Studs," he whispered quietly and then moved off with Dooley.

They followed Beauchamp as he made his way to the rear and found that Vance Wickham had been brought in and lay on a stretcher.

As Thad stopped a few paces away, Major Lee said, "Let me say a word to Captain Wickham, Lieutenant."

Lee went over to the stretcher and Wickham opened his eyes. "Captain," Lee said quietly, "I owe my life to you and your fine men."

Wickham's face was pale and the shot had already done its deadly work. He whispered, "Thank you, sir! They are brave soldiers."

"You led them well, sir," Lee replied.

Wickham nodded and a smile touched his lips. Then he saw Thad and called his name.

Thad came forward and at a nod from Major Lee, the corporal knelt and put his head near Wickham's mouth.

"Tell Belle—I loved her to the last!"

"I'll tell her, Captain!"

"She was—the best thing—ever happened—to me!" Then he took a deep breath and sighed.

"He's gone," Thad said.

"A very brave man," Lee replied sadly. Turning to Beauchamp, he ordered, "Have Captain Wickham carried on the retreat, Lieutenant."

Thad and Dooley found some shoes, picked up their muskets and joined in the retreat. It was a covert movement, according to order, not full scale. They left in small groups, the others keeping up a sharp fire to convince the Yankees they were digging in for a long defense.

Dooley and Thad were among the last to pull back, and by that time the Yankees had almost stopped firing. Thad stopped at the crest of a small rise to throw one last look at the spot where he had last seen Mellon—and a shot rang out!

He felt a searing pain in his right flank, and as he fell to the earth, the last thing he heard was Dooley crying, "Thad! Thad!" And then he sank into a black pit that had no bottom and no sides.

He was the last casualty of their company at Sharpsburg—the bloodiest day of American history. From sunrise to sunset, almost 24,000 men fell on the field. The North counted it a victory, for Lee had been stopped. But once again, the Army of Northern Virginia had escaped—not intact, but capable of being restored.

CHAPTER TWENTY-EIGHT

THE LIEUTENANT

★ ★ ★ ★

He tried to move his legs, but they were like lead. Pain began to trickle through him like water, and as he struggled to turn on his side, the pain intensified until it shot waves of agony through his middle. He felt nauseous and grasped the covers with his hands. A voice came out of the uncertain gray fog that enveloped him: "Thad! Be still; you mustn't move!" Cool fingers touched his steaming brow, and again he fell into a sub-world the living and healthy never see.

He seemed to float endlessly through space, at moments drifting near consciousness. Sometimes he heard voices and felt the cold pressure of a hand cool his brow. Time was nothing to him—a vapid endlessness that refused to remain fixed. It seemed to roll aimlessly—from days to weeks to years . . .

Consciousness arrived softly, and he opened his eyes. For the first time he saw the wall around him, the gray blanket over his body, and Pet beside him.

"Hello, Thad," she said.

"What time is it?"

She smiled at the question. "Ten in the morning."

"What morning?"

"September the twenty-fourth." She leaned over and brushed

his hair back. "You're in the hospital at Richmond—Chimborazo. How do you feel?"

He didn't answer, but lay there staring at her. Her lips were red and her eyes were moist. He whispered, "Bend forward," then lifted his hand and caressed her cheek. "You're real," he murmured, searching her face. After a moment he added, "Vance Wickham is dead."

"I know."

He stared at her for a long time, then as though the single gesture had worn him out, he drifted off to sleep. She tucked the blanket around his shoulders, kissed him, and sat nearby, her lips moving and tears streaming down her face.

When he awoke again, he saw that Belle was beside him. She was wearing a simple black dress, and he tried to speak, but his lips were dry. She poured a glass of water and held his head up while he drank the refreshing liquid.

"Hello, Miss Belle," he said, and knew intuitively why she had come.

"You're better, Thad. For a while, we all thought you'd die."

She was different, he saw. Not just the plain black dress, but there was a change in her eyes, in her face. She was no less beautiful, but there was something missing, and he recognized that it was the joy that had always flowed from her in a steady stream. Her dark eyes were filled with sorrow, and he felt the anger and bitterness that lurked beneath them.

"I'm sorry about Captain Wickham," he said softly.

"You were there when he died, they say."

"Yes, ma'am." He closed his eyes and the memories of the battle rolled over him. He didn't want to think of them, but knew he must—for the captain's sake. "He saved us all, Miss Belle . . ." he began, and told her the entire story, minimizing his own part. As he spoke, her eyes devoured every detail, clenching her fists until they were a waxy white. "So," he finished, "just when the Yankees had us, Captain Wickham was there with his men. He killed their officer and two or three more with his pistol, then took them back up the hill." He hesitated, then said, "That's when the ball hit him, right when he was at the top."

"He was very brave, was he not?"

"Oh yes, ma'am!" Thad hesitated, then continued. "I got to

him as soon as I could. Major Lee was there, thanking him for saving his life, and then he saw me and called me over."

"What did he say?" she whispered.

"He said, 'Tell Belle I loved her to the last.' " She closed her eyes, and he went on, "And then, just before he died, he looked up and smiled, and he whispered, 'She was the best thing that ever happened to me!' "

Belle's head jerked slightly as if the words had been a blow, and her face was paler than he had ever seen it. She sat like a stone, her fingers digging into his arm unconsciously. Finally she rose and murmured in a tight voice, "Thank you, Thad." With that she walked away, her body stiff and her head held at an unnatural angle.

He felt terrible, and when Pet hurried in a few minutes later, he said, "Miss Belle—she's taking it awful hard."

Pet looked toward the door and said slowly, "That Yankee bullet, Thad—it killed her just as sure as it did Vance!"

"Are your brothers all right?"

She smiled. "Yes. Tom was shot in the side, but it was just a graze. Mark didn't get a scratch."

"We lost a lot of men. You remember Studs Mellon?" Thad told her of the heroism of the big man, and finally said quietly, "I sure am glad he called on God."

"Dooley told me about you baptizing him. I wish I could have seen that!"

He grinned sheepishly. "A man does strange things some-times."

"That wasn't strange, Thad," Pet said firmly. She got up and walked to the door. "Now don't go to sleep. I'm going to get you something to eat. You've got to be on your feet for the victory ball."

"Victory ball?"

"Yes. Lincoln announced after the battle that all the slaves were free, so President Davis asked for a celebration for all of us. There'll be a review of the troops and then a ball. And this time, Thaddeus Novak, you *will* dance with me!"

———

Although Thad's wound was serious, it healed cleanly, so the doctor did not argue when Pet took the young man out only three days after he first awakened. He protested that he was not able to walk, but Toby came with her and carried him out to the soft bed that she had made in the carriage.

"Seems like we done dis befo'," Toby grinned as he put Thad down gently. "But you is done growed a mite since I pulled you outta dat snowbank."

Pet had Toby carry Thad up to a spare bedroom at Belle Maison, and for several days he was pampered beyond anything he had ever known. Pet couldn't do enough for him, and he loved having her around. "I should have gotten shot sooner," he said one morning as Lucy cleared away the breakfast dishes. He settled down with a sigh in the feather bed and closed his eyes.

"Never mind getting comfortable," Pet responded in a bossy voice. "Get out of that bed. You can't dance with me at the ball if you can't walk." She yanked the covers back and he let out a yell.

"I don't have any pants on!"

"Well, aren't *we* modest all of a sudden!" she said, standing there with her hands on her hips and a saucy smile on her lips. "Who do you think bathed you while you were unconscious?"

He reddened, but said stubbornly, "I'm not unconscious now —so you just scoot out of here. I can put my own pants on, woman!"

She sniffed and moved over to the large wardrobe. Taking his clothes out, she tossed them on the bed, and left the room, threatening, "If you need help to dress, I'll be right outside."

As Pet waited, her mother came down the hall and asked what Thad was doing.

"He's trying to put his clothes on," she grinned. "I offered to do it, and now he'll either get dressed by himself or die trying."

"Does he know about the surprise Major Lee is planning?"

"No, and everyone better keep quiet," Pet warned firmly. Just then, Thad called out, and both women went in to find Thad shaky, but on his feet.

"Whole room is spinning!" he complained, holding on to the bedpost.

"Help me, Mama," Pet said, and they took position on either side of Thad. "Come on, now. You've just been lying around too long. Time to get you're dancing shoes on," she teased. "Let's go for a walk."

He felt ashamed of his weakness, but was delighted to be on his feet. They steered him out to the porch, and he breathed the fresh air. "Oh, glory, but it's good to be out of that room!" They walked him the length of the porch twice, and then his legs folded and they seated him in a rocker.

"I'm shelling peas and you can help me—that is, if you're able," Pet laughed. "I'll go get them."

As Pet left, Rebekah said, "Thank God you're getting well, Thad." She took a deep breath, then spoke quietly. "All my boys are well—except Vance. Some women have lost all their sons in this war."

"I'm real sorry about Captain Wickham," Thad replied. "He was a friend to me right from the first. Remember how he taught me to shoot?"

"I remember." She looked across at him. "You came here as a boy. Now you're a man."

Just then Pet returned with the peas and Rebekah got up, asking, "What would you like for supper?"

"Catfish and greens," he answered.

Rebekah laughed and agreed with his choice, then left.

As Thad faced Pet he accidentally twisted his body and felt a twinge, but said, "I'm gonna keep wearin' my pants from now on. They're too hard to put on—besides, you don't have any notion of a man's modesty."

She laughed and looked up as she heard someone coming down the road. "Look, there comes Dooley."

Young came tearing across the yard at a dead run, pulled the chestnut mare up so hard she almost reared, and slid off her back in a fluid motion. "Hidee, Thad. See you got your breeches on for a change." He mounted the porch and sat down on the rail. "Thought I'd say hidee to the big hero of Sharpsburg."

"Pet, kick him off that rail, will you?" Thad snapped.

Dooley grinned at the threat. "Thought you'd be interested in the war." He saw Thad's eyes light up, and Young began telling of the retreat of the Army of Northern Virginia from Maryland.

"We wasn't singin' 'Maryland, My Maryland' like when we rode in," he remarked. "I hear quite a few sayin' 'Damn my

Maryland' now, though. We lost a lot of our fellers, Thad. Out of about 600 in the regiment, we lost nearly 200."

"How many out of our company?" Thad asked.

"More'n half," Dooley answered shortly. "We come back mighty thin, but recruitin' picked up some, so I guess by the time you git back, we'll be up to nigh a hundred. Lieutenant Winslow is captain now, and Beauchamp is first lieutenant."

He went on to tell how the whole army was resting and reorganizing, drilling new recruits, and rebuilding its strength. "Longstreet and Jackson was made lieutenant generals. The Army of Northern Virginia's gonna be two corps: Longstreet headin' the first and Jackson the second."

Pet let them talk for half an hour, then seeing that Thad's face was weary, she shooed Dooley off.

"Come back tomorrow, Dooley," Thad pleaded as Pet steered him back toward the bedroom.

"You better soak up all this easy time, boy!" Dooley called out as he mounted. "When Marse Robert and 'ol Blue Light git movin'—you won't have no fine lookin' girl like that to tuck you in!"

Thad gained strength rapidly, so that by the time the Grand Review took place on August 5, he was able to dress himself in the fresh uniform that Pet laid out for him. He still moved carefully, but when he walked out to where the rest of the family were waiting, he did so without favoring his right side.

Mr. and Mrs. Winslow smiled and made him turn around, and Mark, with his captain's bars, remarked, "You look good, Corporal." Tom stood beside Dan; and off to one side, Belle watched. She was dressed in black, as was her custom now, and there was no joy in her face as she got into the carriage.

They rode in two carriages, and when they reached Richmond, they turned in to the parade grounds and hitched the horses. Thad got down carefully and walked with Pet at his side toward the grandstand. "You have to sit down," she said, and forced him to sit in a chair while she and the others stood beside him.

It was a day of celebration, and as the troops marched by, Thad was proud. Jeb Stuart's cavalry led the way, followed by the artillery and dozens of field pieces. Finally, unit after unit in their best uniforms marched by with their flags flying and their company bands bravely playing.

"There's the Third!" Pet cried, and Thad got to his feet as his own brigade went by, with Colonel Barton and Major Lee at the head. "Look, there's Company A!" she said.

Thad saw many new faces in the ranks, which were headed by Captain Winslow and Lieutenant Beauchamp. "Aren't they wonderful!" Pet breathed, and he nodded as they passed.

After the parade, there were speeches. President Davis addressed the army; then Robert E. Lee stood before his troops, and they gave him a resounding cheer. When it was quiet, Lee said, "Since your great victories around Richmond, you have defeated the enemy at Cedar Mountain, expelled him from the Rappahannock, and after a conflict of three days, utterly repulsed him on the plains of Manassas. Without halting for repose, you crossed the Potomac, stormed the heights of Harpers Ferry, and made prisoners of more than 11,000 men. While one corps of the army was thus engaged, the other insured its success by arresting the combined armies of the enemy. On the field of Sharpsburg, with less than one-third of his numbers, you resisted from daylight until dark the whole army of the enemy and repulsed every attack along his entire front. The whole of the following day you stood prepared to resume the conflict on the same ground and retired the next morning without molestation across the Potomac." He paused and a vast silence lay on the entire army as he said in a ringing voice, "History has recorded few examples of greater fortitude!"

The troops cheered wildly, and when their officers calmed them down, a great many medals were awarded. Thad stood there as the citations were pinned on, and then the officer in charge said clearly, "Corporal Thad Novak, will you escort Mrs. Belle Wickham to the front."

Pet gave the stunned Thad a push, and he blindly moved forward as Belle took his arm. Actually, it was she who led him, for he could not think clearly. He stood beside her as Robert E. Lee came to stand before them, with Major Shelby Lee at his side.

"Captain Vance Wickham paid the full price of devotion on the field at Sharpsburg . . ." he said, and in a few words traced

Wickham's heroic act. "I give this citation to the wife of Captain Wickham, well aware that her grief can in no manner be assuaged by this act. But it is all that a grateful nation can do, and we award it with a full heart."

Belle took the medal, curtsied to General Lee, saying, "In my gallant husband's name, I accept this award."

She turned, and Thad moved to go with her, but General Lee said, "Corporal Novak, I would like you to wait." He turned to his nephew and said, "Major Lee, would you read the citation?"

Major Lee read something from a paper, but Thad did not understand a word of it. The shock of being in front of Robert E. Lee and in front of the vast army addled him. He heard words about "heroic conduct," "in the best tradition of the service," and then Major Lee stepped back.

General Lee stepped forward and pinned a piece of ribbon to Thad's blouse, and then he put his hand out, saying, "It is always good to hear of the bravery of our men, but it is especially gratifying to hear of a young man who shows great initiative under the terrible pressures of battle." He stepped back and Major Lee handed something to him. Lee's deep eyes were happy, Thad thought, as he said, "On the recommendation of your officers, I appoint you brevet lieutenant of Company A, Third Virginia Infantry."

Thad took the lieutenant's insignia, saluted, then turned blindly as a cheer went up, which included a wild rebel cry that he was certain originated in the throat of Dooley Young. He made it back to his seat, but was grabbed and embraced by the Winslow family; and after the troops were dismissed, Company A descended on him like locusts, led by Dooley.

"You ain't got them bars pinned on yet, you scudder!" Dooley laughed, and his comrades crowded around, laughing and shaking his hand. "Jest remember, we brought you up right, so we're expectin' good things from you—like a furlough every week!"

Pet was watching from the sideline, and she whispered to Mark, "You take care of him, you hear me!"

"I guess we'll take care of each other," he remarked, and he and Pet walked forward and spirited Thad away from the men who surrounded him.

The conspiracy had been well planned, for Thad found a brand new lieutenant's uniform waiting for him in a hotel room where Mark took him before the ball. He put it on slowly after Mark left, then sat down, feeling unsteady. He was still there an hour later when Mark came back, saying, "What's wrong? Everybody's waiting for you!"

Thad got up and said, "I can't do it, Captain!"

Mark came over and spoke kindly. "You're still in shock, Thad. But you have to go. Come on, now; it won't be so bad."

He steered Thad out of the room as if he were a sleepwalker, leading him down the stairs and into the large ballroom. The thousands of candles and lamps blinded his eyes, and the colored gowns of the women dazzled him. He followed Mark across the room where he saw Mr. and Mrs. Winslow standing beside Major Lee. "Well, here he is!" the major said. "And looking very well—the last Confederate!"

"The last Confederate?" Sky asked with a puzzled look. "Why do you call him that, Major?"

"While I was lying wounded under that horse at Sharpsburg," Lee said, "I didn't have much hope. I could see dying in a Yankee prison camp as a real possibility. Then, just when I'd given up hope of any of our men getting to me—up popped this young fellow, and that's when I thought, *This has to be the last Confederate!*" He looked fondly at Thad and said, "I know other young men will join our army, but I guess that's the way I'll always think of Thad Novak."

Thad felt utterly miserable and out of place, and they all saw it. "Thad," Rebekah suggested, "come along and have some of my fresh peach cake before it's all gone!" And the two walked away.

"The boy looks more frightened than he did when he came to rescue me in the battle," Lee commented in a sympathetic voice. He turned to Belle and asked, "Will you have this dance with me, Mrs. Wickham?"

Belle, dressed in black, was the most striking woman in the room. Her black gown set off her jet black hair and piercing eyes, and the single pearl she wore at her throat on its golden chain glowed as if it were alive. She replied quietly, "If you don't mind, sir, I would rather not."

"I understand," he murmured. "It is very hard."

She looked at him and there was something hypnotic in her gaze. "I will not dance with any man until the Yankees are driven from our land," she responded. Her voice was quiet, but there was a vein of iron beneath its softness. "I have been too careless in the past, but from this moment I will live only for one purpose: to see the Union destroyed."

Something in her voice disturbed Lee, and glancing at her father, he saw that Sky, too, was disturbed. "We live in terrible times," he said, "but we must never lose our humanity."

Belle Wickham gave him a steady stare, and whispered in a steely voice, "I once had that, sir, but now that my husband is dead, there is nothing left in me but a desire to see as many Yankees in their graves as our armies can put there." She turned, saying, "Excuse me please," then left the ballroom.

"Belle's got to learn gentleness," Sky said, shaking his head sadly. "She's never had any sorrow in her life, so when it came, it destroyed her ideals."

"She's young. She'll change," Lee replied gently.

Sky shook his head. "She's a different woman. Not at all the warm-hearted girl she used to be." Sadness filled his voice, and he said quickly, "We will pray for her, Major—and for all who have been wounded, in spirit as well as in body."

"Amen," Major Lee agreed, and the two men turned to watch the dancers.

———

Thad gulped down the cake, not tasting it. After a while he groaned, "Mrs. Winslow, I feel awful! I don't belong here."

"Nonsense!" she rebuked him. "You're an officer now. You must learn to act like one. Go dance with a pretty girl."

He looked around the room and asked pitifully, "Which one?"

Rebekah gave him a sly smile and asked, "Why don't you start with the one Mark's bringing this way?"

He stared at the pair, and panicked. "Oh no! She wouldn't— and I can't dance very good."

"Ask her!" Rebekah urged, and gave his tender side a nudge with her elbow.

Thad swallowed, and muttered, "Ah—may I have this dance, Miss. . . ?"

The girl was wearing a white gown trimmed in royal blue. It hugged her tiny waist, flaring out to the wide hoop skirt below and outlining her womanly form above. Her hair was pinned up in a mass of dark curls held by a blue ribbon. Her eyes were bright as she looked at him. She curved her full lips in a smile. "Why, Thad, of course I'll dance with you. I've been waiting for you."

"Pet!" he gasped, and stared at her until both brother and sister laughed.

"If you don't close your mouth and put your eyes back in your head," Mark whispered as he handed her over, "you won't be able to dance. Besides, you look silly!"

"Leave him alone, Mark," Pet scolded and held her arms out. "Now, after all this time, I'm going to have this dance."

Thad put his arm around her, his head whirling, and somehow he made his feet move. She had taught him the simple steps while he was recuperating, but it was nothing like what he was doing now.

He was so serious that she laughed. "It's supposed to be fun, Thad!" she teased. "You go at it as if it were a battle!"

"Can't help it!" he gasped. And she saw that he was pale and took pity on him.

"I've been feeling a little warm," she said. "Why don't we get a breath of air on the balcony?"

"Sure!" He had no idea where the balcony was, but she led him in and out of the crowd and through a pair of double glass doors.

"Now, this is better, isn't it?" she sighed. He looked around and saw that they were on a very small court, with flagstones and plantings. The yellow light from the candles streamed through the doors, and it was very quiet compared to the room they had just left.

"You look so handsome in your uniform!" Pet told him. She ran her hand over the bars on his shoulders and said, "I'm so proud of you!"

He stared at her, fascinated by the way the soft light of the harvest moon turned her gray eyes to silver. "I didn't even *know* you!" he said, wonder in his voice. "You're so beautiful, Pet."

"I—I'm glad you think so, Thad," she whispered. He seemed very tall as he stood there, and her lips trembled as she added, "You don't usually think of me as a woman. I've been like another boy to you most of the time."

"Well . . ." he replied uncertainly, "nobody would take you for a boy now!"

She waited for him to go on, but he seemed to be paralyzed, and she said, "Thad—do you remember the night you got saved, and we rode home together?"

"Yes."

"You said there were things you wanted to tell me, but you couldn't." She leaned against him, and the pressure seemed to fluster him. "I want to hear them now, Thad—*please!*"

The last word was spoken in a gentle tone. He remembered that night and their expressed love for each other. He bent his head and kissed her tenderly, his arms around her. As he held her in a tight embrace, he felt her hands go around his neck. For a long moment they stood there, taking and giving, and neither of them ever knew which it was who first drew back.

"Pet, I love you so much!" He choked over the words, and added, "I guess I've loved you from the first time I saw you; but I know one thing—there'll never be another woman for me!"

"Oh, Thad!" she cried, and she bit her lower lip, then tilted her head back to study his face. "Will we be married?"

"Yes. Someday," he said slowly. "I couldn't ask you to marry me that night before I left to return to the army, and I can't now. There's a war to fight first. I don't believe in some of the things the South is fighting for—but I can't quit."

"I know!" Pet replied, and touched his face. "I know, sweet!"

They stood there in the moonlight, talking of the future—about Belle Maison, about Belle and her hatred for the North that threatened to destroy her, about her brothers.

"We'd better go inside, Pet," Thad finally said. But both were reluctant to return to the ballroom. He took her in his arms once more, saying, "I love you!"

She held to him fiercely, unable to let go. She wanted to sob like a forsaken child, but knew that she must not. At last she lifted her head and kissed him.

"We'll outlast this war!" she said firmly. "God put us together, my love, and no matter what happens—we'll have each other!"

Then they turned and walked out of their own solitary world of love and joy into the world of war and suffering.

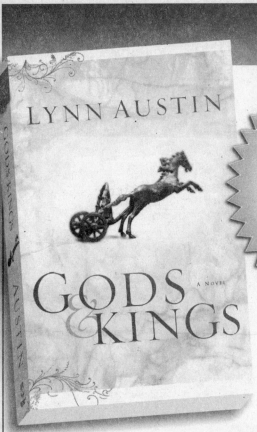

LYNN AUSTIN

GODS & KINGS

A NOVEL

BIBLICAL DRAMA,
Historical Insight, Powerful Faith!

Acclaimed historical novelist Lynn Austin offers riveting biblical fiction with this retelling of the life of King Hezekiah. In her CHRONICLES OF THE KINGS series, Austin wraps historical realism, grand drama, and faith into a memorable story readers will love.